HOT BOY SUMMER

JOE JIMÉNEZ

Entertainment
BOOKS

NEW YORK LONDON TORONTO SYDNEY NEW DELHI

MTV
Entertainment
BOOKS

An imprint of Simon & Schuster Children's Publishing Division
1230 Avenue of the Americas, New York, New York 10020
First MTV Books hardcover edition May 2024
Text copyright © 2024 by Joe Jiménez
All rights reserved, including the right of reproduction in whole or in part in any form.
MTV Entertainment Studios, MTV Books, and all related titles, logos, and original characters are trademarks of Viacom International Inc.
Simon & Schuster: Celebrating 100 Years of Publishing in 2024
For information about special discounts for bulk purchases, please contact Simon & Schuster Special Sales at 1-866-506-1949 or business@simonandschuster.com.
The Simon & Schuster Speakers Bureau can bring authors to your live event. For more information or to book an event contact the Simon & Schuster Speakers Bureau at 1-866-248-3049 or visit our website at www.simonspeakers.com.
Jacket illustration by J Yang
Interior designed by Ginny Chu
The text of this book was set in Cochin LT Std.
Manufactured in the United States of America
2 4 6 8 10 9 7 5 3 1
Library of Congress Cataloging-in-Publication Data
Names: Jiménez, Joe, author.
Title: Hot boy summer / by Joe Jiménez.
Description: First MTV Books hardcover edition. | New York : MTV Books, 2024. | Audience: Ages 14 and Up. | Summary: Four gay teens in San Antonio have the summer of their lives while discovering the true meaning of friendship.
Identifiers: LCCN 2023040533 (print) | LCCN 2023040534 (ebook) | ISBN 9781665932059 (hardcover) | ISBN 9781665932066 (paperback) | ISBN 9781665932073 (ebook)
Subjects: CYAC: Gay men—Fiction. | Friendship—Fiction. | Belonging—Fiction. | Mexican Americans—Fiction. | San Antonio (Tex.)—Fiction. | Romance stories. | LCGFT: Romance fiction. | Novels.
Classification: LCC PZ7.1.J53 Ho 2024 (print) | LCC PZ7.1.J53 (ebook) | DDC [Fic]—dc23
LC record available at https://lccn.loc.gov/2023040533
LC ebook record available at https://lccn.loc.gov/2023040534

for us

When you become the image of your own imagination,
it's the most powerful thing you could ever do.

—RuPaul

Chapter 1

"EY, YOU GONNA READ YOUR LETTER?"

"Shhhhh. I can't hear the man."

Camilo, aka Cammy, aka Cam, takes his phone from his bag and lays his "fresh tips," as he calls them, beside his letter. Modeling his very best gel pen, he focuses the camera on the neatly handwritten page on his desk and snaps a pic.

We're in second period, Mr. Villarreal's notoriously difficult AP Language and Composition class. It's the last day of junior year. Finals week. Stressful. Tense. High stakes af. Yes, all of the above. In front of me sits my letter. It was between Ariana Grande and Michelle Obama, and ultimately, I decided on Michelle Obama, though I seriously believe I could've written a great letter to both. #growingconfidence #forthereals

At the front of the class, Villarreal paces. He's this really smart, really down-for-his-Brown teacher who went to UCLA and USC, with his plaid shirts and his dark Mexican tío mustache, his fierce bow ties and his brilliant-ass laugh, which can light up the room, and of course, his notorious Instagram, which I feel guilty looking at, but I do anyway, and he's gay and funny and is all about anti-racism and women's rights and no homophobia or transphobia and doing something real with your life, something that makes the world a better place.

Sipping his Coke Zero, Villarreal walks row by row, glancing at the letters. "Each of you should have composed a persuasive letter, a composition that establishes and, using the rhetorical techniques you've learned, supports the claim that your letter, and you, as the writer and speaker, are proposing. Not just any letter—no, the most important letter you've ever written in your lives."

If our classroom had a soundtrack, this would be the perfect moment for a very dramatic crescendo. Sure, we've presented our asses off in this class, but today is different. More significant. "It's like the New York Fashion Week of high school English," Cammy said at lunch the day Villarreal gave us the exam topic.

"I'm quite eager to hear these fierce letters. Me siento muy . . . muy . . . muy . . . excited."

We laugh. I mean, it's a *Selena* reference, so how can you not at the very least crack a smile? Anything for Salinas.

"Now, remember, this letter has to ask the person whom you've addressed to take an action, to not take an action, or to continue an action. Again, this is *the most important letter* you've ever written. Even more important than those letters you wrote to Santa all those years ago, or last year, in the case of Mr. Michelangelo Villanueva."

The class chuckles.

Michelangelo, who goes by Mikey, stands up. "Ey, I wanted a new PlayStation 4, sir. Really bad. Everywhere was sold out. Santa was my last resort."

The class laughs. Mr. Villarreal smirks.

Mikey moved here from LA at the start of second semester. He's tall—well, not that tall, actually—but he's taller than I am, which isn't saying much, because at five foot six, pretty much everybody's taller than me. Mikey's Filipino, and he's hot. Like supes-hot af. And he wears nice-ass clothes and smells good, he always has a crisp, fresh-ass fade, and he wears this shiny-ass gold chain that dangles between his big pecs like the first star showing up in the night sky. He also has giant arms. #swoonaf #fanclub. Yeah, I've noticed.

"Thank you, Michaelangelo. Now, take your seat, please. Unless you'd like to read first?"

Quickly, Mikey leaps back into his seat and turns away.

"Will you be taking volunteers, Mr. Villarreal? If so, I'd like to go first." It's Montgomery Suarez, the smartest girl in the universe. Always the first to volunteer.

"Patience. Before we jump in, I just have to take a moment and say this." Villarreal pauses. "It's kind of hard to think the year is over, isn't it?"

I nod. Seriously. The year's flown by.

Across the room, I notice Hot Mikey, as I call him whenever I talk about him to my dog Kimber, nodding too. And I know.

I know. Who has full-fledged convos about hot boys with their dogs, right? Well, I do. #handraised #notashamed. Besides, Kimber's listening skills are top-tier, and I can't really talk to anyone else about these things. Maybe my sister B, but she's hardly home anymore, now that she practically lives with her girlfriend Clari's family, and definitely not Cammy, whom I've watched use people's crushes against them. So nope. Not me.

Speaking of Cammy, I look over, and he's giving this serious, introspective vibe that I don't usually get from him. Noting that I'm watching, Cam looks over at me and serves me his biggest, fakest smile, which I absolutely effing love. I don't know why exactly fake smiles light me up. But then we both smile real smiles, the kind that good friends flash at each other when they understand that the shit they're experiencing is special. And no doubt, thinking about junior year coming to an end is definitely a moment.

Mr. Villarreal sets down his drink. "You have been a wonderful class. One of my all-time favorite classes." A few *awwww*s emerge across the classroom, and I typically don't get into this kind of sentimentality, but I hear myself being one of the voices going *awwww*.

Villarreal then adds, "And for those of you who plan on asking me for a letter of recommendation, you'll need to ask in a formal email with at least two weeks' prior notice. No email, no letter." He looks directly at the front row—Montgomery and Hermelinda, Florencio and Frank and Lulu, all the top kids—when he announces this. "And now, returning to the business of the day, the letters."

Instantly, like seven hands shoot up.

Mr. Villarreal chooses Montgomery to begin. As expected, she delivers a badass letter, written to Supreme Court Justice Sonia Sotomayor, praising the justice for being such a powerful model for mujeres and then urging her to rule in favor of students' safety if an automatic weapons ban ever comes before the Supreme Court. Mr. Villarreal is "gagged" by her letter, as Camilo would say. And while I'm not a huge fan of Montgomery personally, homegirl works hard and her letter takes on a real-ass problem, and so how can I not respect that energy?

After this, a few other students share their letters, and while they're fine, none of them are "stunning." That's another one of Cammy's words that I've stolen. Along with my sister B, who's a beast point guard and also a big lesbian, Cammy's a huge reason why I came out, not to everybody but to Cam and B and Kimber and most importantly, to myself. Coming out to my dad—that's another story. My dad is my dad, and I love him, most days, even if he's a major conspiracy theorist and a racist and a misogynist and a homophobe and even if he thinks "immigrants are ruining our great country" and "Democrats are all Communists" and "drag queens are groomers." It's a lot. So, one day, but not anytime soon. Baby steps, right? Cammy tells me there's a lot to learn about the gay world and not to jump in too fast because then you just look thirsty and "overdone," another one of his words that I'm making mine.

As class continues, I start to get a little bit a lot bored listening to these letters. Honestly, I just want stunning. Like who doesn't love stunning? I'm semi-hopeful when Rita Arevalo starts reading her letter to a supermodel about beauty standards. Her intro starts off really intense, because she's describing waking up in the morning, looking in the mirror, and not feeling good enough or pretty enough and having issues with her body, which grabs me by the balls. I mean, come on, that's like most of my life story right there. But then, it's like she suddenly became afraid of what she was writing and the ideas kinda just fall off the page. So, not stunning. I wanna be gagged, and nobody is gagging me. Until Mr. Villarreal calls on Florencio Martinez.

So, Florencio's one of those pretty boys. He has the longest, darkest eyelashes, which Cammy says look "fake af." They look real to me, but what do I know? Florencio's my friend Benny's younger brother, and he's quiet and polite, which is completely different from Benny, whom I've played baseball with since like first grade and who can act like a major ass and also totally enjoys having all eyes on him. Florencio is friends with, like, all the girls. Even the girls who've hated each other since kindergarten somehow put aside their differences to talk to Flor, as well as some of the really churchy ones who are brainwashed into hating gays.

Wearing a perfectly white, white button-up, tight dark indigo jeans, low-heeled boots, and gloss, Flor walks up to the front of the class. He looks expensive. At Mr. Villarreal's lectern, Flor arranges his papers.

The room goes quiet.

"Good luck," Kennedy Lozano says.

Flor takes a deep breath. He pulls out a tube of gloss from his pocket and rolls it across his already very glossed lips.

Someone in the class snickers, which Hermelinda Vasquez responds to by looking around protectively.

"Ugh. Lewk kween," Cammy mutters under his breath.

With all eyes on him, Florencio shakes a little, then picks up his letter. Watching his wrists quiver makes me sit up. *Oh, shit*, I think. *Is he gonna crack?*

Looking out at the class, Florencio smiles, or attempts to smile, though the shape on his face is less a sign of happiness and more an arrangement of glossy lips and powdered skin that says uncertainty, which is totally different from all the confidence he has given every other time he's presented before. When Flor finally begins talking, I struggle to hear him.

"You're going to have to speak louder, please, Florencio." Mr. Villarreal's voice moves over the room smoothly, like a cloud.

Florencio clears his throat.

Even from the back of the room, I can feel Flor's nervousness, and now I feel nervous too, and I'm not even the one up there.

Florencio just stands there, holding his air inside him like that's the only way to hold himself together.

"She's not gonna be able to do it," Cammy whispers loudly, causing Chelsea Figueroa to lean back, give him a shitty look, and shush him.

Not liking this, Cam shushes her right back.

And that's when I hear someone singing: "Just keep breathin' and breathin' and breathin' and breathin'."

I recognize these words, recognize them with all the parts of me that are afraid to say out loud that I'm different. A million times at home in my room on my bed with Kimber, I've heard them and even sang them out loud, which is a shitshow in and of itself, because, if there's one thing I can't do, it's sing. Trust me on this one. I strain to see who's singing—and #wow #supeswow—it's Hot Mikey, apparently throwing out a lifeline to a pretty-ass boy with thick-ass eyelashes and bangs that bounce a little each time he moves.

Florencio smiles for reals, then. Like an effing Invisalign commercial.

"Just breathe, sis." From the front row, Kennedy jumps in.

"My, my air. My air," Flor sings quietly, and with that, a few of us in class giggle a little, because a lot of us in that room, we know exactly where these words are coming from.

"Yasssss!" Cammy snaps. "Come through, Ariana Fan Club!"

"You can do this, babe," Hermelinda, who's good friends with Florencio and captain of the dance team, says. Honestly, Hermelinda has the best hair in the whole school. Like maybe in all of San Antonio and maybe even in all of Texas, which says a whole lot, because there's a lot of good hair in Texas.

Come on, I think. "Come through." I meant to think it, but I'm pretty sure I say it out loud.

After a few seconds, the air in Mr. Villarreal's room shifts.

Florencio keeps breathing. He pushes the bangs away from his eyes and blinks.

"OMG. Okay. I didn't think this would be so hard . . . So, this letter I wrote," Florencio begins, "this letter is to a performer I love and respect with all my heart. She has given me strength that I did not know I had. She has been a light in my darkest times. Her name is Valentina. For those of you who don't know Valentina, she was a fierce competitor on *RuPaul's Drag Race* Season Nine and *RuPaul's Drag Race All Stars* Season Four. She's a star. She is beautiful. She is glamorous. She is gay, and she is Mexican. She is diva everything. So, this is for you, Valentina, mi amor."

"Yasssss!!" It's Hot Mikey who blurts out his affirmation.

Then Cammy follows: "All right, Miss Valentina stan!!" and "Come on, sis!! Werk!"

Hermelinda and Kennedy chime in too. "We love you, Flor!"

Sitting at my desk, I've never heard anything like it before. The cheers of high school gay boys and their best straight girl-friends. I wanna scream out something supportive, but I don't know what to say or how I'd even say it. The only phrase that pops in my head is "Let's gooooo!" which we'd yell in baseball all the time, but here, somehow, it just doesn't fit.

As Flor reads his letter, I forget that I'm sitting in my high school, in Mr. Villarreal's class, in my hometown. I forget that I'm seventeen and anxious most days to be gay and a little bit lonely af. But right now, I no longer feel small, like I might never be understood or have friends I can show my whole life to. Friends who just let me be without telling me how to be or what to do. OMG. Friends who listen, who actually listen! I want laughter that shoots up from the reddest part of my heart. I wanna kiss a boy and hold his hand, feel him up with my fingers and breath. I don't confess to anyone that I want these things, not even to Cammy, but I want them, and listening to Florencio's letter, I can feel something inside myself clicking.

"... so, Valentina, I urge you to keep performing, to keep giving them all the Miss Colombia pageant realness you have to give," Florencio continues amid a wave of snaps and yasssses. "Keep living your best life, Valentina, because when you do, people like me know we can live our best lives too. To be honest with you, Valentina"—Florencio takes a deep breath here, his voice snagging somewhere inside him—"sometimes I think of those minutes in my life . . . when I would sit in my room alone, feeling so . . . ugly and so lost, and I wondered if maybe . . ." Florencio pauses here and looks out at us, and we can all feel it. Like a fist made of air grabbing that whole room. The tension in Flor's body is apparent.

From his seat, Mr. Villarrreal interrupts. "Florencio, you can sit down now if you like. You've done a fierce job."

"No. I'd like to keep going. . . . I'd like to keep reading, please."

And that's exactly what Florencio does. He takes a big-ass breath, exhales, and goes on: "I wondered if maybe I just did not belong here, if maybe I should . . . not be alive . . ."

Deep, hard-ass gasps. That sound of people not knowing what to do with heavy news. I feel like a boulder has crashed on my chest, slowly moving all its weight into my throat.

Just keep breathing, I think, though I don't know if I'm saying this for Florencio or for myself.

"But, girl," Flor says, "in those dark moments, I thought of you, Valentina. My hero. My French Vanilla Fantasy. Mi amor.

I thought that if you were here sitting beside me, you would grab my perfectly manicured hand—" Florencio stops here and holds out his hand like he's inspecting his nails and smiles.

Mikey, Chelsea, Hermelinda, Kennedy, and Cammy all "yasss" simultaneously.

Flor's smile glows.

Looking at my own too short, crooked-ass nails, I kinda smile too.

Flor continues, "—and you would look me right in the eye with your Latina goddess face and Latina goddess hair and your Latina goddess smile of strength and Latina goddess bravery, and you'd just say, 'Girl, love who you are and love what you do.' And I would take every word and live it. Because of you, I can love myself and I can love what I do. So, in conclusion, Valentina, mi amor, I am so 'Into You' and I always will be. Forever and por vida, I thank you, Valentina. I thank you with all my heart. Girl, thank you for giving me my life."

And then, just like that, it's over.

And then, just like that, my life is changed. And I don't know whether I should cry my ass off right there in the back of the classroom or jump to my feet and shower Florencio with applause.

One by one, people get up from their seats and put their arms around him, first Hermelinda and Kennedy and Chelsea and then Montgomery and then Cammy, who I thought low-key hard-core disliked Florencio, and then Mikey . . . and then me. I take Florencio's hands, I look him in the eyes, and I say, "Wow. Soooo good. Full-on max pro beast-mode letter. And the

Ariana reference! F-word brilliant. God, I love Ariana Grande. She's my favorite. OMG. Seriously. Top-tier peak letter. I'm rambling. I'm sorry."

"It's okay." Florencio smiles, squeezing my hands real tight. "And Ariana's my fave too! Moment. Vibe. And diva everything. I mean, she is everything, right??!!"

It's almost instantaneous. The connection. It's like, one minute we're virtually strangers, and then *bam!* Chorizo, baby!! We're suddenly like almost kind of related, which is crazy, because honestly, I've known Flor for nearly my entire life. I've been over to his house to hang out with Benny and our friend Duncan from baseball like ten thousand times, and yet, all those times I went over to Benny's, Flor would just disappear or go off with their mom. He never spoke a word to me. And even when we've had classes together, I've gotten this vibe, and maybe it's all in my head, but I've kinda felt maybe Florencio thought he was better than me. From the fancy-ass clothes he wears, his good phone, and the rich girls he hangs out with. It's like we were from two totally different worlds.

But today is different.

Today, it's like we're standing in front of the same window. Breathing the same air, fluent in the shared language of icons we love. Today feels like we might actually come from the same place.

Mr. Villarreal calls for a five-minute "brain break," which means he knows we need a moment.

Amid the chatter, the phone-checking, and the nervous energy about who's going to read their letters next, Cammy's going on and on about how effing gorge Hermelinda's hair looks. "You're like giving me full-on Adriana Lima, girl. Stunting. And I'm sure you already know this, because you're like the hottest girl in the school," Cammy says, which strikes me because he says it while looking directly at Chelsea Figueroa, who most people say is the hottest girl in school. Chelsea looks up and conspicuously rolls her eyes at him.

When I turn away from Cam's drama, I notice Flor motioning to Mikey Villanueva.

"Mikey, do you know my friend Mac?" Flor asks.

Okay, stop the music. First, did Flor just refer to me as "my friend"? And secondly, and more gag-worthy than that, is Flor actually introducing me to Hot Mikey?

Of course my hands start to sweat, and my pits get steamy af.

Mikey reaches out to shake my hand, and what do I do? I give him a fist bump. Ugh. It's awkward, because my fist misses his hand, and we try again, reversing roles, with my palm open and his fist balled up, reaching over to connect, and again, we miss.

It's ridiculous.

Flor laughs.

Mikey smiles. "This shouldn't be that hard."

I hold my hand out then. Leave it there open, waiting. It's the only thing I can think of doing, aside from shoving my hand in my pocket or running out of the room screaming.

And when Mikey puts his hand in my hand, I look him in the eyes, and he looks right back at mine, and I think it's a little bit like magic right then, that moment, maybe, that first feeling of the world stopping for a whole second so that all the stars

can look right at me and say, *This is for you. This is what life can be.*
And it feels like that. Beyond ordinary, like magic.

I smile.

It's all I can do. It's all I know how to do, let my face be my
face, since I don't have a game plan or a strategy right now, all
of this coming at me so fast, and I think that's probably a good
thing, because otherwise I might've overthought this moment
and tripped myself up. Judging from the glow coming from
Mikey's eyes, I think it's enough.

I'm not sure what to do or say next. But I don't have to say
anything, because before I know it, Cammy has abandoned his
conversation with Hermelinda and squeezes himself between
Mikey and me, grabbing Mikey's hand too.

Cammy's handshake is extra af and almost topples Mikey
into Flor, who graciously grabs onto my arm for support while
helping Hot Mikey stay on his feet. Flor looks at me like,
Ummm. What is she doing?

Pulling back his hand, Mikey laughs it off.

I look at Mikey and think, *Holy shit, he's got the best laugh.*

I smile more. Instantly, Mikey returns the smile, flexing
his hand, like he's trying to relieve the soreness from Cammy's
too-aggressive grip. When I try to meet Mikey's eyes again, I
get the sense he's looking right at my chest instead of at me.

"You know, we should hang out." Flor taps my arm, and his
invitation pulls me back into the moment.

"That's a great idea. It can be like our very own Fierce
Bitches Club," Cammy jumps in.

Flor looks like he doesn't know what to say or do.

"Bitch, you're too much," Mikey says.

"Thanks, boo. I get that a lot," Cammy says.

Mikey makes a weird face—like he's both rolling his eyes and smelling something gross at the same time—which is funny af, and I'm nodding. OMG. I'm smiling and nodding like my head is on a permanent swivel, a seesaw or a lever. I don't know. All I know is that I feel excitement and eagerness swelling inside me, and it's the last day of school, and here I am making friends—making gay friends—on the brink of what just might be the best summer ever.

Glancing at the clock, Mr. Villarreal announces, "If you can hear my voice, clap three times," which is the signal that we're reconvening.

Beneath the shuffling and the sighs of relief, including mine, Flor says, "Really. Y'all should come by my house tonight. We can make gourmet pizzas. Girl, we can kiki."

"Pizza's my love language," Mikey jokes.

"Bitch, count us in." Cam looks at me, grabbing my arm. I totally wanna go, but I have work. Also, I don't even know what a kiki is.

"Seven thirty, eight-ish? Message me on Insta." With that, Flor takes his seat, and Cam and I go to ours, and the whole time, I'm thinking, *Holy shit. Did I just flirt with Hot Mikey? And OMG! Did he just flirt back with me? And OMG! Did Hot Mikey just check out my chest? And OMG! Did Cammy just crash Flor's invite? And OMG! What do you even do at a kiki? And ummmm OMG! Did I just make gay friends?* #buryme #foundmypeople #webelong #valentinamiamor #summervibes #newfriends #friendshipsreallydochangetheworld

Chapter 2

"**G**IRL, PLEASE. WHAT DO YOU MEAN, 'RULES'?" Cam asks as we're sitting around Flor's bedroom for our first kiki.

"Yes, girl. Rules. You know, like guide points." With a hand on her hip, Flor looks like she's on the main stage accepting a critique. She smiles.

Cam returns the smile, and it's sooo fake. Like top-tier, next-level max pro ultra fake af.

It's eight-ish, and I'm starving. Like my stomach is literally talking major shit about how it needs to eat, which makes me hope that we can expedite this friction over rules. I yawn and take a look around. Flor's room is very "modern mid-century design meets devout Ariana shrine," as Flor characterized his aesthetic when I arrived. I mean, the room def has a 1960s vibe with spacey knickknacks, vintage-looking pink and purple throw pillows, and professionally framed Ariana album cover posters.

I'm sitting on the rug next to Hot Mikey, who's wearing a bright green tank top and giant headphones. Staring at a colorful af, highly technical remixing screen, Mikey taps his finger like he's counting. As it turns out, Mikey's a DJ. Sitting so close to him is a total mood, and I want it to last forever, or at least until we kiss and kiss again and then again, which I hope happens, because every time Mikey makes an edit to the song he's working on, his arm brushes against me, and needless to say, I'm all about this closeness to a boy working on music who I think is super, major hot af. #supermajorhotaf

Catching me watching, Mikey squeezes my arm firmly, like his whole hand grabs the belly of my arm muscle. Instantly, my whole body heats up. My heart starts flinging itself back and forth in my chest, and what do I do? Ugh. I flex, which I know is a total douche move, but I can't help it.

When Cam sees Mikey touch my arm, he shakes his head at me and mouths the word "No" twice.

I don't get Cam's attitude, but I'm excited by flirting with Mikey and Mikey flirting back with me, and also, I'm curious af about these rules Flor's talking about, and so, when Flor clears his throat, I'm all ears.

Grabbing a dry-erase board, Flor announces, "Okay, let's get started." He sets the whiteboard on his dresser. Sheets of copy paper neatly obscure what he's written. Flor's holding a hyper-bright, mega-pink, glittery dry-erase marker, which he wields like a wand. Slowly, he removes the first sheet, and my eyes are glued to his every move.

Dramatically, Flor reads the revealed text. "Rule number one: Ariana Grande is everything."

And I am gagged.

For the reals, I think my jaw drops, and immediately, Mikey's all in. "Ha!! Girl, werk!!!" Excitedly, he grabs my hand, banging his feet against the rug.

"I'm sooooo into this," I say, and I think maybe I'm talking both about Rule #1 and Mikey's hand in mine. From across the room, I hear Cam sighing. Noticeably, loudly. Like this is painful for him somehow, and he needs us to acknowledge his suffering.

Tossing a long imaginary ponytail to the side, Flor reveals the second rule. "Okay, now. In case you are wondering . . . for your consideration, rule number two: Valentina is Kween."

"Come on, French Vanilla Fantasy!!!" Mikey's voice booms across the room, bouncing off the three perfectly placed Ariana Grande album cover posters that adorn Flor's wall.

Flor runs his fingers through his very long, very imaginary high ponytail, and Mikey's on his feet. He drops in and out of recognizable Ari choreo, adding some of his own original moves. #soooohot #damnpa #giveittomedad

Like, okay, I totally thought these were gonna be a much different set of rules. I was expecting "take your shoes off when you come into the house" and "don't eat my dad's chips" or some shit like that. But now, this is an effing vibe.

Cam, on the other hand, is sooooo not living for this.

Glancing over his way, I see him lean back in Flor's fancy-ass love seat. He gives me a fake-ass smile and starts scrolling through his phone. #ugh

"And rule number three." Flor pauses, waiting for us to quiet down, which really means he's holding for Mikey to stop popping and for me to stop doing whatever it is I'm doing. Seriously, I'm getting the sense that this is gonna be a really, really important rule. #megadramaticpause #waitforit #braceyourself

Once we calm down, Flor declares in his most Robin Roberts voice, "Rule number three: Loyalty is life. Love is forever. And friends are your family."

#effinggaaaaag. It's like a window in a stale-ass, closed-up house letting in some air, and I don't know what exactly is happening inside me, but hearing these words, thinking about loyalty between us and love and just the idea of having people who are there for you and get you, no matter what, and don't turn their backs on you or put you down, por vida and forever, it's a lot. And I think, *Yes. I'll take it. All of it. Right here, right now, and always.*

"*Girl!*" It comes out of my mouth like a breath I've held for too long. On the reals, I just keep nodding and clapping, because I feel overcome with something better than happiness, and nodding along with applause is the only way I can articulate what I feel.

When Flor's done reciting our rules, he takes a deep-ass, self-centering breath, shuts his eyes, and shakes out his perfectly manicured tips.

"The rules have spoken, girl! Let the music play!" Mikey

disconnects his headphones, and immediately, the room floods with "7 rings," or a version of it that sounds faster, with extra effects, all of which amplify my feels.

Naturally, Flor busts into her "7 rings" choreo, working that iconic invisible chongo. Next to me, Mikey pops to his knees, bobbing his head and dancing from the waist up, still holding on to his laptop with one hand, and even though I'm a shitty dancer, I just copy Mikey's moves, or attempt to, with a few more fist pumps and considerably less neck action. I am feeling myself, as Cam would say.

And why? Because these rules are giving me hope in big-ass flashing neon lights and pyrotechnics, smoke machines, and five hundred background dancers. Seriously. It's like a whole new world, a world I need to be a part of. Before Flor read the rules, we were all chatting about massively important topics like reducing our carbon footprints, bingeing shows, and the irrefutable fierceness of Ariana Grande's ponytail, and right now, I can see us having like ten thousand other massively important conversations in the future. To me, hope is every-thing. Like no matter what goes on at home, I know there's more to life out there, and so, I just have to get through this temporary shitshow to get to where I really need to be.

Staring at the rules on the dry-erase board on which Flor has documented the guideposts for our new friendship, for the summer, for the rest of our lives maybe, I can't help but think this is all somehow meant to be, and I effing love this journey for myself. Just this morning, life was less . . . well, *my life*.

"So, girl, what do you think?" Flor stands beside me, pointing at the rules.

"They're perfect. I mean, Ariana Grande is the moment. And Valentina. Girl . . ." I pause because I'm smiling so big my teeth feel dry.

"Girl," Flor repeats, connecting smoothly to my crunchy thoughts with one word. "I 110 abso understand what you're saying. She's the icon, the energy, the vibe, and the moment, hunny. It's like sometimes I don't even have the words for this level of gorge. Valentina really is top-tier goddess energy. #absocertified."

Talking to Flor is effortless, like talking to Kimber—well, only different because Flor doesn't just stare at me, he actually talks back and says intelligent, insightful shit and doesn't fart or slobber on me.

"She's iconic. OMG. The mask!" It's a *Drag Race* moment I've replayed over and over on YouTube.

Flor gasps. "Girl. No. First, 'Greedy' is fire. One of my faves. Uff. But I can't. I can't. No. No."

Thinking I did something wrong, I halt, then realize Flor's just going through it, reliving Valentina's elimination. "Girl."

"I know. I know." Swallowing a deep breath, Flor calms himself, holding his hands out like he's balancing.

Behind Flor, Cam stares at me, like *wtf is she doing?* and I shrug.

"Babe, it was self-sabotage," Mikey interjects from across the room, returning to his music, which supes focuses him. "Her inner saboteur. We all have one."

"110 abso," Flor adds. "These are life lessons. Girl, life wisdom. This is the reason for the rules. For the reals, how many times do we get in our own heads and—"

"Fuck shit up?" Cammy blurts.

Flor nods. "Exactly." Pulling out his phone, Flor scrolls through @allaboutvalentina.

I lean in, and Flor leans over, resting his head against my shoulder, both of us sighing as he lands on a stunning image of Valentina's 2017 *Preview* magazine photo shoot. I'm kinda self-conscious about Flor being so close, because I'm still in my work pants, which smell like barbecue and beans, yet Flor doesn't seem to mind, so why should I?

Mikey comes to stand beside me. "I know that shot. It's from the Philippines. Girl."

I look up and smile, and Mikey smiles too, then reaches down and says, "Boop" as he bumps the top of my head with his computer, which is simultaneously immensely sweet and strange and nerdy all at once. I do this to Kimber all the time. Only I boop her little wet nose. So, obvi, I approve.

"She looks good. But that's not my fave pic of her." Grabbing Flor's phone, Cammy scrolls through Valentina's IG.

For reals? It's kind of a lot effing rude just snatching somebody's phone like that, and I see Mikey roll his eyes as he goes back to his music.

If Flor is bothered by this grab, she doesn't let it show.

"I would literally effing give three to five years of my life to meet her. Maybe more," I confess.

"Valentina on the cover of *ELLE México*. Now, that's the

lewk, mamas. Icónica. Period, girl." Proudly, Cam holds up the phone.

"She does look a lot stunning there," Flor agrees, tilting her head to stare admiringly at the shot of Valentina in a glamorous af poofy red dress. "Literally the 'Mexican Cinderella.'"

Flor retrieves her phone. "Girl, she is soooo the vibe I want in my forever life, and this is exactly why she's rule number two."

"My forever life" sounds like exactly the vibe I need, and it's cathartic just watching Flor go through it. Like okay, so we've all been through a lot of emotions today, and on top of that, junior year was really hard, and now it's finally over, #giantbiggayyay, and on top of that, I went straight from school to work, where, after four hours of slinging barbecue, I told my pervy manager, Julio, that I had "stomach issues" and needed to go home. It's a trick I learned from Benny, who faked having diarrhea for years so our coach would let him sit out practice.

So here I am, after my long-ass day, after two final exams and my work shift at Mr. Bill's BBQ, and I was sooooo looking forward to leaving work so I could come over to Flor's, so that when Cam picked me up from work, I didn't even shower when I got home. Pronto fast, I just ran in to let Kimber go potty, fed her, put on a new shirt, and then jumped back in Cam's mom's car.

Now, with dried potato salad and barbecue sauce still smeared on my pants, I'm sitting on Flor's fancy-ass duvet, smelling like somebody else's sausage and still feeling fresh af. Why? Because I can think of no better way to start the summer than exactly like this, the four of us together, about to become BFFs, maybe, I hope, possibly—it's already happening—and making some fierce-ass extra af rules for how to run our lives this summer. Also, we're making little gourmet pizzas soon, I hope, because I'm hungry af.

With my stomach grumbling, I ask in my most polite voice, "Girl, not to be rude, but are we gonna eat?"

"Yeah! I'm starving," Mikey says. "You know pizza's my love language."

"We know, girl. You told us earlier," Cam blurts out.

Ughhh. *What's that about?* I think.

"Then let's go downstairs. But first, we have to vote." Pointing back to the rules, Flor steps toward the whiteboard.

"Vote?" Mikey asks.

"Yes, girl. Vote."

Like she's president of the gay universe, Flor declares, "Okay, girls. Because this is America, let's vote. All in favor?"

Immediately, I raise my hand and say, "Aye."

But Mikey, in his deepest voice, unable to shift his eyes from his laptop, blurts out, "Me." Like, who even votes like that?

Meanwhile, Cammy leans in, cocks her neck, and snaps a selfie with our three whiteboard rules perfectly positioned behind her, and she doesn't even vote at all. Girl.

It's sloppy. It's uncoordinated. It's sooo not the fantasy. And it's triggering Flor, who by this point is serious af. Looking all of us dead in the eye, she claps, "Y'all bitches need to vote. This needs to be official. Officially."

#buryme #lovingandlivingforit #pickingthisup

"All in favor?" Flor repeats, looking at Cammy and waving that pink marker like a gay gavel.

And then it comes. The facecrack.

Holding a fancy faux-fur lavender pillow, Cammy gives Flor the full-on, up-down, *bitch, please* look. Girl, it's a lot. Like, a lot a lot. Then Cammy clears her throat, looks right at Flor, and says, "You know, I'm not actually comfortable with voting like this. I think we need discussion. Last time I checked, this was a democracy. And democracies, from what I remember from Ms. Grauer's US history class, actually have an electoral process."

Mikey peers up from his laptop and gets real severe, like he's asking, *Is this bitch for real?*

No, girl. I don't wanna discuss. It's been a long day, and even though I could've eaten at work, I purposely didn't eat, like not even once, okay maybe a couple of bites of Rebecca's bean and cheese taco, but that hardly counts, because Flor invited us all over to kiki—which I think means get to know each other better and kick back—and to make pizzas.

"Which rule, girl?" Flor's voice rises a bit, like maybe she thinks Cammy isn't serious.

But not today.

"All of them." Cammy looks Flor right in the eye.

Girl, my eyes are rolling soooo hard and staring in disbelief. Simultaneously. #mycorneashurt #girlno #ughhhh #nomaam

"Well, tell us, girl. You seem to have a whole lot to say. Spill the tea," Mikey jumps in, removing his headphones completely.

"What exactly do you wanna discuss?" Shutting his laptop, Mikey signals that he is not playing.

Cammy inhales. Deep, too. Then lets all the air out. The kinda air-drama that tells anyone listening that somebody's about to pop the f off. "Well, first of all, it feels like since before Mac and I even walked in, these rules had already been decided. Like, why even vote? Girl, the rules were already written on the board before we got here. Literally. So that's not even democracy if the choice has already been made for you! And I can't support fake voting or fake-ass democracy. That's all I'm saying. That's what my gut, my instincts are telling me, and I've learned that *my* instincts, girl? They're usually right. So, in the name of true democracy, I just think we should actually hear the reasoning behind these 'rules.'" Cam puts air quotes around the word "rules." "Second of all—"

"Girl, nobody says 'second of all.'" Mikey's fast, sharp.

"Second of all . . ." Staring directly at Mikey, Cammy stresses what she said, throwing down each syllable like a hand in the face. "I recommend that for rule number two, we should add 'mothatuckin queen of the whole tucking goddamn universe' in front of or immediately following Valentina's name. I kinda like the ring of that."

"Girl, that's very . . . rough," Flor replies. "And I don't really believe Valentina would actually say it that way. It's completely off-off-brand for her."

Obvi, Mikey totally agrees, nodding wholeheartedly. Girl, that disapproving look on his chiseled brown face says everything (big muscles, honey skin, impeccable smile, smoldering eyes, girl, even his earlobes and baby toes, I bet, are perfect #husbandgoals #110). And I'm starting to think that maybe Mikey and Cam are really not going to be besties. "Girl, please. She'd never say anything close to that."

"Whatever, girl. Because you're from LA, you know every-thing about Valentina, right? Ugh." Cammy exhales like she's being forced to accept an unjust verdict.

As for me, girl, I'm gagged and not getting involved.

"Oh, and one other thing," says Cam.

"Really, girl?" Mikey's voice peaks. I can tell he's bothered.

"I'm just saying what needs to be said. That's me. All T, no shade. Girl, for example, why is it that Ariana is the only artist mentioned? What about Cardi? What about Doja? Nicki? What about Megan?! They're talented af. Why can't they be on 'the rules'?" Cammy makes air quotes again, which I know triggers Flor, because her forehead stiffens and her upper lip quivers like it wants to jump right off her face and slap the shit outta Cam.

But Flor holds it together. Glances at her nails, which have immaculate white tips and are rounded like on a hand model selling wedding rings in a magazine.

"Well, girl? What do you think, Mac?" Cam turns, looking right at me.

#ughhhhhhh. Girl, what is she doing? Why does she have to drag me into it? I get it. We've been friends the longest, so maybe she expects loyalty. I mean, ironically, it's the third rule—loyalty, right? The very same rules she's making drama about voting on. So I try to be loyal and fair at the same time, which is possible, but it isn't easy. "Well, girl. I 110 see your point about Cardi and Megan. I mean, 'Grab a bucket and a mop . . . macaroni in a pot . . .' 'WAP,' that's like an American classic, don't you think, Mikey? Out of everybody here, you know the most about music."

Enthusiastically, Mikey nods. I hate that I put him on the spot, yet I think he appreciates the compliment, and also, he knows it's a fierce-ass song. #notdebatable #abso110

"And I agree that Valentina would play it classy. Girl, she's been on the cover of Mexican *Vogue*." I look over to Mikey and Flor, who nod in agreement. I don't look at Cammy because I don't want to see the knife in her mouth when she hears me support Flor's logic.

"Bitch, you haven't even watched full episodes," Cammy barks. "All you do is watch the free shit online. Just clips and recaps."

Flor's room goes silent. I think everybody's gagged, and I'm unsure if it's because they're gagged that I haven't seen full episodes of *Drag Race* or because Cam went full-on hard at me like that. Maybe both.

I'm kind of a lot embarrassed, and I don't wanna look like a dumb-ass, so I start up again. "On the other hand, I also think it's not that serious. Like, can we just vote? I just wanna eat my little pizza, kiki, go home, shower, and get ready for tomorrow, because I work. Is that too much to ask? Girl, I smell like barbecue. I smell like chorizo. And I have potato salad on my pants. Can we just vote?"

Cammy rolls her eyes. Like she rolls them so hard I think

they might never stop fluttering inside her thick head. "Fine. Fine. Just vote, then. Erase my voice. Vote so Mac can eat and go home, and everybody can be happy. Fuck my drag, right? And just for the record, this is how democracy dies."

"That's a *Star Wars* reference," Mikey interjects. "He stole that from *Star Wars*. The line's actually 'This is how *liberty* dies.' Padmé says it in Episode 3."

The room gets quiet again.

For a fast minute, I think Cammy's gonna get up and walk out. She's done it before. One time, Cammy got into a rowdy-ass argument with her sister Michelle over something that happened when they were like three, and Cammy threw a bowl of beans at her. Girl. Charro beans, too. You know that shit was messy. Surprisingly, tonight, Cammy stays seated, holding on to that furry-ass pillow.

Girl, silence.

Mikey being Mikey says, "Okay. This isn't awkward af. I think we need some music." A remix of "no tears left to cry" starts to play as Flor says, "All in favor?"

I'm like, Really, girl? You wanna vote right before "no tears left to cry"? That's, like, my sixth favorite Ariana song. Seriously. But I raise my hand and so does Mikey, and looking across the room, so does Cammy, half-heartedly, with a look on her face like she just got the wind knocked out of her.

"Are there any nays?"

Silence.

Well, almost silence. Cammy clears her throat like something's stuck.

Flor triumphantly tallies the count. In pink glittery dry-erase marker. #naturally #extra #naturallyextra. "Then it's official. Welcome to Senior Summer, bitches!! Okay, sis, let's go make some pizzas!"

It's a vibe and a moment. For the reals. And I'm sooo here for it, and I'm #soooverygagged.

Trust me, girl, I can gobble, so when those little gourmet pizzas with fake-ass nonfat ranch are ready, I am picking it up. Loving it and living it. And picking it all up. All of it. Why? Because, girl, this group of my possibly new gay bffs is like a hand starting some fire, and I am sooo here for it!

Chapter 3

"OMG, BITCH! I LOVE THESE!" CAM REACHES across my kitchen table and grabs the box of Berry Crunch I set out for B. I just finished my work shift, and Cam was nice enough to pick me up and drive me home. He cracks open the cereal and pours himself a heavy-ass bowl.

"Just don't finish them," I say. "B's coming over later."

"Girl, please. I'm not you. I'm not munching down an entire box of cereal. I just want a little taste." Cam sticks his tongue out at me and winks.

Passing Cam a napkin and spoon, I force a smile.

My house is hot af, so I turn on the fans and crank the window unit to high, hoping it'll make a difference, which is unlikely, because it's summer, it's two in the afternoon, and girl, this is Texas. Behind me, Kimber huffs and squeals, squirming across the floor to get my attention like she does every time I get home. I let her out to go potty. When she's done pooping, Kimber follows me inside. I pet her and hurl her pink piggy toy across the house, which she effing loves.

Slurping milk, Cam flicks her tongue and gives me an inquisitive smile. "So . . . what's going on between you and Mikey?"

I blush a little. "What do you mean?"

"Babe, for reals. Not gonna lie. But you were sort of all over him last night. It was kind of a lot, if you ask me. I mean, no shade, but were you wanting to give desperate seventh grader first time around boys?" Cammy laughs.

My face gets kinda hot, and my hands knot up and feel like they're about to fall off.

Cammy must see me going through it and says, "Oh, bitch. I'm sorry. I don't mean it in a mean way. I'm just trying to look out for you. Girl, come here."

I go over, and still chewing cereal, Cam wraps me in a big-ass, slightly sweaty hug.

Remembering Cammy mouthing *no* last night, I ask, "You sure about Mikey being a no?" I rest my head on Cammy's shoulder. "I mean, he's superhot, right? And girl. Seriously. It did seem like he was into me. I don't think I'm hallucinating."

Camilo chuckles and breaks the hug. "I mean, I guess he's not ugly? But, girl, eyes open. Mikey's soooo easy to read. All about lewks and image. Girl, her muscles aren't even that big, but she swears. And I'm sure he's into lotsa guys. I mean, have you seen her IG?"

I have seen his IG—his stories, posts, and reels—and I really liked what I saw.

"I just don't want you to get your hopes up. I know guys like him—they love attention, but there's nothing genuine about them. Girl, for reals. You deserve better."

Cammy reaches over and rubs the back of my head. It's sweet of him, and I nod, because I don't know what else to do. Part of me thinks it's my decision and I don't need his permission, and another part of me feels that Cammy's 110 being the kinda friend that straight-up tells you what you need to hear, not what you wanna hear. #ughhhhh. But on the reals, Mikey's smile definitely felt genuine to me.

Cam goes on, "And what did you really think about Flor? Girl, can she be any more full of herself? OMG. Girl. Puro fake friend realness. Mija."

For a moment, I half convince myself I've fallen into a wormhole and jumped to some alternate reality where Cam didn't just make a group chat for the four of us today and now, mere hours later, is already talking mad shit about the same people she made that group chat for. Girl. Meanwhile, I have like a hundred unread messages.

"Wait. I thought you wanted to make friends with them."

"Girl, yeah, sure. I mean, it's just networking. Mikey's whatever, but Flor? You know she's friends with, like, all the girls, and so, she gets invites to all the best parties. It's summer, bitch. Do you see my vision? Besides, she drives that fierce-ass Jeep, which could totally be funsies, right?"

On the reals, I effing love Cam. For lots of reasons. Yet, at times, Cam's all about what other people can do for her, like talking to girls she doesn't even like to make sure she knows everybody's T and so that she gets invited places and always knows who's hooking up with who. But this feels different.

"Wait . . . are you jealous?" I ask.

"Ay, girl?! Jealous of them?"

"You are!" I can see it on his face. "OMG, seriously," I say, laughing. "You're kinda giving middle school I'm a little bit mad because my bff made another friend, but I won't admit it. Girl, calmate—you're my ride or die. Nothing's gonna change that. And maybe if we all hang out, you'll see that they're not bad people. I mean, I'm good for making new friends."

"Define friends." Cam rolls her neck, pops her tongue, and when her eyes meet mine, she's serious.

"Umm. People you bond with because y'all have major things in common? People who love you for who you are and who'll have your back no matter what and will always be there for you—"

"Girl, try people who can get us into some really hot parties this summer and all through senior year. Try connections, networking. Fun times and invites. Broadening your socials—"

"No." I cut Cam off, the taste of his shitty definition of friendship making my mouth sour. Hurling Kimber's pink pig over the sofa, I'm shaking my head. Cam laughs, twirls her spoon in the bowl, and looks at me like I don't know what I'm talking about. It's a look I'm very familiar with.

"No? Girl, if you think we're all gonna hold hands and tell

each other secrets all summer, I think you're gonna be disappointed. A lot."

Seeing my dissatisfaction, Cam continues, "Babe, I'm just saying, don't get all these high-ass hopes. Those girls are fake af. But fuck all the fake bitches, we got each other, right? That's what I say."

The air in the room goes thin.

I bite my tongue, and my lips collapse on top of one another, because I don't have a response.

"Ey, don't be getting all sad girl now. I'm just saying, we'll hang out with them, have our fun this summer, but don't let your guard down with girls like that, pa. For the reals. Let your guard down—that's how you get burned."

The AC sputters.

By my side, Kimber whines. The piggy squeaks.

Cam comes around the table, throws his arms around me from behind.

"I'm just looking out for you. That's what real friends do."

I nod. I lean back against Cam, who squeezes on me with one arm and pets Kimber with the other.

Honestly, I shouldn't be surprised by Cam's hard-ass stance on friendship. Even though he can be chaotic and kinda superficial af, I've also seen his other side. If Cam considers you his people, he'll throw hands in a heartbeat and talk mad, major shit to defend and protect you. I've witnessed it. Firsthand. For the reals, Cam's come through for me, and I've seen him come through for others, and that's why we're friends.

So, maybe Cam acted up at Flor's because he saw something

I didn't, and maybe he was just anxious, because now, looking back, I can see how Flor can kinda be a lot. But there's a lot more to Cam, just like I know there's a lot more to Flor and a lot more I hope to find out about Hot Mikey.

Looking at the clock in the kitchen, I remember that B should be here soon.

"Okay, well, I should clean up before B gets here."

"Anyways, girl. You do that. Oh, and the FBC is putting together some plans for the summer, so I think you should be part of that convo. Flor's drafting a calendar. Of course she is."

"FBC?" I have no clue what this means.

"Fierce Bitches Club, Mac," Cam snaps. "That's what we're calling ourselves. From the group chat?"

I just shrug. "I was at work — I haven't had a chance to look at my phone."

"Well, while you were at work, Flor and Mikey were all putting together these plans of things they wanna do this summer, and like the true friend that I am, I said, 'Wait. Girl, we should really include Mac in this convo.' If you scroll down, you'll see the link to the calendar Flor made. It's a lot of fluff like dinners and coffee, but I have to admit, she had some cute ideas about going to Pride and doing a pool party at her house for her birthday, and of course, there's the Ari concert in August, which she and Mikey and Hermelinda already have tickets to. . . ."

Cam holds his voice then.

My head starts to spin with all this info. I totes love that Flor and Mikey are planning stuff for us to do for the whole summer.

Like, I've never planned something other than baseball more than a week in advance, much less with a group of friends. And yet, after what Cammy just said about them, it feels kind of a little bittersweet. "Wow. Sounds super fun. I love pool parties, and Pride sounds good too. Girl, you know I've never been. I'll just have to see with my work schedule. Oh, and thanks for including me."

"Of course. We look out for each other, right?"

I nod as Cam serves poses for Kimber, who just stares blankly at him.

"So . . . I know we already talked about Ari's concert," Cammy says. "Just to be clear, you still don't wanna go, right?"

"Of course I wanna go. Girl, do you know me? Like I said before, the tickets are way too effing expensive."

"See, bitch. I do know you. I knew you'd say that. So, what if someone who really, really, really wants you to go got a ticket for you? Like maybe an early birthday present from a very good, true af, down-ass, ride-or-die, I-will-always-have-your-back bff?"

I pause.

Cam grins, poses like he's looking at his tips.

"What are you saying?"

"Like what if *I* get you a ticket, bitch? Then we all can go!" Cam screams. He stomps his feet and does a little happy dance, and this makes Kimber get up from where she's lying, and she runs over and stomps her feet and does these ridiculous little jumps with Cam, and I'm like, OMFG!! Is this really happening?!!

For a second, I think, *Wait, no. I don't want Cam spending all this money.* Girl, I seriously don't wanna feel like I owe Cammy or like he can hold this over my head. But then I remember he said friends look out for each other, and besides, he said it's a gift! And with this, I think I feel okay af with Cam getting me an Ariana ticket, because god, OMG, I really, really, really wanna go, and now that all my friends are going, ughhhhh, I abso 110 need to go to this concert, and so I say, "OMG! Yes!!! Thank you soooo much. You're the best! I love you sooo much. I promise to get you something good for your birthday too!" In no time then, I'm on my feet, doing my version of a happy af/I f-word love my life dance, with Kimber at my side doing her own happy af/I don't know what's going on but I love it dance.

Before Cam leaves, we agree that he'll get us tickets kinda sorta close to Mikey and Flor and Hermelinda, who bought tickets with them.

"Nothing too expensive," he agrees, acknowledging that the others likely have expensive af tickets, and we shouldn't break ourselves to keep up.

Hugging Cam tightly, I feel lucky af.

Meanwhile, Kimber paws and baby-cries like nobody ever loves her until Cam finally leans over and gives her a dozen sweet kissies goodbye and tells her to "Stop relying on that body, girl!" which makes me lol my ass off and kinda wish Cam didn't have to leave.

At the door, watching Cam drive off, I wave and pull Kimber back so she doesn't push her wet-ass nose through the screen, and I can't effing believe it: *Holy shit! I'm going to see Ariana Grande!!*

Chapter
4

I'M SITTING ON MY BED WHEN B SHOWS UP.
Kimber bolts to the door, barking her ass off.

I find B in the kitchen. Her fade is fresh af, like she literally just had it done. She's wearing a white-and-maroon floral button-up, which looks really crisp and new, and she smells like those expensive colognes Clari buys her. Kimber's really giving us desperate seventh grader being around boys for the first time, and girl, I know for a fact that I looked abso nothing like this when I was flirting with Mikey last night, no matter what Cammy says.

"I can only stay for a second," B says when she notices me. She hugs me after getting Kimber to chill and then rummages through the sloping heap of envelopes on the table, moving the box of Berry Crunch and the laundry I was folding to the side.

"Clari and KT and Naomi are waiting outside. We're going to the movies."

I lean against the fridge. "How's everything?"

"It's good. Everything's good" is the response I get, simple and flush, flat like a pebble, and I wish, now, like I really, really, with-all-my-body wish that B wasn't always in a rush and didn't have ten thousand more important things to do and that she could stay longer and hang out, like we used to, so we could talk and laugh and she'd tell me about everything that's good in her life. But it's different now.

"Will you do me a favor, Mac?"

Of course. Anything, I think.

"Don't make a big deal about graduation with Dad."

I shrug. "Okay."

It seems like a ridiculous thing to ask.

"Like, don't even bring it up."

"Ummm. Okay. But why?" I'm pretty sure my dad plans to go to B's graduation tomorrow. I mean, all he's talked about since forever was B going to UT, which she is. I know they've had their disagreements, but girl.

"I'm just saying I won't be hurt if Dad doesn't go. I highly doubt he reads the emails the school sends out, and he hasn't asked me about it, so . . . if he shows up, whatever. But if he forgets or doesn't wanna go, I'm okay with that."

"Well, I doubt he'll forget that you're graduating. Seriously. And to just state the obvi, ummmm, #awkward. Like for reals. This isn't like you."

B sighs. "Please, Mac. Just don't make a big deal about it."

I stare at the sink full of my dad's dishes that I still need to wash and put away. I think of the last time B was here, when she still lived here—the argument she and Dad had over B taking a knee with her basketball team during the national anthem. My dad's anger, roaring like a furnace. B's adamant stance—justice and standing on the right side of history—unwavering. Yelling, then, and my dad putting his whole fist in a wall, then smashing a lamp. It's no wonder B doesn't wanna be here.

On the floor, Kimber sits and stares at us like she has something to say.

"You'll be there?" B asks, gathering the mail she's taking and picking up her keys.

I nod and I smile, and at the same time, I feel something like shittiness coming over me. It's like I have a thousand things I wanna tell her, and I don't know how or when to bring any of it up. I feel like B's doing her own thing now, which I totally effing get. But does she realize she's cutting me off? I wanna vent to her about Dad and talk shit about my job, and yes, OMG, I wanna tell her all about Flor and Mikey and how Cam's coming through big-time by getting me a ticket to the Ariana concert and all these new shiny parts of my life. . . . I don't get it. For so long it was just me and B, and now?

B hugs me from behind and kisses the back of my head. She does that stupid little break dance she used to do whenever we'd get good news when we were kids, and I remember, then, that I love my sister, and I remember the sound of her laughter and all the times we'd sit in her room and she'd fill me in on all her drama with her team and tell me all about her girlfriend Clari. Things are so different now, and I wish that I could get it back, even for a minute — our closeness, doing tons of shit together, all our jokes, eating mangonadas and frito pies, doing push-ups in the backyard and pull-ups on the metal bar our dad installed on the door to the back porch, keeping little scorecards and PRs in my dad's old spiral notebook, and then it just comes out. "I miss you. We need to hang out."

"Yeah. For sure. You know you can come over whenever you want."

"I mean, just us. I really miss you."

B calms with this.

I wait for her to say something back.

But headlights flash into our living room, and Naomi honks her horn.

Instantly, Kimber's ears perk up, and she darts to the front window.

"Yeah. We need to. Okay. Ey, I gotta go. They're waiting for me. But we'll talk."

Before I can say another word, B jets out the house, and I'm left at the table, fixing the pile of my dad's mail, calling Kimber back away from the glass, staring at the box of Berry Crunch and my underwear and socks and a few T-shirts, all waiting to be put away.

It's after midnight, and my dad's not home yet. I have work in the morning, and maybe I shouldn't be waiting up for him. I mean, he's a grown-ass man, after all, but I worry about him.

Like a lot. But waiting also gives me an excuse to stay up and get into the new group chat, so here I am on my bed with Kimber, the cutest bed-hog ever, sprawling out over almost the entire mattress, texting with Mikey, Cam, and Flor with a show about serial killers playing in the background.

Flor is texting about the importance of Rule #1, which she explains is all about being true to yourself, just like Ariana. She adds that "Rule #1 means using 'your instrument'"—which I had no clue is what Ariana calls her voice—to give the world the fierceness that you and only you can give it.

Group Chat Exhibit A

Flor: That's what she means. Be fierce. Be yourself. Be the icon. Be the energy. Be the moment.

Mikey: Yassssss. Preach, girl. 🔥 🔥 🔥

Mikey: like positions, that's the energy

Cammy: omfgag. She executive now

Flor: All. Of. This.

Me: Yassssss

Flor: Ooooooh. Yes, mama.

Flor: A top-tier presidential lewk. Peak performance. I'd vote Ariana Grande for president.

Mikey: bc she's all democracy 👏 👏 👏

Flor: 🏹

Flor: OMG. Okay. Assignment: Top 5 Ariana vids.

Mikey: And go.

Cammy: she wanna fight

Flor: Not debatable. Personal truth only.

Me: . . .

Mikey: Easy af. 5 Break up w ur gf 4 positions 3 In2 U 2 Rain on Me 1 ntltc

Flor: Girl, you're fast.

Mikey: she's passionate about her music

Me: 😊

Me: ❤️❤️❤️

Flor: #5 "Into You"

Flor: #4 "Love Me Harder"

Flor: #3 "no tears left to cry," "breathin," "Break Free" (tie)

Flor: #2 "positions" and "thank u, next"

Cammy: omg so predictable

Cammy: girl can she count????????

Flor: Ties, girl.

Cammy: ugh she swears. I guess so let mama play this

Flor: #1 "7 rings"

Mikey: girl take a seat

Cammy: bish pleas

Cammy: she jelly much

Mikey: girl no

Cammy: she real serious dont be mad bish

Cammy: my tops. any 4 Queen Cardi songs also bang bang

Mikey: not the assignment girl she can't read

Cammy: maybe 34 35 remix bc doja and megan til the daylight booboo

Mikey: get your moment girl

Mikey: then take ur chaos and take sev seats

Cammy: she thinks she cute wait til she get read. filth bish

Flor: 😑😑😑

Mikey: this one swearing hahahah. girl please

Cammy: ugh why she so triggered. Sweetie calm down girl need some waterr

Mikey: somebody teach her how to act

Flor: This is not fierceness.

Flor: Okay. Time to change the energy.

Flor: Assignment: Ariana ponytail selfie using whatever you can find as luxurious hair. And go.

Okay, now, maybe I'm just new to the whole group-chat-with-friends thing, but these assignments are coming fast, like I haven't even started my top five Ariana Grande videos list, and Flor's already giving a new assignment? Girl. On top of that, the little comments. #ummmm #helpmekeepup. Like where did they learn this? Is there a YouTube tutorial that I've missed? A TikTok account teaching up-and-coming gay boys how to be fierce? Because I'm gonna need to enroll in a class. Seriously, girl. It's like they're professional gays already, and I'm amateur af.

So what if all my fierceness is inside? It's true. I'm a thick brown boy who eats a shitload of breakfast tacos and tuna — they're good sources of protein and cheap, and I don't have a lot of coins. I do tons of push-ups, I wear boots and baseball caps and hate shopping, and I love barbacoa with Big Red on Sundays and get my tía Ruby to do my fade every other Friday. #predictable #puroSanAnto #southeastsiderealness — I know. And on the reals, I'm good with it. This life is not for every-body, but it's mine af.

It's like I felt so fake for so long being friends with Benny and Duncan, who were okay, I guess, but could be a little bit a lot douchey af some days, many days, most days, if I'm being honest. I'd fake laugh at their shitty stories and disrespectful jokes about girls and the way they constantly clowned on "homos," the whole time secretly rolling my eyes and throwing up in my mouth and feeling bad for not telling them to stfu. I just don't wanna feel like I have to be somebody I'm not, just to fit in or to be invited places or to belong. Been there, done that, girl. And yet, reading these group texts, I'm realizing that I'm in over my head and I'm gonna have to suck it up and hustle, which feels necessary and weird and contradictory all at the same time. I shouldn't have to change to be with my new friends, so why do I feel like I have to? Ughhh.

Looking around my room, searching for inspiration for Flor's challenge, I tell myself, *Don't be a fake. Just do what comes to you and go with it.* I mean, seriously, being true to yourself is the whole point of Rule #1, right? Is it really that hard to be myself?

I want these guys to like me. When I'm with them, I feel more like myself than I ever have before. And though I feel insecure that they know so much more than I do, I don't feel judged by them. I mean, sure, Cammy judges me, but that's different—best friends look out for one another. I guess what I'm saying is that I wanna be more fierce, and not for them, but for me. And so, girl. Here it is. My chance to show my fierceness.

I spot a towel hanging on the closet door.

"Is a towel ponytail fierce?" I ask Kimber, who doesn't care.

On the reals, though, "Keyword: luxurious" just doesn't match up to a bath towel my tía gave us because ours were all tearing, so I better keep looking.

Excitement fuels me.

But before I can put together a ponytail or spend fifteen minutes taking and retaking selfies or before I can edit my idea and find something better with which to craft my luxurious hair, I hear my dad in the hallway.

Concern in her big brown pittie eyes, Kimber raises her head.

"Shit," my dad grumbles. His voice gravelly, slow.

He drops something, which hits the wooden floor with a dull blank thud.

"Goddamn it shit fuck!!!"

The Ariana ponytail challenge is gonna have to wait.

I step into the hallway and find one of his work boots. Thrown toward the bathroom, his pants remind me of some creature that's lost its bones. In the very middle of the floor, a wadded-up wrapper of something he ate. By his bedroom door, his other boot. Light spills out of his room into the hall.

I pick up his pants and set his boots by the bathroom door and toss the wrapper in the trash.

In the kitchen, my dad stands at the counter, shirtless, in blue basketball shorts that used to belong to me. He stuffs a lump of ham between two slices of white bread. He chews, looks at me, and says, "What?"

"Nothing. Just heard you."

"Okay. And?"

I can see the slobbery mass of food in his mouth. I don't know why this bugs me, and I don't know why I even look, why I don't just ignore him or walk away like he doesn't matter, or why I even try with him.

We're silent. We're usually silent, and between us, the silence is dense. A forest, difficult to move through.

"How was work?" I ask.

My father eats and says nothing, opening the cupboard and taking out a deflated bag of potato chips. He holds the bag upward, his lips open, and what crumbs are left fall into his mouth. Thinking maybe I should give him some time to finish eating, I sit at the table. Briefly, I think of the Ariana challenge waiting for me. I'm gonna have to do better than a towel.

When he's done eating, he leaves the bread open on the counter but shoves the pack of ham back into the fridge. He burps, scratches his leg, and walks right past me.

At least he's not throwing shit or yelling, I think.

I return to my room and try to shake off my dad's silence. I sigh, like pushing out the air in my lungs from the other room might actually change something. Kimber has taken claim of the bed. I lock the door—not that my dad will come looking for me—and I grab my phone, and I'm gagged, like beyond gagged.

Girl. For the reals. Laughing louder than maybe I should when I see the pics my friends have sent in response to Flor's assignment, I'm on my knees, covering my face, hacking from the burst of laughter.

Girl. First, Mikey. Ties. Yes, girl. Neckties. Blue, light maroon, paisley, yellow and red stripes, pink-and-black plaid, white polka dots. Ten or fifteen or maybe twenty of them. In his pic, he's wearing a black baseball cap like the one Ariana wears in "Side to Side," with all the neckties sticking out the back of the cap. His shredder shirt is tied in a knot above his belly button, and he's leaning forward on a bike. #inhisgarage. Lips pouty, head tilted, flexing. Yes, girl. Flexing. Okay. I can't even with that flex. This pic is totes getting saved. Also, his cap doesn't even have to say ICON, because his face and body-ody-ody say it for him.

I show Kimber the pic, but she's not impressed.

Then there's Flor. Of course, she's beautiful. She looks like a model. She looks like Linda Evangelista. Only with an Ariana iconic high pony made out of a long fountain of gold tinsel streamers, which makes it look like New Year's just exploded from the top of her head. Girl. It's a gold waterfall cascading over Flor's shoulder, and the lighting is perfection. #seriouslygorge

And then I read Cammy's response.

Cammy: love this filter girl so pretty

Girl. Here she goes again, I think. Thankfully, Flor doesn't bite; it's Mikey who responds next.

Mikey: Macky!! Dont be shy where you at??????

Macky? Ugh. *No,* I think. *Please don't call me that.*

Flor: Girl, just post. It's all fun. Let us see!

But I can't type fast enough, and I fumble my phone, dropping it on Kimber, who lifts her head, stares hard, and sighs like she's judging me.

Me: Was talking to my dad. Hold up.

I won't say it's panic that settles over me, but something more like a bunch of scorpions fighting over a chicken bone inside my head. Like, I see my green bath towel hanging on my closet door, and there's a bunch of medals from baseball, hanging off trophies on my dresser and on hooks in the wall. But girl. No way I can fashion these into a fierce Ariana ponytail. The clock's ticking, and I can't think of anything. Suddenly I can feel my skin start to shake, like it's going to separate from my muscles and ligaments or something. Now, it *is* panic, panic that I'm gonna miserably fail this assignment in front of my new friends and will immediately be ostracized from the group. I look at Kimber, who's busy snoring and seriously gives no shits about my situation.

And then I remember. Like a gay miracle. Girl, trash bags. Girl, yes. Trash.

Running to the kitchen, I grab a handful of off-brand Hefties from underneath the sink and a pair of scissors, and in three minutes, I have cut enough strips of tall kitchen bags to rubber band together a very long, very crunchy Ariana ponytail. Knowing enough about selfies from watching Cammy over the past year, I know not to go in for a close-up.

Keep it far.

Face the light.

Self-timer, I remind myself.

Balancing my phone on my open dresser drawer, I'm nervous and have to pull myself together.

And *three, two . . . pose.*

Wait. Not yet. I need a lewk. I need to level-up this lewk.

I can't think of any other Ariana than "thank u, next" Ariana, which is my third all-time fave song and video, so I run to B's room to snatch her old pink Adidas hoodie, and I quickly throw on my gray backpack and then grab a pile of books to hold in my arms while I stare at the camera. *Three, two . . .* I toss my ponytail . . . *one.*

Girl. Mess.

Top-tier peak mess!

Girl, in my bedroom at one a.m., I am literally giving a master class in messy mess, and for a whole second, I convince myself it's cute and fulfills the assignment. I immediately hit send, which is altogether a commitment, a choice, and a moment, and which will either be my own personal gay triumph of belonging or social self-sabotage death wish during the first week of having new gay friends.

Apparently, it's more than enough.

Apparently, looking like a chonk deer in headlights with a long, crunchy chongo is a moment and a vibe, because my friends are living, and in my room, having to wake up for work in four and a half hours, so am I.

And what do my friends have to say?

Flor: Girl!!! She is giving!!! 👏👏👏

Flor: Effing diva everything loves it, sis!!

Mikey: #giving she's beautiful. She's gorge. Is she linda evangelista??

Flor: Yasssssssss!! Give her a diaper, sis! Hurrrrrrrr!! All. Of. Hurrrr!!!

Cam: Eat bitch!!!!!!!!!!!!

Mikey: 🔥🔥🔥

Cam: Come thruuuu bestie!!! Serve the bitches girl!!!!!

Flor: Sooo making Ari proud! 🖤 🔥 🖤 🔥 🖤 🔥

Mikey: Fukn love this lewk so much!!! 😍😍😍

Cam: Puro Pinche Slay!!!!!

Cam: Iconica.

Cam: Period bish.

And with that, girl, I'm just gonna say it. Reading my friends' gay approval, my heart swells. For the reals, it's like I'm rocketing off into the gayest atmosphere and loving it. Flor's "diva everything" and Mikey's three flames gas me up, and as I toss my trashy chongo back, I run my hands through the dark, crooked strands, reading Cam's praise, like it's the truest vouch I've ever needed to hear in life. Girl, I'm no Hermelinda and I am no Ariana Grande, but I am def 110 abso living all my fantasy realness right here and right now, because in my trash-bag high pony, I feel like I belong.

Chapter
5

"*G*IRL, YOU BETTER NOT GET YOURSELF arrested." I fold an order of sixteen bacon-and-egg breakfast tacos and then hand each taco to Rebecca, who shoves them in a brown Mr. Bill's BBQ bag.

"Ay, you're right. I can't hit that bitch anyway. Caca splatters!" Rebecca cackles, throwing handfuls of napkins and green chile containers into the to-go bag.

On the reals, I effing love Rebecca. I mean, I kinda so very a lot live for her stories and all her endless drama about grown-ass women, teenage sucias, and even babies who hate on her. We work the same shifts, and even though she gives hard-ass old-school chola, she's sweet af nearly almost all the time. But girl, don't try her, because she will talk mean mad rowdy shit and knock your effing teeth out if you disrespect her, her kids, or her cats, Whispers, Mousy, and Sad Girl. Rebecca swears she knows the way the world works, and she readily hands out life advice to me or to anyone else who'll listen. Once, she told this girl Maria Susana to break up with her boyfriend for cheating on her, and Maria Susana did, and then Maria Susana found an even better boyfriend and now has a baby, a husband, two Chihuahuas, and a three-bedroom house. It's like Rebecca's almost a psychic *and* a counselor.

Sometimes I wonder if my mom was like Rebecca. Or maybe if she was quieter and more serious, like her sister, my tía Ruby. I was a baby when she died, so I don't really know. And other times, I wonder if maybe my mom was like somebody I've never met, a person uniquely her own self. It's not my favorite topic to think on, but sometimes I don't catch myself in time, and I find myself thinking about these things even if I don't want to, before I can push them away. Like right now.

But I'm brought back to my San Anto barbecue realness when both doors to the restaurant fly open. Cammy and his eldest sister Denise hold them open for their mom, La Señora Dionara, and literally, the entire restaurant comes to a halt. Like all the tables of old people actually stop talking, which doesn't happen often, and grown-ass men stop eating, mid-bite, to stare. Some of their jaws drop so low that their wives have to tap their mouths shut. Even the little baby being held by her mom is gagged, and she's a baby.

"Dios mío! Is that Laura León?" an old lady in a Spurs shirt gasps.

"Can it be?" a woman with an enormous sunflower glued to her sunhat asks.

"She's so glamorous!" exclaims a man in a Selena shirt.

At one of the viejita tables, two women take out their phones and snap pictures.

Girl, I would never say this to Cammy's face, but if his mom ever went on *Drag Race*, she'd def have a really good shot at making Top Four—no shade—she's a total glamazon. Even though it's Saturday at nine a.m., Cam's mom's wearing an extremely formfitting white blouse and white leggings that have a shitload of crystals glued to them, a gold belt, fifty thousand gold bangles, and dangerously tall white heels. She's like, *Who doesn't wear heels to breakfast?*

When my manager, Julio, comes out to see what all the commotion is about, he recognizes La Señora Dionara right away. (Cammy and his mom visit my work often.) Girl, it's like Julio is so f-word mesmerized, even though he knows she's not Laura León, even though he's seen her a dozen times before.

"Girl, this is nothing. You should see when we go to Mexico," Cammy says to Rebecca, ordering two potato and egg and a bean and bacon.

Denise orders for their mom, who's busy chatting with Julio, which results in Julio's big-ass smile and then punching a bunch of numbers into the register and comping their food.

"Damn, she wears a lot of makeup," Rebecca whispers when we turn around to grab more tortillas, and she's right. "Like even her makeup has makeup on. How can she even hold up her head?"

"Stop," I tell Rebecca, kicking her foot. She kind of has a point, though.

They're on their way to the mall, Cammy tells us, adding, "Girl, then we're at the salon all afternoon doing nails and hair for graduation. It should be más interesting."

Cammy's mom and his mom's friend own a salon together off Military Drive, and Cam works there doing nails and hair and helping run the place. According to Cam, it's a much more high-paced and fascinating work environment than my barbecue job.

"What are you doing after work?" Cam asks me.

"Probably nothing. Just kicking back with Kimber until it's time to head to graduation," I answer.

When they're done eating, La Señora Dionara allows a few more pictures and insists that Julio let her pay for their meal, to which he responds, "No, señora. You've already paid us. With your presence."

Girl. Gag. Asco. Más gag. Más asco! #forthereals

Before they leave, Cammy and Denise get refills, and their mom waves goodbye to her fans.

At the counter, Cam compliments Rebecca. "Ooh, girl. Love your brows. Are they tattooed? I mean, they're sooo perfect."

Rebecca shakes her head and focuses on her job, like she isn't moved by Cam's compliment. "No, I draw them on every morning."

"I just love an old-school homegirl brow," Cam tells me.

"Hand-painted," I add. "Now, that's talent."

Out of the corner of my eye, I can see Rebecca smile, and I ask Cam, "Have you talked to Flor or Mikey?"

Cam sighs, and now she's the one acting like she can't be bothered. "Girl, please. Those perras prob don't get up until noon while the rest of us . . . already on our grind."

This makes Rebeca chuckle.

I tell Cam, "Text me. If you wanna hang out before graduation, I get off early."

"I'll try. Girl, you know today's gonna try me on every level."

By this time, Denise has her hand on the horn.

"See. Already trying my last nerve. Have fun working, girl. Text me," Cam says, sipping on his Dr Pepper.

As I wave, Rebecca's already rolling her eyes.

"Ugh. So fake," she goes, where no one but the two of us can hear.

"Girl. He's my bff. Don't even," I tell her.

"Excuse me. I was talking about the mom," she says, giving me a look.

And seriously, I'm kinda gagged af because here I'd totally assumed she was talking about Cammy. Girl.

Back at our house, it's noon, and my dad munches the tacos I got him, and he's "gonna pick up a little money" by helping out with his homeboy's landscape job, "so we can take B someplace real nice." I guess he did remember.

When he's done eating, he actually says, "Ey, thanks. And umm, how was your shift?"

Maybe it's that he appreciates his favorite tacos.

Maybe it's that he sees that I'm really not that bad a guy.

Maybe he sees that I'm trying or that he realizes B's gonna be gone soon, and I'm all he's gonna have left. But also maybe he's just tired of being a dick all the time.

Girl, I have to admit. It kinda makes me happy that he asks. I mean, seriously, my dad and I used to talk all the time. About baseball mostly, or really, I guess, now that I think about it, that's the only thing we ever talked about. Like the one thing we had in common. But we talked about it every day, and so, I guess I just miss it, now that we don't have anything to talk about.

"Fine. We were busy. Somebody ordered a bag of sixteen tacos," I reply. I'm sitting on the couch, Kimber at my feet. I'm still wearing my uniform pants, but I've taken off my work shirt and kicked off my shoes. For a second, I think about telling him all about Cammy's mom. However, I think my version of the events will come off as really, really too f-word gay for him.

"Damn. That's a lot of tacos."

It's not much, but it's something. Better than silence, I guess.

We agree that we should try to get to the Alamodome by six thirty, maybe a little earlier in case the truck gives us trouble, and he asks, "Did you tell B we're taking her out to eat? What did she say?"

I can't lie. I want to, but I can't.

"She hasn't responded."

"Text her again. Or tell her to her face."

"I already texted three times, Dad."

My dad gets quiet.

I jump in: "You need me to wash anything for you? I'm gonna iron my shirt for tonight. I can iron your shirt too. And your pants. Starch them up real good."

"Yeah. You can do that."

This makes me a little bit happy.

"Which shirt you gonna wear?" I ask.

"I don't know. Something."

"I'll pick out a few. Iron them. So you can choose."

My dad nods, and for a moment, I think he's gonna say something more. Like I can see the words right there between his teeth, but nothing. "I gotta get going. I'll be back around five."

I can't really explain it, but even though he's been such a dick to me, I wanna get up and put my arms around my dad, hug him, tell him this is all gonna be all right. It's the wrong move, though, and so, I leave things as they are. "I'll try again," I tell him as he walks out the door.

"Yeah." Putting on his cap, he replies, "Good idea."

After my dad takes off, I'm in my room, and I'm baby-talking with Kimber while rubbing on her belly, which she effing loves, when I get a message:

Flor: Girl, tacos at my house? I think you're off now, right?

Needless to say, tacos and hanging out with my new friends are two of my favorite things in the world, so no need to ask me twice. Girl, what I do need to ask myself twice is why Flor texted me directly instead of in the group chat. I'm fixing to ask

Flor if it's cool if I invite Cammy, but then I pause. Cam said he'd be supes busy at the salon, and today was gonna work all his nerves. Maybe he'd appreciate the invite? More likely, though, he'd get pissed and start moving his mouth that I'm bothering him while he's sooooooo busy, and also, and on the serio-serio, I kinda don't wanna invite Cam because what if he decides to leave work, and how's he gonna act in front of Flor and Mikey? #facts. And girl! What if he gets mad that I wanna hang out with them when he's apparently already decided that they're fake? Girl, seriously. And also, as much as I like hanging out with Cam, I don't want drama, and on top of that, it feels like I'd be asking for approval to eat tacos at Flor's, and that's not my vibe today.

Mac: Girl. Pues, duh. Can y'all scoop me, tho? Pretty, pretty please. I just need 10.

Flor: Mikey will come get you!

Okay. So, yes, girl. You heard that right. Hot Mikey's gonna pick me up. #bishhhhhhhhhhhh #gaggery #puropincheyesssss #magicalaf

Pronto fast, I'm showering and throwing on clothes. Now, I've never been somebody to worry too much about what I look like or how I dress. Today, though, for the first time in maybe a long time, I'm a little bit kind of a lot stressing over what I'm gonna wear.

Finding myself in a jam, where do I turn?

Naturally, I look at Mikey's IG. Mikey has tons of hot lewks. And scrolling through his pics, I'm like, he's half-naked a lot. Ufff. It's like spank bank treasure trove hottie with a body-ody-ody realness. I throw on a pair of B's Jordan shorts and a shredder, which I have tons of and which looks similar to something Mikey's wearing in one of his pics.

In no time, I'm getting a text that says: Here.

Damn, that was fast.

I quickly brush my teeth and put on deodorant. Before I run out, I grab my favorite Astros cap and pull it on backward, and when I catch a glimpse of myself in B's mirror, I try to picture myself like Mikey—shirtless, flexing, confidently showing myself. I flex too. Not as impressive as Hot Mikey, but a flex, nonetheless. Good enough for me.

When I get in the car, Mikey turns down the music. He looks at my shirt, which has a gray wolf on the front of it, neck tilted upward, howling at the moon. It's an old shirt, well-worn. One of my favorites. "You like wolves, huh?"

I nod, and I try, for some stupid reason, to quell this big-ass smile happening to my face. Mikey looks good.

"Yeah. Wolves are pretty badass," Mikey says. "Me. I like eagles. National bird of the Philippines. I got one on my shoulder and back."

Mikey points to his back and tries to pull up his shirt, which is a struggle, since he has his seat belt on, and the shirt is tight. Unsuccessfully, he attempts again to pull up the back of his shirt to show me the eagle tattoo.

He shifts into park and tries again.

Above us, shade from the giant-ass oak my dad hates covers the car.

"This isn't going the way I thought," he laughs, and undoes

the seat belt. "Shit, I'm gonna have to take the damn thing off."

"Let me help," I say, which I mean and don't mean all at once, and suddenly, I feel my body fill with hot embarrassment for having said this.

"Yeah," he goes. "I'm struggling."

I reach behind him as he leans forward, and tugging upward, I pull the shirt above his neck, nearly over his head. Mikey's sunglasses fall off, hit the steering wheel, and land in his lap, and his big-ass arms get caught in his shirt, above his forehead. Stuck, Mikey chuckles.

"Well, that could've gone better."

"At least I can see the Filipino eagle now," I tell him, which is kinda fake af, because girl, I've already studied the f outta this tattoo by scoping his IG.

Seriously. The detail is stunning, and I'm gagged looking at both the marvelous bird on Mikey's marvelous back, which ripples in brownness, and how the bird's feathers extend over, across, and down his shoulder, too. Mikey has wide-ass lats. And whenever Mikey makes a small movement, it seems like feathers are moving, like the whole bird is moving with him.

"Damn. That's intense." Wanting to touch his back, I refrain. Like I literally grab my own hand, because I imagine tracing each plume. I imagine counting each dark gray feather.

"Philippine eagles are rare. Less than five hundred of them are left in the world. Ey, you know, my arms are kinda stuck up here. You think when you're done you can help get me free?"

Captivated by Mikey's eagle, I'd forgotten about his arms.

Helping him pull his shirt back down, I'm thinking a lot of

things. I'm thinking Mikey is rare—I've never met anybody like him. I'm thinking I feel comfort being next to him too. I'm thinking he didn't have to show me his eagle, but he did. What does that mean? I'm thinking Mikey's skin is smooth, so different from my own, which is covered in dark black hairs sprouting all over my brown chest and under my arms and down my belly and thighs. I think of a tattoo I'd get—where and of what and how?

Mikey grabs his sunglasses, tucks them in his collar.

He opens the door, steps out, and fixes his shirt.

"I think maybe I overdressed," Mikey admits, running his hands over his polo shirt.

"Naw, pa. You look good" is my response. Trying to change the subject, I go back to his tattoo. "I like how they made the wings and feathers curl around your shoulder, like to capture the delt. The shape of it. That's skill."

"Thanks. My mom's homegirl's brother did it for me. Back in Cali. It was for my birthday."

"Happy belated birthday."

"Yeah. It was a good one. But I think the next one's gonna be even better." Mikey flashes his teeth beneath a wide smile.

"Oh yeah?"

Mikey's grinning, which makes his eyes speak to me. "Yeah. November 1, baby. Scorpio energy."

I like his confidence, and although I don't know anything about star signs, when Mikey turns up the music, it's Ariana and it's "Forever Boy," which, girl. Seriously. I mean, come on. That's the song Mikey decides to play when he picks me up. I'm no detective, but it doesn't take a detective to see inside Mikey's smile and dark eyes. I know I'm not an expert on hot boys, but it definitely feels like Mikey is abso 110 flirting with me. Girl. And nothing I'm doing is giving seventh-grade desperada. Girl, really? Maybe that was Cam's opinion at Flor's house, but it's sure the f not mine. I push out the negative thoughts and just listen to the song, which is fire. Not debatable. And driving off in Mikey's ride, hearing Ariana go on about "be forever mine, you and I," the only thing I can do is hope something good and fierce happens between Mikey and me. That and sing along.

Chapter 6

*T*HE FIRST THING OUT OF FLOR'S MOUTH WHEN
we arrive is, "Girl! OMG. Get ready for this one. My
brother's taking us to get tacos. Ughhhhhhh." Flor's sigh is
bitter af and longer than all of Mikey's megamixes put together.

"Sweet," I reply, wondering how these new group dynam-
ics will work out. I mean, I haven't hung out with Benny since
last summer, after I quit baseball, and he tried to get me to
come back.

Mikey just shrugs. "Okay."

"*And* he's bringing Duncan."

Girl. Ugh. Okay, so I'm a little gagged by this.

One-on-one, Benny and Duncan are okay, I guess. Girl,
but the two of them together. #doubleughhhhhhhh

It'll be fine, I tell myself, resting assured that my burgeoning friendships with Flor and Mikey are enough to make this inter-action tolerable, if not possibly even enjoyable.

"Girl, I know you know Benny, but you haven't really seen him around his friends," Flor says to Mikey. "My brother and his friends equals top-tier cringe realness, girl."

Now I'm really gagged.

Is this what Flor thought of me all those years when I hung out with Benny?

"Ummm. *All* his friends?"

Flor looks at me. "Girl. I didn't even know you back then."

"And now?"

"Bitch, you know I love you. Don't try it!"

Flor throws her arms around me and squeezes. And then she pulls Mikey in and squeezes as hard as she can, which girl, isn't very hard at all. So, Mikey being Mikey wraps his huge arms around both of us and squeezes so that Flor's back pops, and the three of us suddenly panic, thinking she's broken some-thing.

Just then, Benny and Duncan bounce down from upstairs. Looking surprised to see me, Duncan flashes me a half-smile, but Benny doesn't say anything. He gives Mikey and me a nod and turns to Flor. "Let's go. I'm hungry."

For as long as I've known Benny, it's been abso obvi af that there's major tension between him and Flor. I never really paid much attention to it, but now, it's all I can notice. I mean, for reals. Flor makes a full-on vomit sound when she sees him and fully ignores what he says and instead starts applying gloss. And girl, she is getting extra glossy for our little taco trip.

Looking herself over in her phone, Flor applies a heavier coat while her brother glares at her as he waits with keys in hand. #facts, she likes her lips full and wet-looking.

Feeling her oats, Flor runs her fingers through her hair, fluffing her bangs.

"I just love a bouncy bang. Don't you?"

I smile. "Yes, girl. She has bangs."

"She sure does." Inspecting her face in the phone again, pouting her lips, Flor makes her bangs jump some more.

Annoyed, Benny jangles his keys and grunts, motioning for Duncan to follow him outside. Shortly after, he's honking. Two short bursts, which Flor ignores, and then a longer, angrier horn.

"I think your brother's waiting outside." Mikey points out front.

"She can wait" is Flor's response. Unbothered.

Girl, I get the sense Flor is on the reals trying to push buttons. #onpurpose #givingslownessforreals #triggering

While we wait, I think about Cammy again. A flicker of guilt starts up inside me, and I ask, "So, have y'all talked to Cam today?"

Mikey yawns and shakes his head, digs into his phone.

"Just the group chat. She said she was 'waaaaaaaay busy' today or something like that." Flor's voice trails off when she says this, and maybe I'm reading too much into this, but she sounds irritated and dismissive.

And then I see it. Girl. Flor looks over at Mikey, and I think, *Am I seeing things? Or did Flor just roll her eyes?* And I'm gagged, like a lot a lot, because why is she rolling her eyes like that? Is she rolling them at me or because of Cam?

Quickly, I reply, "Yeah, he's doing nails and hair with his mom at their salon. For graduation. They're gonna be slammed. I think Naomi—y'all know Naomi, who's with KT—yeah, she's getting her hair and nails done. Or that's what B told me."

"Ohhh, I love Naomi. She's so pretty. I'm glad she won homecoming queen," Flor chirps. "You know, I think Hermelinda's totes gonna win queen this year."

Mikey just nods. He's focused on a video.

Benny honks again, louder. Longer. More obnoxiously.

A smirk escapes Flor's mouth. "Girl, do you like this shirt? What do you think?"

It's a bluish-purple flowy thing. Looks fine to me.

"Yeah. Looks great," I say.

"I don't know." Flor spins around. The fabric flies. "Girl, I feel hot in this. I mean, I love blurple, but girl. What was I thinking? It's like 150 degrees outside. I better change."

And with that, Flor hops upstairs.

"If he comes to the door, tell him I'm changing! And he better not leave us!!" Flor yells from somewhere else in the house.

Fifteen minutes later, we finally emerge from the house. Flor goes first. In a romper. Yes, girl. A white summertime romper. And a straw hat with a wide-ass arching brim that shades her face so all you see is gloss. She carries a small red clutch and sports a pair of dark tortoiseshell glasses that look rich af. And girl, Flor is giving it in the middle of her neighborhood, turning that summertime sidewalk into a runway to be stomped.

Mikey and I follow.

Girl, this isn't at all what I expected when Flor said come over for tacos, and from the look on Mikey's face, I think he expected something much, much different as well.

Duncan rolls down the passenger window. "Took you ladies long enough. What's up, Mac?"

Judging from the scowl on Mikey's face, I don't think he appreciates a random straight guy referring to him as a lady. Sure, we do it to each other all the time, but it just hits different when it comes from outside the group.

"Hey." I say it flatly, and Duncan extends his arm through the window for a fist bump.

The engine idling, the music thumping loudly, I just stare at Flor and think, *Girl, what the f-word is happening?*

Flor tips up her fancy hat and pushes down her sunnies to look right at me. "My mom said I have to watch him today. Also, he just wants me to pay and tell my mom that he behaved himself. That's why he was willing to wait. He always does this."

Benny laughs. "Yeah, I'm doing Mom a favor taking you."

"Yeah, that's why Mom gave me her card, right?" Flor taps her well-polished index finger against the body of her cherry-red clutch.

"Ey, stranger. Come on. Get in. What you waiting for?" Duncan chimes in.

I try to smile at Duncan. Girl, he has his moments and is def a giant mamón, but we'd been friends so long that for a lot of the time I didn't notice his shittiness. Most times. Or I overlooked it or something. And besides, no matter his shitty moments, Duncan has done me some solids over the years.

Benny and Duncan open their doors, and Flor insists that his brother open the car trunk so she can lay her hat in it "so that it doesn't get smashed," which is another squabble that takes longer than it should to resolve, and after standing in the hot-ass sun, sweating, until Benny finally opens the hatch, we finally pile in, half-drenched, squeezing in back. Quickly, Mikey claims the middle of the back seat, which is odd to me because the smallest person, Flor, would usually take the most uncomfortable space, but Mikey insists, and I'm sooo fine with this, because this way, my leg touches his.

"Just drop us off after tacos, and y'all go do what you want. I'll tell Mom you were with me the whole time," says Flor, trying to find a comfortable position. "But one condition."

Duncan and Benny look at each other.

"What?" Benny grunts.

"You have to play Ariana."

"Fuck no!" Benny barks back. "Hell no. Fuck that. I'll go hungry."

Duncan laughs.

"Go hungry, then. Go make yourself a shitty-ass Pop-Tart," Flor scoffs.

"Fuck it," Duncan responds. "I'll listen to her for some tacos. Besides, she fine as fuck. She can carry my baby."

Flor rolls her eyes and pretends to throw up in her mouth. "Girl, please. Like she'd ever give you a chance."

Benny snorts from holding in his laugh or expelling it too fast.

"This is what I have to live with," Flor mutters loud enough for the whole car to hear. But by this point, she's already synced Ariana's "Love Me Harder."

And girl, I love this song. Seriously. Like all her songs are so, so, sooooo good. It's hard not to say they're all my favorites.

Because Flor knows all the words to every Ariana song ever, she performs right there in Benny's car with all the video choreography you can fit into the back seat of a Ford Mustang with two other gays sitting beside you—one of them with big-ass arms and the other, me, serving thickness—which says a lot about Flor's precision and body control.

Girl, like for reals, I can see Flor with kitty ears on that bed and in that chair. #nuanceaf #trueaffan #Rule1. Flor is seriously giving it, and maybe she's playing it up in front of her brother and Duncan, but maybe this is the real-ass energy she brings to the world. OMG. Yes. Girl. All of Flor's gay-ass energy! #lovesit

Meanwhile, Benny speeds, as always, weaving in and out of traffic, honking at a minivan, and throwing the finger at a little wiener dog that takes too long to cross the street, all while nodding enthusiastically and cheering Duncan on as Duncan goes on and on about this new girl he's talking to. Benny fuels Duncan's story, asking questions about her tits and her ass and if Duncan had already "smashed her." And "could she walk after?"

"Seriously?" Flor isn't having it, interrupting her Ariana performance. "I mean, why do girls even like them? Why do guys even want to be like them?"

I'm not saying anything.

Mikey grabs my leg, squeezing it hard, and I'm starting to grasp that he can't effing stand these guys. He leaves his hand on my leg, though, and relaxes his grip, just rests it there, like that's where his hand needs to be. #fyes #swoonaf. Girl, this is a lot, and I am soooooo into him. And of course, I'm sweaty af, and so is everybody else, so Benny cranks up the air, the AC blowing full-on in Flor's face, giving her the bouncy bang she lives for. A perfect detail for her Ari performance.

In the back, we ignore the boys in the front, lip-syncing to Ari and scrolling on our phones, Mikey liking pics of DJs and parties and frowning at others, showing me good ones and bad ones, and asking my opinion on everything from high-tops and swimsuits to hairstyles and pics of puppies in little police uniforms.

"OMG. *Paw Patrol* is so cute." Flor reaches over during the chorus to point to Mikey's screen.

All the while, I just keep thinking about sitting so close to Mikey, his leg pressed against mine, his hand on my thigh. I think I'm getting sweat all over him, which isn't the moment, but maybe it is? I can't tell.

What I can tell is that we're cramped af, and because of this and also because I just wanna touch him, I take my arm and place it over Mikey's shoulder.

"You smell good," he whispers.

"It's my deodorant," I whisper back.

Mikey nods and takes a deep breath, and I think maybe he's immersing himself in my smell or that he's okay with my arm around him, perhaps both. And I'm very a lot thinking that Cam was totally wrong about Mikey, and I can't wait to tell her, not in a like ooh, bitch, you're wrong kinda way, because that could potentially start a clash, but more like see, girl, sometimes you just gotta give people a chance, because people have different sides, which we totally miss if we jump off a cliff of conclusions and judge bitches right off the bat. Seriously. Cammy def knows a shitload about life, but I know some shit too. I take a breath and relax, and beside me, I can feel Mikey relax too.

In the taqueria drive-through, I lean into Mikey and tell him, "OMG, I love this place. They serve breakfast tacos all day."

Meanwhile, Benny's indecisive af as Duncan keeps repeating to Benny that he wants "three country sausage and cheese and a giant Dr Pepper, bruh."

Instinctively, Flor takes over.

"Ma'am? Give us just a moment, please. I do apologize."

In no time, Flor assembles the group order and calls the woman back so we can finally request our food, and when Benny tries being difficult, complaining, "No!! I want two beef fajitas with no onions and no cilantro on corn, and then give me two carne guisada with cheese on flour, it has to be flour because the gravy, and then, one bean, potato, rice, and cheese," Flor just says, "Four carne guisada and cheese. That's what you're getting. Mom's not here, so you don't get to make some special-ass order and waste everybody's time. Four carne guisada and cheese, please. On flour."

I'm like, *Wow, bitch.* #thinkshesdonethisbefore #bossbish #taqueriagirlrealness

The drive-through's fast, and before we know it, we're stuffing our mouths. Everybody in that car deep-throating the shit outta their all-day tacos, except Flor, who stands firm that she'll wait to eat her one soft chicken taco at the table. "I'm not getting food all over this outfit. Girl, have you seen how she drives?"

Driving back to Flor's, the car is quiet af, except for the sound of chewing and Ariana giving us "One Last Time." Babe, as much as I wanna sing, I can't eat my tacos and serve lyrics simultaneously.

"These are yum af," I say to Mikey.

"You're yum af," Mikey replies softly, winking at me, and I smile so big I think my mouth's gonna pop off my face.

"Thanks. You too."

We're almost back to Flor's house, and Duncan, turning around to look at me, starts in on me. "Ey, Mac. You're looking happy af. Come on. Tell us. You get you some last night, bruh?"

Girl, first of all, I'm like, *Ugh. Don't call me bruh.*

Secondly, I think, *This is your moment, girl. Either you be a fake-ass bitch and lie, or you say it. You grab your balls, and you pick your head up and you tell the truth.*

This second feels as big as the universe, and I'm ashamed to admit that for a millisecond, I actually contemplate lying about who I am.

Girl, but here are my friends, my *real* friends, right next to me, and here is Ariana and here is "Break Free," and girl, I know that song's not really about coming out, it's totally about something else, but girl, in the back of Benny's Mustang with Mikey and Flor and Ariana Grande, and with Flor giving us diva everything lewks and choreo, and Mikey pressing up against me, looking right at me, Ariana tells me all I need to hear: "Tried to hide it, fake it. I can't pretend anymore."

Girl. All. I. Effing. Need. Thank you, Kween. Right there. Rule #1. Everything.

"Come on, bruh. Spill it. Tell the tale. Who the lucky girl?" Duncan's determined.

And so, looking right in Duncan's eyes, mid-bite and balancing my half-eaten taco on foil in my hand so none of it falls apart — eating in cars is a talent, you know — I reply, "You know me, papa. I'm not a talker. Besides, *he's* hot af, so I'm the lucky guy."

Girl, gagged.

Shoving my face with a thick-ass potato and egg taco with salsa verde dripping out the sides and dropping a bomb-ass pronoun — *he's* — with one of my all-time fave Ariana Grande songs playing in the background, this is how I come out to my old friends.

Beside me, Flor's clapping, nodding her head, holding her fancy-ass red clutch up to the gods, saying, "Good for you, sis."

Mikey grabs onto my thigh tightly and then slaps my leg over and over, because he's living for this moment.

Girl, this coming out feels like a major flex.

"He's?" Confused, Benny shakes his head. "What the . . . ?"

"Ha!" Duncan exclaims. "He said 'he's'! I told you. I fucking told you, Ben. You dumb-ass. I told you he was. I win!!"

Gagged, Benny looks at me in the rearview mirror and then at Duncan and then at his taco.

But not Duncan. Duncan gloats. Duncan claps and hollers. Duncan celebrates.

Girl, Duncan acts like an ass, like he just won the lotto, like typical Duncan, but a supportive ass. He tells me, "Bruh, I'm so here for you. My mom's sis is gay. She cool af, too. And you know me, I don't judge." He points to the tattoo on his biceps that reads *Only God Can Judge Me* and flexes. Classic Arnold pose. Classic Duncan. #hisarmsaresmallerthanmine #noshade #okaygirlalittleshade

And that's when Benny opens his big mouth. "Wait a minute. What do you mean you're gay? I mean, I know *he's* gay. Just look at him." Benny points at his brother, and I don't know if it's Benny being straight-up rude af or just that play-fight way siblings so often do each other.

Girl, but Flor smiles, does that gay-ass hair toss I effing love. Then tilts her head. Places both hands beneath her chin like she's posing for some portrait and smiles, while slowly, precisely, pointedly extending both middle fingers simultaneously toward Benny, the whole time never breaking her smile, never breaking the pose.

Girl. Dying. #effingburymenow

Struggling so hard to keep myself from bursting into laughter at Flor's soft, wordless read of her brother, I lock eyes with Benny. "Want me to prove it?"

Girl, Mikey and Flor are laughing their asses off, but Benny frowns, puts his hands out in front of him, a wall between us, as if to block the gayness from coming for him. "No. No. No, no. Fuck no." And he makes a vomiting noise with a face to match.

"Look who's the drama queen now," Flor jumps in, snapping a pic. "I should post this. 'Caption: Deep-throating, but she's not good at it.'"

I almost spit out part of my taco.

And Duncan. OMG! Duncan laughs too. Hard, deep-ass laughter. The kind of laugh that makes you cough and see stars.

"That's fucking funny," Duncan huffs, battling to regain his breath. "Man, Florencio, bruh. Who knew you were this fucking funny?"

Benny gives his brother the eye of spite af, shaking his head disapprovingly.

Then he turns to Duncan and stutters, "Ey, ey. Bruh. You're supposed to be on my side. Bruhs stick together. What the hell?"

In the back, Flor puts on a show. Holding out her hand, acting like she's buffing her nails. Inspecting them, buffing some more. Blows them out toward the front.

Girl, it's a lot. And it's hot.

Even though he's over it, Mikey can't help but break a smile watching Flor go at her brother's bigotry.

"I always knew. I did. I swear to you. I just wish you'd told me earlier, bruh. On the real. I got you. *We* got your back." Duncan glares over at Benny, who makes a sour-ass face. "Anybody tries fucking with you, you tell me. I'd gladly open up a big-ass can of knucks on anybody messes with my people."

My people? I think. *Wow. Is he being real?*

And as we pull up to Flor's house, Duncan looks to Benny and tells him, "Bruh, girls love it when straight guys are cool with the gays. It's like it makes you seem sensitive and like you're not some homophobic piece of shit."

"Yeah, bruh," Flor interjects. "Don't be a homophobic piece of shit." She smirks at her brother. "Ooooh, girl. OMG! Loves it!!! She's gonna make a fierce hashtag."

Now Mikey's chuckling and squeezing my thigh. He turns his face and presses his big-ass smile into my shoulder, so that his teeth graze my muscle, which sends a throatful of hot breath and a wave of quivers across my body. Uffffffff! #girlforreals #gimme #cantpretendanymore

Chapter 7

"**M**AC! WE'RE OVER HERE!"

It's Clari's mom, who's yelling and waving relentlessly. After taking twenty minutes to find a parking spot, and after paying twenty-five dollars to park in the Alamodome parking lot, a fee neither my dad nor I expected, we finally make it to the stadium and are making our way to find seats when Mrs. Longoria spots us.

"Come sit with us," she offers, but my dad acts like he doesn't hear her.

In his good jeans and the red shirt I pressed for him, my dad keeps walking, the back of his ten-gallon hat bouncing with each step.

Not wanting to be rude, I tell my dad I'll catch up with him.

He points to the row of seats he wants, which is far away from where everyone else is sitting.

"He wants to sit where he can see," I explain to Clari's mom, who hugs me.

"Mac, it'll be your turn next year. Are you excited, mijo?"

"I can't wait," I lie, hoping she doesn't ask about where I wanna go to college or what I wanna study.

"I'm not sure if B told you, but we're all going to eat at Maria Bonita's after. I made a reservation, and I can easily add two more. If you and your dad want to join us."

I've always thought Clari's mom was nice af. Tonight, she seems nicer than usual.

"I'll ask him, though he wants to surprise B by taking her out to eat after."

Mrs. Longoria pauses. "Well, does B know about this? I guess not, right? It being a surprise. It's just that when I asked B, she said y'all didn't have any plans, so I invited her to come with us. You and your dad are more than welcome to join us. The more the merrier, right?" She smiles. Her lipstick is manzana red, and her earrings are small diamonds that gleam beneath the arena lights. "I can talk to your dad, if that would help," Mrs. Longoria offers, placing her hand on my shoulder, which I know would abso not help things. My dad doesn't really like talking to "fancy people," as he calls them, which Clari's mom, who works in the mayor's office, is certainly one of.

"I'll talk to him. It'll probably be late by the time we get out of here. I mean, there are so many seniors. So who knows? Maybe it's better if we just invite B to eat tomorrow."

Mrs. Longoria nods. "At the least, let's all try to get a picture. While B and Clari are still in their caps and gowns."

"Yeah, that sounds great." I force a smile. "I should get back to my dad. But thank you." And here, I don't know why, but my voice starts to shake a little bit, and I have to hold my words behind my teeth before they crash out of me and shatter, and I say, "I just wanted to say thank you. For always being so nice to us, especially B. I just wanted you to know that. It means a lot."

Clari's mom hugs me again.

This time, though, I don't know how I feel about being hugged by Clari's mom, especially with my dad probably watching, especially with this awkward dinner situation and my emotions swelling up in my mouth, but I guess I'm okay with it, because I don't push her away, and I hug her back.

"Your mom would be proud of y'all."

I don't have anything to say when she tells me this.

I don't know why she says it, and I don't like that she says it to me here.

I don't know what to do with her words. Or the feelings that come with them, rising and swirling inside me, threatening to bust out.

So I nod, like I appreciate her comment, and I thank her again and wave and look up into the stands, trying to see where my dad has gone. Explaining to my dad that B will not be eating with us feels like a box of bricks and barbed wire that I have to carry. I'll have to find the right time to unload this on him. The right words, too. On the outside, I know my dad projects toughness, like he doesn't give a shit and like nothing can hurt him, but girl. #toxicmasc #verytoxicmask #ummmmno

The ceremony begins, and I settle in for a long night. I text Cammy to let her know that I'm here and sitting in the nose-bleeds. Fortunately, or unfortunately—I can't decide—our last name is Acosta, so B comes up fast. This also means we'll be here for a while, listening to letters *B* through *Z*, until it's all over and we get to meet up with B.

"She's coming." My dad elbows me when he sees B's row stand up and make their way to the stage, and when they announce B's name, my dad leaps to his feet. He claps fast and hard, like he wants it to mean something, like he wants her to hear him from halfway across the arena.

"Come on, Bonita! Yeah! Hell, yeah!!" my dad shouts, which reminds me of the times we sat in the stands, and he cheered on one of her pressure-cooker jump shots or a game-clinching double OT free throw.

With a swagger, B crosses the stage.

From as far back as we are, my dad tries to take a picture of B. He bungles his phone and almost drops it into the empty seats in front of us.

"Dad, I can buy us a pic. Look. There's a school photographer up close. Right by the stage." I point.

Nevertheless, he tries working his phone again.

"Goddamn it! Mac, take the fucking picture."

I don't wanna argue, and knowing it's gonna be a shitty-ass pic, I take a couple with my phone. "I'll send them in a minute."

My dad grumbles. The glint of his silver belt buckle, which

I dug out of his drawer and shined for him, catches the lights. The buckle is large like a grapefruit and nice—one of the nicest things he owns—and he seemed happy, earlier, seeing the shiny silver waiting for him on the table next to his old Justins polished up, almost new-looking.

Confidently, B shakes the superintendent's hand, takes her diploma, then steps away.

"All-Region First Team! Two-time district MVP!" my dad calls out. He's beaming, and I'm only now realizing how much this means to him.

Once she's a few steps from the superintendent, B dribbles and quick-steps, a show of agility, a pump fake, a gooseneck, fadeaway.

Swoosh! I see B mouth the word as she falls back, arm arched in perfect form.

The crowd goes ham. Girl. Even I'm feeling it.

"All net, baby!" I yell out.

Hearing the crowd howl for my sister, I feel proud, like a shiny feeling rising up inside me that this human being has done something wonderful and is wonderful and that I have the good fortune of not only knowing her but being connected to her, and then it hits.

In a couple of months, she'll move on, like really, really leave us, leave me. B's moving on with the rest of her life and not looking back. She's got her whole future ahead of her, and it's bright af. But that means no more taco runs, no more going over to our tía Ruby's so she can fade up our hair. No more watching B make Kimber twerk or get all happy for weenies and telling me, as much as I hate hearing it, to "get your life together, because if you don't stand for something, you'll fall for anything, bruh." Girl, I effing hate when she calls me "bruh," and yet, I know I'll miss it.

I guess in a way, B's been slowly shifting out of my life, which creates this strange, sooo not-fierce tension between my dad and me, because even though we don't talk about it, we both know that before long, I'm gonna have to decide if I stay here or if I go, and that means it'll be up to me to decide if my dad ends up alone. And it's like, do I really want that power? And do I really wanna keep living half a life, which is what's gonna happen if shit doesn't change? Do I really wanna spend my whole life tiptoeing around broke-ass glass? Ughhhh. It's a lot, girl. And right then, surrounded by applause for my sister, I can see myself up on that stage a year from now, getting ready to launch off to a future that's soooo much better than my life right now, and I decide that I have to do it. B came out to my dad, and it's the right thing to do, to live honestly, not to live some fake-ass life for somebody else. So, whatever this is gonna look like, no matter how difficult and messy it might be, I know I can come through for myself because I can see it—all the better days ahead. New friends, new confidence, new hope. And like that, with my heart jumping up and down, I decide to tell my dad that I'm gay.

"All net! That's right!!" I hear a voice behind me say, and I recognize that voice right away.

It's Mikey, standing behind me in a light blue shirt, a red tie, and khakis.

Damn it, he's handsome. And he smells so effing good.

I think I gasp.

"Can I sit with y'all?" he asks.

I stumble for a second, not sure what to say.

I mean, obviously, yes! I'm thrilled Mikey looked for me and now wants to sit with me, but then I see my dad glaring at him, and uncertainty takes over.

"Sure," I say, and I feel my face not letting itself be my face.

I feel myself becoming rigid, like just seeing my dad looking Mikey up and down reminds me everything isn't happy and smooth and good for me, that coming out to him is gonna be a lot effing harder than I think.

"I'm Michelangelo Villanueva." Mikey extends a hand to my dad, but my dad hesitates, at first, to shake it.

"You on the baseball team, son?" my dad asks.

The crowd cheers as more graduates cross the stage.

"No, sir. I'm more of a powerlifting kind of guy."

My dad shakes his hand, stares at Mikey's biceps, which bulge beneath the blue button-up. The shirt is tight af, and he looks so good in it.

"How much you bench?"

When my dad asks this, I cringe. It's straight-up go-to queso question number one whenever somebody says they work out.

But Mikey seems unbothered.

"Depends. Mostly I do push days and stack up. Start with two plates. Forty-fives, you know, to warm up. Go for twelve to fifteen reps. Build up. Peak two plates, maybe throw on a

ten. Three to five reps. Or until exhaust. I'm old-school, too.
I do a ton of push-ups. To build up core and complementing
muscles, you know, to help with press."

It's clear Mikey knows his shit.

It's also clear my dad has no clue what Mikey's talking
about.

"If you ever want to work out, sir, I'm happy to work out
with you. You, me, Mac."

Mikey looks over at me. Flashes a smile. Knuckles me on
the arm, rests his hand on my back.

Okay, now. There's magic, and then there's this kind of
real-ass magic. Like really? How can a boy putting his hand on
your back make you feel like you've just seen the origins of the
universe? Girl.

Telling me everything I wanna know, Mikey's smile fastens
itself in my head, and I want his hand to touch me forever. I
bite my lip, afraid I'll smile so big my teeth will crack.

My dad shrugs. "Mac don't work out none. He quit
baseball."

More cringe. Girl, why would he say this? Like, what's his
goal in bringing this shit up?

Mikey looks over to me, and I say, "I can still work out."

"For what? You don't play baseball. A lotta years. All those
sacrifices."

"Naw. There's lots of reasons to work out," Mikey cuts in.

My dad looks irritated that Mikey interrupts him talking
shit to me, and I'm comforted by Mikey's support.

"Working out just makes me feel good. Like Elle Woods

says, exercise and endorphins and happy people and all that. So, if y'all ever want to lift, I'm down," Mikey continues.

I smirk at Mikey's *Legally Blonde* reference. It's one of the first movies Cam and I watched after I told him I was gay.

With bitterness, my dad takes off his hat, dusts off the black felt, looks away.

The crowd goes wild again. I clap too, noting it's Cammy's friend Mary-Kate, who seriously is named after one of the Olsen twins.

We sit, and Mikey checks his phone.

"Flor's looking for you," he says to me. "They're sitting behind the band. First three rows."

I tell my dad I'm gonna go look for Benny's family.

My dad doesn't respond, and he barely acknowledges us when Mikey says, "Good meeting you, sir. And let me know if you ever want to train."

At the front of the stands, Flor and Hermelinda peer out from the railing, cheering on people they know.

"Congratulations, Abigail!" Flor screams.

"Get that diploma, Lorena Lee!!" Hermelinda, whose hair looks really, really good today, yells.

When they see us, Flor squeals, throwing her arms around us.

"OMG. Bitch, I thought you'd never find us," Flor says. "Let's get a pic."

Now, girl. I'm not big on pics. I've taken a shitload of team photos over the years, yet this is different. Gay group pics are like this whole enterprise, an exercise in group politics, self-posturing, and persona-building, and I'm not sure I know what—not to mention *how*—to serve.

I think maybe I should just take a knee, because, well, that's what I usually do in pictures. Being one of the short ones, I know I don't stand in the back row.

But before I can kneel, Flor grabs me by the arm and says, "Mac, you stand here on the end. Mikey, stand next to Mac."

"How do I look?" Mikey asks, adjusting his tie.

"Really good."

I wanna say more, but Mikey's body is angled in such a way that his back muscles press up against my chest and his butt presses against my hip. Of course, this makes me breathe hard, and I'm nervous that I'm gonna blow hot breath all over his neck or that I'll grow and then be totally embarrassed because these are my good jeans and they're tight af and everything will show. *Think of state capitals,* I tell myself as Mikey leans back again.

I wish I had gum. Or a handful of mints.

Flor invites a couple of other girls to join in the back row, and then he and Hermelinda stand between everyone, right in the center.

"How's my hair? Babe, check my hair," Hermelinda tells him.

Flor spends three or four minutes intensely, meticulously, zealously working that crown of hair before finally determining that she's Insta-ready, which to me, honestly, looks exactly like she did when he started.

Once everyone's set, Flor asks Kanari, one of the dance team girls, to take the pic and hands her the phone.

"Take several. And hold up your phone with the flashlight on us. For extra lighting. Like last time. And count," Flor orders.

If I were Kanari, I'd be offended I wasn't invited to be in the picture, but she legit seems kind of a lot excited to take the photo.

Leaning back again, Mikey presses into me, and I let him, exhaling and telling myself to relax, not to overthink how I smile, not to worry about where to put my hands, just put them in my pockets, until Mikey reaches back and grabs my hand and places it on his waist, where I leave it, where I hold him. Because I'm in boots, I'm as tall as Mikey, and with my hand on his waist, I'm holding Mikey and pulling him closer to me, and he's the first guy I've ever held like this, which is a moment, the energy, and everything.

No one has to tell me to smile.

Flor counts it out: "Three, two . . . Say 'gorgeous.'"

And snap.

The arena cheers.

Mikey grabs my hand, lacing his fingers between mine, and he holds my hand against his thigh, where no one can see.

Right after, I don't wanna move, but Mikey pulls me to look at Flor's camera, and I kinda feel bad for Kanari, because she says, "Now let me get in one," but by this time, Flor has already applied her filter and is sending out the pics, and people are already posting.

Except Mikey, who calls Kanari over and says, "Here, jump in with us."

It's just the three of us, Mikey holding his phone high above our heads.

"Y'all ready?" he says.

I stand behind Mikey, both arms wrapped around his waist. Mikey rests his head against mine, and Kanari leans into Mikey, pretty-smiling, and throws her arm out like she's opening a show or something, her hair sitting on her shoulder like it's just waiting to come to life.

"OMG. You're the best. Lemme see! Lemme see!" Kanari demands, her voice sweet and high-pitched.

After that, we all take a seat and just watch the ceremony. Flor and Hermelinda narrate the whole affair. It's kind of very shocking exactly how much they know about the senior class. Kanari and Mikey listen intently, for the most part, and Mikey, who's leaning against me the whole time, every now and then squeezes my hand and asks, "You okay?"

We really only break for the *M*'s, when all of us go 110 abso berserk, cheering for Ben Q. Martinez when he walks across the stage. It's a moment. Even though it seems like Flor hates his big brother, it's clear by how loud Flor is screaming that there's love between them. After, Flor desperately needs a drink, which forces Hermelinda to go on the hunt for water that's "not from a public fountain." Girl, Flor is the drama, and I live for her. And I'm also living for Kanari, who starts telling us all about that maybe she's straight, maybe she's gay, maybe she's everything, and Mikey nods understandingly, telling her, "Girl, I've been there."

As Kanari's telling us all about how awesome she thinks Flor and Hermelinda are, Cammy appears out of nowhere and cuts Kanari off with a "You done, sweetie?" giving her the biggest, fakest smile, which I'd usually love but here, now, seems cruelhearted, rude, even intimidating. And I realize, then, that I've made almost zero effort to find Cammy all night, like, it didn't really even cross my mind. I check my phone to see if he responded to the text when I first arrived; he left me on read, which makes me think, *Girl, maybe it's not that deep, and here I am stressing, but also, ummmm, why didn't she text me back?*

"Okay," Kanari says. And it's like I can smell her fear of Cammy. And it's like Cam can smell it too. It's like he enjoys it, like he thrives off this energy.

Mikey tries intervening. "Ugh. Girl, no. Why you gotta be such a —"

"Such a what?" Cammy interrupts, both hands on her hips. "Really, girl. Tell me. A bitch? Is that what you're gonna call me? Because mija, I'm not a bitch. I'm *the* bitch. And you should really do yourself a favor and learn that little lesson, perra." Cam gives a bigger, even faker smile, and the word "perra" hangs in the air like smoke.

Turning his attention to me, Cammy asks, "Mac, can we have a word?"

Mikey looks at me like maybe he's gonna say something to Cam, but then he looks around us, becoming aware of who's watching, which includes a little girl in an Elsa dress.

"I'll be right back," I say to Mikey.

"I'll stay with you." Patting Mikey's hand, Kanari tosses her abundantly fierce-ass hair over her shoulder. Unbeknownst to me, Kanari has this stunningly long, totally full, gorge af cinnamon-brown hair with perfectly placed reddish-blond highlights, which serves a fierce accent to her very tanned skin. She almost always wears her hair in a bun, so I had no idea.

Girl, I'm momentarily distracted, gagging over Kanari's hair, while Mikey glares at Cam.

"What, girl? You have something to say?" Cammy asks him.

"We love you, Robert!!!" the family to the side of us yells.

"Say it, girl," Cammy challenges.

I shake my head at Mikey. I hope he doesn't go for the bait. Not here.

By this point, the people around us are staring. The little girl in the Elsa costume says, "Mama. Look. They're doing drama," and then to us, "Let it go."

Cammy gives little Elsa the fake-ass smile too. "Just so you know, that's a highly inappropriate outfit for a high school graduation. The school colors are red, white, and blue. So, you know."

Girl, little Elsa's mom looks gagged, audibly gasping and clutching her daughter to her chest.

"Okay. Let's go talk," I agree, trying to get Cam out of there as quickly as possible, waving to Mikey as I leave.

"I hope she melts," Cammy tells me loudly as we walk down the ramp, through the tunnel, and beneath the stadium seats.

I suddenly feel as if I'm in trouble. Like I'm being escorted to the principal's office. Only I'm not sure what I've done wrong.

"Girl, so how was lunch?" Cammy asks me in the fakest

voice. "I heard it was really yum and supes fun. Did you enjoy it? Being with Benny and Duncan and your new best friends?"

"We just got tacos." I'm confused.

"'Just got tacos'? Seriously. I love how you make it sound like it wasn't anything, like you didn't leave me out. You know, I should've seen this coming, Mac. Flor, sure. I know what she's capable of. She's a fake-ass bitch. OMG. Soooo fake. Like Chelsea and Kennedy and Hermelinda. All of them. And Mikey? Ha. Girl. Peor. Even worse. She thinks her shit don't stink. You know, Mac, I expected this from them. But you? Girl, we were friends before them. And what do you do? Fuck me over. Wow. Just wow."

Girl, I'm #dumbfounded. I mean, it all comes at me so fast, so unexpectedly.

I try explaining. "You were at the mall. With your family. And you said y'all had all these clients. I just didn't wanna bother you because you said you'd be busy."

"And? And what? You couldn't text or call? And what about Mikey and Flor? They couldn't see if I wanted to join?"

"I told them you were with your family."

"Oh. So it was your idea to leave me out? Wow. OMG. Wow. This just gets better."

With both hands, Cammy holds his head, like if he doesn't hold it, his whole head might explode. He turns around and paces. He looks at me and shakes his head.

And I feel crushed.

And I feel like I've just shit on my friend.

And I feel there's nothing I can say or do to take this away, to make this better, to clear up this wrong, which I'm not entirely even convinced is a wrong. I didn't leave her out on purpose, and I don't even think it's that big a deal. I mean, since we started being friends, Cam hasn't invited me to tons of places he's gone with others. So why do I let Cam do this to me?

"You know what gets me, Mac?"

I'm afraid that whatever I say will set Cammy off even more, so I say nothing.

"You sold me out. And for what? For fucking tacos! OMG, girl, are you for real? Even after I went out of my way to buy you a fucking Ariana ticket. Girl, you chose them over me."

"It's not like that." I hate that Cam brings up the ticket.

In front of the restrooms, Cammy holds his words, because Hermelinda is standing on the ramp, saying, "It's almost over. They're announcing the Z's."

Mikey and Kanari stand behind Hermelinda, watching.

Girl, I don't know why, but Kanari has her phone out and is recording the drama.

"What are you doing? What is she doing?" Cammy asks.

"I'm recording."

"She's recording," Mikey echoes.

Cammy isn't having it.

"Why is she recording?"

Kanari says something, but the crowd cheers loudly, and I can't make out her words.

"Well, I said what I said," Cammy says. "Hope you're happy, Mac."

And as the speaker introduces the graduating class, I can

hear the crowd clamor, and through the tunnel, I can see five hundred blue mortarboards soaring into the air.

The rest of the arena is celebrating, and I feel like I have a hole inside me.

"I should look for my dad," I say to Mikey, who has moved next to me and has placed his hand on my shoulder.

"You okay?"

I nod. "I will be."

By this point, Cam has walked off.

By this point, Kanari and Hermelinda have made their way back up the ramp for the alma mater.

By this point, I just wanna find my dad, knowing he will likely be pissed that I left him alone for the whole graduation.

Mikey walks with me, and when we finally find my dad, he's standing by the arena entrance, holding his cowboy hat in his hands. B's with him. I see Clari's family down a ways, posing together, laughing, embracing. Clari's mom and her dad, her grandparents and cousins, her tías.

I wish we were like them.

I wish that somehow we had what they have.

And when B sees me, her face tells me it's bad.

Mikey asks, "You want me to go with you?"

I wanna say *yes* and *please*, and I wanna hold Mikey's hand and take him with me, for as long as he'll go, for as long as he'll stay. God, I wanna say yes. Yet I know my dad, and I know that bringing Mikey along will only escalate shit. "Naw. It's better if you wait here," I say to Mikey, hoping he understands.

When I walk up, I can tell B's furious.

The anger in her eyes isn't rage, though. It's hurt. It's disbelief.

"So that's it? That's how it's gonna be?" My dad's voice hurls across the air. His voice is a stone, a sledgehammer, a bottle being thrown.

If his intent is to punish B, he's getting his way. I haven't seen B this dejected maybe ever.

"Does Mac know?"

"What do you mean?" B asks. Pins in her voice.

Unsure what exactly is going on, I look to B.

She says, "Yeah. I think Clari's mom told him y'all could come."

Shit. I didn't tell him. I feel panic start to set in, my hands filling with sweat, not knowing what to do with themselves. My heart stomps on its own face, and I scramble to say, "We can all have dinner tomorrow. It's not a big deal, Dad."

"No. That you're choosing them over us. Does he know that? Tell him."

"I'm not choosing them over y'all." B's voice quakes and erodes, like a cliff losing its pieces, and the pieces falling into some vast emptiness.

"You are. That's exactly what you're doing. You're choosing friends over family. All my sacrifices and this is how you treat me?! Don't you have any respect?" My dad strikes his palm against the cinder-block wall. He raises his voice.

A few people turn around.

My dad's shirt comes untucked.

He's beyond pissed, and I hate being around him when he's

like this. I'm not sure where this is gonna end up. Wherever it goes, it won't be good.

"They *are* my family," B tells him.

As much as I hate B for saying this, I know she's right.

"Do you hear this?" my dad says to me. "You hear this bull-shit? After everything I've done for her! Tell her something!" he demands.

B's eyes swell.

I know she's holding it in, I know. I've been there so many times with him. But the tears just start to come out. Hot and unstoppable. In front of everyone. B holds her hands over her face.

"Dad! Chill. It's her graduation. Let's just go eat tomorrow. We can call Tía Ruby."

I reach over to B, but my dad knocks my hand away.

"No! She wants to be without family? Let her see what being without family feels like. What it really feels like."

It's cruel. He's cruel.

Mikey's watching, and I hate that he sees us like this.

Others are watching our family bullshit too.

Clari's mom begins walking our way.

Mikey and Clari and KT start moving toward us, as well.

"Fucking tell her!" he yells.

"Sometimes friends are our family," I say to my dad, and I say it loudly, and I look at him and at B both when I say it.

Hearing me say this, it's as if I've knocked the shit out of him. As if I've swung hard with a baseball bat and struck him right in the gut.

My dad says nothing in response. Seeing people coming our way, he puts on his hat.

"You really fucked this up," my dad finally says, and I don't know if that's directed at me or at B or at both of us. Shaking his head, my dad walks away.

Chapter 8

"**G**IRL, HOW YOU GONNA TELL HIM?" CAMMY asks, honking at a lady who takes too long to go when the light turns green.

We're in his sister's car, a broke-ass nineties Accord, on our way to pick up stuff for his mom's salon—boxes of shampoo and other supplies—which his mom's gonna resell after they clean them up.

For two whole weeks, Cam didn't talk to me, but today's the day, I guess. She's cut me off before but never for this long, and even though I 110 think she blew the taco drama waaaaay out of proportion, I agreed to help. I mean, girl. In the big picture of life, it's not that big a deal. Also, I'm not one to hold grudges. #loyalty #forgiveness #friendshipvibes #Rule3. Also, and perhaps more significantly, I totally believe that part of being a true friend is not giving up on people. People aren't trash, so why throw them away because they melt down or act foolish or get their feelings twisted because they feel jealous?

Over the last two weeks, I did reach out to Cam a shitload of times via text.

Exhibit B

Me: Hey, just checking in. Sorry I didn't invite. I feel bad. 😨😨😨

Me: On the reals, I honestly thought you were busy with work and didn't want to bother. I'm sorry. ❤️❤️❤️

Me: Hey, girl. Izzzzz meeeeee. Maybe we can go get tacos. Just me and you. My treat. Miss you.

Me: Okay, so I know I messed up. Can we talk?

Me: Are you there?

Me: Okay. Just wanted to say Hieeeee!!!! Hope you're having a good day. Miss you.

Cam didn't reply to any of my texts, which, if I'm being honest, kinda punched me right in the dick. Like, girl? Am I *that* disposable? The upside is that I got to spend more time with Flor and Mikey, which was def funsies af. Like, it's so easy being around them. They kept asking me where Cammy was, and I tried to cover for her, telling Flor and Mikey that she was just really busy, you know, with her mom's salon and everything. But then I find out that Cam is 110 communicating with Flor and Mikey and just leaving me out. Girl. #pettyaf #girlplease #bitchughhh. Of course, this fiasco totally makes me look like an effing liar/abso fake-ass bish in front of Flor and Mikey, who are all, "Does she always act like this??"

Girl. Ummmmmmm. It's a lot. I remind them of Rule #3.

So they tried giving me all this advice about Cammy, telling me that I should stop texting her weak sauce and that I did nothing wrong. I tried to steer the conversation away from Cammy whenever I could. Even though Cam was being 110 messy, it didn't feel right talking about her behind her back. Still, some of what Mikey and Flor said made sense. Maybe I am serving weak sauce. Maybe that makes me look desperate af. And on the reals, I don't wanna be weak or desperate af, but I also don't wanna lose my friend, so I kept reaching out because Cam can't or won't. Is this me taking the high road? Is there a point in a friendship where you just have to say, *Sorry, girl. Not for me*? If so, what's that point? And also, why am I the one always trying to fix things? Girl, some days, friendship with Cam can feel entirely one-sided, and I get the sense that my friendship with Mikey and Flor is totally not one-sided at all.

Anyways, before Mikey and Flor, I might've really been wrecked by Cammy's next-level coldness, but now that I have other friends, it's like, sure, I'm bothered that Cam went off on me at graduation, but no way it's gonna destroy me. And full disclosure, I *was* happy af when I saw Cam's text this morning asking me to help her. As soon as he picked me up, Cam asked about B and my dad, having heard all about their drama at graduation—right after our drama at graduation—and I exploded into verbal chorro and just started rambling all the details. Of my friends, Cammy's the only one who knows all the T when it comes to my family. I can talk to him about it, and I know he gets it.

Oh, and I also tell Cam that I'm thinking about telling my dad I'm gay, which semi-gags Cam, who looks at me like I'm full of shit.

"Girl. He's gonna shit himself. Isn't he más homophobic and racist and sexist and xenophobic and dragphobic af? Do I need to go on?"

Cammy's right. It's not gonna be easy.

"If you ask me, you're wasting your time," Cam continues. "He doesn't need to know. He doesn't *deserve* to know."

I sit with Cam's opinion.

"You want my advice?" Cam grips the wheel, speeding by a tanker truck. "If you're gonna say it, girl, be direct. Just tell him. Don't make any excuses. Don't serve any weak sauce. And don't fucking apologize. And I can be there if you want me to. And if he kicks you out—girl, you gotta be ready for that possibility—you can come stay with me."

Cam speeds around a minivan going thirty or some other ungodly freeway speed.

"Thanks," I tell him. I lean my head against Cam's shoulder.

While part of me thinks she just wants to be there to witness all the drama, I mean she lives for this shit, another part of me knows it's more than that. Cam knows how rough my dad is, and she also has no problem standing up and telling people how it really is. Sometimes, I wish I could be more like Cammy. In that way.

And because I really needed to hear Cam support me, I say, "I think you're right—it's not like I owe my dad an explanation of who I am. But I won't keep it a secret, and I won't lie if he asks."

Cam rubs my head. "Your call, papa. Just know I'm here whatever you decide."

And even though I don't think I did anything wrong by eating tacos with Mikey and Flor, I can't explain how or why, but I say it. "I'm sorry I didn't invite you for tacos."

"I know," Cam replies. "Just don't let it happen again. Next time, I won't be so nice. At least you got to see the FBC in full effect. Girl, can they be any more obvious? Like, can they just be any more high-key about trying to steal you away? Girl, not a good lewk and soooo not the T."

"They're not trying to steal me away," I respond quickly, too quickly, I think, because I feel suddenly defensive and hot and gross when the words just fall out.

Exiting the freeway, Cam sneers. "Girl, don't make me look at you one day and say, 'Bitch, I told you so.'"

It takes forever to find the place Cammy's mom's stuff is at, which turns out to be a house behind another house.

"Watch where you step," Cam warns, stepping over a mountain of dog shit on the driveway leading to the backyard.

The backyard is littered with machine parts and a rusted-ass Buick with the windows busted out, a gang of cats lying on its hood. On the back porch, a lopsided washing machine. A clothesline with white towels looking up at the sun.

A woman named Noelia answers the door. She welcomes us in, and as soon as she does, like, five thousand Chihuahuas charge. I'm immediately hit by the stench of dog piss and chicharrones. I mean, girl. For reals. It's Chihuahua chaos. The house has a small window AC unit, and the air feels kind of a little glorious. Cammy talks to Noelia in Spanish and puts his mom on the phone while the Chihuahuas corral me, sniffing and nipping at my socks and shoes. Girl, I'm tempted to stand in front of the AC for a minute, but I also want to get the boxes and get out ASAP, so I fight the urge.

The boxes are sort of heavy and bulky af. I can barely wrap my arms around them, and trudging through Noelia's place is tough since the house is a wreck, and as much as I don't want to step on a Chihuahua, they won't scatter. In all, it takes eleven tedious af trips through tall-ass alley grass to pack up the entire back seat and trunk of Denise's car.

When we're done, both Cammy and I are huffing and puffing and sweaty af. Like my whole shirt sticks to my body from how drenched I am, and I'm dripping a puddle of sweat onto the street. Bent over, I pick off pieces of grass that cling to my leg hairs and stomach and arms. Girl, it's a lot.

"At least there's some shade." Under a pecan tree, Cammy chews ice from his soda cup. "Want some?"

I have my own ice and reach for my cup. I take off my shirt and wring out the sweat, and Cam does the same.

A pack of stray dogs stands in the street, watching us. One of the dogs has lost much of its fur and is scratching. A small one with a limp begins yipping at us, which triggers the five thousand Chihuahuas to go off from inside the house.

Down the road, someone is burning their trash. And farther down from that, someone is taking all the belongings out of a house and dumping them by the road. Clothing and furniture, a television set, a children's mattress, toys.

Girl, this neighborhood is rough, and I'm nobody to talk shit on rough neighborhoods, because some of the places we've lived are rough af too. But girl, this one is next-level rough af.

In the car, we both put our faces up to the AC, which is pointless, since nothing cool is coming out, but we do it anyway.

"Before I forget . . . thanks, bitch," Cam tells me.

It's the most appreciative thing Cammy's ever said to me.

As we drive off, sweat pours down Cam's face. I pass her an ice cube from my cup, and she rubs the coolness all over her face.

"Girl, put on some music."

There isn't a place to sync a phone, just a radio. I mess with the buttons until Cammy stops me. "That one. Girl, this is soooo my mom."

"Ooh, yes, my tía loves this one too."

It's an old Mexican song with guitars and an accordion and a woman with a voice like sap from mesquites, a voice that can tell you true things about loneliness and sufrimiento, which makes me think of my tía Ruby. We listen, and Cammy sings along as she drives, and I forget how effing brutally hot it is, caring only that I'm with my best friend who knows every word to this song that my tía plays in her kitchen.

Feeling empowered af by getting shit done with Cam, I decide to reach out to B. Since the drama with our dad at graduation, we've texted a few times, but that's it. I know that if I wanna see her, I'm gonna have to make the effort and go over there, because no way B's coming back here. So when Mikey picks me up for the gym that evening—yes, girl, I've started working out again—I ask if we can make a stop first.

"I just wanna check in with my sister. It's not far."

Mikey agrees, and as we pull into Clari's neighborhood, I text B: Can you talk? I'm down the street.

Clari's street is nice. It's lined with oak trees the height of scoreboards, with manicured branches that move and dip in every direction. I can see why B likes it here.

From the curb, I see KT and B shooting baskets by the garage, while Clari and Naomi sit in the back of Clari's Jeep.

Walking up the driveway, I give Mikey a rundown of who's who.

"Babe, your towel!" Clari tosses B a white cloth as she approaches Mikey and me.

"This is Mikey," I say to B.

B smiles like her teeth don't fit in her mouth and shakes Mikey's hand. "So you're the one stealing my brother's heart?" Wiping her face and calling Clari over, B gives Mikey a wink.

Suddenly, I'm embarrassed af. "Stealing my brother's heart"? Girl. Why is she saying this? We haven't even talked about Mikey. Who told her?

"I hope that's what I'm doing," Mikey replies. "Though I'd much rather it be given to me than have to steal it."

It's a smooth-ass line. Even B nods in appreciation of Mikey's game.

Over the last couple of weeks, Mikey and I've been clicking for the reals, like at the gym and walking Kimber and whenever we hang out, really. Each time, I think, okay, maybe I should try and take this a little further, because as much as Mikey flirts, I get the sense he's waiting for me to take the first leap, that maybe that's how he likes it, maybe that's just how he's built. So hearing Mikey say that he's down for me giving him my heart, girl. That's huge, and I'm already sprung.

"Ey, Mikey," B says, "this is my bruh KT and my girl Clari. And this is —"

"And I'm Naomi," Naomi interjects, holding out her hand to Mikey. "I'm KT's girl, but everybody knows I run this show. Right, babe?"

Naomi laughs loudly, sticking out her tongue. Short and fiery, she gives off puro Cardi B vibes for the reals.

"You Asian?" Naomi asks.

"Filipino," Mikey says. "Proud, too."

"Same," Naomi goes. "And my dad's Puerto Rican. De la isla. Hey, I like you already. And I like your eagle, too," she comments, tracing Mikey's tattoo with her well-done acrylic. Naomi then turns to KT and says, "See, babe. That's what I want. But bigger. Down from my head, like from behind my ear, all the way down my back and ass to my baby toes. When you make WNBA, cause you know that shit's gonna cost. One of the good ones will anyways."

"That's gonna be a big bird," KT says, smirking. "People gonna call you Sesame Street."

It's as cheese as you can get, but girl, KT has that funny af, confident delivery that makes pretty much anything she says laugh-worthy.

I turn to B. "I hate to steal you for a minute, B, but can we talk?"

B nods, and I walk her down the driveway. We lean against the hood of Mikey's mom's car.

"Y'all gonna work out?" she asks.

"I hope so. I'm catching feels," I admit.

B gives me a confused look. "I meant are y'all going to the gym?"

"Oh, that. Yeah. He wants to do chest and tris."

B's chuckle bounces off the car hood and ripples.

"Good call. You should get back into it. He's cute."

"He's nice, too."

B crosses her arms. "So what's goin' on?"

"Nothing. Just wanted to see you. I'm trying this new thing now where I'm gonna be more direct with people."

B smiles. "More direct. What's that mean?"

"Direct. You know. Get some courage. Say what I mean. Don't dance around."

"Right. You mean shoot your shot."

"You could say that."

"So, shoot away."

"Honestly. I just . . . I just miss you. And instead of staying home and missing you or being all in my head, I figure I better get my ass over here and see you before you leave, 'cause I know you're not gonna see me at the house. Not after Dad . . ."

B opens her eyes really wide. "He's an ass."

For a moment, we don't say anything.

In the sky, dark clouds. A few birds flying behind us.

"Anyways, I was just thinking how you and me used to talk a lot."

"Used to? We still talk, Mac. We're literally talking right now."

"I know. It's just different now. You're about to take this big giant step forward in your life, and I just wanted to . . . I don't know. I just wanna tell you about all these things happening in my life."

"Okay. I'm listening."

And when B tells me this, I don't know where to start.

"What did you wanna tell me?" B prompts me.

"Everything." I smile. "All of it. I think Mikey really likes me, and he's nice and smart and hot and he's showing me all these things in the gym and he's really into music. I'm becoming bffs with him and Flor, you know, Benny's brother, and Cam is jealous, I think. OMG. Sooo jealous. He says they're gonna try to break up our friendship."

B rolls her eyes. "No. Cam making drama? Really? No way."

I laugh because I know she's being sarcastic.

"But I really don't think they're trying to steal me away. Those are the words Cam used."

"Well, you can't *steal* somebody away. People leave because they want to leave or because life changes and you have to adjust. That's what people do."

"Is that what's happening to us?" The question kinda flies outta my mouth. "Adjusting?"

B looks at her shoes and then at the road in front of us.

"Yeah. I guess we're just adjusting to life right now."

"So you don't think we're kinda growing apart?"

B chuckles and throws her arm around my shoulder. "Bruh. We're not growing apart."

"Good. I don't want us to grow apart," I tell her. "You're gonna leave soon, and I feel like you're just gonna leave me behind." It just comes out, like a piece of truth that isn't supposed to be spoken. I *am* kinda very much afraid we're growing apart. And I'm nervous af about the future and about change, and I feel alone, even with my new friends, even with Kimber, in that house with our dad.

"We're not growing apart." B's voice turns into a hammer. The words pound themselves into the air. "Life just gets in the way. I have a lot going on."

I tell myself to be quiet, to listen to what she has to say instead of trying to think about what I can say next.

"You're right. We don't talk, not like we used to. I have things I want to tell you, too."

"Like what?"

"Well, UT summer training starts the first week of August, and I kinda can't wait. You know, I got a lot of my college paid for, but I still have to take out a loan, which is stressing me out." She pauses for a moment. "Did you know Clari's mom has a whole wedding planned for us?"

"What?!"

"It's true! Her mom already has names she thinks Clari and I should give our kids. And she's insisting that Clari needs to apply to UT Law right after undergrad and that I'm supposed to apply to get an MBA there."

"That's intense. Y'all haven't even left for UT yet. Wait. Are y'all getting married?"

B laughs. "No, Mac. No. That's the thing. She has Clari's whole life planned out. And I'm just supposed to fit into it. You know what that's like?"

"Kind of?" I think I kinda know. "Dad sorta built our lives around sports, right?"

She nods. "Remember how one time you said Dad didn't give a shit what we did as long as we played the game?"

I do remember.

"And remember how pissed he was when you quit baseball?"

"Yeah."

The night my dad found out I quit baseball, he punched holes in the walls and knocked me around the house until my mouth started to bleed and my eye swelled up. B called our tía Ruby, but she didn't pick up because it was late, and she also called Cammy, who raced over to be with me. For hours that night, Cam sat with me and even invited me to his place with Kimber, but I knew if I left, I wouldn't ever be able to come back. It's how my dad is, how he punishes you when you don't do what he wants or how he wants it done. I don't like thinking about this moment, so I catch myself before it consumes me, and I push it away.

Instead I say, "Yeah, Dad's got some problems."

"Bruh. That was brave af. I never thought you'd do it."

"I never saw it as brave. I just had to do it."

"I hear you." B pauses.

Near us, a streetlight goes on.

The buzz is electric.

Light spills over the asphalt, touching our feet.

B continues, "Yeah, well, that's life, right. You figure out what's meant for you and what's not, and you move forward. You move on. And if you get stuck, don't blame anybody but yourself. Because you know better."

It's been a very long time since I've held my sister's hand, but there, on the street, in front of her girlfriend's house, under a streetlight, I reach over and grab B's hand.

She holds my hand too.

Somewhere, the sky grumbles, and to the west, the sky lights up for a second.

Chapter 9

GIRL, THE NEXT AFTERNOON I WAKE UP FROM a nap to the smell of gasoline.

The fans are blowing, and my window unit is serving middle-beginning-of-summer, full-blast-survival-story realness, but still, the odor of gas pervades my bedroom. Girl, I think Kimber smells it too, because she looks up and sniffs like, wtf, and when I open the door, there's my dad standing in the hall-way, holding a chain saw.

Yes, girl. A big-ass *Texas Chainsaw Massacre* chain saw. #ughhhwhy

Wearing cowboy boots, tall-boy socks pulled up to his kneecaps, a pair of old denim cutoffs, and a US flag bandanna over his head, my dad holds that big af chain saw like it's a baby he wants.

"Dad, what the hell?"

"We're gonna cut down that fucking tree, Mac. Right now. Today. No more waiting. That storm last night, that was nothing. Bigger one's coming tomorrow. Call over Benny. And Duncan, too."

"I think they're gonna be busy, Dad." It's summer, and they're always busy. More importantly, we don't even hang out anymore.

"Well, call 'em. Tell 'em to come over. That tree's gonna fall, Mac. We gotta cut it. A tree like that could take out half the house. You, me. Kimber."

I think of it then. My dad's scenario. The tree crashing onto us. Losing Kimber. Ugh. Against my better judgment, I text Benny.

Girl. I know. I know. I don't know why I do it. Like I should have just faked it and lied and told my dad they couldn't come. Ughhh.

Breathing hard, my dad caresses the chain saw. "I borrowed this from Tony at work. You understand why this gotta happen, Mac. Better do it now. Before it's too late. Too late and we can't do nothing about it, Mac."

"I know, Dad."

Benny texts back: Helping Ds mom maybe next weak

Girl, he misspells "week." Seriously.

When I tell my dad Benny and Duncan are busy, he just nods and runs his thumb over the chain saw's teeth, which makes me worry that it might suddenly turn on.

"Looks like you and me, Mac."

I follow my dad outside, and Kimber trails after me.

My dad's holding the chain saw in one hand. With the other, he points up to the colossal oak towering above us.

It really is a big-ass tree, maybe thirty feet tall, and over-hangs a large part of the roof above our kitchen, which is good because of the shade it provides in the hottest parts of summer. However, staring up, I realize that my dad really is right. Last night's storm took down a grip of branches and trees in the neighborhood—if one of those bigger limbs falls, it's ball game.

As my dad walks around the yard assessing the tree, I head toward the shed to retrieve the ropes, because if we're gonna cut on this tree, we're gonna need ropes. As I hurl the ropes over my shoulders, my phone rings. It's Mikey, and I stop mid-step, wrapped in ropes, sweating my balls off, to answer.

"Ey, Macky. You busy?"

I hate when he calls me that, yet I'm really, really glad he calls.

"Helping my dad." Balancing the phone between my shoul-der and my ear, I keep moving, dropping the ropes in the shade a few yards from the tree.

"I got you on speaker here."

"Hey, bitch!!" Cammy jumps in.

"Hieeee!" That's Flor's high-pitched squeal.

At first I'm thrilled to hear my friends' voices, but then I'm like, Wait. Why are they all hanging out without me? And why the f is Cam there? Girl, she doesn't even like them. Seriously.

Ugh. It all comes at me fast. And I resent having to placate my dad's crisis fantasy when I'd much rather be with my friends. #crisisfantasy

"So, we were thinking maybe all of us could get together tonight at Flor's," Mikey says. "Watch some Valentina—come on, Season Nine! Plus, we gotta start thinking about Pride. You down?"

Of course I'm down. I envision myself with my friends watching episodes of Valentina's *Drag Race* season, laughing and kiki'ing and gagging over Valentina's stunning looks.

But then, from across the yard, my dad yells, "Get off the fucking phone! You gonna help or not?!"

"I'm coming!" I yell back, and tell Mikey, "I gotta go. We're gonna cut back this big-ass tree that he thinks might come down when it storms again."

"Y'all need help?" Mikey asks.

"Bitch, I ain't cutting down no tree. You know how fucking hot it is out there?" I hear Cam complain loudly.

I stare at my dad, who's struggling to start the chain saw.

"Naw. It's grunt work," I tell Mikey. "I'll just call y'all when we're done. But yeah, count me in!"

"Girl, bye!" Cammy says, and I'm like, ugh. Wtf? And girl, I hate hate hate that I actually feel kind of a lot jealous. #uggghhhhhhhhhh

Flustered, I shove the phone in my pocket and drag the ropes to where my dad's standing. Eyeballing the oak, my dad passes me the chain saw and points at a branch that reaches over the caliche driveway and touches the dark shingles of our roof.

"What're you thinking? Cut back three or four of the long, low ones? You said once those are the ones most likely to come down."

He nods. "Exactly. You do listen."

It's almost a smile that lands on my face. *Perhaps this won't be so bad*, I think.

In one motion, my dad throws a thick rope over the first branch, near the place it connects to the trunk, secures it, then hands me the rope. "Use this to walk up the tree."

"Walk up the tree?" Girl, really?

Against my better judgment, I grab the rope and press my feet against the trunk. Methodically, I lean back and take the slack out of the rope, then start making my way up the trunk. I lose my footing once, and the hardness of the rough trunk scrapes the inside of my left knee and calf, my arm, too. Behind me, I latch the chain saw to my belt loop, and the saw dangles awkwardly, like a tail that isn't supposed to be there.

I calm myself and go up the trunk again, my muscles straining. *Be fierce*, I tell myself, grabbing more rope. #Rule1.

"Keep going. Don't stop." My dad whistles from below. "You got it. What you waiting for?" It's the first time in a long-ass time that my dad has said something semi-encouraging to me.

From the back of the yard, Kimber watches.

I take four, five, six breaths, and I squeeze my big legs around the branch's girth to stabilize my body. And maybe this is how people do shit they don't wanna do. I don't think of myself or what I'm doing. I think of the clouds. I think of the sun burning my back. I think of getting to see Mikey later and how bad I wanna squeeze on his big arms and kiss him. Before

I know it, I've made it to where I need to be. I yank on the chain saw's cord, and the machine roars aggressively, like it's ready to f shit up. Against the branch, I press the blades, and although it takes a while, once I've cut enough, my dad pulls hard, and I can feel the tree give up its hold, a loud crack erupting from the gash.

When the branch hits the ground, an explosion of dust and dirt fills the air. My dad does a little joyous dance, clapping and howling words I can't make out. As the dust settles, I see something unexpected: Mikey, Flor, and Cammy standing in my driveway.

"Okay. So, y'all wanted to see. There you have it," Cammy proclaims, dark round sunglasses covering her eyes. Sipping from a Big Gulp, Cam points with her pinkie to the giant limb on the ground.

Flor looks gagged. She backs up a few steps as the dust cloud blows her way. She's wearing glasses too. Big, round, dark sunnies. Similar to Cammy's, if not the same pair.

Mikey waves to me and steps over a few fallen limbs and then around the main branch. "Dang, papa! That's a beast!"

"We're just getting started!" I shout from up in the tree, wiping my face and neck with my T-shirt. "What are y'all doing here?" I attach the saw to the rope on my waist and begin hoisting myself down.

Mikey smiles at me and then approaches my dad, extending his hand out to shake.

Cammy and Flor remain in the driveway, next to my dad's truck. Cam leans against the truck and scrolls through his phone while Flor fans herself with a small lime-green clutch, using a tissue to dab sweat from her temples and neck.

"These are my friends, Dad," I say when I'm back on the ground. I cringe because I sound uncertain and weak. Girl, these *are* my friends—I know this, like abso 110—but it's the first time my dad's meeting them all at once. I feel myself filling with anxiety, wondering how this unexpected visit will go down. The range of inappropriate comments he might cough up instantly shakes me.

I see my dad take Mikey's hand. Pointing at sections of the tree, he begins telling Mikey the plan to get the rest of the branches, then cut the pieces and haul them out to the side of the road for the city to pick up. "Three more after this big bitch." My dad beams.

I don't know whether to shake Mikey's hand or to hug him. Girl. I'm sweaty af and covered in tree dust, and a bright red stream of blood trickles down my shin. Also, my hands smell like gasoline, and if I touch Mikey, he's gonna smell like gasoline too. Ughhh. Girl, it's a lot. #messymess #literallysucia #dilemmas

On the reals, I don't have to decide what to do about hugging him, because Mikey reaches over, throws his hand on my shoulder, and squeezes. "It's good to see you, papa. Y'all need some help?"

Without hesitating, my dad blurts out, "Hell yeah. Let's get this shit moving. More hands we got, the faster we can move. They can help too. If they want."

My dad points over at Flor and Cammy, who are shaking their heads.

"Dad, you remember my friend Camilo?"

Cam acknowledges my dad by raising two fingers and nodding at him.

My dad nods too.

"And that's Florencio. He's Benny's brother."

With his hand on his hip, Flor waves, the green clutch moving back and forth across the air like a bright flag. "Hi, Mac's dad!! OMG! Y'all really let that tree have it!"

Girl, I won't lie—I cringe. And immediately, I hate myself for it. Like there's that part inside me that notices and wishes, even, that Flor wouldn't have acted so gay in front of my dad, and yet, this other stronger part inside me says, *No, bitch*. Like, how dare I cringe at Flor for being Flor? And for what? To make my dad's homophobia feel more comfortable? To make myself feel less afraid of what my dad might say or do? Girl, no.

I hope my face doesn't give away my discomfort. And I look right at Flor when I say it: "Yes, girl. We let that tree have it."

Clap, clap. Cam puts her hands together, throws back her head, and smirks her approval.

Girl, my dad looks perplexed af and glances over at Mikey, who translates: "He's saying it's a good thing. That y'all did a good job cutting down the tree."

"Oh. Okay. Okay," my dad mumbles.

For a few seconds, I'm unsure what's gonna happen next. Will my dad go off? Will he talk shit to me or start in on his spiels about gays ruining America and how men not acting like real men is destroying the world? All of this is shit he's said before.

"So, y'all know Mac from baseball?" he asks.

"Well, actually, kind of," Flor begins, moving closer to us. She has to hurdle a few smaller branches, which shows both commitment and flexibility. I mean, who knew she could move like that? "We've met before, sir. I'm Florencio Martinez. My brother Ben played baseball with Mac since they were really little. So, I sort of know Mac through baseball, and I met you a long time ago at this one baseball tournament in Corpus. OMG. I was like five, so you probably won't even remember. And it was insanely hot, well, maybe not as hot as today."

Flor holds out a freshly manicured hand to my dad.

Reluctantly, my dad shakes Flor's hand.

And girl. Looking at the two of them, it's like people from two entirely different worlds meeting for the first time. Like first contact or some shit.

"She doesn't even play baseball, but she's a total catcher!" Cam shouts from the driveway, smirking.

Girl. Messy.

"Mac can catch too," my dad adds, like he knows what Cammy's talking about. "They always put him in the outfield, but I always knew he'd be a great catcher since he was a kid. He's got the arm for it."

Girl, Cam loses her shit laughing.

Even Flor, who's trying not to laugh, giggles as she and her bouncy bangs walk away.

Meanwhile, I'm mortified af.

But it doesn't stop there.

"Hey, Mac can pitch, too," my dad announces. "They said

he was too short to pitch, but I don't think so. He's got the mechanics. I always say it's the motion that matters. Your form."

Girl, why is this happening?

My dad really needs to stop.

"What do you mean? Tell us more, please," Cammy urges my dad.

"Well, I'm not a coach, but I just think Mac should give it a try. Pitching. And catching. Both. Maybe if he starts pitching and catching, this is what can get him back into baseball. Where he belongs."

Girl, awkward.

I want it to stop. Yet I stand here, wordless. My hands vibrating, maybe from the chain saw. Maybe from not being able to do shit to stop this.

"What do you think, Mac? Maybe we can get Ben to pitch to you. Or you can pitch to him."

Flor makes a very audible, noticeable vomiting sound.

"If not, then what about Mike here? You can catch for him, won't you?" Turning to Mikey, my dad asks, "You pitch?"

"Ummm. No. Not my thing," Mikey says, which makes me raise my eyebrows.

"Then Mac can pitch to you. Can you catch?"

Girl, by this point, Cam has to lean against my dad's truck to keep from passing out from how hard she's laughing, and Kimber has joined in from the back of the yard, all happy and curious and wagging her tail, wanting to know what's going on. As for me, I want the sky to open up and take me whole. I wanna shove a handful of dirt in Cammy's shit-talking mouth, and for my dad to stop trying to make everything about base-ball. Baseball isn't going to happen.

"Dad, we should get back to working on the tree."

Mikey steps in, helping us get out of this conversation. Walking up to the big-ass branch on the ground, he asks my dad, "So, where you wanna cut, sir? You want us to slice it up into three or four big pieces first and then piece it up small? Or you want us to start turning the smaller pieces now? Tell us how you want it done. I'm game."

I'm surprised by how smoothly Mikey leans into it. Thankful, too.

Pausing for a moment, my dad looks over at me and over at Flor and Cammy and then back at Mikey, who by this time has already started snapping off a few of the thinner branches and stacking them by the driveway.

"Y'all came here to help?" my dad asks, eyeing Cammy and Flor.

Cam can breathe again and plays with his phone like she didn't hear the question. Flor fans herself and smiles, then says, "It sure is hot out here."

"Yessir, we got a couple hours. We can help. All of us," Mikey assures him.

Girl. Just like that. Cammy's instantaneous facecrack!

And Flor, girl. Breaking her neck!

Like the two of them, Flor and Cammy, just standing by my dad's truck, looking at each other stunned af.

Yes, girl, they have just been voluntold to do some yard

work. I hear Flor object to Cam, "Girl, I don't even do yard work in my own yard."

In the end, my dad tells Mikey that he wants us to cut up the branch on the ground into larger sections first and then break those down into chunks we can move, and Cam and Flor agree to help by making a run to get drinks from the Valero.

And girl. Okay. I am not at all bothered by them leaving. In fact, I'm kind of a lot relieved. Girl. At least Mikey's here with me, and he's coming in clutch. This makes shit a lot better.

And on top of it all, wtf with Cam getting my dad all riled up about baseball? She knows it's a touchy subject here, and getting him to go on and on to embarrass me? Girl, please. Those are soooo not friendship-is-magic vibes. #ridicula #wayverynotcute #megaeyeroll #yeahshedidit #anyways

So, as soon as they drive off, I'm back on the tree.

As we work, I try not to stare at Mikey, but I can't help it. At first I worry that my dad might see my eyes on Mikey, and what then? But I stare anyways. Especially when Mikey takes off his shirt. Girl!

In the tree, my back against the trunk, I think that Mikey didn't have to help us, but he did. That means something. It puts a smile on my face and makes me look forward even more to tonight. In the sunlight, he's shining, and I love that he smiles with his whole face, and I tell myself, *I'm gonna kiss him.*

After the second and third branches come down, I have to refill the gasoline in the chain saw, so I make my way down the tree swiftly.

"Ey, looking good," my dad says as I pour gas into the chain saw. "Why don't we start cutting them up, then roll some out to the road? We can go at the rest another time."

"Yeah. Good idea." Grabbing the hose, I turn the faucet, splashing my face and chest and back, even my legs. My dad heads inside to "handle some business," which means he has to take a shit, and I watch the blood coming from my kneecap dissolve. I have wood chips in my mouth, so I rinse and spit, and then I drink. The water feels otherworldly. And thinking it might help the gasoline smell go away, I rub my hands together in a frenzy. But it doesn't help.

Mikey watches.

"I'm gonna have to go soon, but you're gonna come over, right?"

Above us, the sun still clings to the hot sky.

Mikey glistens. Around his neck, the gold chain glints. At the end of the chain, a rectangular pendant, small, heavy-looking. Whenever Mikey bends over or turns to lift or reaches back to manage the rope, the gold pendant swings.

Catching my breath, watching Mikey, I lean against the house.

Taking the hose, Mikey washes his face and spills water over his scalp and chest. The water rolls over his back and over his gold chain and down his big-ass arms, too. In the sun, the eagle looks darker. His back ripples. A kaleidoscope of muscles.

I say it softly: "It is the east. And Mikey Villanueva, you are the sun." And I know it doesn't even really work, because it's afternoon and the sun isn't rising and because I mess up the beats per line, but I say it anyway, because I learned it in ninth grade and because I feel it right now, and because nobody else is around, because it falls out of my mouth like a star that wants to be seen.

"Oh yeah? The sun, huh?" Mikey runs his hands through his fade. Water on his stubble flicks off into the air, creating a mist around him.

"Yeah. A lot."

"Good. I like that," Mikey replies.

And I'm determined to kiss him, right here, under the hot sun, with water on my skin and blood on my knee, with wood chips in my hair and on my neck and chest, with my neighbors playing their loud reggaeton and my heart wanting to show him everything it can do.

"I'm gonna have to go when they get back."

Water droplets. The sun hitting the house like a hammer.

"I know." I squint to see him.

Sun on his shoulders, sun on his scalp.

"You're gonna come over tonight, right?"

I smile, because he just asked me that. "I'll be there."

"I wanna see you . . . every day. If you want."

My heart grows fat, and I smile when I hear Mikey say this.

"Every day?"

"Every day."

I sit on the wide, long branch we haven't yet cut into pieces.

I look over to the back porch. My dad is nowhere to be seen. I pat the place on the branch next to me, and when Mikey sits beside me, I put my arm behind him, along his lower back, like I'm bracing him, like my arm is there just for him.

My arm against his skin.

My shorts dripping on my shoes, in the loose dirt.

I take a breath and lean my damp head against the meaty part of Mikey's shoulder and upper arm. My face pressing into his eagle.

"I like you," I tell him.

On my leg, where my shorts have lifted enough to show my thigh, Mikey takes his forefinger and draws a heart and then another. The hearts are smallish, quarter-size. And then he drops another heart beside the first of them. Three hearts in all. Beneath Mikey's hearts, the dark hairs curl, and inside my chest, my own heart swirls.

Inside me, my heart full of stars.

And then there's the sky in my mouth and all of possibility.

I take a deeper breath, rubbing my hand along Mikey's spine, behind his neck, which is slick from the heat. I notice the fullness of Mikey's lips, too. His face is angular and round all at once, and I like that his eyes are brown like mine. The hairs on his face and under his arms are dark too. I rub the tight muscle in his shoulder, which forms a knot, and he inhales, rolls his neck from side to side. Moistening his lips, Mikey exhales, and his chest rises, and it's fuller than before. And I hope my chest is full, too, that one day he'll lay his head on my chest and tell me his stories.

"Look at me," I tell him.

For a second, my eyes and his eyes, and us together.

For a second, magic that fixes loneliness.

"I'm gonna kiss you. I want to. That okay?"

A smile. "Yeah." He nods.

Light in his eyes. On his chest, gold echoing.

I grab Mikey's hand in mine. But before I can press my lips against his, we hear it.

A long-ass, disruptive af car honking.

It's Flor and Cammy pulling up, and Cammy, reaching over from the passenger seat to press the horn again, yelling, "We're back, perras!! What're y'all doing?!!"

#seriously

Chapter
10

IPARK MY DAD'S OLD TRUCK IN FRONT OF
Flor's perfectly manicured front yard. I'm showered and
sore and exhausted af from moving the tree, but walking into
Flor's house, the first thing I see is Mikey, and so I'm good.

"You made it." Grinning, Mikey puts his arm around me.

And it's like right now nothing else in that house exists
except for Mikey Villanueva standing there in his shredder.
#swoon

"It's about fucking time! OMG, girl! Could you take any
longer?" Cam yells from the kitchen.

"Girl, for real? You've never seen a full entire episode
of *Drag Race*?" Flor says as Mikey and I walk into the living
room. She sounds concerned, worried, even. She sets down her

magazine, gets up from the couch, and places her palm consolingly on my hand.

"No, but I've watched tons of clips," I tell her, a little ugh that Cammy and Flor were talking about me right before I walked in. "And I've seen almost all the recaps multiple times, which is kinda like watching an episode, don't you think?"

"Girl, it's not the same." Shaking her head in disbelief, Flor appears flustered. "Mikey, are you listening to this?"

From the kitchen, Cam emerges with a plate of grapes, strawberries, crackers, cheese, and a bag of almonds, and a magazine tucked under her arm. "Want some?" She holds the plate out for me, then hands the almonds to Mikey.

I grab a handful of grapes and crackers, and well, then I just grab everything, because it all looks so good, and I'm hungry af. I pop a few grapes in my mouth. "I mean, I've always *wanted* to watch an episode. But I just haven't."

"Why not?" Flor presses. She almost sounds offended.

"I just haven't. I guess I missed them when they came on." It's not easy talking with a mouthful of cheese, but I manage.

"You can stream them!"

Girl. I don't say anything. I don't think Flor understands that not everybody can just press some buttons and stream shit, and the idea of downloading shit illegally puts guilt in my chest. I grab another handful of grapes instead of making this awkward.

"Girl, not everybody has your bandwidth," Mikey clarifies, munching a handful of almonds. "Some people just do cable or just basic channels or no TV at all."

"What she's trying to say is that not everybody's rich like

you, girl," Cammy interjects, her mouth stuffed with a strawberry and her face buried in *Vogue*.

"I'm not rich." Rubbing her temples like she has a headache or like this is all too much, Flor paces across her living room. "I get it. But I mean, with all those hours you work, can't you just buy episodes? Girl, you can buy the whole season."

I'm sure Flor means well. And part of me thinks maybe I should explain that yeah, I work a shitload of hours, but my money isn't spending money. It goes to helping my dad with bills and to buy food and to pay for our rent and Kimber's food and sometimes I lend money to B, or give, really, because she never pays me back, and whatever's left over, that's for shit I need or want, and it's not a lot that's left over at the end. I don't think this is a good time to explain my economics to Flor. Or maybe it is and I'm just afraid or embarrassed or I don't know.

"Well, I just figured that a good friend would have cared enough to share episodes with you. Or something. A *real* friend." Flor smiles like what she said didn't just have fangs. And girl. #gag #likewow. So, I know that Flor isn't a fan of Cam, but she's going in kinda shady-hard with the comment about a "*real* friend," and I'm afraid of what Cam's gonna do. And also, on top of that, Flor does have a point. Girl, on the reals. Why *didn't* Cam ever invite me over to watch *Drag Race* at his house?

Munching another juicy-ass strawberry, Cam goes, "Girl, you talking shit? Like for real, was that shitty comment intended for me? Because seriously, bitch—you're gonna have to swing a lot harder than that, mija. And when I swing back, girl, you won't know what knocked you on your flat little ass."

It's a little hard to understand Cam, because the red berry in her mouth is big af, and as she's reading Flor, strawberry juice spills through her teeth and lips and all over her jaw. Girl, she's gonna need a napkin.

Flor rolls her eyes, and she doesn't take back what she said or try to play it off.

"Yes, we know, bitch," Mikey sighs. "Everybody knows you like to fight. Girl, can we just put on Valentina and be glad Mac finally got here?"

"I'm sorry I took so long. It's just that my dad —"

"Girl, fuck your dad. Seriously!" Cam exclaims, wiping her mouth. "You can't live your whole life tiptoeing around him."

Flor's living room goes quiet.

For a minute, it seems like the air has been torn from the room.

"She's right," Flor admits.

My tongue stiffens, and I don't know what to say.

In front of the seventy-inch television, Flor runs her hands through her hair. On her wrist, she wears a black beaded bracelet and a braid of red. Flowy and vivid yellow, her shirt reminds me of the color of cactus flowers in my tía Ruby's yard. In front of the TV's dark glass, Flor moves back and forth across the room, like she's trying to figure something out. Then, finally, she says, "Girl, I mean, we can't go on living our lives for other people. What about us? What about our needs? Girl, I struggle with this all the time. Like what my parents say I need and what I know I need. Girl. It's a lot. I mean, hello, rule number two."

"Girl, stop right there," Cam interrupts. "That TV is making a really fierce background against that lemon shirt you got on."

"I was thinking the same thing," Mikey remarks.

Cammy raises his phone.

"Here, give me cara. Serve me face."

Flor pops into a sequence of poses that look like she's been studying a fashion magazine, which apparently she and Cammy have been doing. I'm all for the impromptu photo shoot, but I thought we'd just decided to watch *Drag Race*. Girl, chaos.

Flor starts over to the couch to look at the pics, but Cam stops her. "Girl. I'm AirDropping them. You pick the ones you like."

Looking over Cam's shoulder, Mikey's impressed. "Damn, Cam. These are hot. I didn't know you could give photography realness."

Wow, I think. Mikey giving Cam a compliment? Maybe we all *can* get along.

"Girl, there's a lot about me you don't know." Cam licks her thumb, turns a page.

Receiving the drop, Flor squeals. "Bitch, these are sooo good! Well, I mean you do have a stunning subject."

"These skills gonna pay the bills, mamas," Cam affirms. "And if you post, which I know you will, girl, give cred."

Excitedly scrolling through her newfound cache, Flor agrees.

"And girl," Cam cautions. She pauses, her voice going very severe. "No filters."

"Ugh," Flor snaps. "Girl, she is filterless. This face needs no filter, hunny."

"Mmmmm-hmmmmm." Cammy bites her lip. "We'll see."

"Back to *Drag Race*. So, you already know all the spoilers?" Mikey asks, and takes the seat beside me, putting his hand on my knee. And it's everything. I mean, girl. The feeling I get, it's like sunlight and joy and electricity and hope and good air all at once, from every direction, and I can smell him—damn, Mikey smells so good, he smells like he's been working out and showered but didn't cover himself in soap, just natural.

On my leg, Mikey traces out a small heart.

I bite my tongue. I stare at Mikey's thumb, at the creases in his skin, at his fingernails, which are short and squared, cut neat. When I kiss him, I wanna feel his fingers on my chest, on my jaw and my scalp and my teeth, too.

Distracted by Cam's AirDrop, Flor isn't paying attention. "Bitch, either that's a really good camera or you know what you're doing. Hunty!!! These are top-tier peak diva everything! #lovesthem!!"

If Cam's flattered, she doesn't show it and goes about perusing her magazine.

"Should we start the show?" I ask.

Mikey agrees, and once he hits play, it doesn't take long for us all to stfu and focus on episode one. And girl, instantly, like right after Valentina gives it to the workroom with her entrance lewk, Flor grabs the remote and hits pause, because "OMFG! I liiiiiiive for this lewk!"

Every time Valentina serves a new lewk, Flor hits pause and delivers a TED Talk. And I. Am. Here. For. It!!!! Grabbing Mikey's hand, I squeeze, because I'm 110 abso living for these Valentina episodes and because I'm also living witnessing

Flor be authentically, quintessentially Flor. Girl. Usually, I hate when people talk while I'm watching a show, but this is different af, and I can't wait to watch each and every *Drag Race* season with Flor and her fierce-ass, insightful, gay af commentary. I mean, her Valentina commentary is the energy and the moment, and I don't care how effing tired I am, girl — I'll binge with Flor and Hot Mikey holding my hand any day, all day, every day. #living. Girl, the passion and love, the respect and adoration Flor feels for Valentina are the real deal. So how can I not live for it? How can I not want more?

Furthermore, when Flor, mid-lecture, catches a glimpse of me holding Mikey's hand, she gives us both a wink, and honestly, I feel empowered by her approval. Girl, I smile, and I squeeze his hand tighter and lean my head against Mikey's shoulder.

And then, Cam. Seriously. She looks up from sniffing a perfume ad and says, "Okay, girl. So, I don't know what's going on over there with you two." He points to Mikey and me, and girl, I know jags, and jags are obvi cutting into that voice. "So, while y'all figure that out, I just need to remind y'all that Pride's next weekend."

"OMG. Yes! We need to start planning!!" Flor says, grabbing a notebook.

"All in favor? Me!!" I blurt out, and I don't think I can raise my hand and jump out of my seat any faster.

"Well, we all know how Mac feels. Basic Becky here needs to calm her tits," Cam quips, and I feel he's being a little bit a lot really effing shady.

But I don't wanna calm down. I mean, why not get excited

af about Pride? I've never been. I mean, really, what does Cam want? Should I just sit here and golf clap? Should I go home and journal? Girl, please. I think she's the one who needs to calm her tits.

The sour-ass look on my face says it all, because Flor jumps in, "So, I suggest we put together a fierce little group lewk for Pride. Come on, friends' group first time at Pride!"

This is when Cam gets up. In front of the TV, with Valentina in her white eleganza wedding gown paused on the screen, Cam stands so close to Flor that she's virtually standing on top of her, and Flor, as a result, has to move aside. "Girl, I already thought of that. I'm thinking total group vibe. Coordinating outfits. Costume change between festival and night parade. Matching water bottles. Ooh, and some of those clack fans. And dangles!! Fucking loves it already, girl. We arrive together, leave together. Group pics. The whole thing. Diva everything, girl! Flor, invite Hermelinda. If she can't attend the whole event, she can just show up for pictures. Mikey, you said you've been working on a summer mix. Girl, have it ready. We can listen while we get ready. Also, I'm thinking Ubers, since parking is gonna be a fucking nightmare."

Immediately, Flor's texting Hermelinda.

Mikey nods, reaching for his laptop. "I got this."

Cam then looks at me. "Mac, see if B and the Bruhhhs are going. We'll need to— On second thought, I'll call Clari. I need this done the right way."

Girl. #ughhhhhhhhhhhhhhhhhhhhhhhhh

I think my mouth literally drops from the facecrack. I don't know why Cam's coming for me, and she's doing it in front of everybody. Part of me thinks she's being pissy af because she saw me holding Mikey's hand and that means I didn't take her advice. But also, maybe she's just being a jealous-ass, though she's already made it very clear she thinks he's a major "N-O," in her words.

"Babe, Hermelinda's asking about themes. For the coordinated outfits," Flor clarifies. She holds up the phone screen showing Hermelinda's messages.

"Girl, seriously? It's Pride. Rainbow shit. If she wants more specifics, she can text me. Make sure she has my number." Cam then turns his attention to Mikey. "Listen. We'll do neon for the night parade because it's illuminated. Neon necklaces, we can weave them into crowns and whatever. Bracelets, too. You can make suspenders for her. She's gonna need help." Cam makes it clear she's talking about me, and I'm like ugh. Does she really think I can't dress myself? "For the group lewk, let's keep it consistent yet fierce. And noticeable, for the reals. Bitches need to break their fucking necks when we walk by. So, look for neon-pink or electric-blue shorts. Not lime green. Michelle Visage would totally agree, and she's an icon. Girl, asco and tacky af! And that's sooooo not our vibe. Is it?" Cam glances over at Flor, and I vaguely recall Flor's lime-green clutch. Ummm, wow. "Get on Amazon, girl. Same-day delivery. And no glow sticks—too basic." Turning back to Flor, Cam says, "But it's not like Hermelinda's mom is gonna let her stay out past dark. Girl, for reals, we'll end up meeting her ass at some Starbucks to get a pic because that's like the only place her mom lets her go alone."

It's true. Hermelinda's mom only lets her go, like, three places without an adult chaperone—Target, Starbucks, and Sephora.

Mikey shrugs, already scrolling through images of hyper-bright shorts. "I've never been to this Pride. It sounds like a grip of fun, tho. LA Pride—I've been to that one. And Long Beach. Intense. Music everywhere. Crowded, all types. Bears and cholos, power lesbians—"

Cammy interrupts, "Yes, girl. We know. You lived in LA—we get it. Bitch, focus."

Mikey rolls his eyes, breathes out, shakes his head.

"You'd like it," he whispers to me, pushing off Cammy's criticism.

"Hermelinda's in. But she has to clear it with her mom first." Flor appears joyed. I mean, she was his bff before we came into the picture.

"Yeah, not gonna hold my breath." Cammy reaches over and picks up the *Vogue* again.

"OMG, we should invite Kanari, too," Mikey gasps.

"Who?" Cam asks.

"Kanari," Mikey repeats.

"She's on the dance team. You know, the 'showstopper.'" Flor utters this sarcastically, using air quotes.

"Girl, whatever. Invite her if y'all want. You handle that." Rolling his neck, Cam points to Mikey. "So, like I was saying, let's really put this on point. If we're gonna show up together, this needs to be the moment and the vibe. Bitch, I'm so hyped. And I'm getting hungry. You know what I feel like?

Whataburger. We need to continue this little planning sesh there. Girl, she's craving some Whataburger fries and spicy ketchup."

Gathering her phone and keys, Flor nods.

And honestly, girl, Cam's shitty attitude toward me really has me going through it. So much for bingeing *Drag Race*. I guess we'll just have to watch more of Valentina's season another time.

"How short?" Mikey asks then, looking up from a hot male model wearing neon-pink shorts that barely cover his balls.

He's joking, I think.

"Shorter the better," Cam orders. "The babiest of the baby shorts you can find, girl. In the right color, of course. It is Pride, after all."

Cam holds out his leg, does a half twirl, cocks her hip. Cam has long legs, and she's proud of them.

"See if they have anything recycled or high-waisted," Flor adds, staring into the air like she's visualizing. "Or babe, just send me the link to what you're getting, and I'll match mine. I bet I can find something from FARM Rio or thredUP."

By this time, the group is heading for the door and Mikey's car and talking over each other, going on and on about what we'll wear for Pride and how incredibly effing unbelievably hot it's gonna be, and I'm here, like, ummmmm, baby shorts? Seriously. The whole baby shorts thing makes me uneasy. Girl, I don't know. Baby shorts just don't feel like me. It's just not my vibe or my energy. And I can't really see myself shoving myself into something that barely fits me. On the reals, I'm more of a basketball shorts kinda guy. Maybe it's that I like my balls to breathe? Maybe it's that I've never worn baby shorts so I'm just prejudging? Maybe it's just not me. All T, I thought the whole point of Pride was to be yourself and not have to pretend to be something you're not. #realness

Chapter 11

WALKING INTO WHATABURGER, THE FOUR OF us might be unstoppable. Flor and Cam float in ahead of Mikey and me, chatting it up about bomb-ass Pride lewks, while Mikey's talking fire, listing off all the potential mashes of remixes he might assemble for his Pride set. Girl, as soon as we're in, who do we see at the counter ordering? KT and Naomi.

"Just grabbing some grub. You know, before it rains," KT tells us. "Picking up apple pie, too. For my moms. It's her faves."

Next to KT, a group of señoras take their time discussing the menu options with a cashier whose fake lashes remind me of two tarantulas clinging to her face. Girl, I know I shouldn't judge, but damn. Meanwhile, the señoras look expensive af with their perfect hair, their big-ass purses, sophisticated shoes, and color-coordinated jewelry, and I love their bold-ass laughter and OMG! I live for the way they keep patting each other's arms and completing each other's sentences, how they get along. Girl.

While my friends go off about our upcoming plans for Pride, the four señoras make me think that maybe the four of us—Flor and Cammy, Mikey and me—will be friends for a long time. I wanna ask the ladies how long they've been friends and who's who and what's their secret, how have they made it all work? Life, you know.

Meanwhile, Cam, Flor, and Mikey are telling Naomi all about our Pride outfits, to which Naomi responds, grabbing KT's arm, "Babe! We are so doing a theme! We can get you and me and B and Clari. Definitely gonna be part of our Hot Girl Summer."

"Come through, Hot Girl Summer!" Doing this little shimmy, Mikey points up at the restaurant lights or at Naomi, I can't tell for sure, but whatever he does, it looks sassy and hot.

"Y'all need to have y'all a Hot Boy Summer or something," Naomi says, clapping. "Show all them muscles, and serve them hungry bitches the real lewks."

"All this fashion, hunny!" Like a spokesmodel highlighting an exquisite prize on a game show, Flor runs her hand up and down the length of our friends group.

Girl, she's good. And I don't know what those old ladies standing next to us in Whataburger are thinking, but it's a show Flor puts on, and I'm here for it. In the front row, too.

"Mijo, échale gas! You go, girl!" the señora with a

purplish-gray helmet tells Flor in her smooth-ass Spanglish. All the señoras clap and cheer, going on and on, endlessly complimenting Flor's skin, nails, bag, hair, teeth, earlobes, brows, cheekbones, and shoes. I mean, girl.

"Anyways," Cam cuts in with Naomi. "If y'all are serious about Pride, let's talk. OMG. My vibe is sooo on. Bitch, this Pride just got sooo much better!"

"It's our turn," Mikey says to the group, then proceeds to order up a #1, no onions, and fries.

Not wanting to be complicated, I ask for the same, and knowing that my aim is to put my lips against Mikey's mouth later, I also insist on no onions.

"Get me a number four, girl. Extra spicy ketchup. With cheese. Girl, I'll pay you back," Cam instructs me, then pops back into his convo with Naomi and KT.

We order a kid's chicken strip meal for Flor like she asks us to, while she gives the señoras a little session on skin care.

While Cam walks Naomi and KT out, Mikey and I snatch a booth by the window.

Having just let Whataburger have it, Flor slides into the booth and sits across from me while Mikey takes the cups to get our drinks. Flor's glowing, and I effing love it.

"Girl, those señoras were living. You know, girl, sometimes I'm afraid old people just don't get who I am, but maybe I'm wrong," she confesses. "Maybe, like with those señoras, we just have to be ourselves and give people a chance to accept us."

"Maybe. But, like how can we know if they're gonna be respectful? Like how do we even know if they're gonna treat us like humans?" I pause. "By the way, Mikey got your chicken strips."

"Thanks, babe."

I go on, "But really, aren't you ever scared somebody's gonna throw hate when we're just being ourselves and then tell us we're gonna burn in hell or punch us in the face?"

"Scared? You mean to be myself or scared of bigots and haters?"

"Both, I guess." As much as I want Flor's and Cam's confidence, it just seems to come at a risk. A hard risk.

"Sis, on the real, what I'm actually scared of is not being myself. Being some fake, watered-down version of me. To live my whole life serving other people's versions of me and then waking up one day and saying, Ugh. I lived a fake-ass life. And for what? Girl, please."

Listening to Flor, I realize making gay friends and coming out to my dad are just the tip of the iceberg. I mean, can I really change my whole life in one summer? Maybe I can't change my whole life, but maybe I can change some parts that really need changing, some parts that are really holding me back from the life I deserve to live.

"Girl. The thing is, we don't always know who's gonna embrace us and help us slay boots and who's gonna come for us. But I'd rather be myself and be pleasantly surprised by people like those señoras than spend my whole life hiding." Reviewing her IG likes and comments from the pics she posted earlier, Flor exhales.

I see her point, but I also think it can be waaaay dangerous af. "I mean, people get their asses kicked just for being who they are. It happens all the time."

Flor puts her phone down. She's shaking her head. "Girl. Wait. No. No. Nooooooo, mama. It's not because of who they are. It's not because of who *we* are. People get their asses kicked because other people hate us. Because they want to make us go away, because they want to erase us. No, girl. How does me giving girl cause violence? It doesn't. People who feel rage just looking at people like us—that's what causes violence, girl. Don't let it sound like it's our fault for getting bashed, because it's not. We're not the ones with the problem."

"What is the problem?" The question jumps out of me.

"Hate's the problem. Girl, please. Don't even get it twisted. Making us believe that we're the problem. No, ma'am. Painting these exquisite cheekbones, carrying a fierce-ass bag, pushing consistently hot high femme lewks, loving myself—girl, how does any of this hurt the world? Soooo not the problem. Girl. Bigots, toxic masculinity, misogyny, having hate in your heart, fake Christians. Babe, that's the real problem."

I sit with Flor's ideas for a minute, because in the middle of Whataburger, she's giving me her magic. Like she's giving me wise-sis-passing-out-self-love-and-life-knowledge vibes, and I'm here for it. #allofit #listenandlearn #girlelevate. "I never thought of it like that," I say. "Like, why blame ourselves for other people hating us?" Ugh. And OMG. Girl. For the reals. I have to pause here for a second. For several seconds. Because girl, this is a moment. Like for so long, even though I've 110 accepted that I'm gay, I've believed somewhere inside me that I needed to tone it down and not act gay so that people wouldn't talk shit to me and so that I wouldn't embarrass my dad. Like what's that even about? That's soooo fake, and Flor telling me to be who I wanna be because if people hate me, that's on them, not on me, girl—everything! But also, and maybe it's just me, but I think Flor makes it all sound so easy, like with the flip of a switch, I can just change my life, my whole way of thinking. And so, although I believe her 110, and I hope with every bone and ligament and blood cell in my body that Flor and I will be friends forever, por vida and always, I think my journey may take a lot longer than hers.

Seeing that I've gone inside my head, Flor nudges me. "Girl, you okay? Bitch, tell me. Que te pasa?"

I wave my hands in front of my face like that might clear the air for me.

"It's just a lot. It's just . . . ugh."

Reaching over, Flor pats my hand, which I've clenched into a ball of knuckles.

"I love how you see the world," I say, "and I love how confident you are and I wanna be more confident. I just think it's a lot to take in and yeah, I wanna change my life. Ughhhh. Girl, what's wrong with me? I'm getting all these feels."

"Nothing's wrong with you. Girl, let yourself be a human."

There's a lump in my throat, and I can feel water start to push up behind my eyes, but I don't really want to cry. Not here. Not in Whataburger.

"I think it's just that I have all these thoughts going around inside me, and B's leaving and I need to come out to my dad and what am I gonna do with my life after that? And I'm just so glad I met y'all—I didn't realize how good things can be. And I'm sooo excited about my first Pride and I just want us all to get along. And girl, for the reals, when we're old, I hope we're just like those four señoras with their big-ass fancy bags and ten thousand bangles."

"Awwwww. Girl, yessss! That's sooo gonna be us. Girl, rule number three, remember?"

"Rule number three," I repeat.

I hold on to Flor's hand, which feels like a handful of cotton compared to mine.

"Girl, this is just the beginning . . ."

". . . of the rest of our lives." I complete her sentence.

"Yes, girl. The rest of our fierce-ass gorgeous lives!"

My heart jumps into my throat again, and I catch my voice and hold on to it before it breaks into a thousand parts and I cry all over this booth.

Outside, the sky darkens.

A mom swiftly pushes a stroller across the concrete.

Two boys with a football jump off the bus at the VIA stop.

In the parking lot, Cam's standing next to KT's truck, running her mouth a million miles an hour about something. Naomi looks like she's listening, but KT looks like she couldn't give two shits about whatever Cam's saying. Flor and I watch from the window, and I like Naomi, I really do, but like Cam, Naomi says she hates drama, yet, at the same time, she's always around it. #youknowher #isshethedrama

Behind us, a baby starts to cry.

I feel a little calmer now, but I still have a million questions about my future and the life I deserve to live.

Soon Mikey comes back with drinks.

"I hope it doesn't rain too hard," he says, looking out the window. Squeezing in beside me, he places his hand on my leg.

Of course, this excites me, and I make sure my chest rubs against his arm.

When the food comes, Mikey attacks the fries, and Flor asks, "Should we wait for her?"

"For Cam?" Unwrapping my burger, I look out to the parking lot, and girl, no surprise — Cam hasn't stopped moving her mouth.

"She's a big girl. She can catch up." Mikey chews, then dips a handful of fries into the black container of spicy ketchup and shoves them into his mouth.

Maybe we should wait? I second-guess myself, because part of me knows that Cam will 110 abso no doubt move her mouth that we didn't wait for her to eat. And yet, this other part of me doesn't care. I mean, really, girl? She can't expect us to let our food get cold so she can talk massive amounts of shit — and that's exactly what she's doing with Naomi. Girl, I see her.

So I eat. Besides, girl. Cam was a major shady bitch to me at Flor's, so why wait?

Girl, boundaries. I'm not good at them. But boundaries af.

And so, we're pretty much done eating twenty minutes later when Cam finally comes inside. Mikey's washing his hands, and Flor's taking a break from responding to comments on her IG, having passed me a near-entire meal after delicately nibbling on a few fries and one whole chicken strip, without the crust, of course, which she asked Mikey to peel off.

Flor says, "And so, my whole thing with rule number two, girl. It's passion. Like, to me, Valentina is Kween because her whole outlook about passion is to find what you love and do that thing. Make it yours. Make it your life and your mission and your energy."

"Like you said in your letter."

In agreement, Flor smiles. "Yes, girl. Like I said in my letter."

"Really, girl? Y'all fucking ate without me?" Standing at the end of the table, Cam glares at the pile of crumpled food wrappers and empty fry cartons.

"The food was getting cold." Making a point to look right at Cammy, I just say it, because it's true and because I'm trying to be direct and girl, because Rule #1. I know I need to be fiercer, and standing up for myself more is a way to embrace my fierceness and live the life I wanna live.

"And? Let it get cold. Y'all still should've fucking waited for me. Real friends would've waited. Ugh. Couldn't even wait five minutes to eat. Move." Cammy motions for Flor to scoot over, which she does.

I'm getting tired af of this rude-ass tone Cam talks to us with, so I tell her, "Ummmm. More like twenty minutes."

Girl, #deathstare.

Even though Cam's throwing daggers at me, something inside me says, *Don't back down.*

Irritated af, Cam takes a bite of her burger. She chews,

swallows, locks her eyes on me. Not taking her eyes away from me, she takes another bite. Jalapeños and lettuce fall from the sides of her bun. She bites hard, and I stare back. Girl, I know what she's doing. She's trying to make me fear her, and any other day before this one, I might've been afraid, because Cam's mean af. I've watched her tear girls apart with just three words. And I don't want her to dismantle me here in the middle of Whataburger. But how do I stand up for myself and not piss her off any more than I already have? Girl. #challenge #impossibility #wtf

Maybe kindness?

She has mustard on her face, so I give her a napkin. I hold it out, but Cammy doesn't take the napkin. "You have something on your face." I point to the corner of her mouth. Realizing that she's not gonna take the napkin, I place it on the table next to her tray.

"Really, girl? I've been more of a friend to you than anyone. Girl, I even got you a fucking Ariana ticket. Do I need to remind you?"

I hate that Cam says this. I hate that she's pissed at me, at us, for something so small and trivial. Like seriously. First over tacos. Now over french fries! Girl, please. Her whole argument about "real friends"? Girl, a real friend wouldn't be asking us to wait twenty minutes for her to eat. A real friend wouldn't tell us to let our food get cold. A real friend wouldn't choose shit-talking in the parking lot over spending time with us at a restaurant that it was her idea to come to in the first place! #gross #ughhhhh #icant. And on top of all that, a real-ass friend wouldn't throw buying concert tickets for my favorite artist in my face whenever she gets mad at me.

At this point, Mikey returns to the table. "What's going on?" he says.

Flor messes with her phone, and I refuse to break my stare at Cammy.

Confused, Mikey asks again.

"Nothing. We were just talking about real friends," I say.

"And fake bitches." Shoving a fry into her mouth, Cam chews furiously.

"Sounds deep," Mikey remarks, taking the seat in the booth next to me.

Outside, thunder. Loud enough to rattle the windows.

In the parking lot, a car alarm goes off. It's enough to break my stare-down with Cam.

For a few minutes, the four of us sit in silence.

Under the table, Mikey rubs my leg with his leg, which I can't even really enjoy, because girl. Tension af. It surrounds us.

"Can I take your trays?" the cashier with two tarantulas on her face asks.

I nod, and she begins pulling away the trays and the trash, except for Cammy's, because she's still eating.

"I like your bangs," the Whatalady tells Flor. "I'm thinking about cutting mine."

Flor embraces the compliment. "Thanks, girl. I'm an avid supporter of bangs. But please don't cut them yourself. Friends don't let friends cut bangs alone. Just some advice."

I wipe the table with a napkin.

Mikey scrolls through a page of neon shorts.

"Thanks for the advice," tarantula eyes tells Flor. "And thanks for wiping your table."

For a second, it feels like the tension has subsided. Like we'll all just let this moment go and Cam will not destroy me in front of Mikey and Flor.

"Well, I'm hyped af for Pride," Mikey says. "I'm sending everybody three options for shorts. Respond with your top two. Winning lewk gets delivered in two to three days."

I peek over at Mikey's screen and groan to myself. All three options—baby shorts. Ughhh. Not. What. I. Wanted.

Girl, Flor and Cam study the choices.

"The second one." Cam's voice is level; she sips from her drink. "I'll need a medium."

Flor takes her time. "Option two. Yes, girl." Affirming Cam, she leans over and says, "Good choice, babe. I love nylon-spandex mesh."

Cam doesn't budge.

"Scroll down," I tell Mikey. Studying option two, all I see is my panza flopping over the waistband of the bright pink shorts and my thighs stretching the leg holes and people staring at my bulge. Girl, I'm not convinced.

"What's the matter, girl? Not liking Mikey's choices?" Cam slurps the last of her drink.

"It's not that."

"Then what? That bitchy cara you're making says you're sooo not having these shorts."

If I look up, I'm afraid I'll say something I'll regret. Or that my "bitchy" face will say it.

Trying to defuse the escalating drama, Flor asks Mikey, "Is Venmo okay, babe? Or you want us to use Apple Pay?"

No one responds.

"I'm fine with whatever y'all decide," I finally say. Girl, I feel I've sold myself out. It's like how can I go from standing up for myself and setting a boundary one minute and then letting it all go to shit?

"Good. Then it's decided. Option two. Short neon-pink button-fly, four-inch neon-spandex mesh. They will eat." Cam glares directly at me as she speaks.

"Nylon, girl."

Cam looks at Flor like wtf.

"Girl, you said 'neon.' But it's 'nylon-spandex,' babe. It says so in the details." Flor points to the phone screen.

Girl, the look Cam gives Flor could flatten an 18-wheeler. And right now, while a storm is brewing outside, an even more ferocious storm is brewing inside Cam.

"Just facts, girl." Flor returns to her phone.

Cam's jaw and brow stiffen. She takes a deep breath. In her neck, the muscles grow taut, and I can see them thicken.

"Girl. It's. Just. A. Textile," I add. "Seriously."

"Well, this Pride's gonna be hype-lit af," Mikey maintains. He squeezes my leg. Trying to relieve whatever strain has formed, he adds, "Bitch, I can't wait. I'm so ready to dance with everybody. And just to feel the whole vibe."

"I know, babe," Cam says. "I just hope the music is good. I

mean, sometimes these Prides just play the same old tired songs over and over. Like give us something new, right? You're an expert on music, what do you think, Mikey?"

Mikey nods like he's suspicious. "The post said they're supposed to have three music tents at Pride. One for country and Tejano and then another tent for hip-hop and one more for dance-pop and circuit, which is totally soooo my vibe."

Cammy nods, like she's fully invested in Mikey's explanation, but I know her, and I can see that she's plotting something. Then she turns to me. "And you, Mac? What do you think?"

I have no effing clue where Cam's going with this, but I can see the cogs spinning in her head. Girl, one time I saw her read Harper Moreno to filth over wearing chanclas to school — Harper never wore anything close to chanclas to school again. Ever. Not even slides during soccer season!

Nerves hit me suddenly. And it's so stupid. Like, why am I getting all anxious and jittery just giving my opinion about music? Girl. Wtf. So I say, "Yeah. I think everybody should get to hear their music at Pride. That's what Pride is, right?"

"Exactly," Cam butts in. "Different styles. I couldn't agree more."

A few booths away, a little girl throws french fries on the floor while her mom's on the phone.

A hot guy in a cowboy hat with a dad beard and a big-ass silver buckle walks in.

Outside, a few drops of rain.

Across the restaurant, the table of señoras laughs loudly.

But none of this distracts Cammy. And she tells us, "Like

girl, please. Don't give me the same old fifty thousand tired-ass Katy Perry and Ariana Grande songs. Change it up."

Bitch.

Gasp.

No.

Did she really just?

"Seriously, Cammy?" Trying not to trip over the stunt she's pulling, I sigh loudly. "Girl, you know you love Ariana."

I look at Flor, and I almost say out loud to her, *Babe, don't fall for it! Don't take the bait!*

But it's too late.

Flor claps back, "Really? Tell me, girl. What exactly do you mean?" From the rise of her impeccable brows to the serrated edges of her voice, she knows exactly what Cam means, and she's ready to battle for her diva.

No, I think. *Not here. Not in Whataburger. Not today. Not in front of the señoras, not in front of the hot cowboy, and not in front of the little baby who already threw up once.*

"It means what it means," Cam replies. "Sometimes you just gotta change things up. Change up your surroundings. Change your energy. Your style. I mean, you can't just go around wearing the same tired-ass high ponytail all your life."

I'm gagged. Like my heart stops beating for a whole second, and I see the storm that's coming.

Mikey starts to say something, but Flor, with outrage in her eyes, speaks over him. "Her ponytail is iconic. Iconic," she argues, putting the word down on the table like a jewel, some ruby or sapphire that we can all stare at.

I nod. She's right.

"And because her ponytail is iconic, that's why she'll never change it. She doesn't have to!" Flor's voice rockets into the air, and her jaw is resolute.

Cam comes right back. "Girl. Take a breath. Compose yourself, mija. It's gonna be okay. You want some water? All I'm saying is what if. Girl, really. What if? Like a short little bob. Or maybe kinda sexy-stringy and loose, like Bebe Rexha. That might be cute on her. Or what if she maybe talked to Selena Gomez's stylist? Like what if Ariana just served us something different? Could you imagine? A new look. Madonna did it all the time. Now that's iconic."

Flor's face freezes.

Girl. I can't. I glance over at Mikey, and even he's face-cracked.

Then Flor's brow tenses up, and her eyes get very small. Perilously small, girl. Like they're flexing inside themselves, or making a fist.

Girl, I'm sooo not having Cam throwing down like this. I give her a look, like, *Girl, stop!* But she ignores me. All night, Cammy's been on the rampage. Girl, my food hasn't even digested yet, and Cam's got her claws aimed at Flor and why? Because she corrected him about the name of a textile. Girl, I'm no Velma, but I don't have to be a detective to know my bff is way beyond going through it and needs to stop. For reals, girl. But how do I stop Cam when she's already in deep?

I can't help but feel like Cam is threatened by Flor, and trying to make her look small in front of me is Cammy's way of showing us all who's boss bitch. Or maybe she's still pissed at me for flirting with Mikey earlier. Maybe it's everything? Seriously. It's a lot.

I'm hoping that Cam's done, but then she stares directly at Flor and goes, "You know, I want y'all's opinion, Mac and Mikey. I really think Ariana should do something different with her hair. The ponytail. Ya. Girl. It's been done. I think she needs a new lewk."

"I disagree," Mikey says immediately.

Cammy just rolls her eyes, and then she looks at me.

Girl, sooooo not cute. I can see it. What Cammy's doing now—she's testing my loyalty. I just want this convo to end. I wanna go home to let Kimber out before the hard rain really starts falling. I wanna drive home with Mikey and hold on to his hand and kiss him deeply, my breath on his neck. Girl, I'm sooooo over Cam being messy!

Before I can answer, Flor takes a big-ass deep breath and comes back even harder. "Girl. Maybe you just don't understand branding. Ariana's known for that ponytail. People think Ariana Grande, and they think two things—range, impeccable range, voice of a generation. Gorgeous, gorgeous beauty. And high-top ponytail. It's bible, hunny. She's iconic. I can look up the word 'icon' for you, babe. Dictionary.com might help."

Now, I've never seen Flor so on it. Like the bitch is glowing from her vigorously devoted defense of Ariana, and that little vein in her forehead throbs and peeks out from behind her flawless skin and bouncy bangs like it has hands to throw for Ariana too.

But Cam keeps her eye on Flor. "First of all, that's three things, sweetie. Learn to count. Second of all, girl, I definitely understand—"

"Ughhh. Nobody says second of all!" Mikey says.

"*Second of all*, I definitely understand branding. And if a brand doesn't change, it will die. It's called keeping up with the times." Sticking her straw in her mouth, Cammy slurps the last drops of Diet Coke and melted ice from her cup. "Now, Cardi B. Megan Thee Stallion. Nicki. Doja. That's goddess. Those bitches, they slay it perra fierce 24-7 down. Mija, that's iconic."

Mikey jumps in at this point. "They're all iconic. You can't compare. As a DJ, I—"

Suddenly, Flor jumps up, pushing her way through Cammy to get out of the booth. Girl, Flor's small af but chooses violence and pushes Cam so hard to get out of that booth that Cam almost falls on the floor, and her tray slides off the table.

From across Whataburger, the señoras stop their conversation and look over.

"Ay, mija. You okay?" the señora in the pinkish viejita hair asks as Flor, rattled af, runs right by the señoras, storming into the bathroom.

"We're okay. Thanks," Mikey replies, picking up Cam's tray.

The whole restaurant stops and stares.

"Girl, why the fuck are you like this?" Mikey barks.

Cammy smirks. Looking at me, she shrugs like she can't be bothered, like she's pleased with herself. "Girl, I'm just keeping it real. Not my fault she's so sensitive."

But Mikey's hearing none of it. He grabs Flor's keys and phone and follows Flor to the restroom, and that leaves me at the table, staring at Cam's mess.

"Bitch, for real. I don't know why she's so sensitive," Cammy tells me. "She needs to learn how to take a joke."

I say nothing. I mean, inside myself I'm saying a million things. Like, I wanna call Cam out and tell her she's making unnecessary, ridiculous-ass drama with Flor and creating a public spectacle of us. Like girl. Who does that?! And for the reals, everybody knows Flor loves Ariana. Why mess with her head? And also, the ponytail is iconic af. And besides, Rule #1! And more than that, I begin to feel a barb of anger toward Cam, this bitterness that's been building and now feels sharper, dangerous af, because here, she was rude af to me all afternoon, and now she's just intentionally hurt my friend, and it's like Cam *enjoyed* hurting Flor. Ughhh. Gross. Asco. Más asco to the highest power, girl. I don't know what to do with this bitter-ass thing I feel toward someone I still, for whatever reason, consider a friend, and honestly, girl, I don't know the right way to be pissed off and angry at somebody I love.

"Don't tell me you're gonna be all sensitive af too. Girl, please." Cam sighs.

I dump Cammy's trash, then refill my Powerade and gather myself. When I get back to the table, I throw a crumpled-ass napkin at Cam, hitting her in the chest. "Girl, ya. Stop it. You're being messy."

"OMG! Ay, girl. She's gonna need to grow the fuck up if she wants to kick it with the big girls. If not, life's gonna chew her skinny ass up and spit her out with the rest of the weak sauce. Don't you see I'm doing her a fucking favor?"

I shake my head.

Running her hand through her hair, Cam groans like she's soooo waaay over it all.

"110 straight up, girl," I say. "I'm your friend to the very end. But the way you're acting? Earlier, you were out to get me, and now, you come for Flor. No, girl. You're not slaying. You're not giving it fierce boots perra or however you say it. Girl, you're just being a dick. And why? What are you doing?"

"Do you know what *you're* doing?" Cam turns it back on me. Plainly, she asks it, and I can't help but notice something like sadness or maybe hurt or disappointment, even, wrapped up deep inside her question.

I back down a little. "I'm trying to be a friend."

"Ha! Girl. Trying. Yeah. Good one. She makes two friends and thinks she's the expert on friendship."

Ignoring me, Cam watches the storm, then messes with her phone.

By now, Flor and Mikey are walking out.

In the car, no one says a word, so Mikey puts on a mix he's been working on. And yes, it's "Side to Side," and yes, it's Ariana, which I take as a solid vouch for Flor. But it's also Nicki, and I don't know if Mikey plays this mix on purpose, but this way, with this track, he's serving both Flor and Cammy.

In the front seat, Cam plays on his phone and sings along to the Nicki parts.

In the back, beside me, Flor looks out the window at the rain. I think maybe I should say something, but I also think saying something would just get everybody riled up again. Instead I watch the rain collect on the car window and listen to

Ariana, thinking of the video with her on the bike and remembering Mikey's selfie in response to Flor's Ariana challenge at the beginning of summer.

I text Flor.

Me: You ok?

At first Flor doesn't pick up her phone. So I text again.

Me: Just checking on you.

Me: Just want you to know I'm here.

After the third message, she responds.

Flor: Yes.

Flor: Thx.

Flor: I know.

Flor: ❤

Me: ☺☺☺

Flor: Also, I'm so over her. Total chaos. Totes mess. I can't with her.

I pause before I message back. Girl, I know Cam is chaotic af, and I know she's sloppy. Like a lot a lot. But she's my friend. And for some reason, I feel I need to defend her, even when she's doing rowdy effed-up shit. Girl, *especially* when she's doing rowdy-ass effed-up shit. Like for real, nobody's perfect. I mean, she's not all bad. Who is, right? Girl, on top of that, I'm literally sitting right behind her, and if I talk shit about her, isn't that like the literal definition of talking shit behind her back? Girl. #forreals #toomuchdrama #notfake #weaksauce

Me: I'll talk to her.

Flor: Ugh. Girl, she's toxica. NOT GONNA CHANGE.

Me: Girl, let me try.

I see Flor read the message, but she doesn't respond. She puts her phone in her lap and just stares out the window.

Mikey drops Cam off first, even though Cammy tried to insist that he start with me. As we approach Cam's neighborhood, she calls her sister Denise to talk about nothing. When we're at her house, she gets out of the car and slams the door, yapping loudly as she trots inside. Girl, she doesn't even say bye. When we get to Flor's, it's still drizzling, and she reaches over and hugs us, then quickly exits the car, muttering, "Thanks" as she shuts the door.

"Awkward," I say to Mikey as I jump to the front seat.

"You think?" Mikey replies.

The whole ride to my house, I keep my hand on Mikey's leg like it belongs there. The rain falls around us.

Above us, the sky and its dark sheen.

I think to message Flor or Cam or both, but I don't.

Right now, I just want it to be Mikey and me.

We pull up by the piled branches. Mikey parks in my driveway and turns off his headlights. He unlocks his phone and taps the screen, and Ariana's "Let Me Love You" starts to play. I feel my heart quaking like a jar full of stars.

"Sorry about all that chaos at Whataburger," I say.

"Why are you apologizing? You didn't do anything wrong."

"I know, but Cammy's my friend, and she was messy af. I don't know why she gets like that."

"Yeah, she's a lot." I know Mikey wants to say more, like, maybe talk shit about Cammy, but he doesn't.

Honestly, the last thing I wanna do right now is talk about Cammy, so I sit quietly, listening to the song.

Just let me lo-o-o-o-o-o-o-ve you, you.

Taking a deep breath, I say it: "I like you, and I wanna kiss you. I've wanted to all day, actually since the first day you talked to me."

Liking this, Mikey moistens his lips, and I put my fingers inside his hand, and when I pull his knuckles up to my mouth, I kiss the soft parts between his fingers. I rub my stubble on the skin that's on the back side of his thumb, and he exhales, which makes a sound that reminds me of the rain falling outside so that I lean my body in toward his, and like that, with his hand in mine, with the whispering of soft rain around us, I kiss Mikey Villanueva. His mouth is warm and steady like I didn't know a mouth could be, and he tastes like cinnamon, and when Mikey reaches over and slides his hands under my shirt, he squeezes on me and then traces a heart on my chest, in the middle of all my dark hair, and he says with the music, "Goddamn, you the best, best, best." Now I put my lips against Mikey's neck. Now I slide my hand in the back of his shorts and hold him like we fit together, which we do, and I think life is exactly what it needs to be right now. The rain and my hands on his body and Mikey's tongue in my mouth. For the reals, I could kiss him every day for the rest of our lives. I could kiss him in rain and sunshine and droughts and ice days. The windows fog, and my heart opens up, releasing a whole sky full of stars.

Chapter 12

*G*IRL. #PRIDEVIBESAF #PRIDESGIVING #LIVING #everythingisfierceness

Pride's finally arrived, and I'm hyped and happy and moisturized af! Girl, I'm so f-word excited, I might not even care that much if I have to wear those uncomfortable-ass baby shorts. No lies. The day's gonna start with Cam and me meeting Mikey and Flor at noon for a hot little Pride Brunch that Mikey's mom is putting together for us. A Pride Brunch, my first-ever Pride festival, an illuminated Pride night parade, and girl, with all my bffs, and Mikey, who I'm totes getting the deep feels for, and B and her friends! Ufffff. Girl, gimme!!!

First, though, Cam wanted to stop at Target so we could look through all the Pride stuff and maybe find something extra for the festival. And Target is giving! Just as she always does, girl. I mean, seriously, there's a shitload of Pride gear to look through.

Since the Whataburger drama, Cam has come over to the house once. While we walked Kimber, we chatted about her vision for Pride, and I listened to her talk a whole lotta shit about her sister Denise. She sent me a few opossum and raccoon memes, which she knows I live for, and because she's been feasting on the group chat with all her concepts and logistics for Pride, I kinda figured that she wants to move past all the conflict at Whataburger. Girl, easier said than done. Because Flor isn't having it. Adamant that Cam's in the wrong, Flor insists that "she needs to change her energy. 110 abso. If she's unwilling to change her toxic vibes, then maybe Mikey and I need to just hang out with you when she's not around."

Girl, ughhhh. I was a little bit a lot very gagged by that stance. I mean, that's sooo not an option.

And yet, while I've promised Flor and Mikey that I'd have a serious check-yourself convo with Cam, I haven't. And it's not that I haven't wanted to. Okay, honestly, maybe it is precisely because I haven't wanted to. It's just a volatile topic, and I've been working a lot. And for the reals, I'd much rather spend most of my time with Mikey instead of managing stupid friends-group drama, and yet at the same time, I want us to somehow all get along. How's that for complicated realness? Girl. So, while Cam's looking through a display of Pride mugs and Pride toothpaste, I figure now is as good a time as any and say, "I'm glad we have some time just for us before Pride. Today's gonna be a crazy-ass day."

"I know, right?" Cam agrees. "It's like I've been working a

lot and you've been working a lot. We're working girls, hunny. OMG. Is this what being a working woman feels like? All work so you can spend your own coins and only see your bffs on the weekends? Girl. Anyways, I think I might be looking for a boyfriend today. Mac, you should really watch and learn. Girl, it'll be good for you to know about flirting, so you don't come off desperate."

I bite the shit outta my tongue when Cam says this, leaning against the shopping cart and thinking about Hot Mikey and how every day this week he's given me a ride home from work and how we've made out like a hundred times on my bed and on his bed and in his car and outside the gym in the parking lot under the hot yellow lights, none of which Cammy knows about. I guess I'm not that bad at flirting, now am I?

"Yeah." On the verge of dislocating my eyes from rolling them so hard, I look away.

We try on a couple of Pride hats, and Cam passes me a pair of futuristic-looking rainbow sunnies and an oversized silvery button-up, which make me look like some kind of cyborg cholo clown. I try them on and watch Cam posing in the store mirror. "So, girl. What did you decide about Mikey?" Pursing her lips, Cam's giving angles to the mirror. "At first I totally thought that maybe he might actually possibly be a little bit into you, but after the other night, I think he's losing interest, which is 110 a good thing. Like I said. Not a good choice for you."

And here she goes. She *never* thought he might be into me. #girlplease

Then Cam picks up a rainbow romper, scowls like she's smelled something rotted, and hands the garment to me. "Try this one on. Or why don't you get it for your new best friend Flor? She's sooooo into fashion."

Girl. Okay. So, like she's totally throwing me caca right now, and although I seriously wanna clap back at her, I don't, because this morning as I was walking Kimber around the block, that tired, raggedy-ass Chihuahua named Precious Moments started moving her mouth at Kimber, and I suddenly had this much-needed epiphany that Cam, like Precious Moments, is predictable af. And jealous, sure, but mostly threatened. Very threatened. I mean, girl. Obvi af, right? Honestly, why did it take me so long to figure this out? And if Kimber can get by without letting Precious Moments push her buttons and not get all defensive and not go the f off on that little predictable-ass sucia, then I can do the same with a beloved bff, right?

Listening to Cam talk her shit, I remind myself that my path forward is not to battle Cam but to show her that she has abso 110 nothing to worry about—Flor and Mikey are not gonna undermine our friendship. Like B said, you can't "steal" somebody away. People leave because they wanna leave or because life happens, right? And so, using B's logic, Cam has no reason to feel threatened by new friends.

"Ooooooh, and look. Here's the perfect rainbow thong." Cam holds up the tiniest rainbow-polka dot underwear. "Extra small. It's virtually dental floss, girl. Perfect for your boyfriend Mikey. Though it's more than he wears on his thirsty-ass IG stories, don't you think?"

I laugh. A fake-ass, uber-mega-obvi-ultra-max-pro-to-the-highest-power fake af laugh. Girl. And I sigh. And then, still wearing the homo-cyborg sunnies, which I'm kind of a lot very loving on my face, my drive to defend Mikey takes over, and I say, "Girl, you don't have to be jealous of them. They're not a threat."

"Jealous? Girl, you think I'm threatened by them?"

I'm holding the rainbow romper up to my body, sizing it up, doing my best not to feed Cam the reaction she wants. All the while, I'm thinking, *Okay, so much for not letting her push your buttons, girl. That strategy lasted a whole three seconds.*

"I'm not jealous." Cam smirks. "Uhhhh. What's there to be jealous of, girl?" Her voice rises high, over the racks of Pride beads, water canteens, beach towels, and tote bags, and into the fluorescent lights and white ceiling tiles.

Nearby, a tall, gorge, fabulous old-school chola wearing a giant feathered pompadour and severely bedazzled baby shorts with impossibly high heels glances our way.

I don't wanna make a scene. Not today and especially not here in the Pride section of Target in front of a West Side glamazon eyeing us through the Pride racks. Yet I promised Flor and Mikey that I'd talk to Cammy.

I clear my throat. "Okay, girl. If you say so."

"Well, I said what I said." Cam glares.

"Okay, girl." I return the rainbow romper and the iridescent button-up to the rack.

"You're imagining things, girl."

"Am I, though? You sure looked like a jealous-ass the other night at Whataburger." I don't mean to come for her, but I can't help it.

Cam's mouth drops open.

"I mean, seriously, what was that about? Babe, you totally started high-impact drama over a ponytail. A ponytail! And why? Because she corrected you on the name of a fabric."

"Ughhhh. Calm down, girl. It's just a joke," Cam stresses. "Can't she take a joke?"

I take off the intergalactic Pride sunglasses, and I'm looking right at Cam. "Girl, no. Just admit it. You don't like her."

"Girl, she really has you fooled. You just can't see it yet, but she's totally turning you against me. It's what villains do."

"Really, girl? You think Flor's the villain?" I swallow my disbelief, which almost emerges as laughter.

"Mac, yes! And the worst kinda villain, girl. The kinda villain that pretends to be all nice and sweet and angelic but deep down is just as rotted a bitch as anyone else. Girl, if you're gonna be a villain, embrace that shit. Be a bad boss-ass bitch."

"I get it. You don't like her. But you're not even giving her a chance. You've been going at her since the first night."

"OMG, Mac! Why are you taking her side?" Cam's voice comes out crooked, anguished, like it's pressing down on itself and trying to be heard simultaneously.

Seriously, this conversation is más fast spinning outta control.

This is sooo not how I planned this convo to go.

"Look, papa. We've been friends longer, and I don't want that to change. That said, girl . . . I think you're being really harsh with Flor. And I think it would be fierce if we could all just take it down a notch and chill and have a good-ass time at Pride."

"*I'm* the one being harsh with her? Right. Keep defending her, girl. Forget about the shady-ass shit she says to me."

"Like what?" I run through my recent memories of Flor's comments, and the only thing I come up with is her comment about only hanging out with me if Cam's not around. No way I'm mentioning that right now.

"Like reading me for not being a 'real friend' because I didn't watch Valentina with you."

I'd forgotten about that, and I think my face shows it.

"Exactly. So I guess she's getting what she wants. Because yeah, girl. She's inserting herself in our friendship and turning you against me. So, here, lemme give you the answer you want. No, I don't like her. But jealous? Ha! Babe, there's *nothing* to be jealous of."

"Well, actions speak louder than words." I cringe when I hear this come out of my mouth, but I'm feeling hella defensive right now and put on the spot and like all my plans for uniting my friends group have straight-up gone to Toilet City, Ready to Flush.

Girl. This is sooo 110 abso *not* giving. I mean, I promised Flor and Mikey that I'd talk to Cammy for, like, self-awareness and growth and to encourage her to calm the f down, but girl. Why did I just get Cam to flat-out admit that she doesn't like Flor? #counterproductiveaf. Seriously not in my game plan. So maybe this isn't gonna be one of the best days of my life after all. Already, after this exchange, I'm feeling all sorts of ways about how Pride is gonna go today and whether I can pull off the unthinkable—getting the four of us to get along, no drama.

I feel like maybe I'm trying too hard, like I'm pushing together two north poles of magnets that will never go together and then getting all pissed because I can't make shit happen the way I want it to. I mean, is Flor's suggestion that we hang out without Cam even possible without hurting Cam? Girl, can you even imagine Cam's reaction if I say, *Sorry, girl. I have plans with Mikey and Flor and not you?* I mean, can you really have two sets of bffs who hate each other? And should I even have to choose between my friends? Just because I've been friends with Cam longer, does that mean he has rank or that I owe him something? How f-word is it that I feel like I have to choose? And on top of all that, I'm all, how do I even begin to wrap my brain around everything Cam's saying? I mean, why is she constantly hanging out with Flor and Mikey? Like, if she hates them so much, why is she always trying to make plans with them, especially when I'm not around?! Girl, I don't get it. And above all, Cam seriously believes I'm turning on him. I 110 abso hate hate hate that my best friend questions my loyalty. Ughhhh.

I feel like I'm having emotional chorro, and I'm in serious need of a Dude Wipe.

Cam's breathing a little heavier, and sweat collects on her face and neck as she fumbles through a pile of Pride stuffed animals.

I pick up this cute little Pride stuffed narwhal that Cam just knocked over, thinking I might get it for Mikey, and although I'm really loving that I stood up for myself to Cammy instead of just letting him talk shit to me, I kinda really hate seeing my friend going through it. Still, her whole idea about Flor being a villain? I just don't see it. #projecting. The way I see it, Flor genuinely likes me. Girl, I'm all about actions, and Flor's been kind and sweet and generous and inclusive of me from the day she read her letter. If Cam feels that I'm turning against her — and I don't think I am, I'm just being honest and direct for a change — then she needs to take a long look in that store mirror, because it's her own actions that are to blame, *not* Flor's. On the reals, girl. #actionsspeaklouder

To distract myself, I scope this very más cute black tank top with two pit bulls holding paws, wearing rainbow bandannas, classic pittie smiles, and aviator sunnies. Very Kimber. Totes my vibe. Mikey and me. Major want. #gimme

"Girl, say something." Cam throws a stuffed Pride teddy bear at my back.

I shake my head. I'm seeing that ignoring her really gets Cam bothered, and honestly, a little piece of me is living for this. If only I'd known this sooner.

"Girl, hello? Don't you hear me talking?"

I wait a little longer.

Cam is piqued. His face looks misshapen, as if someone's just telenovela-slapped the shit outta her. A part of me wants to get her back for every shady thing she's done to me this summer, and at the same time, another part of me hates that I'm making her feel bad. Girl, I totally know what it feels like to have somebody you care about shit on you — why would I ever wanna make anyone I care about feel that way? Maybe so she can finally learn a lesson? Maybe so she can get a taste of her own medicine? Ummm. Is this the person I really wanna be?

Girl, I am not Cam, and I refuse to engage in villainy. Not today, not ever.

"Girl, what do you want me to say? That it's Pride, and you're my best friend? That I don't wanna argue with you, and I wish we could all just go with the flow and not have all this conflict and go stuff our faces at Mikey's brunch and then go live our best lives at Pride? Is that too much to ask for? I like Flor and Mikey, Cammy. And I think you would too, if you just gave them a chance."

Cam sighs and tosses a handful of Pride beads in the basket.

And since we're being honest, I decide to be fully honest.

"You know, I kissed him."

Slowly, Cam starts chuckling. "Yeah, I figured. But whyyyyy? I told you—"

I cut Cam off. "Because I like him. Because he's nice to me."

Cam swallows a deep-ass breath, and I think there must be nothing left in her lungs when she's done exhaling. "Well, I think you're making a mistake. On the reals, good luck getting your heart smashed, mija. And in the end, when you come back crying to me, don't you dare say I didn't warn you."

"Right. Wow. I guess I just hoped my best friend would actually be happy for me, *mija*." I nod with my big fake-ass smile.

And while I'm biting my tongue, figuring out what to do or say next, Cam keeps on, "Girl, seriously. Who are you? This is not the friend I know."

"Girl, I'm the same person."

"Are you, though? Seriously? When you tell yourself that, do you really believe it?"

"And when you tell yourself you're not jealous af of Mikey and Flor, do you believe it?"

For a whole second, Cammy goes quiet. It's like the earth stops, and she can't pull together a comeback. Finally, she says, "Girl. The old Mac would never try to make himself feel better by talking shit to me. And that's the real T. So, you know what? I'm gonna take my ass to the other side of the store, and I'm gonna look for a Rockstar 240 mg sugar-free Fruit Punch energy drink for me, and I'm gonna see if they have a Rockstar 300 mg sugar-free Kiwi Strawberry for *my friend* Mac because that's his favorite, and they're really hard to find, but I'm gonna try to find one, because I'm a real friend. I just hope that when I come back, *my best* friend—the one I know and love, the one I've been through some hard, serious shit with, the one I'm going to the Ariana Grande concert with—I hope he's the one here waiting for me. Not this other person. Not this Fake Bitches Club whatever it is they're serving you, girl. This mini-Flor and Mikey minion. Ughhhhh. Asco. Girl, please."

As Cam walks off, pushing the cart ahead of him, I admit I'm gagged.

And in the middle of Target, I feel like I'm gonna lose my knees and cry my ass off right here, which is exactly what I don't wanna do.

"Things are really getting heated over here. You doing okay, mijo?"

From behind the kaftans, I see her.

"You know, my best homegirl and I fight like sisters too."

It's the West Side glamazon. And she's flawless af, like a

lowrider car show goddess standing before me. She's giving tower-high-ass bangs and brows sharp enough to slice wind. A shiny-ass, thick af gold nameplate that reads MASOTA hangs from her neck.

"I don't mean to get all up in y'all's business."

"It's okay. We're just having a . . . disagreement."

"Well, mijo, that's just how it works sometimes when you care about people." The West Side glamazon fixes a couple of barely-hanging-on kaftans on their hangers, then places them neatly back on the rack. "Like my bestie and me. I know she loves me, but girl. Sometimes, we just need some space or else I'm gonna grab that beautiful chestnut hair of hers and strangle her with it."

"I mean, I just want my friends to all get along, but I think they all hate each other? And so, what if I can't get them to get along? I feel like it's either we all act fake and pretend we like each other or it's gonna be drama 24-7."

Homegirl smiles. "Welcome to life, mijo. No easy answers here." She places an armful of Pride water bottles in her basket. "You'll figure it out. And until then, don't be so severe with each other. Mijo, there's enough people out to get us. We don't need to be coming for each other. Me entiendes?"

I nod. I wish Cammy was here to hear this.

"Okay, mijo. I gotta get going. It's a big day, and my best homegirls are waiting for me. Enjoy Pride, mijo. Wave if you see us."

As she walks away, I feel like I've just met a movie star.

And when Cammy returns, she's holding two cans.

He hands me a bright green and pink can, my Rock Star. "You know I love you, bitch," Cammy says.

"I love you, too, pa," I say, and I mean it.

At the register, Cam throws his arm around me as the cashier rings up our stuff.

"Friends to the end, bitch. Mwah!" Cam squeezes me and kisses me hard on the side of my head, by my ear.

The cashier smiles. She's youngish and pierced and wears a loose red vest with high-waisted pants, which gives off kind of a relaxed coastal grandmother vibe. "Happy Pride," she says.

"Happy Pride," I say back. "It's my first Pride."

"How exciting! Say hi to all the hot girlies for me." The cashier winks.

Grabbing our bags and strutting for the door, Cam twirls, then shouts, "C'mon, Mac's first Pride! Let's get sickening!! Okurrrrrrrrrr."

Girl, I love the fact that I think the whole world can hear.

Chapter 13

So MIKEY'S MOM HAS GONE FULL 110 ON preparing a feast. Girl, the table is like the kinda extravagant spread you see on ads for cruise ships and casinos. Cleo (short for Cleopatra) has served up a vibrant selection of ROYGBIV fruits with rainbow flags and a sparkly rainbow tablecloth and rainbow napkins and rainbow plates and rainbow utensils and rainbow centerpieces, and girl, it's diva everything. Like Pride is here, and she is here to stay, hunny!

When Cam and I see the spread, we both stop in our tracks, and Cam grabs my hand and whispers, "We belong at that table, sis."

"You sure do," Cleo replies, opening her arms and hugging us both. She smells like tangerines, and I am holding her too long, I think, but she doesn't mind.

Girl, Mikey's mom is beyond glamorous. It's barely noon, and she's in a fully painted face. On her left hand, she wears this giant-ass diamond that looks like it fell from outer space.

"You look 110 abso stunning, Ms. Villanueva." Looking closely at the dress, Cam asks, "Is this peach? Fuchsia? Watermelon?" I think she's talking about the colors assembled on Mikey's mom's dress, which form an elaborate, almost geodesic design.

"And coral. A friend at work made it. Well, refashioned it. This used to be a much longer dress she found at an estate sale, but with a little vision and a whole lot of skill, she whipped this up for me."

"She sure did. Yes, mamaw!!" Cam snaps three times above her head, and seeing Cam so vibrantly happy, it's hard to believe we were about to throw hands at Target. Girl, I'm so effing in love with this gay-ass energy! This is the Cam I love.

Shortly after we arrive, Flor's at the door. When she sees us, she screams in excitement and does her little runway walk and wastes no time in telling Mikey's mom all about the vintage shorts she found online. Cleo piles our plates high with watermelon, pineapple, papaya, coconut, mango, and plums, along with fried eggs, rice, and turkey bacon, because "Mikey loves my Filipino breakfasts, but he only eats turkey bacon," she tells us.

Just then, Mikey makes his way out of his room, and I am floored. Mikey looks soooooo damn good! From head to toe, he's dressed in orange—orange tank top, orange visor, orange baby-baby shorts, orange socks, his gold chain and gold-rimmed aviators, and lastly, and perhaps most significantly to me, these gorge white Adidas high-tops with these bright-ass orange laces that I abso effing live for. Like shoe game 110, girl. Master class in style. Uffff! Hot, talented, and a good kisser. No wonder I'm feeling him like a lot a lot.

When Mikey sees me, he shuffles over my way and throws his big arms around me. I see Cammy watching us, but he quickly shifts his eyes when he sees me clock him.

"Happy Pride, babe," Mikey says as I balance my plate and chew on my rice and egg.

And I'm obvi thrilled af! Taking the seat right next to me, Mikey bites the slice of mango I'm holding in my hand and sneaks a kiss. It's kind of a lot like magic, and I want more!

From the kitchen, Cleo calls out, "Leave Macky's food alone. Come make your own plate, hijo!" to which I say, "Yeah, make your own plate!" and smile big, play-biting at Mikey's hand when he reaches in and tries to snatch another piece.

Our group theme for the day event is Pride, right? So, we decided, or well, Mikey and Cam decided, that we'd each wear a color of the rainbow for the festival and then change into our pink shorts and illuminated accessories for the night parade. Cam chose red, of course, because she told us that she's the "fiery one" #accurate. Mikey chose orange, obvi. Flor selected yellow, though she pointed out that she easily could've worked all the hues, because she looks fierce in any color. Luckily for me, I got blue, which I have a lot of, so I didn't have to buy anything new. Blue is my fave color. Basic, I know. But #izzzzzmeeeeee. And to finish off the rainbow, Cam decided that Hermelinda could wear purple and that Kanari could have green, stressing to Flor that "you better make sure Hermelinda and the other girl show up for the picture. You can't have Pride with missing fucking colors."

So, my lewk for Pride consists of royal-blue Champion basketball shorts and a Carolina blue shredder that used to belong to B, along with my favorite Justin Boots ball cap. I think I look kinda fierce for Pride, though after Mikey sits down to eat, he asks, "How attached are you to those shoes?"

I don't take it personally. My shoes are old and ratty-looking and covered in clouds, but they're comfy af and they're mine. I tell Mikey I'm open, so he takes me to his room to "elevate my lewk."

When we get there, Mikey shuts the door quickly behind us, and I kiss him, his lips easy and soft. "Damn, papi. You look really good," he tells me, tossing my cap on the bed. I kiss him again and again, and I press myself against his leg, and he whispers, "What's that?" and grins as he shoves his hand in my shorts and grabs me.

My heart spins.

I take off his gold-rimmed sunglasses and place them on his bed, and I kiss Mikey again. Then, pushing him back onto his bed, careful not to crush his glasses, I caress his face in my hands. The sound he makes when I press all my weight on top of him fills me, and with his fingers, Mikey traces my big Mexican nose and my lips and chin. Against his thumb, the stubble creates a bristly sound, which I wanna feel and hear over and over.

"Again, pa. Kiss me again."

I bury my face in the brownness of Mikey's neck. I want the blue sky to see us and the whole moon and all the clouds to watch too. I lift my shirt and his so that I can feel his skin. Underneath my hands, his chest is firm, like a place where I can hold myself still and not have to keep moving. I like this feeling. It's a solidness that Mikey carries in his arms and in his back and down to his ass, which I grab, both my arms wrapped around his waist, both my arms telling him I want him here with me. I can feel the breath going in and out of his body against the dark hairs on my belly, and I think this can last forever, or I hope.

But then, there's someone tapping on the door.

"Cam's looking for you," Cleo says through the white-painted wood.

"Just a minute," Mikey says. "Mac's changing."

I kinda laugh at this because I have all my clothes on, still, and yet he's right. I feel like I am changing. All of me, parts and places, spots inside me I didn't even feel before or know. And all because I've met new friends, including this boy from LA who moved to my city and finds a place with me, in my arms, in his bedroom, in the middle of summer.

"We should go," I tell him.

And Mikey agrees. Staring at my old workout shoes, he says, "You're a ten and a half, right? Here, try these on." He goes to his closet and passes me a pair of pristine Adidas, still in the box, like his almost, only gray. "And what about these socks?"

I put on the socks he tosses me, which are bright white with blue stripes and extend up to my knees until Mikey leans down to bunch them up around my shins and looks up at me. Damn, Mikey looks so effing good on his knees. I feel myself growing again, so I cover myself with my cap and think about the names of all the states.

Seeing that I'm covering myself, Mikey smirks. "You look good," he tells me, flinging my old sweat-stained hat on his bed.

We wait a minute so I can go down. At the table, Cammy's going through what I assume is Cleo's makeup kit, her plate stacked high af with mango, which she loves, and asks, "Y'all got any Tajín?"

"Of course. What kinda house do you think this is?" From her cabinet, Cleo retrieves a bottle of the tangy spice.

When Cammy sees me, she smiles. "Ooh, look at her glow up! Mikey's a DJ *and* a stylist!" Cammy gives me a little wink, and it feels good to see him making an effort. "Girl, you don't think those shorts are a little too long for Pride, though?" Cam asks, looking at me.

"No, if Mac likes them, I think they're perfect for Pride," Cleo says, defending me. "Just like I think your crop top is perfect, as long as you feel good in it."

Speaking of, Cammy has changed into her first Pride outfit and is dripping red. She has on cherry-red baby shorts and a bomb red headband, a red slasher crop top featuring the phrase PAPI AF. Girl, she's giving. Red-rimmed sunnies hang from her collar, and red glitter covers her arms and legs, which look smooth and perfect and shiny. Her lips are glossy af, and she wears a gold earring that flares.

Flor is a vision in yellow: a yellow top that's loose enough to billow and gives movement with Flor's slightest gesture. Matching shorts. A collection of long necklaces drizzle down her chest—yellow and white beads, a black cord that dips down her chest and ends in a fancy-looking tiger's eye of a stone. An array of crystal bracelets adorn her wrists. And of course, she's carrying an enormous yellow handbag. "Citrine and chartreuse," Flor tells me, pointing to her bracelets and top, twirling.

How very Flor, I think.

Mikey says, "We should get going."

Flor nods while touching up her face.

Cam chews and does her little twerk, which takes talent, twerking while balancing a full plate of food and eating.

"Okay. Okay. I want a picture first," Cleo insists. "Mikey, help me find my phone."

As Cleo and Mikey search for her phone, Flor tells us that Hermelinda and Kanari are gonna have to meet us at the Starbucks by her house, which isn't that far from Mikey's, but still.

"What did I tell you? I'm not stopping at Starbucks. Tell her to just meet us at Pride. And be there ASAP," Cam orders. "She better not fuck up our pic."

"It's on the charger, Mom," Mikey groans, pointing to the device.

We gather in front of the Pride Brunch table (or what's left of it) to get a group pic. We pile in near the big hand-painted glittery HAPPY PRIDE!!! sign and bouquets of rainbow Mylar balloons—the four of us together and happy, giving it fierce, and yes, girl, proud af.

In the middle of the group, Mikey's standing with Flor perched on his left and me on his right. I have my arm around Mikey, my hand grabbing his ass, which is round and firm like I'm palming a football.

"Cam, honey, you're the tallest," Cleo says. "You want to stand in back?"

"Yeah . . . that's not gonna happen," Cam replies. With that, Cammy shifts to the front of the group and drops into the full splits.

Girl. Yes. I know.

After gagging over Cam's split, Cleo takes the pics, all of us holding our smiles and our poses as Cleo insists, "One more. One more," and then proceeds to take a dozen more pics.

It's no surprise we get four or five fierce shots from Cleo's batch.

In the Uber, Cam takes the front seat, because she's the tallest. Sitting in the middle, Mikey holds the backpack with our night parade lewks between his legs, syncing the "Senior Summer First Pride Mix" he's arranged for us. Girl, I'm gagged, because Mikey's mix starts slowly with what sounds like old-school Superman music with heavy symphony vibes, and then, seemingly from out of nowhere, the voice of God announces, "You are listening to DJ Mike Villanueva," and then *bam!* Girl, he's giving us the intro beats to a slowed-down "7 rings." The whole car (even the driver) gags at how fire Mikey's mix is. Like, girl. I knew he was into his music, but holy caca! Yes, fire! Girl!

Even Cam looks a little bit a lot in awe. "You made this?" she asks.

"Why you gagging?" Mikey asks back. "You wanted a summer mix. Here's your summer mix."

Cam gives me a look, like *Bitch, I see you.* Like it's finally starting to click why I'm so into Mikey. More and more, I'm so happy Cammy and I had our talk at Target.

Bopping, holding up her yellow handbag while keeping her sunnies balanced, Flor remarks, "Girl, this is severely good. For the reals!"

"It's because he's a girl with tattoos who likes getting in trouble," I add, which gets the car yasssssing!

The Uber driver laughs.

And Flor's right. Girl, Mikey's mix is everything. I had no clue he was soooo good. I mean, Rule #2 — I know music is his passion, but maybe I just don't know how deep passion can take you, because I still haven't found mine. From the look of pure joy on Mikey's face as we all gag over his mix, deejaying is the vibe made for him, and he feels it 110 más deep.

Feeling it too, I reach over to Mikey and tell him, "Damn, babe. You're really, really good."

Unthinkingly, Mikey kisses me right there in the back seat, and with his mix going, we're singing along to "Don't Call Me Angel" and posting the group Pride Brunch pic to all our socials. And while I'm usually good at thinking up hashtags and captions, even if I don't post all that much on my IG, girl, I'm kinda stuck. Seriously, I only have seven pics on my IG— they're all of Kimber, tacos, and baseball #cringe. Instead of stressing about what to type for the caption, I make it simple and type in: *Happy Pride! #happiness #friendshipvibes #equalmeansus #belonging #firsttimeatpriderealness*

It's a moment.

Chapter
14

EVERYWHERE YOU LOOK, VAQUERO QUEENS and Cardi B lesbians, fifty million rainbow flags, and drag queens galore, girl. Old burly guys with hairy chests, giant arms, furry backs, and silver beards. Skinny boys and big boys and buff-ass lesbianas with stacked backs and biceps the size of grapefruits. Everywhere I turn, I see people like us and guys I hope I look like when I'm old and girls who look just like B. There are even little kids running around waving inclusive Pride flags . . . and strollers. Girl, strollers! Like, who knew there'd be babies at Pride?!

For the reals. Surrounded by fierceness. Immersed. Basking in it. Hydrated and living!

Immediately, Cam leads us to the main stage, where a queen giving major loose blue cascades of hair and a space-age metallic-pink costume works a full-on "Technocumbia" number. She kicks off her heels and leaps into the air and off the stage, landing in the dry-ass South Texas grass . . . in a perfect split. Patas, dirt, and a cumbia! The crowd goes wild. Girl, she even makes a dust cloud. #sanantosgottalent

"Wow." Flor's gagged, mouth open like a window.

Mikey's speechless too. Then says, "Give her all the dollars."

But Cam just yawns. "I'm bored. Let's move on."

We follow, and girl, the booths are selling everything from T-shirts and doggie Pride collars and hankies, even healing crystals, essential oils, candles, and Pride art. Girl, Pride shopping is definitely a vibe. Just kinda expensive. Nonetheless, Flor and Cam go wild when we see a booth serving silver dangle earrings, because "Dangles are the icon, the energy, and the fucking moment!" Cam shrieks as she jets toward the booth.

"These are the ones I was telling you about!" Flor screeches.

Before I know it, Cam's trying on like ten dangles, swearing they all look good on her. Some of the dangles are so excessively long, they could be mistaken for metallic hair, which gasses Cam up, as she swings around repeatedly like she's wearing good extensions.

"This is realness, mija." Cam pouts, passing me her phone, urging me to video her and her extra-glossy af lips. "All. Of. This!"

Flor gets a "Summer Party Girl Starter Pack," even though she's not even that into partying, but at Mikey's prompting and with the owner's encouragement, she goes for it.

"For the record," Cam tells me as we walk off, "I was into dangles first."

Girl.

Flor pauses in front of a booth signing people up to vote, surveying what's ahead but also taking a moment to look in a mirror and admire the three silver feathers dangling from her ear. Flor's glowing, because she's living the dangle fantasy but also because she's sweaty af. "Ugh. I think I should text Hermelinda. We need to get that pic before this sweat destroys us." Flor sips some water and swings her fancy-ass yellow "Saffiano bag," as she calls it, which Cammy and a handful of queens have all gagged over today.

"Bitch, look! Fans!" Cam blurts out, pointing toward a booth selling vibrantly hued fans with irresistible phrases like THIRST KWEEN, ONLY GOOD BUSS HERE, and SAS! CULERA!

"They're called clack fans," Mikey begins to fan-splain, but I'm not sure Flor or Cam hear him, because they race away to the booth, Mikey and me chasing after them. Flor snatches a fiery hot-pink fan with ornate lettering that reads BIEN PRETTY while Cam goes for the candy-apple-red fan with Old English lettering that proclaims PERRA. Of course. #accurateaf

"They're used at parties to cool off, but they're also used to clack on beat. You'll see better once we get to the dance tent," Mikey promises.

"OMG! I thought we'd never find y'all. Okay. That line was intense!"

It's Kanari. She's stomping her feet excitedly and dressed in lime-green booty shorts and a tie-dyed, sparkly-string green top and matching boots, her long hair pulled back with a silvery-green clip.

"I brought sunscreen," Hermelinda announces as she steps out from behind Kanari. She's in tight purple shorts, a lavender tie-back top, and a giant-ass indigo cowboy hat, whose brim she has to lift up so that Flor can hug her. "SPF 70. It's Coppertone."

Jumping up and down, Flor squeals. "Babes, you made it! And you brought SPF. She thinks of everything."

"The DJ tent's over there." Mikey points. "I think I can hear it."

At first I can't hear anything. I mean, I hear an old George Strait song coming from behind us where the country and Tejano tent is, but I'm pretty sure none of my friends are gonna want to head that way, so I don't bring it up. Yet listening more closely, Mikey's right. I can hear the bump coming from behind the beer tickets booth and the PrEP table.

"They're playing Dua Lipa!" Kanari howls delightedly.

Without hesitating, Mikey pulls off his shirt, lifts his gold chain, shields his eyes, and extends his arms toward me. "Spray me, babe."

"Your glasses," I remind him, and he hands over his aviators.

Hermelinda passes me the sunscreen, and I start spraying him, admiring how effing hot Mikey looks. And more than this, like right here, under the sun, Mikey's doing his smooth-ass little dance moves, and I understand fully and clearly that Mikey Villanueva is exactly who he told me he is, exactly the boy who loves music and loves life and likes me, and in my eyes, somebody who knows who they are—no hiding, no pretending, no shame—that's sexy af. So, girl, this really is #perfectday #perfecteverything! My closest friends. The music!! The boy I like. The sunshine that can't be stopped. Babe, if this is what Pride feels like, I want it every day. #gimmemore #everydayrealness #theworldiswhatwemakeofit

"Wait. What about our pic?!" Flor chirps.

"Yes, girl. But hurry. Let's make it fast. Let me spray Mac first." Mikey grabs the sunscreen. "Babe, your shirt?"

I hesitate. Until this moment, I hadn't thought about taking off my shirt. But perhaps it's because Pride and because I'm surrounded by this small and marvelous group of my friends, people who somehow, because of our connection, because of their fearlessness, because of our mutual love of Ariana Grande and Valentina and my want—yes, my deep, hard want—to belong, have made me feel like a person . . . I peel my shirt off.

And maybe the feeling in my body is belonging.

And maybe this is the part of belonging that I didn't even know about myself.

And I feel like I've taken this big, open breath now, shirt in hand, sun on my skin, and maybe this is it? Maybe this is the fierceness I'm feeling, that spark that fires up Rule #1. Maybe my fierceness is a feeling, like accepting who I am both when I'm alone and also when I'm shirtless and sweaty af in front of my friends along with total strangers at a Pride festival and moving with it. Just going for what feels right and makes me smile, makes me feel like I'm part of something that clicks.

What I know is I'm a short, thick-ass Mexican boy with

body hair and ganas for days, and here I am, right in front of the turkey legs and mini-tacos booth at Pride, and I'm feeling myself like maybe Ariana feels herself onstage or maybe how Valentina feels herself in front of a camera for *Vogue* or maybe like Mikey feels himself with his laptop and his remixes and a big-ass speaker thumping loudly or how maybe like Flor feels herself painting that gorgeous face that was made to be painted for the gods or like Cam feels whenever she reads somebody for the dirty and feels royal and fierce af. Whatever it is, girl. Feeling myself is one of the most exquisite feelings I've ever experienced.

As the cold cloud of sunscreen hits my skin, Mikey says, "Babe, you look amazing."

"Babe, I feel amazing." The truth of it, like a feather in my hand. And I scoop my arm behind Mikey's waist, and I kiss him full and hard on the mouth.

And a queen behind us yells, "Werk, baby boy!!!"

And "Come on, love is love!!" somebody else cheers.

And Flor with her dangle leans in and snaps a pic, squeezing us and saying, "OMG! I love y'all! I love y'all sooo much!"

Babe, it's like all the moments of my life coming together all at once, and holding Mikey in the middle of Pride, I can hear nothing but my heart and maybe some of his heart beating too, alongside mine, and he tastes like spearmint and a little bit like the chemical-ness of sunscreen, but I don't care.

"I really like you, DJ Mike Villanueva. A lot a lot," I sigh, and today, the world feels different somehow, like an echo I can actually hold in my hand after hearing it for a really long time.

Mikey smiles, and it's the kinda smile I wanna see every day of our lives. On him. On all the people I love. On everybody.

Mikey folds our shirts, and he tucks them in our waistbands.

We can hear the bass coming at us from behind, and I'm dancing in the full sun.

Clacking her fan, Cammy bucks on beat with Kanari and Flor and Hermelinda, and seeing everyone together and happy af, I think that maybe it is possible that we can move past all the conflict and shade, that we might just pull off a friendship where I don't have to choose.

"Yesssss, bitch!" Flor cheers. "Now, pixies!"

"Come on, photo shoot!" Cammy yells.

Hermelinda takes her phone from her fancy-ass shoulder bag and instructs us all to "Say cheese!"

Squeezing together, we pose and push the word out between our teeth. Except Hermelinda's not in the picture, and so, the pic is not complete.

Thank God, this very painted queen with a mullet-perm stops, passes her cocktail to her half-falling-over sis, and says, "Get in there, girl. Yo la tomo."

Quickly, Hermelinda hands off her phone, and pushing the brim of her giant hat back, she gracefully leaps next to Flor, and they fall together, fitting naturally, having posed hundreds if not thousands of times beside one another over the years. I look over at Cam, who, in all her vibrant red, makes sure she has the center spot filled up. Arms raised over all of us, she pivots and extends one of her long-ass legs between Flor and

Hermelinda, and I just know that shit is gonna look stunning in the photo. I have my arm around Mikey's front, and I'm leaning on him, my face on Mikey's strong back, right near the dark feathers of his tattoo.

"Happy Pride, babe," he whispers, reaching back and putting his hand on my dick.

For reals, my whole body quakes, and my face gives more than happiness.

"Now smile, bishes!!!" the queen growls, snapping a shitload of pics.

Usually, I don't care about "pixies," but today, I can't wait to see what we've made.

I squeeze in next to Cammy and Flor to see how our pic came out, and then we hear it.

Girl.

Ariana.

Then it's like God just spoke each of our names.

A chorus. A collective squeal. A marvelous roar.

Girl, a stampede.

Flor snatches Hermelinda by her thin little wrist, heading straight in the direction of the queens and best straight girlfriends charging toward the dance tent. And with as much fervor, if not more, Mikey grips my arm, hurling me toward the tent, and I grab Cammy's hand, and he then clutches Kanari, because it's true—girl, from across the festival, over the tops of paleta and handmade Pride dream-catcher booths, through hundreds of prideful queens and butches and strollers with babies eating mangonadas and little dogs in overpriced Pride hankies too, you can hear it: the opening beats of "Into You."

Bitch, I can barely breathe.

Mikey aims straight for a stack of mega-speakers pushing out that bass line we've heard thousands of times, but today is different. Listening to Ariana at Pride is different. I can't explain. It just is. #facts #intuition #youeitherknoworyoudont

As soon as we get to the dance floor, Mikey makes his way to the very front of the stage, and his smile glows brighter than all the suns in the universe. "It's DJ Rue-D!" he yells. Meanwhile, Flor's slaying it fierce for all the femme boys of the world with her fan, while simultaneously holding on to both Hermelinda's hand and that big giant yellow-ass purse. Excitedly, Mikey leans against me and puts my arms around his waist. Kanari reaches over and draws an air heart around Mikey and me. I blow a kiss Kanari's way, and looking around, I realize that I've lost Cammy somewhere in the crowd.

"OMG! It's Pink!" Mikey yells, and I don't even know how he can tell, because we haven't even heard the lyrics. Mikey's living for it. Like 110,000 percent living. Nothing can stop Mikey's joy as he taps the beat on my chest with his palm open and kisses my neck. It's everything, but I'm also sweating my balls off and getting jostled and bumped because the tent is filling up fast, and I want air.

"OMG, babes! It's soooo effing hot," Flor pants. Fanning herself, she points to one of those ginormous industrial fans on the perimeter of the tent. Flor, Hermelinda, and I start moving toward the cooler air, but Mikey motions for us to move farther into the center of the dance floor. And I have to choose. Cool air or Mikey. Girl, I choose cool air. #noquestion #sorrybabe #selflovewins

Kanari goes with Mikey while Flor, Hermelinda, and I camp ourselves right in front of the fan and all its big air energy, or "BAE," as Flor names her. With my T-shirt, I'm soaking up as much sweat from my face and body as I can while Flor performs major facial paint reapplication. And girl. You know, standing here, I'm a little bit a lot surprised at myself for not following Mikey.

"Is it crazy? I mean, not following Mikey?" I ask Flor as she glosses.

"Girl, what are you talking about?"

"Like not going to dance with them? Just doing my own thing?"

"So y'all are together-together?"

I don't know how to answer. Something's happening between Mikey and me, but we haven't named it yet.

"No. Kind of. I mean, we haven't talked about it."

"Girl, clarify. And it'd only be crazy if you felt you *had* to follow him."

I'm struck by the idea that somehow feeling compelled to follow a boy someplace you don't really wanna go is categorically wrong, and I think also maybe this is what I like so much about Mikey. Girl, with Mikey, things feel smooth and unforced, like I'm not all hyper-worried about doing or saying the wrong thing, which is sooooo way effing different from hanging out with Benny and Duncan or even my dad and even sometimes B, and OMG, Cam, for sure, because with them,

I've kinda always felt like I needed to put a leash on my words so as not to say something they'd disapprove of, not do something they'd mock me for. So, yeah. Maybe this is what comes next, right? On the reals, maybe this kinda comfort and assurance is how connections and relationships are really supposed to work?

Looking out at the dance floor, I spot Cammy, who is giving full-on 110 diva everything. Girl. Living. Cam and her fan. Werking her best Naomi Smalls, launching face, and def giving the sidelines of the dance tent every inch of perra she has. It's Cam's moment, girl. And she is having it.

Suddenly, Flor marches over to Cam and begins serving it up right next to her, and I immediately think, *Shit, what's gonna go down with these two?*

But then Cam looks over my way, nods with a big-ass smile that I can't really tell if it's fake or authentic, but the way she and Flor are kiki'ing and fanning for each other, I sure the f hope it's real.

Hermelinda leans over to me and says, "Wow. Are they actually friends now?"

"I hope," I reply.

"Watch out, world, if those two ever get their shit together and team up."

"Seriously," I add, imagining a senior year where Flor and Cam run shit.

Okay, maybe that's a stretch, and before I can enlist Hermelinda in helping me manifest this vision of the future, B's behind me and Clari, too.

"Bruh!" Squeezing me from behind, B presses an ice-cold water bottle against my chest. "Damn, you're sweaty! Here, take my water," she says, letting me go and shaking out her hands. Sweat droplets fly everywhere, and as I hold B's cool bottle against me, the idea that she'll be leaving at the end of summer appears in front of me like a small fire.

It hits me full-on that this is probably one of the last times I'll get to hang out with B before she moves away, and as I grasp this thought, I reach over and tap her arm, and I say, "Ey, I love you," and I squeeze her hand and I look her in the eyes and lean my face into her shoulder while holding on tightly to her like I used to do when I was three and six and eight, and I honestly don't remember when I stopped doing it, or why, but I wish, now, that I never stopped leaning on B and holding on to her arm.

B throws her arm around me and squeezes me as hard as she can, and I'd forgotten how effing strong she is, and for these seconds, I feel that nothing at all has changed between us. Flexing, B gets Clari to take, like, ten thousand pics of us, and we chitchat and crack jokes, and everybody asks about Mikey.

The Bruhs aren't so into the dance tent vibe and decide to head over to the country tent. As Clari and B walk off with their arms stretched behind each other's backs, hands tucked in their waistbands, I think, *I want it like that. Their cariño.*

Just then, Mikey comes up from behind me and places his chest against my spine. He's solidly wet and sooo happy. He devours my water, and I rub him off with my damp-ass shirt, and I realize maybe wiping sweat off each other is Mikey's and my version of the cariño B and Clari share.

I spot Cammy and Flor taking pics with hot boys I've never seen and wave them over. Cam has a big-ass grin on his face, and I can't wait to ask him what happened with the boys he was talking to.

"Let's go back in. Please, please, please," Mikey begs.

The crowd has started to disperse, and Cam and Flor find a place for us up front by the stage — for once, I think we've pulled this off, all of us clicking, no drama, no shady comments, just the four of us living our lives together and joyful af. So, when Gaga's "Always Remember Us This Way" comes on, girl, I am ready for it. Looking around at my best friends — Mikey and Flor and Cam, who's moving her mouth a million miles an hour to new people she's met, all while taking a grip of pics, punching ten thousand keystrokes on her phone, and giving it perra fierce with her fan, and then Hermelinda and Kanari, too — it's love. That's what I feel. Girl, I love my life. And I don't think I've ever really believed this as much as I do right now. It's Rule #3. Forever and friendship and love. Personified, girl. Made into a photograph.

Chapter 15

"*I*NCREDIBLE. BUT ALSO EXHAUSTING, GIRL." That's my response when Rebecca asks me how Pride went. #thedayafter

It's just before noon. Rebecca's standing by the fountain drink machine, pretending to wipe it down. "Wait till you're my age. Have some kids, some ungrateful cats. Then talk to me about exhausting."

A yawn consumes my face. I shove a stack of napkins haphazardly into a napkin holder.

"And how about your boy?"

"Mikey? He's good." Just saying his name, I feel like light's shooting out of my mouth and eyes.

Rebecca laughs. "I bet he's good." She hurls the cleaning rag, but I catch it before it smacks me in the face.

"Well, get you some, mijo. Get some for both of us!!"
Rebecca cackles.

Girl, I laugh too. I wipe the counter surfaces, and Rebecca
pours herself a big-ass Dr Pepper and takes a swig.

"You know, I think my little Brandon—I mean, he's only
seven, but I think he's gonna be one of the LGBTs. So one
day, you just might see my fine ass out there at Pride, werking
and getting werked! Supporting mijo, you know. 'Cause I'm a
down-ass mom."

Looking up from my brisket cuts, I see Rebecca staring out
the front door, squinting like she can't figure out a math problem. And girl. I almost drop my tongs, because I can't believe
my eyes. "Holy caca! Is that Cammy? Is she . . . running?"

With a line of lunchtime cars forming behind her, Cammy
jets across the parking lot as if her life depends on it. And who's
behind her? Flor. And girl, that little bitch is running too. And
Flor NEVER runs.

Rebecca is all, "Do we need to call 911?"

I shrug.

When Cam finally reaches the entrance, she pulls so hard
I think the whole glass door might come off its hinges. Cam's
soooo out of breath, she almost topples over onto the dining
room floor right in front of my feet. Propping herself up using
the poles for the cords that keep customers in line, Cam huffs,
"She's coming. Girl . . . she's coming. She's . . . coming!!!"

"Girl, who? Who's coming?" I urge Cam to complete the
thought.

"*She's* . . . coming." Cam's gasping for air.

"I'm gonna get him some water," Rebecca says.

But before she can move, Flor bursts through the door, half hurdling—yes, bitch, I said hurdling—over Cammy's back. "She's coming, girl! Valentina is coming to San Antonio!"

Bitch, I die.

My heart drops right there and lifts itself up again. #buryme #resurrectedmyselfhunny

If anybody in that restaurant didn't already know that I'm gay, they do now.

I scream. Like scream scream. Customers are staring, but I don't care. Flor throws herself into my arms and starts crying. Yes, girl. Crying. And I don't know why, but then I'm crying too. Yes, bitch. I am full-on crying. In my barbecue uniform, in a hairnet, plastic serving gloves, and a black apron, still holding my tongs.

"Valentina's coming," Flor sobs. "We tried texting you, but we know you can't use your phone at work, so we drove over here to tell you. Girl, she's gonna perform at the Aztec Theatre. My mom's getting us tickets. We have to go." Flor pauses, staring at my forehead. "Girl, you have barbecue sauce on your face."

Before I can check my face, I look up and Cam's on her knees, hugging Flor from behind, and she's crying too. A deep weeping that goes straight into Flor's butt cheeks, the tiny, flat, barely there bit of cake that Flor serves. Girl, as the restaurant gawks, we're all crying, because Rule #2. Rule #2, girl. All of it.

"This is the happiest day of my life," Flor mumbles, with Cam pulling so hard on Flor's vintage vanilla-and-polka-dot shorts that I think her bottoms are gonna come right off.

By now, Julio emerges from wherever he's been and orders me to take my "freak show" to the back of the restaurant and to "clock out immediately, because you aren't gonna get paid for this."

But I don't give a caca. Valentina's coming, and that's all I need to know. And when Mikey finally walks in—after parking the car, I assume—he verifies everything. Two Thursdays from now, at eight p.m., Valentina will perform at the historic, the legendary, the renowned Aztec Theatre in downtown San Antonio! But girl, not just Valentina—Naysha, Anetra, Mistress, Angeria, Vanjie, and more!

"Girl, it's gonna be a mothatucking show!" Cam declares, her eyeballs as big as cherries.

Girl, this is everything.

Flor is so gagged, she almost faints. Like her little body goes limp. Her breath, or her soul—I can't tell the difference—leaves her body, and her DVFs almost fall off her head, but I catch them in one hand and, with the other, steady her body before it hits the floor. All I can do is pass Flor over to Mikey, who holds her up long enough to drag her little body over to a table and set her down in the back of the restaurant, steadying the DVFs on her face, because Flor's little legs have ceased to function from the overwhelming joy coursing through her body, though somehow she maintains a tight-ass, otherworldly grip on her fancy-ass new orange clutch and phone.

Once we've propped Flor up in a chair, that's when I grab Mikey, and I kiss him, right here, in the back of my restaurant. I'm holding him so tight, I swear I hear his back pop.

"Maaaaacccccccc!" I can hear Julio yelling my name, but I'm unbothered.

"We're gonna get to see her, babe!" Mikey says.

Rule #2, girl. We're gonna see the Kween. #livingforit #goddessstatus #miamor

Chapter 16

"**M**ESSY. LIKE, WHY DOES SHE HAVE TO BE SO sloppy?! Girl, I can't with her. It's like she's one of those girls who claims they f-word hate drama, but then she has f-word drama all the time. Girl, no." Criticism of Cam rockets from Flor's lips, as her legs pump vigorously on the elliptical machine.

In the middle of Gold's, hair tied back and wearing an Ariana Grande "sweetener" shredder that I cut for her, Flor is going off.

"Okay, so maybe I'm lost, but . . . I thought y'all were starting to click?" I say. "Like, wasn't there a total change of energy at Pride? And then you and Cammy got coffee with Mikey and went to Sephora the next day, right before y'all came to the restaurant and were super big-time way excited about Valentina." That last part comes out a little crunchy af, and I hope I don't sound as bitter or jealous as I feel.

Flor gives me a look, like *Sis, wtf are you talking about?* "I mean, yeah, we all had a great time at Pride—girl, it's Pride. How can you not have fun at Pride? But that was kind of a lot in spite of *Cammy's* presence. Like sis, come on. What am I gonna do? Be a bitch and ruin Pride for everybody? Girl, duh. *And* I only hung out with her because she was suddenly at my house, screaming about Valentina. Which, to be clear, I don't blame her for. Icon. Period. And also, I invited Mikey so that I wouldn't have to hang out with her all by myself. And if you think that Cammy's performance at Pride was genuine, girl . . . Babes, hate to tell you what you already know, but girl, she's fake."

I get quiet. I really thought things were getting better.

"Am I wrong?" Sipping from the multi-use water bottle in which she's placed half a carton of sliced strawberries, Flor stares at me.

Honestly, I'm gonna listen to Flor tell it like she sees it, yet I have some real, hard-ass doubts about moving my mouth to Flor about Cam when Cam's not even here. #backstabberrealness #Rule3. Girl, this feels a little bit a lot like the very definition of betrayal.

I watch Flor's strawberries swirling around.

"Feel what you feel, girl. I'm sure Cam has her reasons," I say. "And like I started to tell you at Pride, she and I had a good conversation about her energy."

"Reasons? Girl, her reasons for what?"

"For being so . . . bitchy." The moment I say the word, I regret it.

Flor sinks her teeth into it.

"OMG. Thank you. Girl, you're so right. She *is* bitchy. First, she's a major bitch to you and to Mikey, and all T, not to play the victim or anything, but she really is a giant bitch to me. OMG. Like a mega-bitch. Girl, at Whataburger. Seriously, like what was that? Talking all that madness about Ariana's ponytail! Not even to mention all the drama she made over our rules!" As the sentiments surge, Flor's voice amplifies, and she's stomping down so hard on the elliptical that the machine wobbles a little. "Girl! She's chaotic af. From day one, she's been giving tóxica! And then at Pride. Girl. OMG. I mean, I was way into dangles before she was. Babes, she didn't even know what a dangle was until she met me. But then she goes and tells Naomi that dangles were her thing and I just copied her and then she f-word hogs like most of, if not the entire, convo with those mildly hot guys we met and then she ignored us to play on her phone. Did you notice that? Bitch, I did and no. Girl, please. Like she barely even paid attention to us after she met those guys."

I consider Flor's point. From my perspective, Cam was genuine af during our difficult convo at Target, and she was super fun while we were getting ready, and she really seemed to be connecting with Flor at Pride. And yet, Flor sees her as fake? Am I missing something? Is it possible that Flor isn't giving Cam a fair chance?

"Don't even get me started on everything I taught her about handbags and sunnies," Flor continues. "Like, does she realize Mikey and I didn't even want her to hang out with us, and the only reason she got invited in the first place is because of you?"

Girl, it's a lot. I mean, when Flor invited me to the gym today, I figured we were just coming to play on our phones and pretend to work out, maybe do some half lunges and talk about how fierce it is that we get to see Valentina. This is definitely an unexpected turn of events. Like, how do I even respond? Maybe she's just venting. But also, maybe it's no different from Cam talking all her shit about Mikey and Flor behind their backs. Girl, are Cam and Flor two parts of the same person? Uffff. I wipe my face with my towel, and I increase the level on my machine.

"Don't just sit there all silent. Girl, tell me what you think. You've known her longer. She's a total bitch to you, too."

On the reals, I agree with virtually everything Flor's saying about Cam coming for her repeatedly, yet I know that agreeing out loud could be interpreted as picking a side, and that's not at all how I wanna handle this conflict.

"She's not a *total* bitch," I reply.

Flor rolls her eyes. She's pushing buttons, her machine is going faster, and I sigh, because I wanna say a hundred things — like explain that Cam wears a thick-ass skin because she's had to, and she believes others need to grow a thick skin too. From what I've seen, Cam grew claws to get by in life, and sometimes, maybe Cam uses those claws on the wrong people. Like on us. But you don't just throw somebody away. And I know that Cam's waaay envious that Flor has it so easy — even though I'm very aware that Flor doesn't have it all that easy — but having money definitely makes so many things easier. Cammy def feels threatened by people who have more than she does, so she tries to make them feel small before they can do the same to her. Yet I don't say any of this right now, because it's not really my place and because, although I trust Flor, I kinda think I'd just be throwing gas on the flames if I start feeding Flor negative info about Cam, whom she already doesn't like, when all I want is for us to get along. #counterproductiverealness

"I don't get why you're defending her." Wincing from exertion, Flor exhales.

So, what do I say? Do I say, *Girl, I defend you, too? That's what real friends do for each other*? Do I try to argue that I'm not defending Cam, just giving context, trying to help Flor understand a complicated and chaotic but lovable person? Yet before I can respond, Flor asks, "Can I show you something?"

"Sure?"

She scrolls through her phone and turns to me and sighs. "Girl. Read this," she says as she hands me her phone, which is opened to an album entitled RECEIPTS.

There are dozens of screenshots: text conversations, DMs, Snaps, a few tweets, a pic of a hot-pink Post-it with the words *KM IS A GROSS FKN HOE* written on it. Girl, for a second, I think, *Who's KM?* Girl, Flor even has highlighted comments from IG posts, complete with big giant red arrows pointing out words, like she has annotations and shit.

"Girl, what am I looking at?"

"Bitch, just read."

I click on an image of a group convo titled "The Real Hot T." It's between Flor and two people whose names have been scratched out. I think I can use the word "redacted" here. Girl, I've always wanted to use that word (in a non-militaristic or espionage setting).

Redacted Name A: all the time. she has lots of opinions about everybody. 🙄

Redacted Name B: Does she talk about Flor? What does she say about Flor?

Redacted Name A: Mostly that hes fake and full of himself, stuff like that he says Flor tries to buy friends bc he can't make friends on his own and that he wears too much makeup, like Flor says his skin is so flawless but he has to wear so much makeup bc his skins not flawless

Flor: OMG. How do I buy people's friendship?

Flor: Too much makeup? Omg.

Flor: Girl, please. I know how to paint. Quite well, in fact.

Flor: Sweetie, she needs to check a mirror, because she's not that flawless.

Redacted Name A: He says you bought him Burberry sunglasses, same pair for both of you and you get people to hang out with you by paying for everybody when you go out to eat and he feels sorry for you bc you told him that you never had friends

Redacted Name B: Shade.

Flor: Yes, I bought us matching glasses. Big deal. He asked for them, and it's not like he could afford them, so yes, I bought them. I was just being nice. #charitywork

Redacted Name A: I'm just telling what he told me, and don't say I said any of this

Redacted Name B: I told you that you're too nice, girl. People take advantage of niceness.

Redacted Name B: I also told you Cam was so FAKE!! And toxic!! From the very beginning I told you to watch out for her.

Flor: Girl, seriously sooo gagged. Is this really what I get for helping the less fortunate? 😵😵😵😒😒😒

I look up when I read the part about the "less fortunate." It sounds snobby af, and I hate shit like that. Glancing over at Flor, I wonder wtf she says about me when I'm not around. Girl, if I ever found out she referred to me as the "less fortunate" or as "#charitywork," I'd be wrecked.

From the convo, Person B sounds a lot like Hermelinda. Girl, she's totes gassing Flor up. I have no clue who Person A is, and although I'm tempted to ask, I don't. Like, do I really give a shit? What I really give a shit about is that I feel guilty af reading these screenshots. Is this what friendship is? Reading shitty things you say about each other, saving screenshots in case you need them for later? And on top of that, why should we even believe Person A? Does she even have credibility? Ughhh. I mean, on some level, isn't she being shady af too? No better than Cammy, because here, she, he, or they are listening to Cam talk shit about Flor and then sharing what Cam very likely believed to be a private conversation. It's a lot. Girl, this is why I stay outta shit like this.

I bring my elliptical to a stop.

"I'm sorry." Handing Flor back her phone, I shake the feeling that she would ever look at me as inferior, figuring she probably just said those things because Cammy was being a bitch to her. "I don't believe you buy friends."

"Girl, there's more where that came from. Look." She goes to hand her phone back to me, but I shake my head.

"I don't see the point of showing me receipts that she's shady. Girl, I know."

Flor sighs and slows her machine to cool down. "Well, it's not your fault, girl. I gave friendship with her a chance, but I think I'm done."

"Done?"

"Yeah, done."

I don't know exactly what this means. Like, is Flor gonna cut ties with Cam? Or maybe she'll just distance herself, put up a wall, not trust Cammy? Whatever Flor does, can I still be friends with both of them? Ughhhhh.

As we leave the gym, I think I should ask Flor not to say anything about me calling Cam "bitchy" or maybe promise her that I won't tell anybody about her folder of receipts. Yet each of these avenues feels ridiculous in its own way. I feel like I'm giving major weak sauce, and giving it to myself, which is waaaay worse than serving it to others. Seriously. If Cammy didn't want us talking about her shitty behavior, maybe she should've treated us better. Furthermore, if Cam wanted to keep us as friends, maybe she should've actually nurtured these friendships instead of sabotaging them over and over again. But what if that's just it, what if maybe Cammy can't change? What if this is just the way she's built? I mean, should I really wanna change my friends or should we just accept people the way they are?

Once we get into Flor's car, we FaceTime Mikey. Even with the bad lighting of FaceTiming someone in a car in a parking lot at night, the excitement all over Mikey's face is visible. F-word, he's even handsome in shitty lighting!

"Come over tomorrow," he says. "My mom's gonna make her wings. We can watch more of Season Nine."

We agree, and Mikey adds, "And we can make our plans to go see Valentina."

As we pull out of the parking lot, I feel joyful af because I get to see Mikey, yet I also feel stressed the f out, because well, girl, seriously, #allthisdrama. It's like, I just had this really super-intense convo with Flor about Cam being a bitch, and then Mikey invites us to his house.

As if reading my mind, Flor asks, "Do we invite her?"

Babe, on the serio, Flor's a smart girl. She's number two in our class. She's been the keeper of girls' secrets and a sounding board for girl drama for as long as she's known Hermelinda. Clearly, Flor knows exactly what she's doing. And right now, all T, Flor's trying to start a war.

Already, these plans to meet up at Mikey's tomorrow to binge more of Season 9 — which I 110 abso cannot effing wait for — seem to be in jeopardy. Like bad. Cammy's gonna freak out if we don't invite her. Ummmm. #breakfasttacos

"What do you want me to do?" Mikey asks me.

Flor looks over at me as she drives.

Girl.

"We could all just say we're doing different things," Mikey suggests.

"You want us to lie?" The question bursts out of me.

Flor bites her lower lip. On the steering wheel, her grip tightens. "It's your call, Mac—she's *your* friend. Do we invite her or not?"

She's your friend. Hearing Flor say that sucks.

I stare at the freeway in front of us. Red taillights, a large green sign announcing an exit ramp. There's the Tower, too, all lit up, glimmering over downtown.

And then it happens. Inside me. Like a far-off blinking light that's been growing brighter, hotter, and within reach, this feeling that I am here and part of this and alone, too, at the same time. Yes, I really, really like my friends, but I don't like what they're doing, and it feels shitty and fake and gross af. Ughhh. I tell myself to slow down, but the world around me swirls— lights and skyscrapers and cars zooming by—and the feeling that I want no part of escalating this conflict magnifies. "I call shade. And if you don't invite her, then go ahead and uninvite me, too."

"You're kidding," Mikey replies.

I hear Flor take a long-ass deep breath.

But I'm not kidding. Not in the least. It's like how effed-up would it be just to not invite somebody over a screenshot with some so-called "facts" provided by a person who won't even identify themselves? Girl, this isn't witness protection.

"Two wrongs don't make a right. And you can't just not invite somebody based on what some person whose name we don't even know says. At least give Cam the chance to tell her side of the story."

"It's a very reliable source." Her voice quieter than before, Flor shakes her head and drives, not looking at me.

"You really wouldn't come?" Mikey asks. "The whole reason we're doing this is for you."

"Girl, I don't know why you stand up for her so much!" Flor counters.

"Because Cam's one of my best friends. Girl, you don't think I'd stand up for you, too?"

"But babe, think about it — is she even really that nice to you?" Flor seems determined; her hands grasp the steering wheel tighter.

I feel sweaty and suffocated and defensive — I just want this convo to end.

"I don't have to think about it. Cam's been there for me for a long time. I —"

"Like at graduation? We all saw what she's capable of."

I hate that Flor says this, because she's right, and I don't have anything I can say. Nothing constructive at least. And sitting in the passenger seat on my way home, I don't think Mikey or Flor will ever understand why I'm defending Cam. Shit, I don't even fully understand why I'm defending Cam. But he's my friend, and he's been there for me, and yeah, she acts like a mega-bitch, and I'm probably very sure he said all those things those text messages accuse him of saying and worse things probably, too, but that's just who he is. Take that away, and then what? It's like Cam has these claws that she grew to get by in a shitty world, and can you really take away somebody's claws? Throw them back into a hard-ass world without the one way they've learned to protect themselves?

The car goes quiet af.

Girl, it's literally Pearl-staring-at-RuPaul-level tense, and the only thing I have on my face is a mouthful of disbelief and all of Rule #3, so I say, "Y'all are real quick to cut somebody off. Like damn. Let's hope I never act human and make mistakes around y'all. Whatever happened to friendship and loyalty and forever?"

Girl, nobody says shit. And maybe they're not used to me being so up-front and direct, but wrong is wrong, and purposely making somebody feel like they don't belong is twisted af. For reals. Like who does that? That's some Benny and Duncan and Regina George and Rolaskatox bullshit all in one. Like, girl. At least have a conversation with her before you decide to give her the chop.

Finally, Mikey swallows some air, clears his throat. "Yeah, not inviting him would just make a shitty situation even shittier. And he is coming to Valentina, so he should be there for that convo."

I think Flor's stunned by Mikey's reversal, because in front of that steering wheel, Flor's eyes are big as saucers, and girl, she looks completely wrecked, and then she's shaking her head a little, and suddenly, I'm getting the feeling that maybe Flor and Mikey have been talking about this issue, and Flor was expecting a much different outcome. I could be wrong, but girl. If Cam thinks they're trying to turn me against him, Mikey just proved him wrong. As for Flor, did she just prove Cam's accusation right? Girl, maybe she does have it out for Cammy. After Whataburger, can I really blame her, though?

As Flor exits the freeway, I realize this drama over Cammy backstabbing Flor isn't just gonna go away. Maybe space is what this friends group actually needs, because peace really might be too much to hope for. But if there's one thing I'm good at, it's being hopeful af. So that's my play. I'll be the one who tries to make sure things are fair, that Cam isn't walking into an ambush, but also and maybe more significantly, the one who helps her see she can do better and has to if she's gonna be friends with us.

As Flor turns down my street, I hold the idea of "us" in my hands. Like, am I seriously already separating the group between Mikey, Flor, and me on one side and then Cammy? Ughhh. I don't like the way this sounds, and when we pull into my driveway, Flor doesn't say much. Already, Kimber's going ass at the window, and when I walk over to the driver's side of the car to hug Flor goodbye, she doesn't open her door, and the embrace she gives me through the window is awkward af and lukewarm, at most. Girl.

Chapter 17

WHEN I WALK INTO MY HOUSE, I FIND MY DAD in front of the TV, his hand on the remote and Kimber hovering beside me, offering up her slobbery pink pig for me to play with.

"Day was good?" he asks, and I'm surprised af. Girl, my dad doesn't ask about my day.

I nod, petting Kimber, tugging at her piggy.

"You off tomorrow, right?"

"Yeah. Why?"

"I thought maybe we could grill something for B. Or take her out. To eat. Maybe go to Luby's. She's always liked it there. I talked to her today. Said she might stop by tomorrow. In the evening. She asked if you'd be here."

Instantly, I imagine like five thousand things that can go

disastrously wrong with this invite. The last time we were all together . . . #Alamodomegraduationshitshow. When I think of B and the dejected af look on her face as my dad went off on her at her graduation, all I can do is ask, "And you're gonna apologize?"

"Apologize?"

I stare at him. He takes a swig from his beer, and Kimber's rubbing her sloppy-ass pig against my leg hair. Ordinarily, this is the part where I'd walk away or back down or say, "Never mind," and then apologize for even bringing it up. But girl, after my conversation with Flor and Mikey, I'm feeling emboldened af to stand up for what I believe in. Seriously. I'm kind of very a lot over keeping some fake-ass peace by making myself small and never resolving anything, so I tell him, "C'mon, Dad. We both know you crossed the line. But ey, we all make mistakes, right? And I know B loves you, and I know you love her. So yeah, Dad. You should apologize."

I wait for him to blow up. But nothing comes out of his mouth. He just bites his lip and stares at the dog.

"You know she's leaving soon," I continue, feeling even bolder, "so y'all should really work it out. Before she moves. Anyway, I'm going over to Mikey's tomorrow night. His mom's making me dinner." This is a big thing for me to say—huge—because every other time I would've put my own wants and needs aside to do the "right thing" and be there for my family, but tonight, I'm choosing myself over them. Girl. I kinda even gag myself, because if this is what growth feels like, then #gimmemore.

For a second, it looks like my dad might go the f off on me.

But all he says is "She needs to apologize for shit too" and goes back to his beer and his show.

I leave him with the TV, and Kimber follows me. Back in my room, I'm replaying the conversations with Flor at the gym and in her car and the half-ass hug she gave me in front of my house. To calm myself, to keep myself from overthinking, I listen to the fan, which pretty much makes the same sound as those white-noise relaxation apps that Flor likes. It doesn't work, though. My brain is running a hundred thousand million miles a minute, so I get on the floor, like I used to do when I'd get stressed during baseball, which was literally like all the time, and I do as many push-ups as I can. I go until fatigue, and I do this several times. Sets of fifteen and thirty and as many as my arms and chest will allow me to do.

Gasping, I lie on my floor. It's like my head is full of Rule #3, and my heart is telling me to listen to some Ariana, because Rule #1, right? No-brainer. What's loyalty if there's no joy? Girl. And also, because in the past, when I didn't have my friends, Ariana's vibe usually did the trick.

"One Last Time." Uffffff. Girl. So good.

On my phone, I watch the video, and then I lie back with the phone on my chest and just listen to her voice. I find myself letting go of the shitty feeling I have, and Ariana even gets Kimber to chill the f out and fall asleep. It's all good, until my phone starts blowing up.

The FBC group chat. A barrage of texts, all from Cam.

Cam: Omg so xcitd so so so xcitd girls to see Vals show.

Its gonna be the fiercest hunty and theres a meet n greet

220

2 before that will be cute 2 maybe sometimes those aren't
that great but I hope this one is girl

Cam: Soooooo gagged hunty

Cam: Wy bishes doin??????

Cam: You whores betta not b sleepin onme

I play "One Last Time" again because my heart rate has
skyrocketed. Just as the song ends . . .

Cam: Can you believe she's coming?? I wonder what she's
gonna perform

Cam: ?

Cam: Helloooo I bet she's doing two ballads old song like
Selena bc this is tx prob Como la Flor and I hope she does
Ariana Greedy

I call shade on that one, girl. Everybody knows Valentina's
history with that song—it's the one that got her sent home—
and on the reals, I think Cam's trying to provoke Flor.

Girl, nobody responds.

And honestly, I wanna jump in. I mean, there's def shit
Cammy and I need to discuss, but not via text and certainly not
on the group chat, where things can go soooooo f-word wrong.
Seriously. And besides, this needs to be a private-ass, face-to-
face convo, and I should probably put my thoughts together
before I try going at Cam with any of this.

Cam: Omg omg omg I cant wait

Cam: Ugh yall whores really betta not be ghosts, this izzz
why I need new friends

New friends? Ugh. Girl. And then, not even a minute later . . .

Mikey: Yeah, girl. We're getting together at my house

tomorrow night to get our shit together for Valentina. Stop by.

Cam: Finally a bitch gets a response. Yassss girl!!!!! If I'm not busy I can make an appearance. I might have plans tho so we'll see

I stare at my phone, cringing at how flippant Cam sounds. Like an hour ago she almost got cut the f-word outta this friends group. And this is what I saved her for? So she could act like an ass? And like, can she even fathom what an f-word bitch she sounds like right now? #selfawarenessMIAmija. I mean, is she oblivious? Tired of swallowing my words, I FaceTime Cam so we can talk this shit out right here, right now.

Do better, I think.

The call rings and rings, and no answer. Of course, I'm bothered. Girl, it's like I know she's available because she was literally just texting us.

I try FaceTiming her again. Same response. Girl.

Tired of the bullshit, I finally just shoot Cam a text. No group chat. Just us.

Me: Why aren't you picking up? I was gonna say let's get food tomorrow. Me and you. I'm off.

I keep my eyes on my phone, and I can see Cam's leaving me on read. Waiting for those three little dots to appear, I wonder if maybe her mom's talking to her or Denise could be asking her to help with her kids or with something in the kitchen. Cam's family is very demanding. And maybe I'm desperate for a rationale.

Me: Tacos or pancakes. At IHOP. You pick. I know you love IHOP. ❤❤❤

But girl, silence.

And at the same time that I'm texting Cam, Flor's texting me this:

Flor: Girl. She really needs to stop.

Flor: Babes, you know why she's doing it. Shade, girl. #notcute #sonotadorbs

Me: Girl, don't escalate shit. I'm trying to make this work.

Flor: WERK! Tru tru, sis. 🔥🔥🔥

Flor: She doesn't have confidence like us. 👑👑👑

Flor: Insecurities are not happiness, sis.

Me: Girl, stop. This isn't helping, babe.

Flor: I know. Okay, girl, so, I didn't want to say anything earlier.

Those three little dots appear, and I'm forced to wait for whatever Flor wants to tell me. Finally:

Flor: But you know she actually told me that somebody should talk to you about losing some weight because she said a lot of the girls are saying you got fat after you quit baseball. I think she's shady x 3,000, sis. Like she said now you have a "puffy" stomach and your arms aren't even that big. Ugh, girl. She kept saying "panzota, girl" and called you a "fat-ass hoodrat" and said she was joking when I said something. Babes, I'm sorry. I'm so over this. #notstunting #beast #gotyourbacksis 😩😩😩

I stare at her message and realize that my cheeks are burning. My eyes sting, and all the air in my body wants to talk shit.

Flor: Also, let's gym again soon. I really want to gain three pounds in my butt, so I can be an even number. Everybody has a butt except me. #cakefordays 😁🍑😁

Flor: But yeah, bitch. I am jelly. Hard jelly, girl. #sadface

Also, #eyesrolling

I can barely focus on Flor's texts, because I am livid. Lose weight? Fat-ass hoodrat? Girl. #ughhhhhhhhhhaf

I can't. I literally have to take myself outside because I'm furious, and I feel betrayed, and I'm so pissed. My heart is going off like a jackhammer. Standing on the back porch, my bare feet on the hot splintery planks, with Kimber pooping somewhere in the dark, I realize this is how it was always gonna go down. Girl, honestly, how did I not see this coming? Like, why am I surprised? One day Cammy was gonna come for me like she's come for everybody else. I mean, it's like the whole time Cammy's here holding a dagger in front of me waving it at all these other people, and I'm all like, it's okay, that's not really a dagger, girl, Cam's just being Cam, nobody's perfect. Uggghhhh!!!!! No, girl. No. No. No.

I'm realizing that this isn't Cammy's chaos era. No. Girl, this is just who she is. And the worst part, maybe she likes it this way? Standing here with my "panzota," watching Kimber sniff fireflies far past the porch light in the dark by the alley, I'm rereading Flor's messages, and I feel ridiculous af. Girl, take me back to Party City where I belong. Serio. I'm giving #clowncity, girl, because earlier wasn't I all twisted about betraying Cam by listening to Flor talk shit while the whole time Cam's been betraying me by making fun of my stomach and arms and calling me a rata behind my back? Girl, please. Fake Bitches Club realness.

Finally, Cam responds.

Cam: OMG yessssss!!! Sounds delish but let's rain check boo I'm already booked and busy babe come on booked and busy realness!!!

Me: You work that early now? Wow. I thought you didn't get up before noon?

Before Cam can respond, Flor's coming back at me with this:

Flor: Okay, girl. I'm going to go put on two more pounds of makeup, because apparently I wear too much.

Me: Just put on one pound, girl. Or three! So you can be an even number!!

Flor: Ugh!!! Gagged.

Flor: Luv you, sis! Mwah! 😘😘😘

Girl, and then this from Cammy:

Cam: Girl come over on next Thursday before we go to Valentina

Cam: I'm getn in drag bitch realness!!!!

Cam: 1st time n drag realness hunty!!!!! For the V show n then we can go with my sis friend who knows cast of show n can get us in backstage at Aztec Theatre hunty luv ya sis

Girl, I'm really tempted to say, "IDK. Maybe. If my panzota and my fat hoodrat ass can come, too." But that would put Flor in a shitty spot, because it would be obvi she's the one who told me this. #restrainedaf

Me: Girl, you really okay leaving people out?

Cam: Hahaha girl why????? there gonna be so boring af!!!! Go with me, my sis friend get us backstage girl backstage vip hunty vip life

Cam: Ugh I hate that tired-ass group chat. For reals
nonsense I can't. And yass leave out the weak sauce girl

Is she for real? Maybe it's because I'm gassed up af that
Cammy called me fat and fake-friended me by talking shit
about me to Flor behind my back and then was too "booked
and busy" to get IHOP with me where I was actually gonna try
and help her — I mean, she doesn't even get up early, and now
she suddenly has early plans and with who? Girl, stop. And
maybe it's because of all the times Cam's shut me down, insults
and not-so-humble brags at my expense, all of them accumu-
lated and steaming furiously inside me right now, or maybe it's
because Cam's personal brand really is fake-ass friend realness, and now she's trying to steal me away from Flor and
Mikey because I'm getting close with them and further from
her and because they treat me soooo much better than she
does, and maybe I'm just mad at myself because it's taken me
so long to stop defending her and just admit that she's tóxica
and fake and bitchy af. Girl, no. So many toxic-ass things
about this toxic-ass scenario with this toxic-ass friendship.

And girl, no matter how many times I remind myself of
Rule #3 — "Loyalty is life. Love is forever. And friends are your
family" — girl, loyalty and heavy, fake-ass shade do not mix,
not in my book. I'd hashtag that line, but it's too long, girl.
#waitnohashtagistoolong. And here on my crooked-ass back
porch, watching my dog live her best life chasing fireflies in the
tall grass by the back fence, I remember how f-word excited
I was at the beginning of the summer for all of us to become
friends and get closer so that I wouldn't be off on my own little

island, living in my own little semi-sad world, with my one kinda-sorta gay bff who I now realize is a major, totes, big-time fake-ass friend.

As much as I'd wanted to be the peacekeeper, after Cam talked shit about my body, I don't know. I feel like Cam just sees me as a belonging, as a pawn, as an accessory. I feel like she doesn't actually want me as a friend, she just doesn't want me to be Flor's and Mikey's friend, and there's a huge-ass difference. Like, I think the one and only true reason Cam's making a big deal about me going to watch her get ready for Valentina is to keep me from Mikey and Flor, that Cam just wants me to be there to watch her put on her face and her hair and to cheer her on as she gets dolled up, just so she can ignore me for the rest of the night as she gets showered with all this attention. Maybe she'll even let me carry something or take pics of her whenever she orders me to.

And so, refusing to make myself small for Cam or for Flor or for Mikey or my dad or for anybody, I give my own perra fierceness and I make a choice.

FBC

Me: Okay. So who else is getting in drag for Valentina?

Cam just told me she's a yes. First time in drag realness!!!

As for me, I'm a no. What about y'all, Flor and Mikey?

🔥🔥🔥

Chapter
18

"**B**ABE, YOU DOING OKAY? THAT TEXT IN THE group chat . . . that was a choice," Mikey says when he picks me up for dinner the following day.

"Babe, ughhh. Don't even get me started." I try to change the subject. "What are we listening to?"

"It's my new day party mix," Mikey says, turning it down. "I'm getting it ready for Flor's birthday pool party at the end of summer. But it can wait. Honestly, babe, tell me the feels."

Leaning back into the passenger seat, I puff my cheeks and blow out my lungs. This whole situation has Mess City, Texas, 7820Mess written all over it. As it turns out, Cammy was somehow able to clear her very busy schedule to hang out, so she's already at Mikey's painting . . . with Flor. Girl, seriously? Last night, as soon as I spilled Cam's first-time-in-drag T, Flor immediately jumped in, announcing that she's gonna get in first-time drag too. I was thinking I was so letting Cam have it by going behind her back and revealing her plan, and yet, from the flood of messages last night and the 117 group texts I woke up to this morning, I think I've created a common ground between Flor and Cam while also simultaneously and inadvertently provoking a full-on fake af frenemies drag war.

As Mikey stops at a red light at the end of my street, I lean over and kiss him, because while going toe-to-toe with Cam will abso need to happen tonight, kissing Mikey is what tru tru really makes me feel good, and that's what I need right now. Cinnamon gum and vanilla iced coffee—that's what Mikey tastes like. And his lips are softer than I remember. I tell him, "Whatever she gives me, I'm giving her right back. Hard, babe."

"Hard? Damn, papi." Mikey grins, grabbing my thigh playfully.

I like it when Mikey flirts. I like all the ways he makes me feel desired and wanted.

"So, did she ever text you back?"

"Nope. She's ignored me all day. I told you the last one she sent me was last night."

2:19 a.m.

Cam: Reals cute, perra!!!

Cam: So I guess shes giving now. Wow.

Cam: Let the games begin. 👏👏👏

7:34 a.m.

Me: Thanks. Can't wait, babe. ❤

From ear to ear, Mikey's beaming his approval. "Babe. She swears."

"Let the games begin," I say, and Mikey bursts into laughter.

Early this morning, while walking Kimber, I put together my plan of attack. First jab Cam throws, I'm saying, "Callete el hocico, girl. Go back to Mess City where you belong." And I'm gonna keep repeating it, like in fifth grade when Hot Cheeto girls would get rowdy and start waving their dusty-ass, crusty orange af fingers and try to argue with Ms. Elizondo, and the teacher just kept repeating the same thing over and over. It worked for Ms. E, and I think it can work for me against Cam, who pretty much still is a Hot Cheeto girl. Seriously.

Mikey's hand on my leg, I tell him, "I know Cam's coming for me, and for the first time, I'm not afraid. It's like, after you get the shit knocked outta you for the tenth time, you can take anything, right?" I don't know if Mikey agrees, but he nods and keeps his eyes on the road.

"Not to criticize or anything," Mikey says, "but what happened to you trying to calm shit down?"

"Yeah, I know. But I'm not gonna just let Cam clown on my body."

"Baby, all serious, Cam is dead wrong. I like your thick-ass... everything," Mikey says. "I think you're thigh-conic af, babe."

Thigh-conic. Mikey's compliment fills me with ganas.

"Don't let Cam get in your head. Babe, that's his MO. Get in your head and make you doubt yourself." Nodding as he turns into his neighborhood, Mikey suddenly becomes the wisest man in the world with this advice.

As we pull into his driveway, I place my hand on his chest, and Mikey holds my hand near his heart, lacing his fingers into mine. I feel like I can tell him anything. Mikey turns off the car, and I say, "You know, I used to wanna be around Cam all twenty-four, and I'd listen to all his bullshit because I thought he was like a king or something."

"What do you mean?" Mikey's eyes shift over to me.

"Like I was desperate for us to be friends. Like I wanted him to like me so bad."

I'm biting down on my lip.

Seeing my stress, Mikey squeezes my hand gently and admits, "Honestly, babe—not gonna lie—fuck Cam."

He goes to get out of the car, but I grab his hand, because I know that on the other side of the door to Mikey's house awaits my confrontation with Cammy. "Can we just sit here for a few more minutes before we go in?"

"Of course." He turns the music back up a little. "You cool if I talk you through Flor's b-day mix?"

I nod. As pissed as I am, I don't think I agree with Mikey's assessment. It's like, I don't wanna stab the bitch, I just want him to know he can no longer talk shit about me and not have me say something back. Maybe Cammy and I just need to throw verbal hands and then everything will be cool after that. Like in fourth grade, when I boxed Duncan at baseball practice, and then he invited me to his birthday party the week after that. But we're not little kids anymore; we're seventeen, about to be seniors. Girl, if Cam and I go off on each other, will that really make anything better? Or girl, will my little first-time-in-drag stunt really be the beginning of the end of my friendship with Cam? Girl. It's some heavy-ass shit, and for this reason, I'm only partially paying attention as Mikey narrates the list of songs he's put together for Flor's b-day pool party, which sucks, because I should abso 110 be listening, but I'm just distracted and frustrated and stressed, which becomes a major issue when Mikey asks, "So what do you think?"

"About?" I have no clue what he's talking about.

"About the mix. Do you think I should keep that opening or the other one?"

Girl. I'm cracked. "Yeah, they're both fine." Ughhh. Why am I lying?

"Fine?"

"Yeah." I try to smile away my discomfort, like maybe smiling will alleviate this tension forming between us.

"Were you even listening?"

When I look up, Mikey isn't smiling, and honestly, if I'm going full 110, I'm kind of a lot resenting Mikey being so abrupt with me right now. Doesn't he understand the strain I'm going through? I mean, yeah, his mix is important, but I'm focusing on a friendship that might potentially die in the next few hours. Girl. I wanna pull my hand away from him, but I feel stupid and petty for thinking this.

"I'm just thinking about Cam drama."

"So, I just wanna be clear. Right now, you're more interested in Cam and her drama than you are in me and what I have to say?"

"That's not what I said."

"It's not what you said, but it's what you did. You literally just ignored your boyfriend when he was telling you something he was proud of."

"Nobody said y'all had to be Cam's friend." I relate this bluntly, like it's a known fact, not debatable. Wait. Did Mikey just call himself my boyfriend?

"No, but I know that's what you want. I don't buy that you're okay with me and Flor being your friends but ignoring Cam."

"Flor and me," I say. And ughhhhhh. Girl, nooooooo!!! Cringe. Like mega-cringe. I hate myself for being this person correcting somebody's grammar in the middle of a disagreement that's on the brink of becoming a big-ass argument. And did Mikey just refer to us as boyfriends?

Mikey just looks at me blankly. "Ummm. Yeah. Flor and me. Wow. This really has you upset."

"I'm not upset," I snap. I pull my hand back, and I don't know why I do this. Like I literally tell myself, *Bitch, don't pull your hand away*, and then I do it. Girl, more cringe.

"Okay, well, maybe we can just listen to this other mix I wanted to share with you. It's tribal house, fast and heavy fierce, a lotta tambores, and I love it. I thought you might like that for working out. It's one of Nina Flowers's new sets," Mikey says.

He's right. It's way different from the high-energy vocal sets he usually plays me, which are great, but Nina takes me someplace else, and I effing love Nina's sound. Aggressive. Hard. Definitely fierce af. I can totally see myself giving this at the gym.

I exhale and go with the sound.

Mikey and I don't talk.

I look over, and he has his eyes shut tightly. He's breathing kind of heavy, his chest moving up and down and full.

Shit. He's definitely pissed. I stare out the window.

Everything looks so hot and dry.

On the sidewalk, a woman uses a newspaper to shield her kids' faces from the sun.

On the other side of the road, a man drenches his yard with a green water hose.

Nina's music is sooo good, and I tell him so, but there's clearly tension between us.

I move the AC vent so the cold air blows on my face.

I stare at the garage door ahead of us. Squares, newish-looking panels, a silver handle.

Oddly, then I start thinking that maybe I shoulda just stayed home today, and I think of Rebecca, who's probably working her extra hours right now, wiping down saltshakers or filling containers with salsa, and with my heart sputtering, I remember that yeah, Mikey did just refer to himself as my boyfriend, which is a moment. Girl. I feel bad that I kinda went off on him, and I feel like I'm kinda all over the place.

I turn to Mikey. "I shouldn't have gone that hard at you."

But Nina's loud, and I don't think Mikey hears me. I don't wanna yell, and also, I don't wanna just turn down his music, either. Like, I'm mad and feeling weird af so let me just turn down this music you just told me you really, really like.

Timing is everything, I remember B telling me once, and even though I think she was talking about basketball, B's advice can apply to a lot of shit in life. So, I wait, and once I can see that his breathing has slowed, I reach over and turn down the music. Mikey's eyes are closed, the sky behind him hot and blue.

"What you do that for?" Mikey sighs.

"I need to tell you something. I need to apologize."

Mikey shifts in his seat. His eyes open.

"I'm sorry. I went hard at you. You didn't deserve that. It was wrong. And I'm . . . sorry."

"C'mon, you don't have to apologize. I'm a big boy," Mikey replies.

"Yeah, I know. But I was wrong. I don't wanna pretend like I didn't act like a dick when I know I just did. I just feel like I'm gonna have to choose between y'all and Cam. And I'm so pissed at him. I'm sooo effing pissed at him right now. And I hate that I'm gonna have to choose."

"Babe, nobody's asking you to choose."

"I know. Not yet. But I just feel like I'm gonna have to choose. Eventually."

Mikey holds my hand. He raises my knuckles and kisses them sweetly.

"Also, and I really hope I heard this right, but did you just call yourself my boyfriend? Is that what we are? Are we boyfriends?"

"Yeah. I said it."

I smile like my face has no end.

I smile like there are five hundred suns in my heart.

Like every bird in the sky and all the stars and the little rabbit in the moon are all watching me hold on to this joy.

"I really like how that sounds." I lean over then and press my mouth against Mikey's. With my tongue, I touch his teeth, and this makes him kiss me back harder. In my shorts, I'm growing, and I think maybe everything's gonna be good, that no matter what Cam comes at me with, all of this might actually work out.

As our kiss ends, I see Flor walking out of Mikey's house. She has one eyebrow, her hair's pulled back in a baby chongo, and she's giving full-on, half-painted face in daylight sun realness. Girl. #itsalewk. She waves and trots casually to her car. She's on the phone, which she holds in front of her.

When I lift my hand to wave back, Mikey's already reaching for his door, and I tell him, "Babe. Hold up. I gotta wait for this to go down."

Looking at my shorts, Mikey coughs up a laugh. He grabs his gym bag from the back seat and goes, "Here, cover yourself with this."

Like she's on a movie set or a photo shoot, the sun reflects off Flor's face. "Hurry, bitches," she says. "We're almost done with the first look. Oh, and my mom made red-pepper hummus and a salad. You know how she is. Can't show up empty-handed."

I'm glad to see Flor, and even though she only half hugs me because she's protecting her paint, she still hugs me like we didn't have any tension last night, which is refreshing because I can only imagine the f-word attitude Cam's gonna give me the second she sees me walk in, and she will most definitely have something to say—she made that crystal af clear on her text. I mean, silent treatment for two weeks over breakfast tacos? Girl. I'm bracing myself for some good, hard-ass library chingasos or worse. Mess City, here we come.

"Y'all need to water this grass," Flor says. "She's thirsty, girl."

I chuckle at Flor's commentary, but Mikey just shrugs.

"How is she?" I ask Flor. "Like, what kind of mood is she in?"

"Actually, she's being pretty chill," Flor responds. "Like, it's kinda funsies."

I'm relieved but also skeptical. How can you kinda have fun with somebody you don't even like and who admittedly doesn't like you? I'm curious—how long is this "funsies" gonna last? Or, in Cam's words, when do the games begin?

Walking in, all I can think is *here we go.*

"Girl, I'm thinking of recreating Valentina's Episode One lewk for next week. All red, head to toe, very Latina—not the same look but inspired by." As much as I want Flor's enthusiasm to be contagious, it's not. Trepidation, that's a good word for how I'm feeling.

"Girl, Cleo left us all these notes and charts about makeup application," Flor tells me as we head to Mikey's dining table.

At the table, Cam diligently studies a tutorial on Flor's iPad, while Doja plays in the background. Spread across the table is an assortment of Cleo's professional makeup supplies, along with a lineup of face charts, which are these outlines of faces printed on sheets of paper that you can try different lewks on.

When I see Cam, I don't know what to say. I mean, do I go all in and play offense or do I wait and see how she's gonna play her cards? I mean, girl. What level of toxic masc aggressiveness or fake-ass mean-girl friendship are we gonna serve the girls today?

"Hey, girl," Cam says. Staring intently into a mirror, she lines her lower lip.

Hey, girl? Ummmmm. Is that all?

I guess we're gonna play it cool and fake af. We'll see how long this lasts.

"Hey."

I'm in no rush for the Cam drama to start, so I follow Mikey to the TV room. We get settled in on the couch with the end of Episode 2, right where we left off. His mom has put out a spread of snacks—nuts and fruit and cheeses and gourmet popcorn and pita chips and hummus and protein bars. It's fancy af. Mikey's house is "very open concept," as Flor comments, so from where Flor and Cammy are set up at the table, they can see the TV and continue painting "for the gods, hunty," as Cam keeps repeating.

Chewing a giant bite of muscle bar, Mikey clicks for the show.

On the couch, a handful of chips in my mouth and my arm around Mikey, I feel closer to him than ever. I'm glad that Mikey was so forgiving with me earlier. I mean, both Flor and Mikey could've been total perras to me about our conflicts, and yet each of them treated me like, well, I wanna be treated, like a real friend instead of someone who wants to punish me and make me feel like shit for mistakes I make, which brings me back to Cam.

Girl, at the table, she's all huddled up with Flor. Giggling and nuzzling up to her, whispering. Every time I look up at her, she doesn't look my way. Girl, she's ignoring me. On purpose. #fakeaf

And on the reals, I'm kind of a lot thrown by this change of energy. Girl, they literally hate each other, and now they're all bff? Whatever. Maybe drag really can bring frenemies together. In a way, I'm like, at least they're getting along. And maybe on some level, Cam is trying to make this work. It's possible. Still, I wonder what time the real Cam's showing up. More than that, I wonder what the real Cam and the real-ass me are gonna say to each other.

Diligently, Flor works her face charts while at the same time watching the show.

"Okay. What about these?" Flor holds up two of her faces.

Girl, they kinda both look the same to me. I mean, maybe there's a slight difference in the cheek colors, but it's hard for me to say.

"What are your other choices?" Mikey asks.

"I think she was talking to me, babe," Cam interjects.

Mikey and I exchange glances.

"This one," Cammy decides. "You don't need high cheek-bones, girl. You're already blessed." She pats Flor's arm reassuringly, and I'm like, okay, what world are we in?

"Do you think I can pull off big red flowers in my hair?"

"Girl, you need hair first." I don't think Mikey means to say this as loudly as he does, and I don't know if he intends for his comment to sound like a read, yet it does.

"Oh, Cam's getting us hair," Flor responds.

"Good hair, mamawwwws." Cammy pops her tongue, then finishes lining her lip.

Girl, Mikey almost chokes up his almond.

"Cam's bringing you hair?" I ask plainly, because maybe I'm hallucinating.

"Big-ass beauty queen hair. Let's be exact, mamawwwws." Cammy snaps. "She's serving a Miss Teen Mexico pageant lewk. Very dramatic. Very Latina."

Flor looks pleased. "Yes, girl. It's from her mother's salon. She's giving several hair options. Girl, I need to feel a connection with my hair. A bond." She turns to Cammy. "Babes, we can also drive around and shop for hair tomorrow or the day after. As long as I get it by next week. It's on my to-do list." Flor taps her little black notebook. "And Mikey, your mom said she's gonna paint us for Valentina."

"Professionally painted, girl," Cammy brags, drawing on eyeliner.

"Umm. When did you talk to my mom?" Mikey shoved too many chips in his mouth, and it's difficult to understand him.

"This morning. Oh, and tomorrow we're gonna pick up some shoes. If you and Mac wanna go. Also, your mom said we can borrow lashes, but that we should really buy our own. And your mom said we can look at some of her old gowns when she gets home tonight, because we're the same size and since I'm really into vintage. Girl, I wish my mom was this supportive."

I'm confused. "Not to be rude, but I don't get it. If Mikey's mom is gonna professionally paint y'all, why are y'all spending all this time practicing putting on makeup?" I ask. It's a fair question.

Cammy looks up, and I think, *Okay, bitch. This is it. She's going in.* But, no, Cam doesn't miss a beat, keeps right on with her paint and replies, "Because this isn't a one-off, girl. I'm thinking long-term."

Beside Cammy, Flor nods. "Same. I'm here to learn, sis."

"Yes, ma'am. Drag knowledge is power, hunty." Cammy snaps when she says this, and Flor laughs, nodding, scribbling something in her little black notebook.

Consequently, I'm only half watching as Jaymes Mansfield sashays away. Distracted by what's happening between Cammy and Flor, I feel uncertain, disconnected, left out, and girl, I don't like how this feels.

Before Episode 3 starts, Mikey hits pause, and we head back into the kitchen. He goes to the fridge to get a drink, and I take the seat at the table right next to Flor.

Watching Flor and Cammy paint is like watching surgery. Girl, they're meticulous and slow af.

"You look great," I tell Flor, thinking I should engage more with this little paint session. If Cammy wants to ignore me, then I'll just insert myself in the convo.

"Thanks. I'm sooo glad we're doing this. I've always wanted to get my drag going, but I thought I'd have to wait until I moved away. Girl, I love this."

Flor's phone buzzes, and I see Cammy put his phone down.

Reading the text, Flor snickers, and I wait for her to tell me what's so funny, but she doesn't. Instead she leans over and slaps Cam kittenishly on the arm. "Girl, you are too much. You better stop." Still laughing, Flor's shaking her head and shining, and I wanna pull her aside and ask wtf happened between her and Cammy that led up to Cam giving Flor hair and Flor getting Mikey's mom to paint them both and them being so damn friendly. Girl, is this even real?

I check my phone to see if Cammy texted me.

Nothing.

Cam cracks her knuckles and says, "Okay. So, you ready, bitch? Let's. See. The hair." She claps each word.

"Okay, sis. Let's get to it. Show. Me. The hair." Flor claps each word too.

Both erupt into laughter.

Sis? Ummmm. Where's this coming from?

I look over at Mikey, who just shrugs, like *I don't get it either*.

Digging in one of her plastic totes, Cammy pulls out two hairpieces, one red and stringy and loose-looking, and the other one dark and full of herself, with the potential for a lot of volume, kinda like Hermelinda's.

"Girl, these wigs are thirstier than that dry-ass grass outside," Cammy laughs. "But they're just here for color sampling. Our real hair will be much, much better, girl. Lace front realness, hunty. Maybe a long high pony for you, girl." Cammy shakes out her paleta-red hairpiece and holds it up against her painted skin, pouts and bats her eyes with only one lash applied.

Flor lives for it. "Yes, ma'am."

"Let's brush them out, sis. See what magic we can work with these right here and right now, girl."

Watching Cammy and Flor, I hate to admit it: if Cammy's goal is to make me feel excluded, she's winning af. Is this Cam's play, stealing Flor from me? But Flor has made it abundantly clear that she doesn't like Cammy. Yet she's acting like they're long-lost sisters, and if it is an act, she deserves an Academy Award, because the performance is believable af. So what's her angle? She seemed legit happy to see me when I arrived, but now she's definitely behaving out of character. Girl. I'm staring, and I can't stop staring, and I hate that I'm staring.

"I really just wanna see how the colors work together," Flor says. "And like I said, we can always go look at hair tomorrow if we need to. I have a whole to-do list. Girl, she has soooo much to do."

"Booked and busy, girl!" Cammy croons.

"High-key booked and busy, girl!" Flor replies.

And girl. Then Flor and Cam swap hair, and sitting side by side, they're brushing each other's wigs and whispering to one another. Girl. Like they are literally brushing each other's hair and telling secrets, and I am gagged. Didn't Cam read me for the dirty at the beginning of summer, telling me this shit was never gonna happen? Ughhhhhhhh.

Instead of just sitting here watching Flor and Cammy bond or pretend-bond, I make a choice. Girl, this is my moment, and I'm having it. And so, feeling like a bold-ass bitch, I say, "Wow. I love all this getting along slash bff energy y'all are giving. It's what I've wanted since senior summer started. So why do I feel like y'all are leaving me out?"

I hear the clank of Mikey dropping something in the sink.

And puro gaggery maxed out, girl. Both Flor and Cam look at me with their mouths open wide. I don't think they were expecting me to call them out like this.

Flor kinda stutters, which is rare, because she's usually so eloquent and on point with her messaging. She says, "I—I . . . I'm sorry. Babes, no. I didn't mean to leave you out. I guess I just got so carried away with all the excitement."

"Yeah, well. It feels like you're excluding me." I'm frustrated af and confused and jealous. Ughhhh. I hate that I'm jealous.

Flor gets up and puts her arms around me.

I stare at my knuckles, because I'm still kinda bitter, and then I hug Flor back, and with some of my frustration dissolving, I smile at Mikey, who's watching from the kitchen. Mikey's brow furrows like he's doing calculus.

"We're still besties, right?" Flor asks with the sweet part of her voice. Leaning her head on my shoulder, I get the sense that she really is remorseful, that she wasn't leaving me out on purpose.

"Yeah. Of course," I reply. "I'll always—"

And girl. That's when Cammy does it.

Dropping her face into her palms, Cammy takes in a deep, aching breath, and girl, she cries. It's like she sucks all the air outta the room, and the sobs emerging from her are loud af and gripping—there's no way not to stare. When Cam looks up, her eyes wet, she struggles to control her breathing, and the mascara is not waterproof, because dark streams stain Cam's powdered cheeks. She says, "I'm so sorry that y'all have to see this. It's just that, sometimes, I feel like no one understands who I am. As a person. My point of view. My sense of humor. My style, my passion for hair and makeup and dance and my love of drag." From her seat, Cammy looks at Flor. "For the first time in my life, I feel like somebody gets me. So yeah, Flor's right. 110 abso, girl. I just got too focused on the happiness I get from painting and having someone like me to paint with and talk about hair, and I just got so excited that we get to see Valentina, and that we're bonding over drag, that I've ignored *my* best friend. Mac, I'm so sorry!"

Above me, I hear Flor mutter softly, "Ummm." She breaks our hug and anxiously runs her fingers through her hair.

From the kitchen, Mikey just looks at me like, *WTF is happening?*

Cammy continues, "I know I can be a bitch sometimes. A lot of times. Believe me, I'm trying. I just have so many things on my mind with all the hours my mom expects me to work and family drama with my sisters and ugh. I don't want to lay this all on y'all. That's not what we're here for. . . ."

Deeply, Cammy sobs again. She's a pretty crier, I think, even with only a half-done face.

"It's okay." Flor stands behind Cammy, then leans over, hugging her from behind.

Flor looks at me and shrugs.

Gently, Cammy weeps into Flor's shoulder, and I don't know whether to throw my arms around Cam or to distrust my eyes, because I know this bitch, she's my best friend, after all, and she might just be delivering an Emmy-worthy performance for Best Fake-Ass Apology to create a distraction and bring all the attention back to herself during a friends group conflict.

Watching Flor, her arms encircling Cammy, I don't think she's buying every single sob Cam's selling. It's hard to tell, and looking over at Mikey, all he's doing is shaking his head while stuffing almonds in his mouth.

So what do I do?

Girl, I hate seeing the people I care about suffer, no matter how shitty they've been to me. Even the doubts I have about Cammy can't change this part of me that wants to fix things and protect people. And so, I walk over to Cammy and put my arms around two of my best friends.

And maybe I'm wrong? Maybe Cammy is pulling a top-tier peak shenanigans stunt and maybe I look stupid af falling más pronto fast for her antics? But what if she's not faking this shit? Cammy never exposes herself the way she is now. Can I really just stand here and watch my so-called bff go through it without offering some type of comfort? If I'm wrong, *I* look like the mega-bitch. Is that really my energy?

Cammy clutches my arm and squeezes me. She squeezes me hard, and I don't know if it's that she wants to hold on to me or if she means this force to be punishing, because as tight as she's grabbing my arm, girl, it hurts. But also, and maybe this matters more, I look over at Flor, who sighs when our eyes lock, because this is all so unexpected and a lot to take in. As much as I wanna see this as a breakthrough and not as a breakdown or a production, I just don't know. Judging by the shrug and the sigh along with the mistrust smearing her face, neither does Flor.

It's a moment, for sure. And with Mikey still in the kitchen, I nod for him to come over, for him to be a part of our moment, which he does, though he hesitates, at first rolling his eyes as he trudges over, then standing beside me and rubbing my shoulder until he finally stretches his arms around both Flor and me and then gives me a face like, *Is this what you want?*

We hug for what feels like a long-ass time. It's hot, and I'm ready to let go, and as Cam sobs a little more, from the corner of my eye I catch a glimpse of him looking at me through the mirror on the table. And, girl. OMG. Girl, Cam smiles. And wtf. I look over to see if Mikey and Flor noticed, but their eyes are elsewhere.

As our group hug concludes, Flor says, "Bitches, look at my paint."

Girl, she's a mess, her one fake eyelash askew, tracks of mascara trickling down her face, her lipstick smudged. And as we all stare at Flor's wrecked paint, laughing off the intensity of the moment, I can't shake the fact that the smile on Cammy's face just a few seconds ago in no way matches the story she's trying to tell. Nope. Not a good lewk.

Mikey puts on Episode 3, and the girls wipe off their faces, because Cleo texted that she was on her way, and "she's gonna need a clean slate," as Flor says. Accordingly, the energy in the room has changed, and I've backed down, determined not to go so hard at Cam, or at Flor.

"Do you think my padding will negatively impact my walk?" Flor asks, giving a *Matrix* af body bend in the high-ass heels Mikey's mom brought for her.

Cam jumps in with a quick and solid, "Fuck no. Body-ody-ody is the era, girl."

Watching Flor and Cam strut, Mikey asks, "Where did you get these shoes, Ma?" He sounds kinda bothered.

"I brought them from work, hijo. They texted me their sizes," Cleo explains from the hallway. Then she says something in their family language and blows Mikey a kiss, which makes Mikey's semi-frown promptly flip upside down and glow.

Clicking her way across the tiles, Flor gives some kinda esoteric-ass Morse code that only the fiercest queens in the world can decipher.

"Babe, I don't know," Cammy says. "I think your walk's still giving too much fashion. We're not in Paris, sis. You're pushing a hot pageant lewk, right? It's coming off . . . inconsistent."

"Inconsistent?" Flor is not pleased.

"Cammy has a point," Cleo agrees.

Flor snatches her phone and frets, and as Cammy showers Cleo with thanks for the shoes and the professional makeup tutorial, Flor low-key whispers to me, "Girl, what was that apology? Do you think she means it?"

"Girl. Who knows?" I certainly don't wanna kick a friend when she's down, but given that smirk I saw earlier, I def have my doubts about Cam's "apology."

"Well, I am kinda living for today," Flor adds.

Now, I don't know exactly why Flor saying that she's "kinda living" irks me, but it does. And on the reals, I kinda wanna remind Flor that didn't she just tell me she was "done" with Cammy and then try to get her disinvited from our little get-together tonight? For a moment, I consider pulling Flor aside and showing her *my* receipts—the messages Cammy sent me about doing our own thing for Valentina and leaving Flor and Mikey out. Would she still be "kinda living" for her cute little paint session with Cam after that? It's tempting af. But girl, what good would that accomplish? Sure, I might feel satisfied momentarily, but do I really wanna watch my bff's happiness turn to drama? I literally tell myself, *Don't be a shady bitch.*

"I don't think Mikey believes her," I whisper.

"I know, right?" Flor nods and returns to practicing her walk through the kitchen, up and down Mikey's hallway and around the couch.

Soon Cammy joins in, and the girls are giving it to Mikey's hallway, each in astronomically high heels that add half a foot to their height. Cam towers over everyone, and even Flor with her petite-ass body looks longer, more elevated. #literally. And girl, they have no trouble maneuvering around in these heels.

"We've done this before," Flor and Cammy say in unison.

I find myself watching Cammy and repeatedly thinking up snarky little reads, like when Cam boasts, "Girl, I'm soooo giving Nicky Doll," and I have to literally bite my tongue so that I don't say, "No, girl. More like Annabelle." And girl, Cam's soooooo concerned about that nose contour, maybe she should focus on contouring that fake-ass personality, too. Seriously. It's like I can't help myself. Like, am I becoming a sour-ass, shady bitch? I feel like I'm going fast from a Basic Becky to a Bitter-Ass Becky, and I don't think this is a good look. No, ma'am. Not for me. Not today. Not ever.

While Cleo sets the wings to marinate before baking them, Flor meticulously studies pageant walks on YouTube, paying attention to every single detail of the detail, and Cam is not playing, asking Cleo like five thousand questions about color-correcting her stubble and highlighting her T-zone along with making angled, "snatched" lewks, as she keeps saying. I nod for Mikey to follow me out back.

"Finally," Mikey says, sliding the patio door shut.

On his patio, I stand with my back to the wall. I put my arms around him and pull him to my chest and fill myself with a deep-ass breath. Now that we're official, I feel like he's mine. Firmly, I put my hands on his back and behind his neck, and I secure his body against me. We kiss. The patio is dim. Night wind brushes through not-so-tall trees in long strokes and short ones, and we'd have to drive out past the city's edges for the stars to see us. In Mikey's eyes, there's a kind of light that I don't know a whole lot about. A kind of light that tries to lay itself on me, not to hold me down or enclose me, no, but to connect, to keep me with him, beside him.

We sit on the bench by the small jungle of tropical plants his mom has assembled on the concrete. I hold his hand. Mikey lays his head against me, and my heart finds its way inside him. We stare at the rooftops and the sky.

Mikey grabs onto knots in my arms and says, "Crazy day, huh?"

I agree. And although I came out here to talk shit, somehow, with Mikey, here, now, that urge goes away, and all I wanna do is be with him, like this, quietly, under the night sky.

"You believe him?" Mikey asks then.

"Cam?"

"Yeah."

"Naw. Maybe. I don't know."

"Well, I don't," he says.

I nod, and Mikey entwines his hand with mine.

For a while, we sit like this. My heart against his back, his breath on my hands because from time to time he'll lift my hand and kiss it. With his free fingers, Mikey draws his three hearts on my chest, and then he rubs the spot above my heart and taps me there, and he says, "Keep them here. Always. Don't ever lose them. Or forget them."

It's sweet af, and I like this a lot about Mikey.

"Of course, pa. Always."

"Good. I really hope so," he tells me.

I could sit with him like this for all the days, I think, and I imagine the two of us as old-ass men, together, how I wanna take care of him and be there for him, cheer him on and help him chase his dreams and never let him down. I pull Mikey closer.

And then, Cleo cracks open the back door, the long yellow shaft of kitchen light scattering the dimness. "Michael? You out here? We're looking for you."

Mikey bites his lip.

"Be right there, Mom," he exhales.

I know we have to go in, yet I kiss Mikey again, and I should've done this sooner. I reach for his waistband, and he lets me put my hand down the back of his shorts and press against him.

"We could . . . you know," I say. "I want to."

Mikey leans in against me. His hand reaches down my shorts. "Oh yeah."

I'm kissing Mikey's ear and behind his neck I taste salt.

He breathes heavily. "You make me feel like I wanna be the only one."

"You are the only one. I promise."

Mikey hangs on me tighter. Listening to him, he sounds softer than usual, and I think maybe being official means something larger than I thought it did to him.

"I want to. So much," I say. "We'll have to plan it. For when it's just us. For when we're alone, for when we have the house to ourselves."

This pleases Mikey, I think, because he kisses me hard on the mouth, and with his thumb, he taps the hairs just beneath my throat, right by the top of my heart.

"Me and you," he says, looking right into my eyes.

"Por vida. Always." I kiss Mikey softly.

He slides open the door, and a few minutes later, once I've gone down, I follow him back inside.

The girls are in full-ass face as Cleo slides two trays of wings in the oven, and bitch, I am gagged. For reals. Walking back into the house, I almost trip, because seriously, Flor and Cam both look stunning af.

"What? 'Ain't you ever seen a princess be a bad bitch?'" Cammy exclaims, quoting "Bad Decisions." Naturally, Flor 110 abso lives for this. Though I can't tell if Cammy's talking about herself or Flor or both, but it's true. #fullfaceslay

While Cleo rushes around the kitchen, Mikey and I set the table without clearing off Cleo's kit, which is a task, girl.

The house smells like hair spray and hot wings, and I'm hungry.

"Mikey, tell me about my walk," Flor says, then stomps across the kitchen in a zigzagging pattern, sidestepping Cleo, who has her hands full.

"It's . . . good," Mikey replies. "I mean, I can see that you're changing it up."

I don't think Mikey has a clue what he's critiquing, though, and neither do I.

Cammy, on the other hand, def has something to say. "Mira. Like I told you, girl. You're giving Sasha Velour when you need to be giving Naysha Lopez. Icónica, girl. Did you even watch those Naysha videos I sent you?"

Flor nods.

"Mija, it's all in the face. First you were too serious. Now you're smiling too much. You need to smile more like you're 'constantly happy,' like the video said. But you're doing better about not looking so constipated . . . or what was the word the lady in the video used? Stoic. And you're still giving too much hip. Watch this."

Cam then demonstrates. Gliding across the floor, she looks like she knows exactly what she's doing. She makes eye contact with us and poses at the end, all while smiling like she has a lithium battery powering all the happiness behind her teeth. "I'm giving Univision weather girl and Miss Universe energy combined," Cam gloats. "OMG, I kinda look like Naysha, right?"

Flor nods unconvincingly.

Disinterested, Mikey turns away and looks at the TV.

But I have to agree with Cammy—she's very effing a lot good at this. And all T, she does kinda resemble Naysha.

Distraught over her walk, Flor sighs and grumbles, which leads Cleo to come over, put her arm around Flor, and say, "Michael, let's show them Lava Walk."

Evidently, Mikey 110 abso loves this idea, because his face lights up like he's swallowed a star. In seconds, Mikey pulls up a YouTube video on the TV.

From the table, surrounded by her instruments and two newborn queens, Cleo starts in, "I'm going to tell you a story about my life back when I was a little girl in the Philippines. I had a friend, who was very close to my heart. We did everything together, and we both wanted to be models."

The house goes quiet af. I love people's stories, and I think Cleo is like super amazing and interesting. Leaning in, Flor and Cam are all eyes and paint.

"All day we would practice posing and walking. We would look at fashion magazines and try to look like the girls in them. We dreamed of walking the runways of the world. My friend's name was Catriona Elisa Magnayon Gray. She was —"

"Miss Universe 2018!" Mikey points to the television, where a gorgeous woman in a red bathing suit, with perfectly long dark hair and legs like Naomi Smalls, walks a runway.

Flor gasps. Like her whole body jerks, and I can hear the breath escape her mouth. Cam is holding a lipstick in her hand like an offering. Her brows arch high, her mouth opening like a doorway.

"Miss Philippines!" the announcer declares. He shares that she is a former martial artist, who earned a black belt at twelve years old. She's twenty-four now and a fashion model and singer, who has raised money for various charities through benefit concerts held in her country and abroad.

"She's beautiful," mumbles Flor, reaching for her notebook.

"Twenty-four years old?" I look over at Cleo. Slowly, I'm doing the math.

"OMG. You're friends with Miss Universe?" Even Cam seems impressed.

Eyes locked reverently on Catriona Gray, Mikey smirks.

"Well . . . no. I just thought it was a great story." Cleo laughs, a fierce, uncontrollable laughter that leaves her coughing for air. "They believed me!" she says to Mikey.

Mikey just looks at his mother. #eyeroll. "She loves telling that story, girl."

"It's my way of grabbing your attention." Cleo exhales. "Okay. I really want you to see this now. Mikey, replay it."

Our eyes zoom in on the screen.

Catriona glides across the catwalk in a sparkly, full-length orange lace and sequined gown with gold cutouts. As Miss Philippines, the soon-to-be-crowned Miss Universe 2018, moves elegantly across the stage, the announcer on the clip tells the television audience how proud Miss Philippines was to renovate an old apartment building in Manila and turn it into a care center that offered free education to children. And this is when Catriona Gray does what only Catriona Gray can do.

"This is Lava Walk." Awe radiates from Mikey's voice.

The video switches to slow-motion mode, and that's when Miss Philippines serves it—girl, a full-on glam catwalk into a slow turn with the most breathtakingly beautiful boss bitch face, followed by a smile that could light up any darkness.

"That's Lava Turn?" Filled with veneration and gaggery, Flor speaks as if she's just witnessed a miracle. "Play it again. Play it again. Please," she urges, stepping back from the table, already practicing the movements. Entranced, Flor's already halfway down the hall when she becomes lava.

"Emulate her face. Look at her eyes," Cleo instructs.

"Mikey, play it again." Now Cam's turning to lava.

Mikey obliges, playing the video about a dozen more times. Each repetition, Flor and Cam carefully study every gesticulation—the smallest shift of the woman's cheek muscles and eye, the way Miss Philippines's body sways perfectly out of the full turn that leads her elbow to rest elegantly on her hip. And that smile. Girl, that smile!

For the next twenty minutes, all Flor and Cam do is practice to perfect their versions of Lava Walk. Up and down the hallway, through the kitchen, in front of the TV and sofa and across the dining room.

Watching the girls live, I still believe I need another convo with Cam about our path forward, especially after that weird-ass smile she gave me, but is tonight really the best night for that? I mean, why f up the vibe? Girl. Still, if we don't address our shit, won't it just come back and bite us all in the ass? But honestly, on the reals, I'm gonna wait, because this gay-ass energy we have right now is the good stuff, and it should be protected at all costs.

Of course, Cleo comes in golden with her bomb-ass wings. We feast. And at the table, Flor and Cam go on and on and on

about the Lava Walk, hair extensions, and the overall fierceness of going to see Valentina's upcoming show. Watching
the girls eat in full face and hair is a lot, and putting aside the
drama and conflicts and doubts, sitting at this table next to
Mikey really does feel kind of exactly like I hoped friendship
with my gay bffs would feel. Girl, we laugh and talk and listen
to Cleo's stories, and it's like the best family dinner I've never
had. #chosenfam #complicatedbutgrateful

Chapter 19

"**A**RE YOU FOR REAL? GIRL. A GREEN LOWRIDER?"
All dolled up for Valentina's show, Flor's checking face
in Mikey's car, and she's doubting me. In the parking garage
two blocks from the Aztec Theatre, we're waiting out the heat
before getting in line for the show, because Flor doesn't wanna
melt. When I told everyone that I heard from a very reliable
source that Valentina and the girls are gonna roll up in a sweet-
ass green lowrider tonight, Flor had questions.

"Well, actually, girl, it's a '64 Impala," I say. "Ragtop. So,
it's a convertible. Looked like some hundred-spoke Daytons.
Lip-lace. Two blade, maybe. Probably twenty inches. And the
paint? Candy green, babe. Metal flake. That means there's
metal chips mixed in with the paint job, so it sparkles."

"Ooh, like sequins?" Inspecting her teeth in the back seat, Flor fans herself.

"Yasssss. Exactly like sequins, girl," Cam quips from the front. "Personally, I just need to see Naysha. People are asking if we're related." Cammy has already pasted herself all over her socials and is scrolling through the comments.

"Oh, girl. Remember you told me to remind you about the tix," Cam says.

"Oh yeah. Gimme a sec, girl." Flor taps her phone, screenshots, sends. "Done."

"So, a car in a gown?" asks Mikey. A remix of "God is a woman" is playing quietly, and Flor subtly lip-syncs to it. Mikey cranks up the AC and tilts his head upward. His brow wrinkles a little, like he's trying to picture an automobile giving evening gown eleganza in downtown San Anto.

"I never thought about it like that," I reply. "I just know people throw their hearts and souls into customizing their rides. The shows have categories, prizes. It's a vibe."

"Ooh, you mean like a car pageant? I love it." Flor seems determined to make a connection she can latch onto.

"Yeah, I guess. Kinda. Sorta."

"I don't know about y'all bitches," Cammy says, "but I can't wait anymore. I'm going down to look and more importantly to be seen. If it's fierce, I'll text y'all to come down. If it's not giving fierce — girl. OMG. What am I saying? I'll be there, so of course it'll be fucking fierce. Bye, bitches!"

Cam gets out and slams her door. Dressed in gold, she

glimmers even in the dull light of the parking garage. She swings a boxy gold-sheen clutch in one hand, and both her arms are adorned with gold bangles. And girl, her shorts are sooooo impossibly tiny-small that it's amazing that I can even call them shorts. And she's tall. With her big-ass Lucite stilettos and the four wigs she's wearing, girl, she towers.

"She'll be back," Flor says. "It's too damn hot. Once the sweat starts soaking through her pads all the way down her crack and thighs, girl. Ughhh. She swears."

"Damn, girl. Tell us how you really feel," Mikey jokes.

"Well, girl. I'm not gonna act all fake. Just so you know. I already told y'all we're only getting along because of drag. You know that. I know that. These wigs know that." Flor flips her long-ass pony, which slaps my chin since I'm in the back seat sitting next to her. "Girl, I guess we just needed something to have in common."

"Like a goal or something," I suggest, removing a strand of hair from my face.

"Right." Flor nods, stroking her ponytail. #bigsurprise #iconicaf #geethanksshejustboughtit. "So, looking fierce for first time in drag was our mutual goal. And goal accomplished, mamas. Besides, it's just a collab. Very transactional. She got me all this luxurious hair, which I can admit is the good stuff, and styled it, and of course, I helped her with those gaudy-ass stripper shoes she wanted and some not-busted accessories. Girl, she wanted to wear her mom's 'gold.' I mean, it'd be cute if it was heirloom, but spray-painted aluminum? Not so much. So, anyways, it worked out for both of us."

Mikey and I nod. They both look fierce. And even though Flor has insisted all week that she's not holding the past against Cam, here we are. And although I'm hopeful that tonight will go off drama-free, on the reals, I'm still kinda stressed that Cammy carries solid beef against me, Mikey, and Flor. After her apology, Cammy pulled one of her little disappearing acts—like, I haven't seen her all week—though she and Flor did go shopping once, and she did come through with the hair. *Maybe* she's letting it go? If that's the case, it's prob a good thing that I didn't force a confrontation. Or maybe she's saving her beef for later, which is a very Cammy thing to do. If that happens, I guess I'll just deal with it when she uses it against me. Either way, I've promised myself not to let tonight revolve about drama and to focus on the real stuff—Mikey and me and seeing Valentina.

Checking her nails, Flor goes on, "So, as for whether or not this lasts, I'm not banking. I hope so. But if *I* get more attention tonight? Girl. We'll see how she takes that. Just like that quote in Mr. V's classroom, the true measure of a person is how you act in times of controversy and challenge. Mm-hmmm. Girl. All T, though. She looks fierce. I've no problem saying that. All T. I do look fiercer." Raising her hand above her hair, Flor snaps twice.

"Werk," Mikey cheers. "You better live, hunny!"

The car fills with our gay-ass noise, and reaching up front, I grab onto Mikey's shoulders and squeeze. At the gym earlier, I promised myself that no matter what, I'd learn from my prior mistakes—the official focus of my night will be spending time with my boyfriend, on this, our official first time going out to a big event together. Mikey got us these tropical-looking button-ups with matching palm trees all over them, and so, I'm 110 kind of very a lot living for his cariño. Mikey really is a sweetheart.

"Babe, anything from Cam?" Mikey asks.

I check my phone. "Nope. Maybe we should just go down?"

"Give her another five minutes," Flor suggests.

"So, back to the lowriders. How do you know all this car stuff?" Mikey asks. My palms on his shoulders, he puts his hands on my hands and smiles at me through the rearview.

"My dad. He was really into lowriders. He would take B and me to car shows when we were younger. He'd pick up all the magazines. It was his thing. And then, at work, Rebecca told me her cousin's neighbor's friend is renting out his ride for some drag queens. So, two and two, babe. Valentina's in town. This car. Who else could it be?"

"Girl, you don't think that's kinda . . . stereotypical?" Flor says. "I mean, Valentina's very classy. Is this really her brand?"

I almost break my neck looking at Flor. Girl. Is she for reals?

Seeing my aggravation, Mikey gives me the *go easy on her* look, and I take a breath.

"Ummm, lowriders are like the epitome of street class. Just because you don't understand the aesthetic doesn't make it not fierce. And yeah, girl, maybe they are stereotypical. But people say doing drag is stereotypical gay-ass behavior or that drag queens are ruining society, when we know that it's fierce and affirming and gorgeously extra and glorious af, so, yeah,

110 I abso support lowriders *and* drag queens. It's giving."

Maybe I've gone a little harder than I intended. Flor looks like she's just gotten too close to a hot-ass stove. "I know, girl," she says. "I know. I'm sorry. I guess that does sound really shitty and snobby and ugh. So cringe. Sorry."

"It's fine. I'm just saying, other people's fierceness is just as valid as yours, girl. Anyways, I'm thinking we should start heading down. I don't wanna miss when Valentina and the girls show up in that green-ass Impala."

Glancing at my phone, I text Cam: WYA?

No response.

"Babe, we have time. Remember, we're staying in the AC as long as we can so we don't melt," Mikey replies.

He's right. It's like a hundred-plus degrees outside. July in Texas. Girl. I can't even imagine if I was the one in full paint and body-ody-ody, and it makes perfect sense why Flor decided to do two looks tonight—swimsuit competition realness for waiting in line and then a super-quick trip back to Mikey's car to change into Cleo's gorgeous vintage white-sequined gown for the show itself. If we're gonna pull this off, the timing will have to be flawless.

Finally, we make our way down to the Aztec Theatre. Now, girl. I effing love my city. I love the river and the brisket and Fiesta every April and the parades and cascarones, the Spurs and menudo and barbacoa with Big Red and all of it . . . except the heat! Girl, whenever my tía says she doesn't remember it ever being this hot when she was little, I believe her. Tonight, even with the sun setting, it's giving climate change realness.

Whereas I'm huffing and puffing, literally trying to push my way through all the heat, Flor marches on, seemingly undaunted. Girl. She is 110 abso giving it to us in her one-shoulder, cutout-midriff fuchsia pageant swimsuit, nude pump, and glittery title sash ensemble. With every step Flor takes, that dark and sultry, sculpted-ass high pony bounces, adding a whole other foot to her dimensions. The sash Mikey made her, which she proudly wears across her bosom, reads MISS TEEN SINALOA, and as we approach the long-ass line that's formed in front of the Aztec, we start to hear the cheers.

"Come on, Miss Teen Sinaloa!"

"Ay, perra!!! Aquí viene Sinaloa!"

"Ladies and gentlemen, for your consideration . . . Miss Teen Sinaloa!"

As we walk, I can't tell who's yelling these gems at Flor, but Flor is living, like A-game confidence and constant happiness.

"Sinaloa. It's the state in Mexico where my mom grew up," Flor tells a woman with a fancy-ass camera, then swings her high-ass pony a full 360 degrees and pops into one of the many pageant poses she's been perfecting all week.

Standing to the side, Mikey grabs my hand tightly. "She's made for this," he says.

I nod, and girl, it really is a moment seeing someone you care about find that thing that life, in all its fierceness, made just for them.

Up near the middle of the line, Mikey spots Cammy. I mean, she's so tall and golden and surrounded by adoring fans, how could we *not* see her?

"Let's keep moving. We gotta catch up to Cam," Mikey tells Flor, who reluctantly waves goodbye to the small crowd assembling around her.

"Bitch, I'm already turning to water," Flor complains. "Girl, these pads are soaked. How's my hair?"

"It's all good," Mikey assures her, and when he does, it strikes me as funny that now we are both looking up at Flor instead of the other way around. I take the BIEN PRETTY fan from Mikey's back pocket and vigorously fan Flor as we make our way toward Cam.

"I'm afraid to smear my face," Flor whispers.

"Just dab." Mikey passes Flor a tissue from his front pocket. "My mom gave me these to give you. And she said to tell you to remember, setting powder is your friend."

Now I kinda melt too, because girl, the thought of Mikey and his mom collabing to take care of Flor really serves me.

When we reach Cam, in her loudest voice, she screams, "Well, it's about fucking time! Girl!! Aaaaaaaaaaaaaaa!!!!!" Cam stomps in her heels and throws her giant hair backward so far that she almost whips bystanders. Her bangles jangle. Her ass bounces. She drops and pops and bucks, calling all eyes to her. Girl, she's giving first lady of the street, and the crowd is here for it.

Next to her, Flor poses. Majestic, statuesque, snatched. Like, girl. They really are the yin and the yang. As I relentlessly fan Flor and Cammy, who kiki with a bunch of queens who're showering them with compliments, I think of all the nights in my life so far and all the ones to come, and I can already tell this is gonna be one of the great ones. Unfortunately, though, due to all my robust fanning paired with my biceps and back workout earlier today, girl, my arms ache, and eventually, I just have to pass the fan over to Mikey, because #musclefatiguegirl #therealness.

As Mikey fans, he strikes up a convo with any and everyone. He has two fingers hooked onto my belt loop, and when anyone bumps me and I move, he moves with me.

"This is my boyfriend, Mac," Mikey tells a couple of guys who go on and on about DJs and beach parties, a language Mikey is clearly fluent in, and although I don't have much to say, I feel good here next to Mikey, proud that we're together. Every now and then, Mikey reaches over and grabs on my arms, and I flex for him a little, which he loves. And whenever he gets close enough, I kiss Mikey's cheek or the back side of his neck, and I wipe away his sweat with the small white towel tucked into the back of my waistband, which I've brought exactly for this reason, and sometimes, when nobody's looking, I grab Mikey's ass and whisper in his ear, "Mine."

If this kind of happiness is what living your best life can feel like, then we're doing it right, and even though the heat is brutal af, and I have sweat rolling down my nalgas, I kinda don't want tonight to end.

"I was just telling my hubby, 'Bitch, either that's Jennifer Lopez's daughter or it's Naysha, because girl, she is sickeningly gorgeous,'" a muscle queen in a Trixie cutoff says to Mikey. "I soooo was convinced she was one of them or both."

Mikey introduces Cammy, and needless to say, Cam feasts

on this commentary. "I get that all the time. We could be sisters, me and Naysha. I mean, I am the one and only Verónica Lopez," Cam says, posing, tossing her hair, extending her long-ass legs like they have all the business.

"Love your hair. Hope it wins," a big girl in a red leather crown remarks, blowing Flor a kiss as she walks by.

This gives Flor joy, and I hold her hand. Covered in sparkles, her arms make me think she's caught a thousand falling stars, and girl, she's keeping all of them.

The energy in the crowd suddenly heightens, and a cheer spreads through the whole line. Mikey leans in and grabs my arm. "Babe, they're here!" He points frantically down the street. Everyone around us gags, because rounding the corner, we can see it—just like Rebecca and I predicted—a candy-ass metal-flake green af 1964 drop-top Impala filled with fierce-ass drag queens. Girl, so what if the car's two blocks away? I see big-ass wigs and sequins. It is undeniable, girl.

"Where's Valentina? I don't see Valentina." Flor squints.

As the car approaches, the queens come into sharper focus. They have their music turned way up, and it's a song we all recognize.

"Giving Doja!" Cam screams. "Okurrrrrrrrrrrrr!! Now, that's what I'm fucking saying!"

"Is that Mistress? Driving?" someone behind me gasps.

As the car gets even closer, it's clear that Houston's very own Mistress Isabelle Brooks is one-handing the wheel, doing her world-famous titty pump as she maneuvers through the downtown buildings, and next to Mistress, girl—Vanjie and

EsTitties up front. And posing in the back seat like a high pantheon of chola goddesses, Angeria, Anetra, and Cam's icon, inspiration, and self-proclaimed "twin," the incomparable Naysha Lopez.

The crowd howls excitement and adulation, and while the crowd fixes their eyes on the queens slow-cruising our way, I press into Mikey, my arm around his waist.

"Werrrrk! You better walk that fucking duck!!!" Mikey screams at the car.

I hear Flor living her life too.

But girl, Cammy has gone quiet as a coin. And when the loudest bitch on the street goes quiet, you know something's up. I turn to look at her, and I can tell that she's staring directly at Naysha. Cammy is awestruck, starstruck, struck by the sacred lightning of bearing witness to the kinda overwhelming and stunning beauty you want for yourself.

I squeeze up beside Cam and place my hand on her back and say, "Girl. That could be you. In that car."

I say it because it's true.

I say it because words aren't happening to Cammy's mouth, and girl, words are always happening to Cammy's mouth.

I say it because I know her, and because it's there, that possibility inside Cammy's stare.

Mouth open, Cammy starts to say something, but it's loud everywhere around us, and she can't finish.

I grab onto her hand.

Leaning toward me, Cammy squeezes my fingers and asks, "You think?"

"Girl, I *know*."

For part of a millisecond, I see Cammy almost feel all the feelings. And babe, Cam never succumbs to these kinda things. With a bubble in her throat, she swiftly shakes off the feels and nods my way. She puts her bangled arm behind me and holds me a little, and I begin to understand, perhaps more than ever, that beneath the hard-ass veneer my bff puts up, there's a softness no one is ever supposed to see, except maybe, in small glimpses, me. And I'm glad I'm here for it. And I'm glad we've made it this far as bffs, that we haven't given up, no matter the conflicts, the jealousies, the chaos that she—and well, to be honest, sometimes I—bring, because I realize that as much as I'm willing to point out Cammy's chaos, girl, I also need to check my ass and fix my own.

Gradually, Mistress rolls up, and girl, this car is everything and soooo much more. On the hood, an exquisite airbrushed mural. Azteca realness, girl. Backdrop of two Mexican volca-noes and the forbidden lovers—the warrior Popocatépetl and the sleeping princesa Iztaccíhuatl—from the old stories my tío Robert told B and me when we were little.

"Where's Valentina? I don't see Valentina." Concern fills Flor's voice.

Mikey shrugs. "Maybe she's already inside?"

And then, girl. Mistress gives it and sticks the switches, just like I hoped she would. Girl, #hydraulics #alltherealness. In three swift movements, the car rises, drops down, and hops. Girl. A bouncy-ass green sparkling lowrider full of fierce-ass chola drag queens right in front of the illuminated red and green marquee of the Aztec. #tonightsadgirl #atthelogsgirl #purosananto

Right when we expect Mistress to roll to a complete stop in front of the theater for the queens to exit, Mistress cruises on by us, and we're all left thinking, *WTF? Where are they going? What's happening?*

The crowd starts to chant: "Bring back our girls! Bring back our girls!"

"Where's Valentina?!" a queen with overplucked eyebrows yells right in my ear.

"She's getting a Big Red and a corn cup!" someone else answers.

Soon the magnificent chrome grill peeks around the street corner, and it becomes 110 evident that Mistress has circled the block and is headed right back our way. The crowd loses its effing mind. Including me. And I never get rowdy-ass and scream my culo off, but girl. Okay. Let me explain. When Mistress makes the full turn, on the glimmering candy-green metal-flake hood, in full-ass Azteca regalia—quasi-quetzal feathers, obsidian, gold—is the queen of gay Aztlán herself, our Valentina.

Flor murmurs, "No words, girl. I have no words."

I can't take my eyes off Valentina. #Rule2

"What song is that?" I ask.

"Amor a la Mexicana," Cam answers. "It's one of my mom's favorites." She powders her cheeks and forehead. "Okay, girl. Watch this." Squeezing her way through the crowd, Cam doesn't look back. People part for Cam, stepping aside for her gold.

I feel mesmerized. Enthralled, captivated. It's a lot, and I have my arms around Mikey, and he's recording Valentina giving it to downtown San Anto atop the glistering car hood. Smiling perfectly, her hair that red auburn color that my tía Ruby loves, only better, more expensive-looking and without three inches of black roots showing, Valentina surpasses each and every expectation I had for what she'd be. Girl, we're gonna need to revise the rules, because after witnessing Valentina's beauty firsthand, Rule #2 does her little justice.

With the car proceeding toward the Aztec, two lines of security have assembled near the entrance. Flor gets this intense, determined af gleam in her eye, and she says, "Girl, come with me."

With that, she hands me her phone, and she runs. Yes, bitch, she runs. In six-inch pumps, a sash, a fuchsia swimsuit, and ten pounds of hair. Across the street, tugging me behind her. Looking both ways, of course.

"Why are we running across the street?!" I cry.

But trust. That beautiful little bitch times it perfectly, because as soon as Valentina's people step out onto the street for her to exit the car, as soon as they use their arms and bodies to keep back the crowd, Flor urges me, "Do it, girl. Call her! Call her!"

So I do.

"Valentina!!!!!" With every ounce of oxygen in my two lungs, I yell. I yell as loud as all the love in my heart for Ariana Grande and Valentina and Flor and Mikey and Kimber and for B and for Cam, yes, for Cam. I yell for every boy like me in

America and all over the world who just wants those few seconds to meet somebody they adore.

And girl, it's like destiny. When Valentina looks up, there's only a fraction of a moment, a nanosecond, if that, for Flor to grab la reina's attention, and girl, she does. With every molecule of eleganza in her petite-ass little stilettoed body, with every thread of spandex sewn into her swimwear, with every fiber of that heavy-ass forty-inch hair, Flor steps onto the street, and she walks.

Girl, she walks.

OMG. Like all the gods and every diva up in drag heaven are all watching, Flor stomps that asphalt like it's the Miss Teen Universe runway. Flor stops traffic, and the gays on the sidewalk have all eyes on her, but the only set of eyes that matter are standing in front of a candy-green carload of the world's fiercest queens, and they're watching too, and girl, knowing that Valentina has seen her, knowing that this is her moment, Flor werrrrrrrks.

Long steps. Natural, elegant. The epic slow-mo turn. Hair that spins like the eighth wonder of the world. Flor is giving lava, and the crowd gasps. Girl, it's audible. They can probably hear it in Houston and Austin and Dallas and maybe even Corpus Christi and El Paso. And in the moment of this collective gasp that stops the world, girl, Flor just walks up to Valentina, who by this point, is so intrigued that she steps away from the green lowrider and into the street to meet this girl wearing a Miss Teen Sinaloa pageant sash.

"Yes, girl!!!" Valentina's voice climbs with the power of a thousand Mexican trumpets.

Standing with her idol, Flor proclaims, "You are more beautiful than I could ever imagine."

In the very middle of the street, Valentina reaches out and takes Flor's hand.

"Thank you, mi amor. You are beautiful too."

And, girl, Valentina runs her hand, her perfectly manicured hand, against Flor's sash.

"Miss Teen Sinaloa. I love it!" Valentina exclaims.

"It's where I'm from."

"Orgullo, girl. Yes, ma'am. I get it."

Light from streetlamps, the headlights of stopped traffic, and the green light that the cars ignore falls over the two of them, because the road is a stage for these few moments, for Valentina and Flor.

"I almost forgot to introduce myself," Flor confesses. "I'm Flor. And it's a dream come true to meet you."

They smile. The kind of smiles that reminds you that yes, ma'am, God made drag queens. The kind of smile that sells toothpaste and makes you wanna go to the dentist, too.

Flor reaches underneath her sash, into her swimwear, and takes out an envelope.

Girl.

"I wrote this for you earlier this year for one of my classes." Flor unfolds the white envelope. "My friends and I . . ." And right here, underneath all the Texas stars and with cars honking, Flor gives that brave smile and points to me and to Mikey on the other side of the street and to Cam, who's gagging in front of the theater marquee, blocked by the line of security.

And on Cam's face, it isn't joy. No, girl. Cam stares right at me, and all I see on her face is a look of utter betrayal.

Flor continues, "We're only friends because I wrote this letter and read it in class. It's about how much I love you and admire you and how we all should find what we love and do it. Valentina, you brought us together. You changed my life. I love you. I love you. I love you so much."

Tenderly, Valentina clutches the envelope. In Valentina's exceptionally manicured hand, Flor's truth gleams. And in the middle of St. Mary's Street, in front of the Aztec marquee, sharing a space in her heart with Valentina, Flor isn't just some baby queen in the diva-everything presence of a beloved international celebrity, no, Flor isn't gagging or starstruck or losing herself in this moment. Girl, Flor's smiling like the only breath she needs is the breath right now. And maybe it's the fierceness of being filled by life's magic, maybe it's the joy of taking in so much iconic beauty all at once, maybe it's that she's simply out of breath, because girl, stomping that ferociously on asphalt in those big-ass heels after standing on your feet on concrete waiting in line cannot be easy on the body. Whatever it is, Flor proves that some nights, life just changes us. Some nights, there won't be any going back, because we are exactly who and where and how we are meant to be.

Chapter 20

"**G**IRL, C'MON. WE GOTTA GET FLOR CHANGED," I urge Cam, who, caressing the massive gold shrimpee earring dangling from her left ear, pretends she doesn't hear me as we're both standing right next to each other in front of the theater.

I try again. "We gotta go. We're supposed to help Flor change."

From across the street, Mikey and Flor watch. I can feel their eyes. Girl, #urgency #wtf

The line of people waiting for the show is flooding into the building. Girl, these bitches are zealous af, and they wanna eat, which after all the thrilling sensation of the build-up, not to mention the intolerable Texas heat, I can sooooo relate to. And it's obvi af that we don't have long—girl, thirty minutes, maybe—to execute this costume change before the show starts. Girl, it's not a lot of time, so I don't get why Cammy's not with me on this. Seriously, we planned this shit out.

"Excuse me," Cam utters to the bougie queen she's talking to. Glancing over at Flor and Mikey idling across the street, Cam doesn't even look at me when she says it. "Change of plans, girl. I think I'm gonna stay down here. She'll be fine." Cammy finally deigns to look at me, anger and hurt flickering in her eyes.

"Girl, what's wrong?" I ask. Truly, I'm bewildered. We've all been living our best lives tonight.

"Did you and Flor plan all that behind my back?"

"Plan what?"

"Oh my gawd, girl. Don't. That! Racing out into the street together, hand in hand, so you could meet Valentina! Without me!"

Instantly, I think, *Here it comes*, what I truly, honestly, with all my heart thought we could avoid—drama at a drag show.

Mikey jogs over to my side, and with a hand on my back, he says, "What's the problem? We're wasting time."

Ignoring us, Cam turns to the side, giving us her back.

"She's not coming," I inform Flor as soon as she can hear me.

For a moment, I think Flor's gagged, but then she rolls her eyes so hard I think they're gonna get tangled in all that opulent, luxurious hair. "Big surprise."

We start racing back to the parking garage, and after a few yards, Flor's struggling to keep up, because heels, because humanity, because heavy-ass hair.

Mikey tells her, "Stop. Here, gimme your shoes."

"I'm not going to walk barefoot! F-word gross!" Flor isn't having it, but she also can't run in these heels.

"Girl, we won't make it. Give me your shoes. Mac can carry you!"

Girl.

"Girl, what are you waiting for? Every second counts!" Mikey barks, dropping to his knees in front of Flor, who, by this time, desperately kicks off her heels into Mikey's awaiting palms.

And I'm like, Okay. Giddyup, girl. Transporting Flor on my back, I'm realizing that all those years of ridiculous-ass lunges and squats we did in baseball, in and off-season, actually serve a purpose—besides giving me a big ass and thick thighs—girl, collectively, they have prepared me for this moment, the moment where I come through and carry my 128-pound bff (extra poundage added for hair) across two downtown inter-sections, up three flights of parking garage stairs, and straight to Mikey's car and her evening gown pageant eleganza destiny.

"Can you believe I met her?! OMG! OMG! OMG! I can't believe I met her! Valentina talked to me! She took my letter!!!" Flor squeals when we finally make it to the car.

Overwhelmed with all the feelings, Flor hands me her sash.

Whipping her ponytail ecstatically, she screeches, "Girl, she knows my name!"

For a minute, we sit with the AC going hard, screaming our asses off, Flor taking deep, steady breaths to compose her-self. It's kinda f-word amazing. Okay, no. It's a lot very f-word amazing!!! Girl, I was like eighteen feet from Valentina! Like,

Valentina actually heard my voice and looked right at me when Flor pointed me out! And girl! My bff actually talked to her, like they had a real-ass conversation, and Valentina said her name! I feel like I just witnessed a modern gay miracle, and because of that, my heart's on fire, girl.

Once we get Flor into her evening look, we hustle back to the Aztec. We're sweaty and outta breath and determined af to take our seats and enjoy this show.

Girl, it's a lot, and it's a moment. Each gay-ass molecule in my body is singing its anthem of an Ariana Grande medley, which is the fierce-ass opening number performed by Angeria, who's letting every seat in the theater have it, girl.

Because we're late, the ushers make us wait at the top of the aisle before taking our seats, which I'm not gonna complain about because girl, from where I'm standing, Angeria is giving me all the Ariana I need right now . . . until two weeks from now when we go to the Ariana concert, which takes me to Cam. Looking around, I see her, having taken her seat alone, looking just a little bit golden in all the darkness, three empty seats surrounding her.

"Excuse me. I'm sorry to bother, but are you Flor?" asks a woman dressed in a black suit and carrying a walkie.

"Yes."

"There's an invitation. From the cast. Apparently, you shared a letter with one of the cast members, and after reading your letter, they'd like to invite you and your guests to sit in one of the VIP balcony boxes."

Girl, cue the gagging. Flor doesn't even have to ask.

In unison, Mikey, Flor, and I respond, "Yesss!!!"

"Miss, we have one more friend—" I start to say to the lady. And then I think about how Cammy chose to ignore me and literally turned her back on me. "You know what, it's fine. We'll find her after the show."

We find ourselves whisked away, ascending red velvet stairs to an ornate private box that gives a stunning balcony view overlooking the entire Aztec along with an unparalleled view of center stage. The only better view in the house is maybe God's and all the drag angels' up in heaven.

Walking up the stairs, I grab Mikey's hand.

Elaborate and vibrant paintings grace the theater walls, reminding me of images in museums and fancy-ass history books. I think Cam would love this moment and would prob want to stop and take a hundred thousand selfies on our way to the VIP box. But I put a stop to these feelings right away.

"Girl, use the railing," Flor instructs, as she wobbles a little making her way in front of us.

Below, the audience rambunctiously cheers for the next performer. "Miss Vanjie! Miss Vanjie! Miss Vanjie!!" We pause to watch Miss Vanjie pop off a fast-and-furious dance number, the stage a sea of crisp hair flips, high kicks, and dips.

"Who'd have thought when you read that letter in Mr. V's . . . ," I say to Flor. "And now, all this!"

Flor glows, and Mikey shows me all the light in his eyes, and it's something real and unreal all at once, and I never want that light to dim. I realize that maybe this is the night that I'll invite him to spend the night together.

When we reach the private box, we find it occupied by a gaggle of drag queens, some of whom I think I recognize from Pride and from flyers I've seen online. Before she leaves, the woman in the fancy suit tells us to make ourselves at home. She points out some waters and sodas and light hors d'oeuvres and a private powder room just for us. "And if you need anything," she says, "let me introduce you to one of the hosts."

She motions for a tall woman with enormous blond hair and giant boobs and a gown that looks like it's been cut from nopales or emeralds, maybe both. Girl, her hair really is a colossus. Girl, like her bangs even have bangs! And her hair is sooo feathered, it's on the verge of flying off this balcony!

"Hola! I'm Elizabitch."

It's the West Side glamazon who lessoned me up at Target.

"I remember you. From Target," I say.

"And I remember you. Mijo, how are you?"

"Living my best life," I reply as Elizabitch reaches over to hug me, which is both true and untrue because as much fierceness as this night is giving me, I can't shake the thought that Cam is missing out on something special and fierce, a core friends group memory, girl, that for years on end will give us all life.

Behind us, the crowd's 110 abso living for Anetra. Girl, they are shaking the air!

"You must be Flor, the writer," Elizabitch says.

Flor nods.

"Ahhhh, Miss Teen Sinaloa." A queen who introduces herself as Kelli leans in, double-kisses Flor's cheeks. "Girl, you're quite the topic of conversation tonight."

Flor smiles, running her fingers through her hair.

"I love your gown. And that sash!" Elizabitch gasps. "Here, lemme touch it, girl, so I don't give it ojo."

Humorously, Elizabitch grabs for Flor's sash to protect it from her "evil eye," making Mikey, Kelli, and me laugh.

While Flor talks with the queens, Mikey and I take our seats to watch Anetra, who, girl. Girl. Girrrrrrlllllll!!! #neongreencatsuitracingrealness #bossbitchenergy #allboots-girl. She is giving the floor a fierce-ass pounding, girl. Ughhh. I think that floor's gonna be sore.

Understandably, Mikey's a major fan, because Anetra's high-energy dance vibe is totally his vibe, and she gives proud Filipino heritage, too. Girl, connection and respect and love.

Once Anetra is done, Mikey and I attack the food table. We race back to our seats to prepare for the next performer. It's Naysha. And obvi, I know Cammy would abso 110 live for the chance to watch Naysha and kiki with all the queens in the VIP box. But girl. To quote the wise and beautiful Tati, "Girl, choices." #accountability

Naysha opens with a ballad, and the whole house goes quiet as silk.

Girl, she's marvelous. Holding the entire theater in her palm, she rivets us with a breathtaking performance and a sapphire-colored gown.

Watching Naysha, I keep thinking of Cam. It was kind of a lot very rash of me not to ask the lady to grab Cammy before we came to the VIP section. The show has only just started, so I'm sure I could ask Elizabitch for help. I lean forward in my seat to look for Cam in the crowd. And when I spot her, girl. She's already filled our seats, like she f-word gave our seats away. I check my phone to see if she texted to ask where we were, but nothing. And now she's kiki'ing and having a fierce time without us. Without me. Any guilt I have about not inviting her to the VIP section evaporates.

Just then, Elizabitch and the woman in the black suit with the walkie approach us. The woman says to Flor, "Valentina would like a word with you."

Flor's thrilled and asks, "May my friends come too?"

Elizabitch interjects, "Girl, this ain't a meet and greet. She's only asking to talk to you."

That's totally fair, and I'm just grateful my bff thought to invite me.

Justifiably, excitement overcomes Flor—I mean, girl, she's getting a one-on-one with her idol—and she can't stop smiling or grabbing at her not-as-styled-as-before ponytail. "OMG. How do I look? My face? Girl, tell me. Mac, where's my clutch?"

Seeing Flor's unease, Elizabitch intervenes. "Mija, chill. Ven. Why don't we just step back here into the powder room? Touch you up a bit. You know, before you go onstage."

"Onstage?" Flor gasps.

"Yes, mija. Valentina's gonna do her solo numbers, and when she's done singing, she's going to read a part of your letter to the audience, and then she's gonna call you up onstage with her. Pa' que sepas, girl."

Flor stands and lets Elizabitch lead her to the powder room. Just before she leaves, she turns back. Her eyes are wide and glistening, and I can tell that she's both stunned and mentally preparing for the moment.

"Good luck!" Mikey yells.

Flor blows a kiss our way.

After intermission, with the house lights coming down, Kelli stands next to Mikey to tell us, "Papi, this is it. Valentina's coming on."

When Valentina walks onto the stage, a single spotlight awaits.

The spotlight gags at Valentina's beauty—a vision in red—and so does the curtain.

At the microphone, Valentina stands silently. And time stands very still in the Aztec.

We're waiting, and Valentina is giving.

Finally, she speaks. "Earlier tonight, outside, in front of this theater—and what a magnificent theater this is . . ."

The crowd cheers.

"Earlier tonight, I was given a letter. By a fan. No, not just a fan, by an icon and a hero. Yes, I think that's more accurate. Right now, in the world, girl—they are coming for people like us. Not for the colors of our dresses or the ways we wear our hair. No, girl. Some people in this world would like to see us erased, because they are afraid that if the world accepts us, then somehow they lose something they believe belongs to them and only them. But girl, this is America, and she belongs to all of us."

Girl, the crowd roars with this statement, and I'm nodding and gripping Mikey's hand.

"And so, when I read this letter earlier tonight, it made me think of bravery and truth and hope and love, yes, love, definitely love, and fierceness, girl, yes, fierceness, which are all things the world needs right about now. All the things that make our lives . . . our lives. I'm telling you this young person who wrote this letter and shared it with me, girl, she's giving me the full French Vanilla Fantasy! Because this letter is hope and it is love and it is truth, girl. And so, tonight, with you, and for you, I dedicate this next song to all the flores of the world, and to you, Flor, mi amor, my new friend, my hero, my icon."

I can feel Mikey choking up, like all the feels inside him are about to gush out.

I get it, because I feel it too.

And then Valentina sings.

And girl, it's fierce, and it's hope she has pirouetting inside her voice, the kinda hope that's built on the need just to be, to live our lives, to belong, just as we are, without apologies, without shame, without fear of retribution or violence. Listening to Valentina's song, I can't help but hold on to Mikey as tight as I can, and I bury my face in the muscles of his back, and I'm breathing into the back side of his heart, because we're together now, and I think also I might be on the verge of losing a friend, which I know is probably a good thing, but it still hurts, and so, I'm feeling all the feelings.

And when the song is closing, Valentina's voice resonates in the muscles of my hands, and I think I need more nights like this one, more songs and rhinestones and new friendships and lowriders filled with drag queens and love.

After bowing, Valentina calls Flor from the wings of the stage to stand with her.

Girl, there's 110 abso no other way to say this: Flor is stunning af.

Under the spotlight, Flor's gown is a galaxy all its own. A swath of night sky where all the light finds a place to call its own. As Valentina hands Flor the microphone, Flor looks up over the crowd and says, "Hi, I'm Flor. And first of all, for those of you who are wondering, I'm not really Miss Teen Sinaloa. But I want to be. . . ."

The crowd laughs.

"I needed to clarify. Because truth matters, hunny. But I love pageants, and so, being Miss Teen Sinaloa is *my* French Vanilla Fantasy."

Tossing her head back and laughing, Valentina enjoys this reference.

Flor turns to her idol. "Valentina, you are an inspiration to me. Living your life on your own terms, the way you believe you deserve to live it, it makes me want to live my life more authentically, honestly, and fiercely. And because of this letter, which I read in front of my eleventh-grade English class earlier this summer, I made new friendships, friendships that I believe will last a lifetime. And so, I take this moment to thank you, Valentina, for showing me how fierce life can be and also to thank my best friends Mac and Mikey, who are seated up in the VIP section. Thank you. Thank you. Thank you so much."

The audience applauds. And girl, when Flor acknowledges

Mikey and me, she points right up at the balcony box, and the whole audience turns to look at us.

All I can think is, *She didn't say Cam*, and I guess I say it out loud, too, because Mikey replies, "Good. Why would she?"

Instantly, my eyes move down to where Cam's sitting, and I see her. Mouth dropped, livid, she's staring directly at me.

Chapter 21

AFTER THE SHOW, WE HEAD FOR THE EXIT. People swarm Flor so that Elizabitch and Kelli have to help steer us out of the theater.

Outside, the city street and the symphony of headlights and horns.

Under the downtown sky, Flor takes a few pics with Elizabitch and Kelli and then with Mikey and me.

The three of them step aside, Flor taking a private moment with Elizabitch and Kelli.

And while I give Flor her space, Mikey says, "Look who it is."

It's Cam. She's walking directly toward us, talking to some guy I've never seen before. Dyed blond, his hair cuts across and back, like it's supposed to look organized yet chaotic at once.

I keep waiting for them to change course, but Cammy bumps Mikey hard af, and Mikey ends up on the ground.

"Girl! What the fuck!" Mikey yells.

"Oh, woooow. Didn't see her," Cam taunts, and the guy next to her laughs.

I help Mikey up off the ground.

"Babe, you okay?"

Brushing himself off, he nods.

The glow of the streetlights marks our faces with shadows. Around us, people gawk.

"Ughhhh. These are them?" Cammy's new friend sneers. "Girl. Can you just scream basic hoodrat realness, mamaws?"

I'm disgusted that Cammy pushed Mikey, and I hate that this guy who I don't even know is making fun of us.

"Girl, they're a 'couple,'" Cam tells his friend, doing air quotes around "couple."

Now Mikey's tugging on my arm, urging me, "Let's just go. Just leave it. Baby, let's go."

"Of course. 'A couple'!" the blondish guy jeers. "Riiiiiight."

Girl, Cam's being messy, and I give him the shittiest look.

By this point, I'm over it. I don't think I would ever knock the shit outta Cammy, but girl, right now, that's all I can think of doing, and it's obvi af, I'm sure, because quickly, Mikey throws his arm around my chest, and Flor's suddenly beside me and grabs my hand.

"Baby, let's go. She's not worth it."

Mikey and Flor are pulling on me, and I let myself be led away.

"Don't even bother, babes," Flor says to me. "She's fucking trash!" And girl, I'm gagged, because Flor never uses language like that.

I'm so beyond pissed, I can't help but turn back. "Girl, you're the fucking villain! Go back to Mess City where you belong!" I yell. It comes out crooked. Nowhere as fierce as I want.

I see Cammy race toward me, stomping in her high-ass heels and throwing her water bottle, which hits me on the side of my head. "I'm the mess? Stupid bitch, you're the fucking mess! Leaving me out again and again, and lying to me, swearing they weren't trying to turn you against me!"

I break free of Mikey's and Flor's grip. "You're the one who turned me against you, Cam! I'm tired of your shit!"

Cam freezes for a second like she doesn't know what to say but quickly recovers. "You think you and your boyfriend are so fierce? Girl, just like I said, he's not gonna be loyal to somebody like you!" Cammy smirks like she won some dumb-ass prize. She turns to her "friend" and starts in, "What do you think, sis? Give it a week? Two weeks?"

Cam's new friend stares at Mikey and then at me. "Less than a month, for sure. They won't last."

My heart punches itself in the face, and I look over at Mikey, who says, "She's trying to push your buttons, baby. Just go."

Unfortunately, it's working.

"Sis, they sooooo weren't my real friends," Cammy says loudly, and more people have stopped to watch the commotion.

"They're so fake! Literally the Fake Bitches Club. OMG. Especially the little one. Girl. Swearing!"

Cam and her friend are now leaning against one another, cackling. Both of them, loud and shit-talking and obnoxious af, snapping their fingers and grinning triumphantly, like they're having the time of their lives. I've seen Cammy like this before, but I've never been the target.

"What the fuck's wrong with you?" Mikey barks. "Bitch, I never liked you, but he gave you chances. He defended you. He was your friend."

"Girl, please. Calm down, sweetie. You want some water?" Cam points at the puddle on the sidewalk.

My eyes are fixed on Cam, and I wanna stuff a rag in that shit-talking mouth.

Grabbing onto me again, Mikey pleads, "Chill, baby. It's not worth it. Come on."

Mikey's pulling on my arm pretty hard, and even though I'm super-beyond gagged by how Cam and this random guy are wrecking our night, I tell myself, *Hold it together. Don't lose it.*

But then Cam takes a step right toward me and says, "See. Just like I said, they turned you against me. *I told you so.*"

And it isn't a sucker punch, not really, and it isn't a full-on right hook or a body slam, but girl. I hate that she says this. And I hate that she says it all smug-ass, like she predicted this shit and has all the control. Girl, I hate that she chooses to do this right now, in public, at a drag show, on what's so far been Flor's night.

Flor then tries going at Cam like she has something to say,

but Cam does her hand up toward Flor's face like she's shooing her away, and she loses her grip on her gold clutch, which falls at my feet.

I pick it up.

Now Cam takes another step toward me.

"When you're ready to talk to a real friend, sis, you know where to find me," Cam says, reaching for her bag.

But I pull back, and with all the air in my body pushing itself out, I hold her bag up beyond her reach, behind my head.

To the side, I can hear Flor saying, "Give it to her, Mac. It's not even fucking real."

But all I can think is, *We used to be friends*. We used to be *best* friends. I'm in too deep at this moment, and I'm spinning. What's done is done.

"A real friend? Ha! OMG. OMG. Bitch, you swear. Like you've been a real friend to me, Cammy? Girl, real friends don't sabotage their best friend's other friendships and they don't body-shame them or manipulate their feelings. And they definitely don't throw helping them in their face every time they get mad! Are you fucking serious?"

Cammy scoffs. "Are *you* fucking serious? Like all the times you left me out on purpose? How is that being a real friend, mija? Tell me. What part of leaving me out tonight makes you a real-ass friend?!"

"I didn't leave you out!"

"Right. So you and Flor just magically decided to go talk to Valentina as soon as I walked away? And then rub my face in it in front of the whole audience?! Girl, no. Take a fucking seat, culera."

"Nobody rubbed your face in anything!" I cry. "You chose not to go with us!"

"And you chose to leave me! How many times will I allow you to leave me behind!? Girl, are you delusional?"

"You chose to leave!"

"Bitch, before me, your only friend was a dog. A fucking dog."

Cam's jab gets me, and I don't know what to say back.

"But now, bitch," she continues. "Naw. I finally see right through you, mamas. And I don't like what I see. Mac, you're not the same. And this new Mac is fucking gross. Me das asco."

"Right. Asco. Like when you talked all this shit about me behind my back. Making fun of my 'panzota' and calling me a 'fat-ass hoodrat'? Oh, yes, girl. Such a good friend. Best friend in the whole universe. Fake-ass bitch!"

Cammy's eyes get small. She glares at Flor, opens her mouth . . . nothing. But I'm not done.

"All the shit you've talked about all of us. All of us! And I still defended you."

"I have receipts, girl!" Flor shouts, holding up her phone and pointing.

"Nobody's fucking talking to you!" Cam exclaims.

"Girl, if the category is backstabber realness, you win!" In front of Cammy's face, I clap my hands. "Congrats, girl. Have your moment."

Cam swats at my hands but misses and wobbles a bit in

her tall-ass heels. "Ya, girl. Keep telling yourself this story to make yourself feel better about all the shitty things you've done to me. And if the category is using your friend to get you an Ariana ticket you can't afford, then, wow, bitch. You snatched that crown, mamaws!"

Cammy's friend tongue-pops, and I'm so over them both. I'm so over all of this. The onlookers, the heat, Cammy's shrill-ass voice.

"You know, Mac. I almost believed you when you said they weren't trying to turn you against me. But exactly like I said. You let them. You turned against me."

"Yes, girl. Play the victim. Act a fool."

Cam lunges again, and Mikey tries to position his body between us.

"C'mon, babe. Let's go."

Sidestepping Mikey, I keep on. "Say whatever you want, girl. Like your fake-ass tears at Mikey's. 'Oh, feel sorry for me while I attack everybody.' Girl, nobody believes you. We don't. And we're done."

Again, Cam tries to snatch her bag, so I pull it away, and Cam mouths off. "Yes, girl. She swears she hates the drama, but look at her now. Bitch, she is the drama."

"Maybe you're right." And with that, I open up Cam's shitty, fake-ass Michael Kors clutch, and in front of all these people who have stopped to watch our sloppiness, plus the ones walking by, I dump out Cam's shit. Right there on the ground. In front of the Aztec.

A cloud of dust rises when her powder hits the floor, like a little bomb has just exploded between us, and Flor, behind me, snaps so loud—girl, it's almost a sonic boom.

Cam's gagged.

And I tell myself stop, but I can't. "Oh, look. That r.e.m. eye shadow sure looks a lot like one from Mikey's mom's kit. And look, an Anastasia Beverly Hills lipstick, which I know she can't afford, so she probably stole it from Flor. Such a great friend." I turn back to Mikey, then point to the pile of makeup and gum. "Sorry, babe. I don't think your mom's gonna want that back. I wouldn't."

Cam's speechless, like all the pistons inside her chaos are trying to fire up a comeback, but nothing's giving. Even her friend's mouth won't close, and it's like Cammy's just walked into a shitshow, trying not to get it all over her good shoes.

I kick the lipstick.

Turning back to Cam, I say it firmly af so that spit flies off my tongue. "I want nothing from you. So here's your fucking purse, girl. A fake-ass bag for a fake-ass friend. Good luck. Have a nice life, mija. Thank you. Next." With that, I hurl the little gold bag as far as I can—which is far, because I used to and kinda still do have a really good arm—it lands on the other side of the street.

Pissed af, I push past the crowd and head toward the garage.

I have a million things going through my mind right now. My heart won't slow down, and I know I've shown my ass, and I hate that I've acted so petty and ridiculous and sloppy af. I hate that I mocked Cammy for being poor, like is that really who I am? Is that really who I'm becoming? Ugh. Girl, I never let myself get so lit. Yet it's like every single one of my demons is stirring tonight. I feel betrayed, laughed at, humiliated, disrespected, all by someone I felt close to, someone I once called a best friend.

It doesn't take long for Mikey and Flor to catch up.

Mikey puts his hand on my shoulder.

"This was a great night. I want a thousand more nights like this one," he tells me, and I look at him like he must be out of his effing mind.

"Girl, he's kidding," Flor adds, rubbing my arm, her face melting a bit.

"Baby, sarcasm," Mikey says to me. "Hello? I mean, I'll take everything up until that last fifteen minutes. Holy shit."

"OMG. Okay. That was like super intense," Flor says, hugging me. "But bitch, OMG. I met Valentina! Pinch me, bitch. Am I dreaming? Wait. Don't pinch me. I don't wanna bruise. OMG. How did I look onstage?"

"Diva everything, girl. You were shining." Chuckling over Flor's theatrics, Mikey leans his chin on my shoulder.

I'm still pissed af, yet I like that Mikey's so close to me, and listening to Flor and Mikey go back and forth about the fiercest parts of the night, I feel myself calming down.

When I'm ready to talk, I say, "I hate how I acted. In public. In front of everybody."

"You were fine," Mikey says. "I mean, it was kinda hot seeing you get all fired up. You're usually so chill."

Flor's yawning. "OMG. Stop making it about her. Let's

keep talking about me and how my French Vanilla Fantasy came true, girl."

This makes me smile a little. My heart is still a box of thunder and knives, and I just wanna fall off the edge of the earth and forget about the last part of tonight. But I love Flor's gay-ass energy, *our* gay-ass energy, and I think/hope maybe shutting down Cammy's bullshit might be part of me protecting my own gay-ass energy. Like ending my friendship with Cam is a necessary part of moving forward with the life I deserve to live. But damn, I feel like the whole world just watched me take a piss on the floor, and even if letting Cammy go is for the better, it doesn't feel that way. No. Even with my two realest friends in the world trying to make me feel better, I can't shake that thing inside me that hums like I've done something wrong, like I've gone too far, like an alarm.

On the ride home, the street and the car and the whole world have gone the color of daffodils and old melon rinds. It amazes me that the world can feel so still, and yet, in the same night, so full of commotion and conflict, too. Mikey puts on one of his Ariana megamixes, but he keeps the volume on low because girl, Flor is still telling her story. Mikey and I exchange smiles, because Flor hasn't stopped talking about all the realness of her backstage fantasy since Mikey started the car.

Gradually, my heart rate settles, and I'm surprised to say . . . I feel kind of a little bit lit. Because I just survived a real-ass head-on peak af collision with Cammy, a juggernaut of drama and reading for filth. Girl. And not just survived, but I served it back ounce for ounce, exactly what Cammy was giving me, and bitch, she was giving it to me perra fierce. And no, I didn't back down or cry my ass off (only a little) or get on my knees and beg him to forgive me. No, ma'am. I stood up for myself. I'd be lying if I said a huge part of me isn't proud of myself right now. And I'd be lying if I said there isn't a huge part of me at the same time that feels terribly, incredibly sad because I've just lost one of my best friends.

Looking out Mikey's window, I see the freeway come and go, and I stare at the rooftops and the highest branches of neighborhood trees, and I see a scary-ass but exciting af possibility — a future where I say shit that needs to be said, where I'm not afraid of being cut off for wanting respect, where I can draw a line and let go of people and things that aren't good for me. Bitch, it's heavy, and it's the real stuff, but it's the life I wanna live.

When we drop off Flor, she can't stop hugging us, showering both Mikey and me with thank-yous "for making this night so iconic." Barefoot and gowned, with her big giant hair, running toward her front door, I can't help but think that Flor herself looks like a Mexican Cinderella.

Patiently, Mikey and I sit in the car and wait until she makes it upstairs and we see the light in her bedroom turn on.

"I had a really good time with you," I say.

"I did too."

I call Mikey over with my eyes, and I press my mouth against his.

"Stay the night with me," I say. "I'll call in to work. I never do, but I wanna. I wanna spend more time with you. To fall asleep and wake up with you. Me and you."

"Just us," Mikey whispers.

"You've done this before?" I don't know how to ask, or if I should, but I do.

Mikey nods. "Yeah. Have you?"

"No."

"Okay. That's okay. I really like you."

We decide to go to my place, since I need to let Kimber out. Plus, it's late, and my dad will certainly be asleep, whereas Mikey's mom is a total night owl. He drives us back to his house first, though. "I'll be fast. I just want to pick up a few things," he says, darting inside.

In the car, I think over and over about how I don't wanna get this wrong. Although we've kissed a hundred thousand times before, and I've felt every inch of his body and vice versa, I can't explain really why I wanted to wait, I just did, and I think I'm the only one who gets to say when it's right for me. I try to imagine what he will feel like. His mouth and his body, the parts of him I haven't seen. Will I feel any different when it's done?

At my place, Kimber acts a fool, running around and wagging her tail like she's never seen Mikey before. I hush her, and we take her out back. Mikey puts his hands in my shorts again, and he kisses me under the moon.

Inside, I look in my dad's room, and he's knocked the f out.

We shower quietly. One at a time. In the tiny bathroom. As I stand beneath the water, Mikey stands at the sink, drying off. Kimber paws at the door noisily, so Mikey lets her in, and she sniffs our pile of clothes, and she pushes her red snout into his underwear, and then she makes circles and lies on them.

In his backpack, Mikey rummages around.

Water running down my face, I reach over and turn off the shower. I smile. I pull back the curtain and stand there.

Mikey stares. He's standing at the sink, and then he's standing in front of me.

I'm dripping. And Mikey can see all of me.

Yet I don't feel ashamed or exposed or vulnerable in a bad way. I don't reach to cover myself with the curtain or towel. I don't hide behind my hands. I don't worry about having a belly or if my arms are big enough. I run my hands through my wet hair, and I feel firmer right now, with nothing on, with nothing between us. Mikey takes off his towel, places it on the sink. The two of us looking at one another, we stand like this for some time.

I step out of the shower, then, and I step over Kimber, who's looking up at me like, *Can't you move?*

In the foggy mirror, I can see our shapes.

I'm breathing like I've just walked a thousand miles, and Mikey reaches over. With his finger, he spells a word on my chest. Three letters. Swirls of my dark hair.

"What does it say?" I can't make out what he's written.

So he writes it in fog, on the mirror. "MIO."

We're whispering, and after a moment, I press my hand behind his head and pull him closer, his face against mine, and pressing my mouth against his, I say it: "I think we're supposed to be together."

"I do too."

I'm afraid we're making too much noise.

"Should we should go to my room?" I ask.

Mikey says, "Okay. I'll be right there. Just give me a sec."

Kimber follows me, and in my room, I check the bed, and I turn on the fan. I turn up the window unit so it's louder and colder.

I stand back and look at the bed, and I wonder how we'll both fit.

Kimber tries to jump on the mattress, but I block her and tell her, "No, baby girl. Sorry. Not tonight."

On the floor right in front of the fan, I throw a blanket.

I text Julio, my boss: I'm sorry. It's late. I don't feel well. I think it's a stomach bug. I won't be in tomorrow. Good night.

I'm waiting for Mikey. I hear him flush. And then he flushes again.

I turn on some music, and it's taking longer than I thought.

When he flushes one more time, I don't understand.

"Are you okay? What's wrong?" I ask, and tap gently on the door.

"Yeah. I'll be right out."

I think maybe he doesn't feel right or that maybe he's changed his mind. We don't have to if you don't want to, I text him.

He writes back immediately. It's all right. It's not that. It's just taking some time. Just prepping. I'll feel more comfortable this way.

I lie on the bed. I try not to feel bad about lying to my work, which is easy because Julio's an asshole and Mikey's here, and I'd much rather be with him in the morning than at work. I try not to close my eyes, but I'm tired.

And when I open my eyes again, it's morning. I look at my phone. 7:32 a.m. I can't believe I fell asleep.

Mikey's beside me, his head on my chest, and he's breathing soundly. I hold his warm body next to mine.

I look at my door, and it's locked.

Kimber's on the floor in her spot by the fan.

Mikey groans a little and rubs his face on my chest. The stubble and the warm push of his breath.

"You fell asleep," he mumbles.

"I know. I'm sorry. I'd been up since five. Is everything okay?"

"It was just taking me a while. You know. To get ready."

And I don't really know, but I pretend that I do.

Mikey reaches under the covers, and I'm hard. "I'm still ready, if you want to . . ."

"Yeah." Without hesitation I say it. "For sure. Just let me check to see about my dad."

The house is quiet. No sign of my dad, and when I come back, Mikey's placed the things we'll need on the dresser. We do it in my bed in the half-dark with a song on the radio that isn't the perfect song by far, but it's a song and it's music between us, my big body on top of his, which somehow feels smaller and unsure of itself beneath me, even though we're the same size. It lasts as long as I can make it last, and I don't want it to end, but it does, and when we're done I lie there holding him and trying to catch my breath, thinking maybe this is the way love and connections and trust all work—there are moments and they come and they go, and so often, we want these moments to keep going and going and not falter, not fail, not end. But they do.

My chest is moving up and down.

I have my arm around Mikey, and I'm thrumming my fingers over his thigh.

I feel spent, and lying next to Mikey in my bed that's too small for the both of us, he asks me if I'm hungry, and "Did you like it?"

"Every second," I say to him, still trying to take control of my breath, holding his hands in mine and kissing the top of his head, rubbing my knuckles over the place in his body where he keeps his heart.

"We should get up," Mikey says, and I can hear the sleep clinging to his voice.

"Sleep some more. I'm gonna let Kimber out and feed her, and then we can eat."

Outside, wind moves the trees, and morning light inches through the branches, across the yard, over the short yellow grass and dry weeds. On the back porch, I'm smiling about Flor's moment last night with Valentina onstage, and I'm thinking about all the bullshit with Cam. If only I'd pushed for a convo that night at Mikey's, maybe we could've addressed our conflicts before all the shit hit the fan. I wonder if maybe somehow we can bounce back from all the drama and look back on all of this one day and laugh. I start to check my phone to see if Cam sent me a shitty-ass text or posted something shady on IG, but I think of Mikey in my room, and there's no reason. At this point, I figure my friendship with Cammy is done. I wanna say good riddance, but I don't believe I'd mean it if I did.

In the room, light falls through the small space between the curtain and my wall.

In the corner, the swirl of the fan, the whir.

Mikey's sleeping, and I stare at the eagle on his arm. I stare at his pile of clothes on the wooden chair by my dresser, and I watch his chest rising and falling like it has someplace to go, and I think about being with him again and again.

After eating, Kimber paws at the wooden door and marches in, looks up at the bed, then plops down on the floor and snores.

I crawl back into bed, and Mikey squeezes over next to me. He breathes against my neck, his heart sending its deep, even sounds inside my chest. For a second, I consider waking him, asking him if we can do it again. For a second, I consider not letting him sleep, not letting him miss the rest of this moment. But I realize that this is, in fact, the moment—a summer day with my honey—and I realize that to protect moments like these and to bring more of these moments to my life, I'm gonna have to keep changing some difficult shit. I'm gonna have to want what I keep.

Chapter 22

IT'S EARLYISH, AND FLOR AND I ARE DRIVING TO meet Hermelinda, Kanari, and Mikey at Starbucks when my phone dings.

It's a text from Cammy, the first I've received since our fight two weeks ago. Tomorrow's the day we're all meant to go see Ariana. I'd asked her, like, ten days ago if I could buy the ticket off her, but she'd left me on read. Until now. I discreetly read it.

> **Cam:** So this is a quiet difficult message for me to write. I'm not gonna talk about how disrespectful and inappropriate yall acted toward me the other nite but I do need to tell you that I can't in my right mind give an Ariana ticket I paid for with my hardearned money to someone who does not act like a true friend. Its prob

best this way since you prob would not ever pay me back. After everything I've done for you. Acquaintances are everywhere but good friends are hard to fine. If anything I have learned from this whole situation that sometimes people change but they don't always change for the best.

At first read, Cam's message kinda kicks me in the teeth. As much as I wanna dismiss it, I can't. For a while now, I've known that I wouldn't be attending the Ariana concert with Cam. The way things ended with us couldn't have been messier. Well, I guess maybe it could've. I could've snatched the hair off her head or she could've talked major shit about me, Mikey, and Flor on her social media or tried sabotaging Mikey and me or outed me to my dad or something equally ridiculous and tragic. But we didn't.

I can't speak for her, but I can say that for me, it's kinda been crazy not having one of my best friends, my first gay bff, around as summer draws to an end. All T, I miss Cammy. I won't say this to Mikey or Flor or even B, but I've told Kimber, who kinda just stares at me, then goes back to licking her paws or her chocha or both. I mean, I would've liked telling Cam all about my first time with Mikey and all the emotions of actually having a boyfriend and how I'm seriously kind of a lot nervous but also soooo excited about senior year and these big-ass decisions I'll have to make, like applying to college out of state and possibly majoring in English and leaving my dad and Kimber behind.

But girl, let's be real. When I really think about it, Cammy wouldn't be down for convos about Mikey and me getting closer, and as for going to school outside of Texas, she'd def probably try to convince me just to stay here in San Antonio and not leave her behind. That's just how she is, and that's one of the reasons why I need to move on.

I take a breath. "I just got a text from Cammy," I say.

"OMG. What does it say?" Flor quickly, and rather dangerously, crosses oncoming traffic to pull over so she can read the message. In front of a fire hydrant with a Chihuahua peeing on it, Flor reads and rereads Cam's text.

"Girl, did she proofread this?"

I don't laugh. I don't give a shit about proofreading right now.

"Disrespectful? OMG. Inappropriate? Ughhhhh. She can't be serious."

"No, girl. She's serious."

"This is quintessential Cam, girl. Soooo playing the victim."

"I knew this was gonna happen."

I stop talking because I can feel my voice beginning to split.

Although the smarter part of me decided to give myself space and walk away from Cam, the more hopeful part was holding out that somehow we might pull off some miracle and be civil, or at least not spiteful. Not that we'd be all bff and shit, but I mean, girl, we have history, and besides, we're gonna see each other all next year at school. I figured Cam might at the very least just let me buy the ticket off her to recoup her coins but also maybe as a signal that we can coexist without hating one another. Well, that part of me just got drop-kicked in the balls, which I hate to admit, because I wanna be stronger than this. Like even though I knew things were over, this text is a nail in the coffin of our friendship. It's proof. Seriously. Still, even though I'm wrecked that I can't go to the concert with Flor and Mikey and Hermelinda and Kanari, it's probably for the best because the ticket was expensive af.

Not far off, we see Hermelinda pull into Starbucks. Kanari's with her. They're both ebullient af, and they're dressed like they're going on a yacht or something. I don't wanna see them right now. I don't want them to see me like this.

"Girl, do you mind if I wait in the car? I'm not feeling it," I tell Flor.

"No, girl. C'mon. You'll feel better once we get you a skinny iced vanilla. The girls will be happy to see you too."

"Actually, would you mind taking me home?"

"Girl, you're letting her win—"

"I just wanna fucking go home!" I bark this at Flor, and she doesn't deserve it, but maybe she does because I'm telling her directly what I need and what I feel, and she's trying to convince me my feelings aren't real.

"Girl. Ummm. Okay. Let me just say hi to them real quick."

I appreciate Flor for doing this, but I'm too cracked to say so.

On the patio, Flor meets Hermelinda and Kanari. Both wave at me when Flor points to the car and says something, then shrugs.

I close my eyes.

I hate the shitty feeling in my body right now, and I hate Cam.

I hate that stupid-ass part of me that gave Cam this power over me, and I hate the even stupider part of me that hoped, even as Cam revealed her true colors, that we could remain friendly. I don't know.

My head hurts. Sighing doesn't help for shit.

As soon as he gets there, Mikey jogs over and knocks on the window, and Flor's not far behind.

"I'll take you home, baby," he says.

I nod and get out of the car. "I'm sorry for talking shit to you," I say to Flor.

Flor grabs my hand and says, "Girl, on the reals, I'm sorry you have to go through this. Y'all really were friends. This must be hard for you."

I can't smile, but I thank Flor and squeeze her hand tight, and somewhere inside me, I feel seen. It's like I've known that Mikey and Flor haven't liked Cam for a while, if ever, but she was my first gay best friend, and I feel like I'm burying a friendship and a part of myself with that friendship, even though I know moving on is for the best, and maybe I sound dramatic af and maybe I am the drama, but it's true. And I'd rather admit this shit than play it off and keep my feels all bottled up like some fake-ass, toxic masc bullshit that's gonna explode everywhere one day. When I get in Mikey's car, he takes my hand and kisses my palm.

"You really wanna go home?"

I shrug. I show him Cam's text.

"Baby, we can get you another ticket. Kanari got one in our section not too long ago. It wasn't too expensive. And if it's the money, babe, you know I'll get you one."

Mikey tries to look at my eyes.

I stare at the road.

"I don't want you to buy me a ticket. I'll buy my own ticket. Or I just won't go."

"Babe, I have money saved. I don't understand."

And he's telling the truth, he doesn't understand.

And I don't even know if I explained it, would he get it? Would it connect with who he is and who I am and how we live and what each of us knows about the way the world works and how it doesn't? I just don't wanna owe Mikey. He's not the kind of person who'd hold it over my head—the total opposite of Cammy—but still. He's already given me a pair of shoes and bought me the matching shirt we wore to see Valentina. He's paid for other shit too, and I hardly ever pay for anything. Brisket tacos from my work, Smoothie King once or twice, the C4 energy drinks he chugs.

"The offer stands. But you know, there's not a lot of time."

"I know." Even though this conversation has me twisted, it feels good knowing that I have a boyfriend who gives a shit about my point of view and is kind and listens.

For a while, we sit in his car and drive.

Mikey plays the mix he's been working on.

"It's the good stuff," I tell him. "Babe, you really know how to hustle."

Mikey shines a little.

After driving around the city, Mikey and I sit around my house for a while. I'm calmer but still angry at Cam. In the backyard, Mikey throws Kimber's pink piggy, and she grabs it twice but then gives up because of the intense heat.

My dad's at work. The house is hot, and the AC and the whir of the spinning fans don't do much.

Inside, we lie on my bed, and Mikey puts his legs across mine, and we listen to a song he's been remaking.

Mikey lays his head on my chest, and he rubs his fingers through the dark curls on my belly. "I know what will make you feel better," he says.

Later, after Mikey heads home, I sweep and mop, and I make some food for my dad. Nothing fancy. Just picadillo, some papas and beans, which my tía Ruby showed me is easy to make.

I sit with my dad as he eats. He's shirtless, and his pants hang open, unbuttoned.

Kimber lies at my feet and begs.

I stare at my mom's name — Cassandra — tattooed in faded black script lettering over Dad's heart. My dad carries my mom's name on his left arm, too. A banneret. A cross, a crown of roses, gray thorns. Praying hands. Most times, nearly all the time, when I think of her, I remind myself to forget. What would she think of Mikey and me?

I heat him up another tortilla.

I eat too, not much, because I'm not hungry. I'm still pissed at Cammy about the ticket, and even though Mikey made me feel better today, I guess Mikey's magic wears off eventually, because I'm back again, feeling bent up and angry and bitter af about Cam.

After a while, my dad rinses off in the shower, and he crashes on the sofa and puts on a show.

"Ey, why don't you get me a beer?"

I toss him a tallboy, and I fall into the old brown recliner with a strip of tattered duct tape covering a hole.

Before my dad can crack open his beer, he looks at the light going off on his phone, and when he answers, he says, "B? Ey, how's it going? What's going on?"

They talk, and I rub on Kimber, who throws her big feet up on my knees, like she thinks she's a baby again and is gonna try and climb up on my lap.

I smile a little, but the smile soon goes away.

"That was your sister. Asked if you and me wanna meet up. Said she wants to talk."

"I don't feel like talking right now," I say.

"You sure?"

"I'm sure."

I think my dad stares at me for a minute. But I don't look at him, and so how would I know?

Now Kimber paws at my leg. She whines like I'm supposed to pick her up or give her something, but I don't.

As he's about to leave, my dad asks, "You going out?"

"Naw."

"You inviting somebody over?"

"No."

"Okay."

I almost feel relieved when I hear the door shut, and when I hear the truck engine clamor, I put my hands on my face and eat all the air I can.

Kimber follows me to my room.

I do a bunch of push-ups. I stand on the back porch, watching Kimber sniff around the floor planks of the shed. I fill a glass from the kitchen tap and watch as the water whirlpools down the drain.

Mikey FaceTimes me; he's working on music. "Listen to this new one I mixed. Listen to how it connects," he says.

I like seeing Mikey's face, but I'm not in the mood to talk.

"Can you just leave it on? You don't have to say anything," he says.

I lean my phone against the lamp on the nightstand and lie back with my hands behind my head. I shut my eyes, and then I lie on my side, and every now and then, I look over and watch Mikey at work on his computer. In headphones, he's shirtless and happy and dancing a little, his gold pendant bouncing up and down on his brown chest like a thimble. It feels like I'm watching a video clip, a TikTok, a story on Instagram or a Reel made by a boy who's too hot and too sweet to be true and is all mine.

Watching Mikey, I consider a million ways to put together enough money to buy a ticket. Pawnshops, borrowing money, asking my tía Ruby and my tío Robert, who've always offered to do what they can to help. But already they don't have a lot, and asking them would put them in a jam.

My eyes growing heavy, I tell Mikey, "I'm crashing. I'm gonna fall asleep."

"Just leave your phone on, babe. Make sure it's plugged in."

"Yeah."

"One more thing," I tell him.

"What, babe?"

Mikey turns down his music.

"The ticket—how much was it when you looked it up?"

Mikey takes off his headphones, and he picks up his phone.

"Four hundred seventy-five. Plus fees, then taxes. Why?

Did you change your mind?" Mikey's grin and his brown skin, his eyes flickering with light.

"That's a lot. I don't know."

"Okay, babe. Just remember like I said, the offer still stands. I want you to go."

In the morning, my dad's up before I am. Hearing his noise in the kitchen, Kimber scratches at my door, and I think I'm running late, but then I look at my phone and I'm not.

I let her out in the hall and crack my door so she can get back in, and I lie back down.

And when my dad taps on my door, I don't understand what he's doing, because he never comes to my room, and then I remember he went to see B, and I worry something's gone bad. Quickly, I sit up in bed.

"Mac?"

"Yeah. What's wrong?"

My dad pushes open the door, the hard yellow light from the hall bulb spilling in.

"You're up really early. What's the matter?" My voice grating, uneven, kinda stalled.

"I'm just going in early. You up? Can you talk?"

Between my dad's legs, Kimber pushes through, and she jumps back on the bed like it's hers.

"Okay."

"I'll be in the kitchen. I need to leave soon," my dad says.

It's not even five yet, and my dad's filling his thermos with coffee, which he doesn't normally do.

I sit at the table, my hands in front of me.

He stands with the yellow thermos in his hand alongside a white grocery bag that holds his lunch.

"I don't know if you saw. I put the rest of the meat and papas into tacos. From last night," I tell him.

"I saw." And he pats the white plastic bag.

Kimber sniffs the thermos like there's something in it for her. "And B?"

"Good. She's good. We went to Little Red Barn."

"Wow. Damn, Dad. That's old-school." I kinda chuckle, and I wipe the crust from my eyes, remembering the old restaurant B always picked when we got to go out to eat when we were young.

"Yeah, her choice. Always was her favorite."

For a second, my dad stands very still, like he's looking both ways before taking a leap.

"So what's wrong?" I ask.

My dad shakes his head. "Nothing's wrong. But she did ask me to help her fix something."

"She asked for your help?"

"Yeah."

"Good."

"Said she's leaving soon. We talked about old times."

"Yeah. That's good. I'm glad y'all talked."

"We talked for a couple hours, and we closed it down. Said she didn't wanna leave with us not talking." My dad pauses. His eyes, muscles around his jaw, the ones in his neck tense up. "I apologized. Like you said."

And I'm gagged that my dad apologized. Girl. Like a lot gagged.

"Okay." It's early af, and this sounds important. My dad never opens up or shares shit like this, so I'm trying to dislodge the sleep from my eyes.

"Yeah. B asked how you were."

I nod. "Okay."

"Said you were upset."

"You told her that? Why? I'm not upset."

"No, she said it."

"Oh."

"Told me your friend, the one who does the gym a lot, he talked to her. Said you had a beef with Cam and you were supposed to go with them all to a concert. But Cam took your ticket and so you couldn't go."

I cringe that my dad knows this, that B, for whatever reason, told him. And why in the world would Mikey be telling B this shit? How do they even talk?

"Dad, it's not that big a deal." I get up to feed Kimber. "Anyway, I'm glad y'all talked. I gotta start getting ready for work."

My dad fidgets. He shifts his hands around in front of his big belly and opens his mouth like there's a breath he needs to get out.

"Kimber. Where's my baby girl? Who wants breakfast?" I reach for her food bowl, and Kimber hauls ass to the counter.

"So we went halves. I figure it's a way to make things better. Or start."

I look at him, confused. "Huh? Halves on what?"

"On the ticket. For that singer you like. Ariana Grande?"

I gag. Bitch, like I literally almost choke on my tongue.

"Y'all did not go halves. Dad, no. C'mon." I'm starting to breathe heavier, like I might hyperventilate.

"Mijo, I don't know how to work the ticket, but I have it here in my phone. A link, I think. I just gotta send it to your phone. Or I think B already sent you it? Check the email."

Immediately, I grab my phone and look at my email, and there it is—a ticket to Ariana Grande. Girl, I don't know whether to let myself smile or call up B and talk mad rowdy shit to her for getting all in my shit and then thank her a thousand for getting all involved in my shit. I think I'm smiling so much that it's making it hard for my eyes to see, and I think I should be thrilled, though I'm hesitant and wanna stay chill until I know everything about this ticket and B and Mikey and my dad.

"Dad. Are you serious? I know for a fact these tickets are too expensive. It'll take me forever to pay y'all back."

"You do a lot around here. You don't have to pay us back."

I go quiet. It's a lot.

Kimber does her little hungry dance. I pour her kibble. She looks at her bowl on the counter and then back at me and whines.

"Why?" I wanna believe him. I do. I mean, I know I pull my weight, and I know I disappointed him after I quit baseball. I wanna believe that my family would just do something for me, no strings, no fine print. "Or, like, why now?" I ask, placing Kimber's bowl on the floor.

Kimber gobbles, and my dad hesitates. He sighs. Finally, he grabs the truck keys from the table, and he says, "Because . . ."

My dad's chin moves up and down. His lips reshape like he wants to say something, but he stands there, shifting the keys around in his palm.

I don't think my dad knows what to say next or if, even, he can say what we both know needs to be said. Getting me an Ariana ticket is a nice gesture—more than nice—and whereas I know B means well, my dad . . . I'm afraid that if I accept this ticket, one day he'll use it against me, just like Cammy did. He'll get pissed at me or try to pressure me to do shit I don't wanna do, and he'll use this as a sign of my ungratefulness. Yet at the same time, my dad just apologized to my sister, and they put together money that they don't have to buy me a very expensive and much-wanted Ariana Grande concert ticket.

And sometimes, I guess the things we need to say will tell us when it's the right time to say them. Sometimes, the truest things are just waiting for their moment, that instance when they aren't manufactured or forced. Looking at my dad, I see openness where it didn't used to be, and I don't know exactly how I draw this conclusion except—maybe it's the even texture of his voice right now, maybe it's the rare softness in his eyes, which don't look away from me or right through me either. And so, I say the things I've been wanting to say.

"I like him," I say.

My dad nods. "Yeah."

"We're together. Mikey and me. And it means everything

that you got me this ticket so that I could go to the concert with him. But I gotta ask you to promise me that you won't ever hold this over my head or throw it in my face if you ever get mad, and if you can't make that promise, then . . . I shouldn't be accepting this ticket from you."

It comes out smoother than I think it will, and for the first time in my life, I'm not afraid of what my dad will say. I have 110 no doubts about the trueness of what I'm saying. So, what's the worst he can do?

By my side, Kimber licks her chops, and she blinks at me like, what's going on and what's gonna happen next?

"So, what you're telling me is you're . . ."

He can't complete the sentence, so I do. "Gay. Yeah, Dad. I'm gay."

My dad's jaw tenses. He breathes heavier now. His chest growing and retreating. Setting down his thermos and his lunch, and with his keys in his hand, he walks over to where I'm standing in the middle of our kitchen, and my dad takes a deep-ass breath and exhales a hefty load outta his lungs, and then . . . he puts his arms around me. It's awkward af because we *never* hug, and I'm unsure how to respond, but I hold him back, just a little. I can feel that I'm stronger than my dad, more solid, stacked, and I don't mean just in the firmness I carry inside my chest and my arms. No, I feel like I have something my dad doesn't or once did but has lost over time, and there's a moment in my body where I feel sadness for him like an echo, like a coin rolling down a sidewalk, not knowing where it's going or when it's gonna end. For those few seconds, my dad holds me in a way I can't describe, and he says, "Mijo, I don't get it. This is hard for me. I didn't grow up where this was okay." Then, looking right at me, he says, "But you're my son."

I suppose this is my dad's way of speaking his truth, and I suppose all you can ever ask of anyone is that they tell you what's inside their heart. Not lie, not be a fake-ass, not tell you what they think you wanna hear. Yet I wish it was more, and I know it can be more, but I think right now, my dad's giving me all he's got.

And I don't think I have to say it, but girl! Girl!!! Girrrrrl!!!!! I'm soooo f-word ecstatic, because I just came out to my dad, and it wasn't all storybook af and no, it wasn't ultra max pro rejection and drama and pain—it just was. On top of that, tonight I get to see Ariana Grande with my boyfriend and our friends, and of everybody in the whole big, giant, amazing, fierce-ass world, the people who came through for me are B and my dad! My dad!! Girl, my dad, who for years has talked endless amounts of bullshit and lies and hate about gay people, and yet, he comes through for me by telling me I'm his son and that he got me a ticket "just because." I'm gagged.

Girl. All morning, I can't stop smiling, like I blow up Mikey's phone and also Flor's, and when they wake up, they both roll outta bed and show up at my work, jubilant af and almost as electrified as me. When I explain to Rebecca that my dad and B got me an Ariana ticket, Rebecca puts down the knife she's using to slice sausage, and she gets a little choked up, and she tells me, "Ey, it's because he loves you, mijo. Deep down. Because when a parent really loves their kid, nothing on some damn news show

319

or what a politician says can ever change a parent's love. And I should know. Look at all the damn kids I got." Rebecca laughs then, like all the wind in the world is behind her, and standing beside her, knowing all the hours she works, it makes sense.

Work blows by, and soon I'm showering and throwing on my best Adidas shorts and a black cutoff I loaned Mikey for the gym one time that kinda still smells like him after he gave it back. #swoonafdadallday #heartswole #forevermine

In the backyard, my dad's drinking a beer in his work pants and boots, sitting on an old chair on the porch. Hurling the pink pig for Kimber to chase down and return, he looks tired and worn like always but not so angry as before. I don't wanna make a big deal about how much it means to me what my dad's done, but I need him to know that I appreciate it — not the ticket itself, which I wanted so much and is great, of course, and perfect and so fierce, I mean, girl, it's an Ariana concert ticket — but my dad's support, his vote of confidence in me, not giving up, his cariño and love, calling me "mijo," calling me his son.

"Ey, they're coming to pick me up," I say. "I just needed to tell you thanks. Dad, thank you."

Lobbing the pig, my dad nods. He wipes the dog slobber on his palms against the wood. "You be careful. Have yourself some fun," he replies. "And tell your friends . . . tell Mike, I hope y'all have a good time."

I smile. It's a start.

On the way to the AT&T Center, Mikey plays his classic Ariana mix, which gives me very-perfect-night and all the friendship-is-magic vibes I need.

In the back seat, Hermelinda and Kanari and Flor.

Mikey's wearing a white Nike tank top and arm bands, and he glows.

I keep my hand on his thigh and stare at his eagle tattoo and gold chain as he drives.

And when we get to the venue, girl, the parking lot is jammed.

"See. This is why we show up early," Flor says.

All around us, girl. Throngs of people marching in to see a goddess sing. It's fierceness. Diva everything. All the gay-ass energy you can want. Like young newbie gayboys and fierce-ass queens, sophisticated fashiony girls and old guys with big biceps, hairy chests, giant mustaches, and boyfriends like mine, too.

"Girl, this concert is virtually Gay Pride," Mikey tells Flor, who claps her hands, then fans herself with BIEN PRETTY and agrees.

"I'm soooo glad my mom let me come. I was like, no way I'm missing Ariana," Hermelinda says, her hair correct and bright.

Inside, we gather ourselves and take pics by the giant-ass illuminated Ariana sign.

"Girl, posting all of them and like right now!" Flor shrieks, quickly plugging away at her phone.

Kanari's thrilled af, in her kitten ears and sky-high boots, hugging and telling everybody she sees, "Can you believe she's here?! Like, she's literally in the same building as us right now??!!"

I'm seated by Kanari, which is kinda right behind Mikey

and Hermelinda and Flor, so Mikey asks Kanari if they can swap, and she agrees.

"Of course, babes. You're my seventeenth favorite best friend," she jokes, and Mikey gags.

The whole night I'm with Mikey, and holding on to him, I can't believe this almost didn't happen.

"I'm glad you came." Mikey kisses me right before Ariana begins.

"Thanks for talking to B," I tell him, and I put my arm around him, where it'll stay for most of the night. Seriously. #closecall #hereforitnowgirl

It's a lot, and I feel lucky af to have Mikey and B, and my dad, even. Wow. Did I really just say that? I did.

And girl, when the show starts, it would be an abso complete 110 understatement to say that Ariana is fierce. Girl, please. Ariana's beyond fierce. Like Ariana is intergalactically, universally, top-tier iconically fierce af! And we're living, and again, I think I don't ever want this night to end. It's like iconic after iconic after iconic moment, and choreo forever and light show for the gods and every single Ariana Grande song I love.

Watching Ariana give every syllable all night, I can't fathom being at home right now and missing any of this at all. I mean, girl. Lip-syncing with Kimber in crunchy-ass trash bag chongos is one thing, but singing along with Ariana and all my best friends at her concert, girl—this is the real gig. We dance and Mikey goes on and on about beats and transitions and drops, and he takes a shitload of photos and videos and talks and talks with all the people around us. We're close af to Flor and Hermelinda and Kanari, and as the night goes on, eventually people shift around so that we're pretty much side by side, in the same row. And when the time comes and Ariana sings her last song, Mikey grabs my arm and looks at me, and I put my arms around him and kiss him with all the arena lights going on, and I say, "You and me, babe. You're mine."

Mikey nods. "Forever mine," he says, and the joy inside me is 110 abso everything I hoped for tonight.

"Babes, let's go eat. I'm starving," Flor suggests then, and the girls both agree.

Surrounded by fandom, we stream out toward the exit, still singing "One Last Time," Mikey holding on to my arm and Kanari and Hermelinda and Flor holding on to him. Girl, it's the good stuff, and I'm happy af. Dancing around with Mikey, I tell them all, "This is the gay-ass energy I need for all of my life!"

Of course, Mikey hugs me with every ounce of his strength, and Flor poses with Hermelinda and Kanari and, of course, gives diva-everything back arches and hair tosses, which produce the very bouncy bang that she loves.

"Get a pic! Get a pic!" Kanari yells, and a mom walking by, who apparently has accompanied her vibrantly dressed son and his best friends, says, "Here. Let me take it. If you take ours."

We pose and they pose, and amid all the compliments and chatter and gay-ass energy, I see her — Cammy.

In black slacks and a dark, expensive-looking top with a cross-body bag that Flor would very likely gag over, she passes by us with some guys I don't recognize. Cammy sees me, and I see her. It's brief. Maybe a couple of seconds, but long enough to acknowledge each other with a simple and unmistakable nod. For a moment, I think she's gonna come at me. For a moment, I think she's gonna lose her head. But girl, she's gone before I know it, and even though I try to follow her group with my eyes, I lose them in the crowd.

The crowd pushes out onto the asphalt, and when we come to the part of the arena where we can see the doors, Flor says, "Girl. OMG. Bitch, I left my fan!!"

"Are you sure? Where did you last see it?" Mikey asks.

"I don't know. Maybe in our seats? Or I guess I could have left it in the restroom," Flor answers. She's flustered af.

"Do you want us to go back and look for it? We can go back," Kanari says, already turning to walk back into the arena.

We decide to go back in search of Flor's fan.

We split up. Mikey and I will head back to the restroom, while Hermelinda, Kanari, and Flor return to check our seats.

Heading back into the arena, girl, I feel like we're on a mission. The AT&T Center seems even bigger now that nearly the whole crowd has dispersed.

Emptied, the hall echoes.

Nearby, a lady pushes a cart and sweeps, an old Mexican song leaking softly out of a small radio she keeps. She sees us, but she leaves us alone.

Mikey walks slowly into the restroom, but nothing.

"It's gone. I'm sure somebody picked it up," Mikey says.

"You think there's a lost and found?"

I pause, because the lady who's cleaning is watching and points at the floor she's just mopped.

"We should find Flor," I say, taking Mikey's hand in my hand.

And when we find Flor and the girls, she's apprehensive at first and asks, "Did y'all find it?"

"Naw." I shrug.

"Sorry, girl," Mikey adds.

"Well, I hope she finds a good home," Flor says, surrendering. She throws her arms in the air and huffs.

As we're walking back out of the arena, Kanari says, "Did y'all see Cam?"

"Girl, when?" Flor asks, her voice dropping to the floor.

"When we were taking pics with those fierce little seventh graders," Kanari says. "He walked by. He was with some guys."

I'm the only one who says yeah.

"And?" Mikey asks.

I tell them, "It wasn't a big deal. She walked by and I saw her and she saw me, and we both kept on doing what we were doing."

I feel as if my friends are all staring at me, as if they expect more.

But then Mikey says, "Well, good. It's better that y'all just go on with your lives instead of holding on to old drama. What good does that do?"

He's right. And in a way, I'm fine with it being just the three of us now — Mikey, Flor, and me — which is not at all how I imagined it at the beginning of summer. The curiosity in me that wants to know how Cam's been doing and who those guys were that he was with and what did he think of Ariana, well, it's dimmer. At the beginning of summer, I would have told you Cammy was my best friend in the whole world, but now I'm able to shrug off the fact that I saw Cam and move on. I mean, maybe that's just how friendships work. Some friendships fire up strong as starlight and Texas solazo, the kind of connections that last over lifetimes, which is the bond I have with Flor and Mikey. Some friendships are lighter, full of goodness and fun times, but nowhere as deep, like my connection with Hermelinda and Kanari, which is fine, really. And still others, girl. They may start up bright as bonfires, full of dazzle, excitement, and promise, only to fizzle out as they run out of air or as people show their true colors. We may think they'll last us forever, but girl, these kinda connections are brief, snuffing out eventually like candles.

I'd like to think Cam and I were all three of these friendships at some point.

By the time we get back to the escalator, it's closed, so we look for the stairs. We're moving through the corridors, and all of this and none of it looks familiar.

Flor continues, "OMG. Do y'all even know where we're going?"

And we don't.

Girl, it kinda just feels like we're wandering around, which I don't so much mind, although I'm hungry af.

Finally, we see a guy carrying some boxes, and Flor asks,

"Sir, excuse me. Sir? I think we're a little bit lost. Can you show us which way to the exit?"

For a second, the guy looks frazzled, like he doesn't know what to do with us.

"This area is not for the general public," he says.

"I know. I'm sorry. We just got a little lost." Flor's using her sweetheart voice, like I call it, which is syrupy and candy-like and helps her get shit she wants.

"I don't know. I can't help you. But you shouldn't be here."

"What do they want?" another, sweeter voice bends around the corner.

The man fumbles the box. "The exit. They're lost and looking for the exit."

"Please, ma'am," Flor calls out. "If you can help us, that'd be great."

And then, from behind the man, who almost drops the box, we see her.

Girl. Girl. Giiiirrrrrrllllllll!!!!!!!!!!!

"'Ma'am'? Do I look like a ma'am to you?" says the one and only, the iconic, the incomparable, the incredibly, 110 abso, undeniably, fiercely gorge, Rule #1 Ariana Grande.

"You're her." Flor's words emerge like daylight breaking free, soft at first but then stronger. "And no, ma'am, you are most definitely not a ma'am, more like a queen, a goddess—*the* goddess!"

Ariana smiles. "You're too sweet. But I'll take it."

Girl, the totality of this moment is starting to hit Flor. I can see little tremors start happening to her fingers.

"Breathe, girl. Just keep breathing," Mikey says, rubbing Flor's shoulder.

"Gasp—you're so perfect," Flor mutters, her hair moving with each syllable.

"Gasp—you're so perfect. And those bangs," Ariana replies.

"Thanks. I'm kinda known for my bangs."

"I get it. I know a thing or two about signature hairstyles." Ariana turns, her ponytail flowing in a magnificent half spiral.

Then the man with the box clears his throat, and Ariana acknowledges his concern. "I'm sorry. I'm just really enjoying this so much. Here, I only have a second, but I think there's an exit over this way."

Ariana calls us over and points down a not-so-long hallway.

Flor can barely walk, so Kanari and I sorta carry her along.

"She's in awe," Mikey says to Ariana. "You're everything to him. To all of us."

Ariana smiles. A sweet, warm, real-ass smile. "You know, I gotta run, but we can do a photo if you want."

OMG. A photo! Why didn't we think of this??!!

At this point, we pull Flor to the side, and Mikey pinches her hard, telling her, "Bitch, snap out of it! You're about to miss taking a pic with Ariana Grande!"

Maybe it's the pinch. Maybe it's the menacing tone Mikey uses. Maybe it's the all-around aura of Ariana's kindness and joy and the fierce-ass high pony brushing against us as we all position ourselves around our diva. Whatever it is, girl, Flor is up and posing, and I can't stop smiling as the man who'd been carrying those boxes says, "Okay. One . . . two . . . three!"

And when the pic comes through, girl, it comes through!

"I love it. I'm done!" Ariana says, hugging and blowing kisses and giving us all the #eternallymeowingrealness we can handle.

Chapter 23

"**H**APPY BIRTHDAY, BITCH!" MIKEY SHOUTS AS he does a little dance up to Flor's house.

Posing in the doorframe, Flor is giving 1960s Hollywood starlet. She wears giant gold sunnies and a kiwi-green kaftan.

I hand Flor our gifts, and she immediately digs into the vibrantly tissued gift bag and squeals, "OMG. My fan!" She gives it a clack with every ounce of her gay-ass energy.

I was able to find a replacement for her beloved BIEN PRETTY fan online.

"OMG, cute!" she cries as she pulls out the T-shirts we got for her.

"They're vintage. And I cut them into shredders for you," I say.

Next, Flor digs a thumb drive out of the bag; she looks perplexed. "Girl?"

"All your fave songs," Mikey says. "One endless summer megamix just for you."

"So you can listen on the elliptical as you werk on getting a bigger butt," I add.

"OMG. Y'all think of everything," Flor says tenderly.

"There's more," Mikey says.

And when Flor pulls out a framed eight-by-ten of our iconic group pic with Ariana Grande, she has a moment.

"Girl, I know," I say, wiping back a strand of Flor's bouncy-ass bangs. "Rule number one, babe."

"And rule number three." Strumming her fingers around the frame, Flor confesses, "Y'all really have made this summer the best summer of my life."

"*Our* lives, babe. All of us," I add, nodding at Mikey, too, and here, Flor gets a little teary-eyed.

I hug her, thinking she smells like really expensive hand cream, and a lot of it, which I don't really wanna get on me, but girl, I don't care, even if it's not for me, because I love who Flor is and how she is and all the goodness she's brought to my summer. #seniorsummerrealness

"Not today, ma'am," Mikey says hurriedly. "Save those tears. I have a live set — now *that's* gonna gag you to tears!"

I follow Mikey to help him to set up under the cabana by the pool.

Moments later, Flor emerges through the sliding glass door,

handing out glasses of lemonade. "It's fresh. Kanari and my mom just squeezed it."

"Flor, you have guests!" her mom yells.

Soon enough, KT and Naomi are strutting back to the pool, with Naomi yelling, "Hey! Is this the all-girls pool party or what?!"

And then B and Clari arrive. I'm really thankful that Flor invited B and the Bruhs to her party and that B came down from school.

Hermelinda arrives next, and Flor and Kanari rush to her side. They all shriek from pure joy. Watching them spin around and hug, it's giving pinwheel of kiwi, bright purple, and gold. Girl. #festive #vibrantaf #allthesummervibes

Girl, for a "low-key, nothing big" get-together of just "a few close friends," Flor's mom has gone all out with the elaborate-ass snack spread. Girl, it's like a Whole Foods extravaganza of colorful fruit cut in an array of geometric shapes and cheeses from faraway continents with names I can't even pronounce.

Who eats like this? I think, stuffing a handful of cheese and baby carrots in my mouth.

From the ice chest, I grab Mikey two water bottles and a Tropical Passionfruit C4, his fave. The drinks drip, and I wipe them with my towel before handing them over to my babe. I know, right? *My babe.*

Behind his table, Mikey's focused af. "What about the video? Babe, I still need a sound check!" With panic in his voice, he nearly drops his headphones, which takes me outta my head and back to the task at hand, which is helping my DJ boyfriend set up.

"Babe, I got you." Hunting down Flor, I borrow the tripod she promised we could use to record Mikey's live set. Benny joins Mikey and me, and as it turns out, Benny knows shitloads about sound tech due to his obsession with massive speakers and explosive car audio. He volunteers to help.

Completing the sound check calms Mikey down, and I figure maybe Benny's not so bad, when he's not amplifying his bullshit and waaaaay playing up his ego next to Duncan's, which I guess, now, when I think about it, really isn't all that different from the way I used to be and am trying not to be, and well, I hate to bring her up, but the way Cam still can be and the way I acted when I was around her.

Now Mikey's looking more relieved, and girl, OMG, he looks soooooo effing hot af in his Miami Heat jersey, his big-ass arms and bubble butt, his golden skin, his fresh fade and clean-ass shoes. Up there with his headphones, rocking back and forth, checking and double-checking and ramping himself up to go, Mikey looks in total control of his set, and it's easy, now, to 110 abso believe him when he says music is his destiny. So, girl, when Mikey's finally ready to start up, he blows me a kiss and nods like, *Babe, this is it*. Charisma, fierce uniqueness, big nerve, and loads of talent are what Mikey Villanueva is giving.

With both my hands, I make the shape of a heart, and then I step back and wait.

"Video's good to go. I got him on sound, too." Benny gives me a thumbs-up, and I think, damn, Benny's kinda coming in clutch and taking this a lot seriously, which I guess is what eventually happens to people when they find something they're passionate about.

Mikey looks down and shuts his eyes. I can see him breathing, gathering, summoning. And then it's immediate, instantaneous, smooth. Eyes fiery, Mikey looks up, and he jumps into performance mode, shutting down the volume to complete silence so that everybody stops talking and looks around.

"What's going on?" Hermelinda asks.

"Hey, what happened to the music?" KT throws her hands up, looking confused. "That's my jam!"

And like that, Mikey knows.

Slow. Melodious. Purposeful. It's Ariana. "Forever Boy." And at first it's a capella. All vocals. Girl. Stunning, of course, right, because it's Ari, and that voice, girl, and all the core memories around her that we've built — Rule #1: Ariana Grande is everything! Seriously. This summer has proven that to be true. Then Mikey throws in these echoing drums, and he heightens the vocals, speeds it up. Slowly at first. A light instrumental joining her vocals. And then nothing. Softness, smooth equilibrium. Pause. But then he's taking us high, so high. Gradually, purposefully. Combining, and then, girl, everything! Full-on rise to rocket bpms and drop into Ari's iconic af goddess diva-everything voice!

Girl, I am living!!

The girls scream, and Kanari and Hermelinda and Clari and Flor are jumping up and down, and girl, then I realize that I can hear my own voice, and I'm singing along.

Clari has her arms around B, and B smiles my way.

Benny comes back to the cabana and says, "I'm not a dancer," and I say, "Girl, me neither," but either Benny doesn't hear me call him "girl" or he doesn't seem to mind, and soon I can see Benny bumping his head and he's tapping his foot, and without even realizing it, I'm doing the same. I mean, I guess we're both dancing, not like Flor, certainly not all fierce af like Kanari, but in our own basic, who-gives-a-shit-if-I-can't-dance, it's-a-great-song-and-this-is-just-how-I-am kinda way.

On the platform behind his table, Mikey's arms are out-stretched, and he's singing along too.

Mikey gives it to us again and again, song after song, rise after rise, peaks and valleys, drops, lifts, and the kind of mea-sured melodic realness that pulls us with him only for him to take us back to the height of this live set that's giving us all life.

After a coupla hours, Mikey decides to take a break and sets his laptop on auto. Flor gathers us all around the cabana for a group pic.

It's not complicated. Like the vibe is so good that we all just fall into place.

Hermelinda, Flor, and Kanari take center.

Naomi serves face and body-ody-ody in the tiniest pink bikini, and of course, KT's "stud shoulders" and buff-ass arms are giving their own version of body-ody-ody too.

Clari and B join in beside Hermelinda.

My babe calls me up next to him, where he fits in my arms like the color blue fits on the sky. I hold him tightly. I press my mouth up against his ear. "Baby, you're killing it up there. It's soooo damn good."

I call Benny next to me, but he declines, which is fine with me; at least I tried.

"On three!" Flor stresses, gleefully wielding her new BIEN PRETTY fan, and we all serve up our best smiles, looking at the mini-tripod Flor has erected right in front of us.

Girl, I am feeling all of myself, and I want this to last forever. I've never been all that into pics, but I would take a million shitty pics if it meant I could live a thousand afternoons like this one.

"Grab my bag," Mikey tells me as he runs to the restroom.

In between his sets, we make it fast. Mikey's kicking off his high-tops and peeing simultaneously while I help him out of his shirt and towel the sweat off his back and his chest and arms. Still, he's sweating hard.

Mikey turns and kisses me. His hands slide off my chest because I'm sweaty af, too, and his neck, salty and slick, is still a good place to press my lips. "Thanks for being here. For helping me," he says, and then Mikey kisses me with the kind of want that stays behind and reminds you of what a kiss can really be.

Mikey pulls out hyper-orange shorts and bright white socks, an Astros baseball cap that he pulls on backward, with the bill flattened and straight back. Quickly, he splashes water on his face and neck, and I dry him off and wipe up the water that's splashed on the floor. In seconds, he's close to brand-new and running out the door. As I'm shoving his dirty clothes back into his backpack, I hear the Superman theme music from the set he made for us for Pride.

"You're listening to DJ Mike Villanueva," a deep, commanding voice announces.

My heart starts doing backflips, because I know what this means to him.

From the patio, I watch, and Mikey's up again, singing along, dancing as he transitions into his next song. By this time, Flor's dad has the grill going, and Benny's beside him, in dark glasses, slouched in a pool chair. Girl, it looks like he's barely alive. Flor's mom comes out with a tray of mocktails, colorful concoctions in fancy, reusable stemware with pineapple slices on each glass's rim, for which the girls are living, except B and KT, who smile politely and say, "No thanks, ma'am."

When the kabobs are done, we all sit around with our plates, and although Mikey wants to continue playing for us, Flor and his mom convince him to take another break so he can eat. Devouring my kabobs, I sit next to Mikey while the girls talk about everything—reminiscing about last year's state basketball playoffs, predictions and plans for this year's dance team, leaving for college, what people are saying about Cam.

"Apparently, Cammy is livid, girl. Like beyond bitter at how everything went down," claims Hermelinda as she nibbles on zucchini from a veggie kabob. "And when she saw our Ariana pics, girl! She's blaming Flor, of course, for everything. Saying she doesn't really care, because Mac wasn't even that real of a friend to her and that Mikey's . . . whatever, but that Flor sabotaged their friendship."

Flor fake gasps. "She's just mad that she finally met a girl who wasn't gonna play games. It's giving very playing the victim."

"Girl, she's a total train wreck. I mean, does she even know how to act?" Hermelinda's voice gets loud. Her point is clear and sharp.

"All the real. Girl, I don't know why y'all even bothered being friends with her in the first place," Naomi chimes in.

I certainly don't wanna talk shit or disrupt this perfect afternoon by Flor's pool with a few of our close friends and awesome food and Mikey's phenomenal af live set, but girl.

So, I say, "Because I gave her a chance. Several chances. And to paraphrase the goddess, 'I don't wanna waste my time on some dumb shit . . . we gon' make some new habits.'"

For a second, the table goes quiet. But then, Flor says, "Werk, new habits." And then clacks her fan like applause.

Under the table, Mikey squeezes my thigh, and he grabs onto my hand.

"Come on, lyrics," says Kanari.

B jumps in. "I gotta agree with Mac. At some point, though, people either admit when they're wrong and they change. Or they don't, and then you just gotta say deuces because they're gonna keep letting you down." Here, B's eyes reach for mine, and she raises two fingers like she's telling somebody goodbye, and it makes sense to me now, kinda, more of it, B and me and my dad and forgiving and not forgiving Cam.

"Good karma. Girl, that's my aesthetic." Mikey says this.

Flor replies, "True true. Send that 'love and light.'"

"That's for sure. Preach, girl," Naomi says, snapping.

People at the table laugh.

I rub my knuckles against Mikey's chest, which is the kinda

cariño that motivates him, because he kisses the round cap of my shoulder. "Baby, I'm gonna go finish off my set."

It's good this way, and I kick back at the table next to B.

By the pool's baby waterfall, Naomi and Kanari are showing Flor's mom how to buck.

Girl.

"You got a minute?" I ask B, who's chuckling her ass off watching the girls lesson up Flor's mom on how to properly shake her ass.

B nods. "How was the concert?" she asks.

"Amazing af. Everything and more. I just needed to say thanks. You know, for reaching out to Dad and going halves."

B smiles, taps her perfectly clipped nails on the metal table, and pops a couple of blueberries in her mouth.

"I'm glad you got to go."

"I told him he couldn't hold this over my head like I owed him. And I came out to him."

B's nodding and a little gagged, and she pats me on the back. "Good. Wow. Damn, bruh. What he say?"

"Just that he didn't understand, but I was his son. I told him about Mikey and me."

"Damn. You really took your shot," B responds. "And Cam?"

"Nothing, really. Kinda miss those friendship vibes, but you know."

"For reals, I'm glad you got unstuck in that bullshit friendship."

I nod. I don't disagree with anything B's saying, except that my friendship with Cam wasn't all bullshit. There was some good stuff.

"You thought any more about college?"

I smile. "I've been looking at some schools."

"Oh yeah? Look at you." B's enthusiasm gasses me up. In some way, I want her to be proud of me.

"Yeah. Someplace small. Flor's looking at Yale. But not me. Too big, too cold. I'm thinking California."

"Nice. I like that for you," B says, lovingly taking a fist to my upper arm. "And your dude?"

"Music," I say. Glancing up at Mikey, he's giving us Miley, the girls are girling, and he's shining. "That's his first love. We'll see."

Above us, the sun's eating all over the sky, reminding us she's a star.

I ask B to get a pic with me, and she does, taking like fifty thousand pics, smiling and cutting up and hanging all over me like we're ten and eleven, and I realize now that as much as shit changes for us, there are some vibes that will always be the same.

In fact, and maybe right now I'm just feeling myself and maybe I'm just all in my feels because it's the end of Senior Summer and so much has happened, but sitting here next to B, my boyfriend giving a sickening day-party set, all my friends gathered around, Flor being unapologetically gay af and me, too, in my own way, giving my own gay-ass energy, girl, it's everything, and I'm like, isn't this the whole point of life, just getting yourself to a place where you can shine and you feel okay to shine and you want other bitches also, just like you, to shine?

And then, girl, I can see something happening. Flor's mom is talking to Mikey, who, for some reason, turns down the volume. We're all standing here, like, *Ummmm, what's going on?*

I think, *Did somebody call the police? Did one of the neighbors file a noise complaint?*

Suddenly the patio door flies open and out steps . . . the one, the only Valentina. Giving for the reals, full-on, daytime pool party gorge redheaded bombshell goddess take-your-breath-away lewks right here on Flor's patio, Valentina shouts, "Come on, birthday girl!! Somebody wanted cake?!"

I feel like I'm hallucinating, and I think everyone else feels the same vibe, because we're all 110 abso stunned by the realness of it all. But then Flor screams, "Mi amor!" and throws her well-moisturized, kaftaned arms open for Valentina, and if there is a word for more than gagged, then let that word be spoken now and known, because whatever that fierce-ass feeling is, this is what I feel at this very moment watching my best friend getting all the birthday love from all our friends and her idol, who was "just passing through town. On a little road trip," as Valentina tells us. Girl, sooooo #Rule2!!!!!

Soon Flor's mom walks out carrying a big-ass tres leches cake, with seventeen lit af candles, girl, and Valentina leads us all singing "Happy Birthday" to Flor, who can't stop fanning herself and smiling.

I seriously thought nothing could get better than lowriders and drag queens, but on the reals, I may have to change my mind after today, because this tres leches is divine af, and right now, I don't know that anything gets better than drag queens, love, and tres leches cake!

And OMG. I look up, my mouth full of Mexican cake, and Mikey's looking right at me, glowing and dancing in the sun, pointing at me, giving us his version of Ariana's "Everyday," which is right now no doubt my 110 abso fave Ariana song ever, and I live. Surrounded by the people I love most, girl—I feel it. I belong. All I've ever wanted is friends who click with the real person I am—friends I don't have to hide from or lie to, friends who hold my hand when I'm going through it or just because, friends who understand that I'm a down-ass friend even if I'm not wild or fabulously funny or the most thrilling or fashion-forward person in the room. And not only that, but friends who help me understand the real person I am and the person I'm gonna become. And I found them. This is my family—my chosen *family*. Girl, I hope it's forever. Love, friendship, loyalty. All of Rule #3. Por vida and always.

Acknowledgments

I am beyond grateful to the following people for their love, support, cariño, and guidance, all of which helped this story become the story it needed to become.

First, mil gracias to Sandra Cisneros, for whose mentorship and encouragement I will feel gratitude por vida and always. I am grateful to the Macondo Writers Workshop and to Reyna Grande, who helped me make the genre jump from poetry to fiction. In writing a story about the very human need to connect, I thank my chosen family for giving me the sense of belonging I longed for as an isolated and incredibly lonely queer kid in South Texas. Thank you to my partner James and to Howie and José, Kole and Preston, Micheal L., John and David, Randy, Tiago, Mehadi, Omar, Joel, Chris and Lee, Jeff and Gabe. I've learned that sometimes, your friends are more than family, and together, y'all can make life more than wonderful. Thank you, Dr. Carlton, for your guidance regarding health and queer identity. Thank you to DJ Tony Moran for sharing stories about his passion for music and immaculately white sneakers, and thank you to DJs Nina Flowers, Roland Belmares, Rue-D, Joe Pacheco, Marti Frieson, and so many others, whose circuit, tribal, and Latin house sets have fueled me both in person and on SoundCloud. For my editor,

Acknowledgments

Christian Trimmer, a thousand thank-yous for helping me build my skills and for the vibrant, much-needed conversations about queerness, fake friends, mean gays, forgiveness, and language. For my agent, Stuart Bernstein. OMG. Thank you for believing in my book about loyalty and friendships and what if my best friends and I were back in high school today. Thank you to Valentina, whose pride, style, and beauty captivated me from the moment she walked into the Werk Room and to the 110 absolutely forever iconic Ariana Grande, whose music inspires me at the gym, at my desk, in big rooms at three a.m., at pool parties and tea dances. Thank you to RuPaul, whose words of wisdom in the Werk Room and at the Main Stage have undeniably made their way into my heart and into my classroom. And finally, thank you to my teachers, especially my small-town Texas public school English teachers—Mrs. Shaver, Mrs. Hedtke, and Mrs. Vance—thank you for creating classrooms where reading, writing, thinking, and respect mattered and where students like me could feel valued and safe enough to actually learn instead of worrying about getting beat up or talked shit to because we were different. The world truly is a better place with caring and compassionate teachers.